THE
INTERPRETER'S
SECRET

Also by Andrew Rosenheim

THE
INTERPRETER'S
SECRET

ANDREW
ROSENHEIM

NO EXIT PRESS

First published in the UK in 2026 by No Exit Press,
an imprint of Bedford Square Publishers Ltd,
London, UK

noexit.co.uk
@noexitpress

ISBN
978-1-83501-460-8 (Paperback)
978-1-83501-461-5 (eBook)

2 4 6 8 10 9 7 5 3 1

Typeset in 11 on 13.5pt Garamond MT Pro
by Avocet Typeset, Bideford, Devon, EX39 2BP
Printed and bound in Great Britain by
CPI Group (UK) Ltd, Croydon CR0 4YY

The manufacturer's authorised representative in the EU for
product safety is Easy Access System Europe, Mustamäe tee 50,
10621 Tallinn, Estonia
gpsr.requests@easproject.com

For Laura and Sabrina and Clare

1

Her name was Mrs Golubova and she was seventy-eight years old.

Three hours before, just as the airplane prepared to pull away from the gate in Stockholm, a flight attendant had come slowly down the aisle, followed by an old woman carrying a cane. *Thump, thump, thump* – with each step the woman brought the stick down hard on the floor, loud enough to be heard over the hum of the now-idling engines. When the attendant stopped by his row, Weaver watched with a sinking heart as she pointed to the empty seat beside him.

By then he could see the old woman clearly. She wore a wool skirt, rough as a horse blanket, that hung down to her ankles, and a sage cloak-like coat with buttons that were undone. Her hair was tied in a bun, and a pair of ancient spectacles dangled from a silver chain around her neck. A classic-looking country *babushka*: all she needed was an unruly bunch of chickens and a pail of corn.

The attendant reached for her bag, and the woman reluctantly handed it over, watching intently, her jaw set, as it was put in the overhead compartment.

By now Weaver had stood up and moved back in the aisle to let the old woman take her seat. Although the plane was almost empty, the seat by the window in his row was occupied by, from the blond looks of him, a Swedish businessman, spruce in a suit and already yawning. Weaver had planned to move to an empty row once the plane was airborne, but this prospect soon evaporated once the new arrival sat down, introduced herself, and began to talk.

Irina Nikolayeva Golubova was Russian – a Muscovite, she explained – and on her way to London, where her daughter was living with her husband and three small children. She gave no explanation for why she was flying via Stockholm, though Weaver assumed she had flown there to circumnavigate the ban on direct flights from Russia to the UK. And she did seem happy to tell him pretty much anything else, including the full names of all three grandchildren. Her English was patchy, so he switched to Russian, which seemed to make her happy and sealed his fate – with Mrs Golubova in full flow, it would be rude to change seats now, especially since her only other possible audience, the Swedish businessman, was either asleep or doing a good job of pretending.

For the duration of the flight, the old woman barely drew breath, only interrupting her narrative to pepper Weaver with questions. *How had he come to learn Russian so well?* He explained the mix of family background and education that accounted for this. *What had he been doing in Stockholm – had it been a business trip?* Yes, he said, wanting to leave it at that. But she continued – *Where did he work?* When he told her, she seemed impressed – *The American government? He must be an important man – a 'big shot'.* He didn't think so, he replied lightly, hoping the questions might cease.

Fat chance. *Was he married?* Not any longer. *Were there children?* No – given his divorce, a good thing too.

His answers were brief because he was not by nature forthcoming – an old girlfriend had once said he should have been English rather than American. He was also tired, and his thoughts still focused on the strange events in Stockholm during the previous day.

After landing at Heathrow, when the plane reached the gate, he stood up to get the old woman's bag down. She thanked him and said, 'You are very good looking for someone so polite and tall.'

'Flatterer,' he replied in Russian, and she laughed. There was no sign of the cabin crew coming to help, and he didn't feel he could abandon her now. He had been brought up to feel obliged to help the old. His ex-wife had always found this embarrassing. 'Sanctimonious', she had called him, adding scathingly, 'You only do it because it makes you feel good about yourself.' Actually, it was to keep himself from feeling bad.

So he carried Mrs Golubova's bag and his own down the aisle, pausing to make sure she was keeping up. Mrs Golubova had said that her son had arranged for the provision of a wheelchair, but there was no sign of it outside the plane on the gangway. When he asked a quartet of airline minions, none of them knew anything about a wheelchair, nor seemed very willing to learn. He was about to remonstrate when Mrs Golubova tapped him sharply on the arm. 'I can walk,' she said firmly. 'I like to walk.' Once he saw the expression on her face, he didn't argue. It combined bewilderment with a surprising determination, as if to declare that, should the chaos of the immediate world prove overwhelming, Mrs Golubova would nonetheless go down swinging.

It took them thirty minutes to make it to the arrivals hall, by which time Weaver wondered what on earth she had in the bag he continued dutifully to carry. Jars of sauerkraut? A samovar made of lead? They stopped frequently so the old woman could catch her breath. 'You are strong and fit,' she said at one point, wheezing slightly. 'Not like my son-in-law,' she added witheringly.

At passport control they waited a further twenty minutes before reaching the head of the line. There Weaver let Mrs Golubova go forward first, saying he'd bring her bag through for her. But once through passport control, there was no sign of Mrs Golubova. Was she in the ladies' room? Or had she gone through in search of her luggage? Weaver figured he could always come back up to look for her, so went down the escalator and into the baggage reclaim hall. The terminal seemed fresh and spanking new; he missed an air of English dowdiness, the faint scent of cheap disinfectant.

He checked the carousel number on a monitor and soon found Mrs Golubova. She was looking slightly stunned as the bags moved past her like the slow-moving floats of a small-town parade. He collected an empty trolley and waited with her until at last she spied her own suitcase approaching; it was a large, battered leather case, with seams starting to split at one end. Weaver lifted it off the conveyor belt with one colossal jerk, then put it on the trolley with their carry-on luggage.

They walked slowly together through customs, emerging untouched, though he was used to getting pulled over – a cousin of his father had worked for immigration at JFK, and Weaver asked him once why he was so often stopped. 'You probably look too sure of yourself,' the cousin had said. 'People think it's nervous people we're looking for, but that's all wrong. It's the calm, confident ones we pull over.'

Not that Weaver was feeling calm or confident today; he was still edgy after his time in Stockholm, still shaken by what he had both witnessed and listened to.

'You will be long in London?' Mrs Golubova piped up.

'No,' he said, which wasn't strictly true, but he sensed what was coming.

'I would hope to thank you for your kindness to me. I believe tea at the Goring Hotel is said to be most pleasant.'

'Thank you, that is kind of you, but sadly I will be in the countryside with friends.'

'A great pity.' She added after a moment, 'My daughter and son-in-law live in Surrey, but can easily arrange for me to come into the city. Should your plans change, kindly let me know.'

'I will,' he said. He was not about to point out that he had no way of contacting Mrs Golubova.

They moved into the arrivals hall, where a line of blue-suited chauffeurs stood, most holding up handmade signs with their passengers' names. Suddenly there was a large cry. Three small children rushed forward, brushing past Weaver and embracing Mrs Golubova in a spinning wheel of tiny limbs. Behind them stood a couple, presumably their parents. The man was short and plump, dressed in a sloppy suit; beside him stood a handsome woman dressed in the universal uniform of the international rich: dark designer jeans, smart white jacket, and the inevitable oversized sunglasses. Nearby a uniformed driver was waiting; now he came forward.

Weaver handed the trolley over to him after first taking off his own bag, then nodded at the couple. Waving goodbye to Mrs Golubova, he decided to leave it at that. Any further exchange would just be awkward. Instead, he made his way through the crowd of people waiting for arrivals. Just short of the terminal's automatic doors, he stopped and took out his mobile phone.

'Yes,' said a man's voice a few seconds later. In the background, there was a mixed duet of wind and water; he must be on the river.

'It's me. Weaver.'

'Where are you?'

'Still at Heathrow.'

'Then you better hurry up, friend. The evening rise waits for no man.'

He ended the call. Most of the chauffeurs were still there, looking bored and a little impatient. There was another man standing there; not a chauffeur, for he didn't hold a sign and he was dressed in a summer suit the colour of old chalk. His profile was familiar. Weaver remembered him from the private house in Stockholm, barely twenty-four hours before. Russian security.

What was the man doing in England? Was it just coincidence that he was here, or was he waiting for someone – like Weaver? Had he missed him in the little throng of Mrs Golubova and her family?

Weaver didn't share his friend JP's untrammelled Anglophilia, but he knew the country well enough to feel at ease there – and to feel safe. Which was why, later on, he was surprised that it was England where they came gunning for him.

2

IT HAD ALL KICKED OFF FOUR DAYS before.

'Have you ever been to Sweden?'

At first he thought the query came from Mac, two workstations along, next to the window on the seventh floor. Mac had nabbed the seat when they'd moved floors six months ago. Weaver had feigned disappointment, yet was secretly relieved, since the windows were floor to ceiling. He could get vertigo just standing on a chair.

But the voice came from closer to home. Turning round, he looked up and saw, not two feet away, the lean face of Pauline Fullerton, raw-boned product of a West Virginia mining town. A place dedicated to 'fighting and fucking', as Mac, who hated Pauline, succinctly characterised it. Pauline was a manager, brought in to run the small unit of interpreters and translators employed by the State Department in New York City. A gifted bunch, at least linguistically, well-paid and secure in their berths.

The group was collectively and often individually maverick, perhaps unsurprising given they were people who spent their time thinking in a minimum of two different tongues. From a management point of view, they were a nightmare: unreliable, rarely modest, and prone to insubordinate forays that ranged from downing tools (an act whose expression, paradoxically, was muteness) to playing the most juvenile practical jokes. Speaking twelve languages didn't necessarily make you act like an adult.

Hence the need for Pauline, who had a coldness in her carriage, a flintiness that made even the most ascetic New Englander — and Weaver knew more than a few — seem downright soft. She showed little appreciation for the work she supervised, and was happy to admit she spoke no language other than English; though Mac, in his cups, liked to say she was fluent in Pig Latin – 'and stronger on the Pig'.

Now, in answer to her question, Weaver said, 'No, I haven't been to Sweden. Why do you ask?'

'Because you're going.' She paused. 'Don't look so excited.'

He turned in the swivel chair and looked out the window along 42nd Street, long enough to glimpse the distinctive art deco tower of the *Daily News* building. When he passed it each morning he would think invariably of Superman, swapping his cape for the humdrum suit of Clark Kent. Weaver yearned to reverse the process, and shed his own humdrum suit for a cape that would give him the powers to fly out of New York, and work on something more noteworthy than Russian statistical accounts of their natural gas reserves.

These were aspirations he did not share with anyone, not even Mac, his closest friend among his colleagues, for to do so suggested a lack of commitment to his job that Pauline would never tolerate. He had moved to Manhattan unwillingly, at his now ex-wife's insistence, but the fact remained that in his last year of living in Vermont he had been laid off by a sporting goods company, translated two books by obscure Russian poets, and enjoyed a gross income of seventeen thousand dollars. Now he was on a State Department salary of $187,000 a year, with full benefits; even in New York City this was more than adequate. He lived in a small but comfortable apartment on the Upper West Side, and despite the depredations of his recent divorce could take cabs and eat in restaurants; more importantly, he could afford every year or so to add to his collection of Tonkin cane fly rods, and travel north at weekends to use them. As he had planned to do in four days' time, travelling to his boyhood home in Vermont for his first fishing of the year. Until Stockholm raised its ugly head.

He cocked a doubtful eye at Pauline. 'What about the Gorky project? I'm only halfway done.' Ukraine's wheat harvest had failed more than once in the 1950s, and a secret Politburo report about it had never been put into English. Such was the excitement of his line of work.

'You'll be interpreting at the G20 Summit.'

'Which meetings?'

'The trade subcommittees. The Russians weren't invited, of course, so you'll be doing French and backup stand-in for Italian. Tractors should be high on the agenda, so brush up your agri-vocab.'

'Why me?' He wasn't asking in order to be flattered; he would not have been in this office if he were not a good interpreter, though his initial accreditation was as a translator – a distinction lost on the world but fundamental in the business. 'And why such short notice?'

'One of the DC crew's dropped out.'

'Who's that?' he asked, trying to think of a reason he couldn't go. Trade talks were very dreary work. Though exacting: if you said a hundred kilos instead of a hundred tons, you could find half a country's steel exports dumped in the Med by mistake. Unfortunately, the trout fishing season was not an adequate reason to decline the assignment.

'Percy. He's got the flu.'

Percy was a fabled long-server in DC, who in his very first year had been the interpreter for a meeting between Nixon and de Gaulle. But now through old age, a charmless manner and, frankly, a failure to keep up (languages moved with the times), he had been relegated to Trade and Commerce, where Weaver also toiled. 'Won't he get over it?'

'Too big a risk. You fly tomorrow. You can join the flight from DC if you'd rather. The plane will be full of our contingent.'

'No thanks.' He had friendly colleagues in DC, but a direct flight from Kennedy beat a change anytime. Besides, the DC bunch always liked to drink on long-haul flights, and remembering the Italian for 'tractor combine' didn't mix well with a hangover.

'Am I in cattle class?' he asked. 'It's a long flight.'

'Afraid so. But I got you an aisle seat,' she added brightly, though without cracking a smile. But then she rarely smiled for anyone, and almost never for Weaver. 'And you'll like the hotel.'

'Really?' His head filled with an image of another soulless tower block, one of many in the hi-tech ghettos that ringed the airports on the outskirts of many European cities. IT companies had a lot to answer for. You could drive half an hour from, say, Munich International Airport, passing the inventors and vendors of every conceivable digital device, without seeing a single grocery store.

Pauline went on, 'It's the Grand Hotel. That's where the talks are being held, and where most of the summit leaders will be staying. Somehow Percy swung a room, and now it's yours.'

'Is the President coming?'

'No. He's going to the UK instead, or at least that's what Washington tells me. He's visiting Wales – where is Wales?' she asked.

'Next to England. How many days will the meetings last?'

'Just two.'

'I'm off next week, you know.' He could go to JP's in the UK and fish there. Fishing from the bank: no wading, genteel, but difficult, and in its own way as good as anything in Vermont.

'I know. See you in ten days. Though you might have picked a better time,' said Pauline, which was not the response he wanted, but it would have to do.

Later he would realise how sharp a preconceived image he'd had of Stockholm – an island-filled Venice of the North, with trees; an even more watery Vermont – yet how little he actually saw of it. He'd had no time to reconnoitre. Within minutes of arriving at the hotel, he was thrown into tense and detailed territorial negotiations between Americans and the EU. Neither was prepared to give ground – or ice, rather, since the territory involved was the Arctic Circle.

When the meeting adjourned, he decided to walk around the neighbouring Gamla Stan, or Old Town, but he was intercepted.

A DC colleague named Donitz had missed the plane from Washington, and Weaver was told to work a session with the Italians concerning cheese imports. This was challenging; his Italian was rusty. As a graduate student more than a decade before, he had spent a summer in Rome doing an intensive course to supplement his undergraduate courses in the language, and back then its gracious musicality had proved easy. But even his love of Dante didn't help much in translating on the fly the differences between authentic and lookalike kinds of parmesan (Parmigiano-Reggiano, he learned at unnecessary length, was the only true bearer of the name). So Weaver struggled.

Worse still, the meeting carried on almost until seven, and he had to run through a fog of jet-lag fatigue to get to the Interpreters' Dinner, a first-night tradition among the veterans at international conferences. Punctuality was a group rule, and anyone late for the meal had to pick up half the wine bill, which for Weaver meant out of his own pocket, since Pauline would never approve that kind of excess on his expenses.

The invitation to join the traditional first-evening dinners at these summits had come the year before and indicated he had arrived, now accepted in the small, pedantic and, to be honest, pretty wacky cadre of international interpreters. But he was flattered enough that he didn't want to blot his copybook now and find himself *un*arrived. In the event, he was just on time, taking his seat near one end of the table as the last arrival, a hapless interpreter from France named Jean Calvert, was coming through the restaurant's front door.

The dinners had a history that stretched back to the UN's inaugural meetings in San Francisco in 1945, and had until recent years been boozy affairs. Bertolini from Italy, known to all as 'Bert' ever since the younger President Bush had got his name wrong, had once overindulged at a dinner held in a Hamburg beer cellar. He showed up the next morning at the conference, dapper as always, and translated without hitch or hesitation the German Chancellor's plenary address – which was not much use to Italy's delegates, since Bertolini translated the entire speech into Estonian.

Now in the woke spirit and sombre professionalism of the times, they dined sparingly. Gravadlax was followed by some kind of fillet – reindeer? Weaver wondered as he chewed through its accompanying unknown berries. Nobody drank very much: a glass of wine or a tall glass of beer. By the time the entrées had appeared, Weaver was struggling to stay awake.

He was sitting next to Elek Tomic, a Hungarian whose parents had arrived in America after the Uprising of 1956 without so much as a spare pair of socks. He too was employed by the State Department, and seemed to know every European language spoken east of the Rhine. Unsurprisingly, given his antecedents, he had an implacable hatred of the Russians, but was otherwise a happy kind of man: balding and built like a bowling ball, entertainingly indiscreet, especially when he'd had a few, which on any evening was more often the case than not. He liked to tease Weaver about the latter's spoken Russian, which Tomic claimed was last heard during the time of the tsars.

Soon they were all talking shop and swapping notes on their inevitable travel travails – some of the Europeans were on the road forty weeks of the year – when another, smaller party entered the restaurant and walked past their table. Among these new arrivals was Sam Blanchett, the DC-based boss of Pauline and overall director of the State Department translation sections in both DC and New York. A slim figure of average height, probably ten years older than Weaver, he was a Midwestern transplant brought east by the White House Chief of Staff, Henry 'Hank' Hofstadter – they had worked together before in Silicon Valley. Blanchett had suspiciously jet-black hair and wore very expensive clothes, which Mac, a terrible dresser who had last worn a tie for his bar mitzvah, maintained must cost twenty-five per cent of the man's salary, though to no great effect. 'You can take the boy out of Kankakee, Illinois,' Mac had declared scornfully. 'But even a Paul Stuart suit doesn't take Kankakee out of the boy.'

Like Pauline, Blanchett was no linguist, and knew nothing about how interpreters operated. He was open about his ignorance, however, and professed an eagerness to learn, asking questions that those interpreters who had been cornered by him found near-inexhaustible – and near-moronic. Weaver supposed there was something admirable about Blanchett's rabid curiosity, though he was glad never to have been subjected to a one-to-one interface with the man.

But Blanchett was not the reason why the table now fell silent. Also walking past was Hofstadter. Watching him, Weaver thought he looked much as he did on television – not always the case with the famous when spied in the flesh – with a box-like face that was tanned from his vacations in Hawaii.

Hofstadter was probably the most prominent member of the White House (except for its elected inhabitant), and he figured constantly in the press, defending the President's positions on everything from Israel to ice-cream cones. An ex-marine who had an MBA from Harvard Business School, he had enjoyed a roller-coaster career in West Coast start-ups before entering the White House. Unlike the President whom he served almost slavishly, he was always good copy, helped by a ropy personal life that involved what Hofstadter himself once described as 'booze, broads and several tolerant wives'. After a deal maker for a President had wreaked havoc in the White House, this President was at pains to act above the fray – leaving Hofstadter to live for a place in the fray instead. He did the President's dirty work; cynics suggested, since the President was so detached, that Hofstadter did most of the clean work as well.

When the new arrivals had gone by, Tomic broke the silence. 'I see the Chief Wild Man has graced us with his presence. The President himself is said to be in Wales with the First Lady.'

'Why Wales?' said Angela Rottmann, a tall and prickly German woman, whose face contorted when she spoke, as if she'd discovered a lump of cheese in her wine glass.

'Maybe his wife wants to buy it,' said Tomic, and they all

laughed. The President's wife, his second, was known in her own right for her business acumen – and wealth, which had been consolidated rather than crippled by the failure of her first marriage and the resulting highly lucrative divorce. She had been introduced to the President by Hofstadter, for a time her colleague in a Silicon Valley start-up, and the President was said to have fallen head over heels for her. Until then a notably staid and prudent figure, he had seemed to find personal liberation in the glitzy lifestyle of the woman – enough to have left a wife of twenty-seven years for the new arrival.

'Is she really so rich?' asked Rottmann.

'Who knows?' said Tomic. 'I am suspicious of any fortune made in the divorce courts. As for Hofstadter, I'm told he was close to going bust before he joined the administration. He had to be rescued, or he couldn't have taken up his post.'

'Who bailed him out?' Weaver asked. 'They must have known they'd never see their money again.'

'Unclear,' said Tomic. 'Some anonymous benefactor.'

'He was not at the summit today as far as I know,' Rottmann noted.

Tomic shrugged. 'He gets to do what we'd all like to do.'

'What's that?' Weaver asked.

'Leave when he wants to.'

Rottmann nodded gravely. She said, 'The Chancellor doesn't like him. Your President always brings Hofstadter with him when they meet.'

Tomic said, 'Interesting. Though since President Morozov seems to be surrounded by bruisers, I think he'd like Hofstadter more than he'd like the American President. Not that those two are going to meet anytime soon.' He went on, looking thoughtful, 'I have a distant cousin from Hungary. In 1956, after the Uprising was put down, his parents moved to the Soviet Union – that tells you what kind of people they were. The son – that's my cousin – works in the Kremlin. Perhaps surprisingly, we get on very well, despite the different paths our parents followed and our own different views. He has a dacha in the Valday Forest; very nice at this time of year. President Morozov has one nearby.' Tomic added with a sly smile, 'Slightly grander, I believe. Sometimes my cousin sees him there. He told me Morozov has a good sense of humour and can be witty, but also icily cruel.'

Tomic stopped talking and looked at the table where Hofstadter was holding court. Turning back to Angela, he said, 'You know, if both Blanchett and Hofstadter are here, then something's up.'

'Really?' the German said, sounding as if any irregularity was disturbing to contemplate. 'Even though the President isn't around?'

'He's sent Hofstadter instead,' Tomic said sharply. 'Something's definitely going on.'

3

WEAVER HAD AN EARLY NIGHT, RETURNING STRAIGHT to the Grand when dinner was over, resisting Tomic's entreaties to have a drink in the Cadier Bar. He collected his bag from the front desk, and took the lift up to his room on the top floor. He soon learned why Percy had managed to nab a room in the hotel, for though his room was beautifully if simply decorated, it was extremely small, with one of the few views in Stockholm that was not of water.

Checking his phone, he found a text from JP in the UK, who sounded well into the after-dinner brandy:

Saw two big browns I decided to save for you.

As if. It went on:

Dinner party Saturday night. Don't worry. Fishing first.

Oh Jesus. JP's efforts to integrate into English society, even after almost ten years there, were inevitably painful, especially for his guests.

There was also an email from Mac in New York, or rather an email forwarded by Mac; it was from Weaver's ex-wife:

Dear Mac, hope you are well. As you know, Weaver kept Parker as part of the divorce settlement, but with the clear stipulation that I could have visiting privileges. I now find Parker is effectively in your custody – NOT part of the agreement. Please bring Parker here this Saturday so I can walk him. Shall we say 11 o'clock? Here is my address in Battery Park...

Mac had simply added in a note to Weaver: *I can't make Saturday anyway, and have said so. I hope this isn't going to be a regular request. M.*

The custody battles of a failed marriage. In this case, canine custody. How could she be doing this after not wanting the dog when she'd moved out of their home and in with her new boyfriend? He hit reply and typed in vigorous capitals: *SOME THINGS BEST IGNORED – LIKE HER REQUEST*, then hit Send.

By the afternoon Weaver was running out of steam, hungry after a croissant-only breakfast and long morning session on French exports. The queue for the lunch buffet had been too long to contemplate, and he had gone instead to a side table, where the waiter had served him a single small shrimp sandwich.

Now he sat on the aisle next to Tomic, waiting for another presentation by a multi-lingual panel. Weaver was covering the Italian delegate again. While waiting, he fiddled with a pen Mac had given him. Mac was mad about technology, and forever buying new digital devices during his interpreting travels abroad. This pen, for instance, doubled as a digital recorder. It was sleek and would have been elegant had it not also been the bright red colour of sour cherries. Mac had given it to him when Weaver had stopped by the office before heading for the airport. 'Your consolation prize for missing the fishing in Vermont,' he'd said lightly. 'You can take notes and record a session at the same time – without anyone knowing you're recording them.'

Weaver idly flicked the recording button; there was no telltale light and he wondered if it was working, but there seemed no way to be sure and he could not exactly play it back out loud in the middle of a session. Usually, he worked with a dedicated recorder, an Olympus, tiny but with lots of memory. He had it in his pocket, but there seemed no reason to record any of this session, where the French delegate was now quacking on in the nasal singsong of Provence.

As he made a note to himself for later – to double-check the

terms the EU used for cubic grain capacities – he noticed one of
the pairs of doors at the back of the auditorium swing open and
a man come through, late for the session. It was Sam Blanchett,
and he stood behind the last row of desks, seeming to scan the
ranks of the interpreters rather than the delegates grouped on a
small stage at the front of the room. Blanchett's eyes were moving
methodically, and when they came to Weaver, they stopped. Then
he pointed in Weaver's direction.

Weaver's first instinct was to turn around, to see the object of
Blanchett's attention. But there was no one behind him, only a
side wall of the hall. Blanchett, he realised, was pointing at him.
He looked back at the director and mouthed a soundless *me?*
Blanchett nodded, then crooked his finger and motioned him
to come.

Weaver got up and walked towards the back of the room,
ignoring Tomic's questioning look. When he neared Blanchett,
the man gestured for him to follow and went out the swing door
into the corridor.

There, Weaver joined him. 'You know who I am?' Blanchett
asked tensely, and Weaver nodded. He was taller than Blanchett,
who was hunching both shoulders as if trying to deny this.

'Good. Come with me,' Blanchett said, turning away to go.

'The Italian delegate's about to start.'

Blanchett spoke without looking back. 'Tomic can do it. I'll
text him.'

'But he's handling the Polish submission.'

'He can do both,' said Blanchett impatiently, turning his head
around to look at Weaver. 'This is more important. Come on,' he
said. 'We've got a little trip ahead of us.'

They walked to the rear of the hotel, going through a set
of doors bearing a decal of the international sign forbidding
entry. They passed a laundry room, where two women in maids'
uniforms were folding sheets, and then walked through the
cleaning store of the hotel: an army of buckets and mops, vacuum
cleaners, and squat floor-polishing machines. Pushing the bar on

an exit door, Blanchett led the way outside, where a black BMW saloon was sitting with its engine running. They got in the back, the driver separated by a glass partition that was pulled shut.

They headed north, joining light mid-afternoon traffic, travelling away from the water, though it was hard to call anything 'inland' in a city built on an archipelago of eleven islands. They sat in silence, Weaver full of unspoken questions, until they came to a large circle of park with a central fountain. 'Östermalm,' said Blanchett, pointing out the window as they circled halfway round and continued west, towards the lowering sun. 'The fancy part of town,' he added. He squirmed against the leather of their seats and turned slightly towards Weaver. 'But you know that already, I guess.'

Why did he think that? Weaver had never been to Sweden before. What was this about? Bemused, he said, 'Are you sure you've got the right guy?' It would make a good story at the next Interpreters' Dinner if Blanchett had got it wrong.

'What do you mean?' Blanchett was irritated. 'You are Weaver, aren't you?'

'Yes. But I'm not a diplomat or an analyst. I'm an interpreter.' They were on a long boulevard now, bifurcated by a wide tree-lined pathway, where a couple were towing an obstinate dog on a lead. This was Karlavägen according to the street sign, and reminded Weaver of Commonwealth Avenue in Boston, where his stepfather's mother had lived years before in an elegant apartment building.

'You're one of Pauline's, right?'

Is that how they were known on high? 'Yes.'

'Then I've got the right man. I talked to her an hour ago; I need an interpreter. The one we normally use, Mrs Macauley, had a fall and broke her leg. So you're coming in off the bench. But don't worry: it's not going to take very long.'

Weaver nodded, but he was puzzled. Mrs Macauley was the State Department's senior Russian interpreter. In the old pre-sanctions era, when the two nations still met, Mrs Macauley would invariably get the call, especially if it involved the two respective presidents. But there were no meetings with the Russians these days, not even low-level trade talks, and thus no Russian work for the likes of Mrs Macauley, much less Weaver. As a sop to her veteran standing, she was given the occasional German trade meeting to work; this despite her German being deeply second rate, according to Mac at least. But Weaver didn't have even second-rate German – he had barely any at all – so why was he being called upon to stand in for her? Maybe she had a side-line in French or Italian; he certainly hoped so.

They had turned off the boulevard now and were driving through a residential neighbourhood, a kind of upmarket Queens of low-level apartment blocks. The sequence of buildings finally gave way to greenery, with small fields flanked on three sides by woodland. Houses came into view, perched at a distance on a low ridge facing the road. They were large houses – villas, really; some the size of hotels. Weaver had lost his bearings. He had no idea where they were.

Slowing almost to a halt at the entrance to one of the villas, they went through a pair of open gates before pausing at a sentry box manned by a solitary uniformed guard. The BMW must have been expected, for the man barely glanced at the car before waving them on.

They went up a paved stretch of drive, lined with silver birch trees, their fresh green leaves just beginning to unfurl in the spring sunshine. Through their sparse branches, Weaver caught glimpses of a large mansion. It was the size of the main lodge at a resort, with windows running across the front; from the oblique angle of the drive, Weaver could see the building was almost as deep as it was wide. Characteristically Swedish, it was built out of wood and painted pale yellow ochre; on the third and highest floor, there were protruding dormer windows. There was something peculiar about it. Then Weaver realised there was no one on the porch or in the grounds; no sign of anyone at all.

'Where are we?' Weaver ventured, as the car came to a halt.

'A German banker lent us this place. It's his vacation home.' Blanchett seemed to regret these disclosures, adding sharply, 'Enough with the questions.'

They both got out, Blanchett on the side nearest the mansion's front door. As Weaver circled round the back of the car, Blanchett quickened his pace, almost trotting as he went up the steps and through the front door, which had been opened by some invisible hand. Baffled, Weaver followed more slowly, noting a CCTV camera held by a bracket above the entrance.

Inside he found himself in a large entrance hall, an atrium two storeys high. In one corner stood a towering blue-and-white-tiled *kakelugn*, the traditional Swedish stove used to heat houses. Following Blanchett, he crossed the pale parquet floor to the impressively wide staircase that rose to the next floor. The house was spookily empty. Whoever had opened the door for Blanchett had disappeared.

On the next floor they proceeded down a long corridor; the doors on either side were all closed. Turning a corner, they at last encountered someone: a man in an olive suit standing in the corridor, talking intently, seemingly to himself. Then Weaver noted the wire of an earphone emerging from his jacket collar.

Seeing them, the man broke off his conversation and stepped forward as they approached.

'Is their guy here?' Blanchett asked.

'Just arriving now. They'll bring him through the back.' He jerked his head towards a closed set of double doors on one side of the corridor behind him. 'The Chief's already in there.'

'Good. No sign of anyone else?'

'Some English guy tried to follow us from the hotel. A reporter, I think. We put a stop to that.'

Weaver pictured a comatose Englishman dumped in a Swedish hedgerow, then told himself not to be melodramatic. Blanchett's tension must be catching.

'Let me know if he reappears,' said Blanchett. They had almost reached the set of double doors when they opened and a man came out. Tall, with a grey pallor to his skin, he had distinctive high cheekbones and a long nose that had clearly been broken at some stage. 'He's translator?' he asked, pointing to Weaver.

'He's not here to serve lunch,' said Blanchett. 'Now let us through. He's wanted inside.'

'I must search him,' the man said. There was no uncertainty in his voice.

Weaver moved forward. 'Fine,' he said. After all this drama, he wanted to know what was on the other side of the doors.

The Russian man came and patted Weaver down carefully, running his hands along every inch of both legs. He stood up, and said, 'Empty your pockets.'

Blanchett interrupted: 'He went through security at the hotel. He hasn't been anywhere else, and they're waiting for us inside.'

The Russian considered this. 'Okay, you may go,' he said, staring at Weaver as if memorising his face. 'But give me your phone.'

Weaver looked at Blanchett, who shrugged. It was not an unreasonable thing to ask, since phones were often banned from meetings. Weaver reached in the side pocket of his jacket and brought it out. 'And your recorder,' the Russian said. 'You will not be using that.'

Weaver dipped a hand into the same pocket, and retrieving the Olympus handed it to the Russian. The man stood aside and Blanchett went through first, followed by Weaver.

Towards the back of the room, Hank Hofstadter, the White House Chief of Staff, was sitting in one of a pair of ornate high-sided Empire armchairs that were slightly angled towards each other. A smaller straight-backed chair was placed between them, set back a foot or so. There was no one else in the room, which was itself immense and formal and light. The pale walls were decorated with indifferent oil landscapes; three tall baroque mirrors hung between the four windows. Opposite them was a marble fireplace with a solitary piece on its mantel: a cobalt blue porcelain lyre clock, crowned by a gold sunburst. The clock was working: it was a quarter past three.

Hofstadter didn't get up as Blanchett led Weaver towards him. 'Chief,' said Blanchett, 'this is the interpreter.'

'Where's Mrs Macauley?' Hofstadter demanded.

'She had a fall.'

Hofstadter clicked his tongue in disapproval, as if Mrs Macauley should have been there anyway. 'So who's this guy?'

'This is Mr Weaver. He's from the State Department, like Mrs M. Excellent credentials.' He paused, then asked, 'Do you want me to stay, Chief?'

'No,' said Hofstadter. 'The General should be here any minute now. I don't want anyone else in the room. Except for Weaver here; my Russian's a little rusty.' He gave a small laugh.

So Weaver would be working in Russian. Normally this would have cheered him, but instead he felt agitated at the prospect. To be thrown into a confidential confab, conducted – half of it, anyway – in a language internationally proscribed, was unsettling.

As Blanchett left, Hofstadter motioned Weaver to sit down. He went and perched on the little upright chair and looked at Hofstadter. The suit the man was wearing could not be faulted, for it was a dark rich blue and beautifully tailored, making its hefty wearer look impressive rather than fat. With it, Hofstadter wore a white shirt with a blue tie that was studded with little vermilion arrows. But it was the hair that was most striking, swept back behind the ears in twin sheaves, like wheat pushed up by a combine just before the cut.

Half-reclining in his chair, Hofstadter stretched out both legs. 'So, where do you hail from, Weaver?'

'I'm based in the New York office. In the UN Building.'

'Okay, but where were you *raised*?'

'Vermont.'

'The Coolidge state. The quiet president, a model I want you to follow.'

'Sure,' said Weaver mildly, taken aback. 'Can I ask who we're expecting to join us?'

Hofstadter said casually, 'Nobody you would have heard of. I'm not sure what he wants to discuss, but you can be confident it's more important to the Russians than it will be to us. They're the ones who are hurting these days. From our point of view, it's a glorified courtesy call, and you just happen to be the interpreter. It won't take long.'

Weaver nodded obligingly. 'I see,' he said, not at all sure he did.

A door opened behind them and then closed. Weaver heard hard steps on the wood floor. Weaver started to get to his feet, and Hofstadter followed suit, though more slowly. The new arrival, a large man in a suit, waved a flat palm to indicate they should stay seated, though there was nothing cordial in his manner.

'General,' said Hofstadter. 'Good afternoon.' The man nodded and sat down in the other Empire chair. He looked briefly at Weaver and nodded again, more curtly. The General was not in uniform, and seemed awkward in civilian clothes. His suit did not look inexpensive, but it didn't altogether fit his bulky frame – he was tall but corpulent.

Weaver realised there was something familiar about him. What was it? This man wasn't a top military figure (generals were two a penny in the Russian forces) or a member of the Politbureau. Those people Weaver knew because once that had been part of the job, and even after the recent ostracising of the country, he always read the State Department's Russia reports, complete with identifying photos, just in case the situation changed. Had this man featured in one of them? Weaver wasn't sure, but he had seen his face before.

As the man settled into his chair, his jowls moved in a wave down his chin and onto his throat. Then Weaver remembered who he was. They called him *Morzh* – 'the Walrus', nicknamed for these pendulous folds of skin. His real name was Kuzmin. A big bluff character of the old school, reminiscent of the military figures so prominent during the Brezhnev regime. If

Weaver remembered correctly, he had recently and unusually been transferred from the military to Intelligence – the SVR. Probably not for any expertise in Intelligence matters, but for his unquestioned allegiance to Morozov, who needed someone both ruthless and unquestionably loyal to snuff out any dissent in that most secret and least transparent part of the regime.

Weaver realised this wasn't his usual world of semi-obscure trade talks; he needed to pay close attention. And as if going back and forth between two world-famous principals speaking different languages wasn't difficult enough, there was the added problem of what Tomic called 'The Third Man'. It was as if another person, invisible to everyone but the interpreter, was there on the sidelines, acting as a distraction; soon the interpreter would find his thoughts straying – finding himself noticing one of the interlocutors' gaudy ties, or thinking about which restaurant to visit that evening, or wondering if the attractive receptionist who'd issued his credentials was single, even available. There could be none of that now.

He sat back deeper in his chair, so the man on either side could see the other. He took out a little notebook from the inner pocket of his jacket, along with the red digital pen he'd been using in the trade talks.

But then Hofstadter said firmly, 'No notes.' The look he gave Weaver was glacial. Weaver slid the notebook back into his jacket pocket, along with the pen. He had unwittingly violated the interpreter's precept that Waverly, an elderly translator now residing somewhere in a bilingual heaven, had often cited: 'You should be of no more notice than the furniture.'

Fortunately, Kuzmin began to speak, in the sterile prefatory greetings of diplomacy, thanking Hofstadter for meeting with him. He sounded solemn, and conventionally insincere. His Russian was educated but essentially standard and accentless, once a necessity for a successful servant of the Soviet State. There was a hint of St Petersburg, which must be his native city – a few pre-stressed reduced vowels and a bit of the famous 'o' roundness in his intonation. He turned to Weaver for the first time, still speaking in Russian. 'You must tell me if I speak too fast.'

Weaver replied that it was not a problem, and then Kuzmin asked where he was from. Weaver told him Vermont, which didn't seem to mean a lot to the Russian, who said, 'You speak excellent Russian. Like a native, if perhaps one from the last century.'

Weaver smiled briefly, in acknowledgement of the truth in this mild insult. 'Unlike the legendary Mrs Macauley,' Kuzmin went on, to Weaver's surprise: if Kuzmin knew the interpreter, then perhaps these two men had met before. Kuzmin was smiling to himself, as if enjoying a joke only he understood. 'To be truthful with you, she was getting on in years,' he said, and gesturing at Hofstadter added, 'the last time she sat with the two of us, her memory was not so good. But at least it meant I did not worry she would reveal anything of confidence.' He was speaking in Russian and didn't smile, but was watching Weaver's reaction to this carefully, as if gauging the new interpreter's own discretion.

Hofstadter looked disgruntled by the conversation going on without him. 'You know,' he declared impatiently, 'we would never have risked meeting you if you hadn't said it was important. But I haven't got long.' He looked pointedly at his watch. 'I'm seeing the Chinese right after this, back at the Grand. About the proliferation meeting next month in Rome.'

This seemed curiously undiplomatic, like telling your girlfriend you were taking someone else on vacation, then detailing the good time you expected to have with the other woman. Was Hofstadter trying to wrong foot Kuzmin somehow? After Weaver finished translating this, Hofstadter continued more gently: 'Naturally, as I said last time, we will want to make sure your interests are addressed.' It seemed an obvious effort to sound respectful, but the effect was condescending; the sentence landed like a bone thrown from a dinner table where the Russian had not been invited to sit.

Disconcerted by the silence, Hofstadter went on: 'If you have any requests for items you'd like us to bring up with them, then please tell me now. I was assuming that's what you wanted to discuss today.'

The General still said nothing, and his expression remained inscrutable. Hofstadter shifted in his chair and stared crossly, first at Kuzmin, then at Weaver, who felt powerless; it was not as if he could make the General start talking.

'I made a special trip for this,' Hofstadter complained. 'It wasn't easy getting here, you know.'

Kuzmin suddenly sighed. He spoke at last. 'I think you'd find the complications of my travel arrangements here rather outstripped yours.' He added, 'I've never been an Austrian before.'

Of course. Kuzmin must have travelled incognito, using false papers and even, it seemed, a false nationality. To travel that way was risky, even for a spy; it meant the meeting must be important for the Russians.

Kuzmin went on: 'Let me clarify at once: I am not here to ask you to pander to the Chinese on our behalf. We have our own confidential relationship with them, which I do not propose to discuss with you.'

This sounded like a mix of bravado and wounded pride; it was also pretty rude by any standard, diplomatic or not, and Weaver paused momentarily before translating it. 'I am not here to ask for favours,' Kuzmin added. His tone was snappish, almost hostile, and Hofstadter stiffened, his face reddening when he heard the translation. He looked increasingly wary, like a boar catching the scent of a hunter in the woods.

Kuzmin paused, then said deliberately, 'I am here about a debt.'

Hofstadter said, 'Well, if you mean the Germans, they had their money—'

But Kuzmin interrupted, saying, 'I am not here about the money, which I understand was repaid some time ago. And there is no problem with the German bank, which is prospering, like so many Western banks. Especially when the dirty clothes that go to them are made clean as new linen. Like the "clothes" you were supplied with.' Kuzmin's voice was now artificially soft. 'But the money was guaranteed by a foreign power; we are no longer talking about Germany. A foreign power that looks on you with friendly eyes, despite our recent misunderstandings. That said, I doubt sincerely your House of Representatives would approve of the country's generosity to you and your... colleague.'

Weaver hesitated, wondering how bluntly he should put this in English; he sensed that Hofstadter reacted badly to threats. But Kuzmin was having none of it. 'Go on,' he ordered Weaver in Russian. 'Tell him what I said. That's your job here, so do it.'

Weaver did as he was told. The ensuing silence was painfully long. 'So,' the Russian said at last, 'I wanted to see you here to remind you of the help we gave you. The bank of Galkin was involved in name only. The true debt was to the guarantor.'

Weaver wasn't sure he had heard this name correctly – was it Galkin or Caulkin? A surname, or a financial term he had never heard before? *The Galkin Exchange* perhaps – it could have been a Len Deighton novel, the kind his father liked. He said the name indistinctly as he translated Kuzmin's words, and Hofstadter looked momentarily puzzled. But Kuzmin was now talking again, so Weaver could hardly ask the Russian to repeat himself.

'Of course, to be candid, the debt was to our President.' He switched to English unexpectedly. 'Naturally, he is aware of the other individual's involvement. I am referring, of course, to—'

'Stop,' Hofstadter interrupted, raising his voice for the first time in Kuzmin's presence. He looked alarmed. Weaver wondered why. 'Not here,' Hofstadter said tersely, looking at Kuzmin but tilting his head in Weaver's direction.

Kuzmin stared back at Hofstadter, and said, 'We are willing to stay silent about this history, but in return we want the arrangement we proposed last time honoured by your President. I have mentioned it before; it is a minor matter to you, and easily accomplished.'

Hearing Weaver's translation, Hofstadter looked uneasy, as if he suspected a full house in the other player's hand. 'Go on,' he said.

Kuzmin continued. 'Our understanding is that an announce-ment is imminent. We want a place on the list.'

'Pardon,' said Hofstadter.

Weaver was surprised that Hofstadter had not understood him; he was taking pains to speak clearly. He was about to repeat his translation of Kuzmin's words when the Russian interjected, exclaiming crossly in English, 'Yes!'

Yes what?

Kuzmin added, 'There is one particular name we wish to see put on the list.'

'You mentioned this last time. Why do you want it so badly?' Hofstadter asked, blunter still.

Kuzmin said, 'We have our reasons.' Hofstadter looked about to protest, but Kuzmin added firmly, 'The individual's importance is to us, not you.'

Hofstadter was shaking his head. 'I have come here as the representative of the President of the United States, at his request – and yours. Yet you seem to want my government to help you in an entirely unusual way, one you won't explain.'

'No, I will not.'

Hofstadter shook his head with fake regret. 'Then I'm afraid the answer is still no.'

Weaver supplied the Russian words carefully, but Kuzmin looked unperturbed, and his voice was steady and cold: 'I have only one superior, Mr Hofstadter. I too am here expressly on his behalf.'

As Weaver finished translating this, Hofstadter was shaking his head again. 'How is that relevant?'

Kuzmin said, 'Can't you tell? You see, if you decide to keep this individual in the US of A, then Comrade Morozov will not be satisfied, but you will be even less happy.'

Hofstadter made a show of shrugging once Weaver put the words into English. 'I don't think publicising an arrangement made years ago is going to strike the world as earth-shattering, even if it can be traced back to Moscow. A bit of a three-day wonder,' he added dismissively.

'Perhaps not, if that were all. Remember our conversation the last time we met.'

Hofstadter looked startled. Kuzmin continued: 'You enjoyed your stay in Moscow a few years ago, I believe.'

'What's that got to do with anything?' Hofstadter was starting to flush.

Kuzmin shrugged. 'In Moscow, the prime entry in our video holdings features your own youthful escapades – I emphasise "youthful". I am not sure if people will be amazed or disgusted by the content we would release. Perhaps both. Informally it is known to the clerks in the registry by your nickname. They are assiduous researchers, those gentlemen, especially if there is something comic about what they unearth. I think in this case the nickname is a prime example of what Americans used to call a Polish joke.'

And Kuzmin laughed, loud enough that Weaver had to raise his voice while translating the words. Kuzmin seemed oblivious or just uninterested in Hofstadter's reaction, and clearly the unspecified joke was at Hofstadter's expense, especially as Kuzmin had used the term *klichka* for nickname, which had derogatory connotations. Weaver did his best to keep his tone completely neutral, while Hofstadter sat stony-faced as the laughter continued provocatively.

Stifling a further guffaw, Kuzmin said, 'All most unfortunate, and for no reason whatsoever – except your own pride and your unwarranted suspicion about our request.' He had stopped laughing altogether now and was staring hard at Hofstadter as he added, 'And your lack of respect.'

Kuzmin allowed Hofstadter to digest this once Weaver had finished putting it into English. When Kuzmin did eventually go on, he spoke quickly, almost breezily, as if only minor details remained to hash out. 'We need this to happen quickly.'

'How much time has the man got left?'

'Two years minimum. Long enough that inducements from your Intelligence people might lead him to do something foolish.'

'Like talking?' Hofstadter asked mildly, but the underlying sarcasm was undisguised.

'Like betraying his Motherland. We cannot take that chance.' He waited for Weaver to finish, then said, 'Dan Berry. That's the one. Here are the details.'

An envelope had somehow materialised in Kuzmin's hand. He reached across Weaver and handed it to Hofstadter, who quickly tucked it away in his jacket's inside pocket. Kuzmin started to go on: 'Sukolov—'

'Who?' Hofstadter interjected; he sounded both baffled and concerned.

'Forgive the native name,' Kuzmin said, sounding entirely uncontrite.

'No more names,' Hofstadter interjected quickly and emphatically. His eyes shifted like swivelling tanks towards Weaver, then back again to the Russian. 'This will be tricky to do unnoticed.'

'It should not be beyond your capabilities. Attention will be on Washington.'

'I hope so.'

'That we leave to you.'

'Are you sure the guy will want to go home?'

'Of course. Sukolov—'

Hofstadter interrupted. 'I said no more names.' He tilted his head towards Weaver while his eyes stayed firmly on Kuzmin; it was a warning, Weaver realised, a warning about him. Kuzmin nodded, unbothered, then said forcefully, 'We expect the announcement no later than this weekend, with the release to follow immediately. Yes?'

The tone was of a measured ultimatum; push had come to shove. Weaver translated very carefully, picking words that were entirely unambiguous to convey the clarity of Kuzmin's expectation. Not that he himself understood what Kuzmin was talking about. Who was Dan Berry? And who was Sukolov? Which normally would be 'Sokolov'.

'But you know, this kind of thing takes time—'

Kuzmin cut him off. 'Yes, and time is of the essence to us. Is that clear? Otherwise, unfortunately I am afraid our secret will certainly emerge, and I do not mean the bank business. Galkin is the least of your problems. Now, is that agreed?' he asked insistently. He leaned back in his chair, waiting for the American to respond.

Which seemed to take an age. Hofstadter bit his lip and looked around the room, as if hoping to find assistance elsewhere. His gaze travelled so slowly that for a brief moment Weaver wondered whether Hofstadter was going to reply at all. But finally, almost imperceptibly, he nodded, clearly and strongly enough to indicate surrender.

Before Hofstadter could add a verbal confirmation, there was a sharp knock and the room's twin doors opened. Blanchett came in, followed by the tall Russian who had taken Weaver's phone.

'Chief,' Blanchett said as he walked towards them. 'Excuse the interruption but you're due back at the Grand. The Chinese will be there shortly.'

'Okay. We're done here,' Hofstadter said, and stood up. He shook hands quickly with Kuzmin as the Russian rose, then crossed the room and stood by one of the large gilt-framed mirrors, where Blanchett joined him. They talked in low inaudible tones while Weaver stood awkwardly by himself; Kuzmin, ignoring him completely and sitting down again, spoke to the Russian security man. Then Hofstadter crooked a finger at Weaver, signalling for him to come over. As he did, Blanchett moved away out of earshot.

In a low half-whisper, Hofstadter said to Weaver, 'I don't know what you think of this meeting with that nobody, but you are to forget all about it. It's strictly confidential. You understand?'

'I understand,' Weaver said dutifully.

'No, you don't understand. That's my point.' This was true enough; Weaver had found Kuzmin's remarks baffling. Hofstadter continued: 'It involves matters of national security, and that's why you would have found it hard to follow.'

He took a step back, as if weighing what else to say. Weaver was struck by the contradictory accounts he had been given in the space of twenty minutes. First this had been a courtesy call with a nobody; now it was a matter of national security.

Hofstadter said sternly, 'Any leak about this could do massive damage to our country. So you can't tell anyone anything about it. Not a soul: not your wife, or your girlfriend or your boyfriend or any kind of friend you have.' His eyes stayed fixed on Weaver's face as if he were waiting for something to appear. He said, 'If you disobey this order, which I assure you has the approval of the Commander in Chief, you will regret it. I'll have you transferred to Alabama in six hours flat. Then you can translate mush mouth for the rest of your distinguished career. Is *that* understood?'

'Yes sir,' he said again, this time genuinely. Hofstadter nodded, seemingly satisfied, and walked away. Weaver started to leave as well. As he walked past the seated Kuzmin, the Russian turned towards him and said, 'I remember this Vermont that was your home.'

'Really?'

'It was once home of the writer Demidov, too.'

'So I have been told.'

'His New Jerusalem,' Kuzmin said acidly. 'Though later he was eager to return to the old one.'

Weaver replied, 'Well, they say that even in Moscow, Guy Burgess lived for the cricket scores in the British papers.'

'Burgess was no Demidov.' Kuzmin's voice was contemptuous. He got up and said something to the long-nosed Russian security man. The security man said to Weaver, 'I want your notebook.'

'And I'd like my phone back,' said Weaver. He realised Blanchett had returned and was now by his side. 'And my recorder.'

'First your notebook,' the Russian ordered.

'I didn't take any notes,' Weaver said, but handed it over.

The man didn't even pretend to inspect the contents, but with one enormous wrench used his hands to tear the moleskin notebook in two, then shoved the halves into the inside pocket of his jacket.

'So much for my coverage of this morning's trade talks,' Weaver said to Blanchett. He noticed that Hofstadter had left for his meeting with the Chinese. Weaver held his hand out to the Russian, and the man gave back his phone and recorder. As Weaver deposited them into his pocket again, there was a small but audible *beep!*

'What was that?' the Russian demanded, speaking Russian. He looked alarmed.

It must have been the red pen, now sitting again in Weaver's jacket. He had forgotten all about it. He said quickly, 'My phone. It's reminding me to take my medication.'

'For what?' asked Blanchett unhelpfully.

'Hypertension,' he said spontaneously. 'I take pills for blood pressure.'

'Ah,' said Blanchett with relief. 'I was worried this guy had bugged your phone during the meeting. Anyway, you're all done now. Let's go.'

But the tall, grey-faced Russian moved to block their departure. 'I need to search you again.'

Enough was enough. Blanchett said crossly, 'Come on, he's already been searched on the way in. The meeting's over. So let us through please, or we'll be late for our next appointment.'

Grudgingly, the Russian moved to one side. Once they were through the double doors, Blanchett said, 'The driver will take you back to the Grand. He's in the courtyard out back. Come on, I'll show you.' He hustled Weaver down the empty corridor, towards the rear of the house. Suddenly he slowed down, and looked at Weaver suspiciously. 'Now listen. The meeting you just attended? Mrs Macauley took it. You weren't here.'

'Really?'

'Yes, really.' Seeing Weaver's face, he shrugged. 'Hofstadter's orders.' So that's what Blanchett and Hofstadter had been conferring about.

'What will Mrs Macauley say about that?' asked Weaver.

'Not a lot,' Blanchett said mysteriously. 'But tell me,' he said, his tone lightening, and innocent. 'Did something weird happen in the meeting? Hank seemed very out of sorts. I'd like to know in case he brings it up.'

He was searching Weaver's face, as if looking for an answer. What did the man expect him to say, thought Weaver, since he had little real idea himself of what had just taken place? He could see now why Blanchett got on people's nerves. He shrugged and did his best to look mystified – easy enough since he was. Blanchett looked about to say something, then thought better of it, and motioned Weaver to come with him.

Ahead, set back in a small recess, there was a lift. Waiting for it was a man in a medic's uniform, grasping the rail of an empty gurney. As they passed, they saw another man at its side. He also wore a white coat, and a stethoscope was looped around his neck. Seeing Blanchett, he shook his head wearily. 'We worked on her for over half an hour here. No good. She was DOA at the hospital.' The lift arrived, its doors opened, and he helped the paramedic push the gurney forward.

'Come on,' Blanchett ordered, shooing Weaver along. They had taken just a few more steps when Blanchett stopped. 'I'm going to leave you now,' he said. He pointed ahead of them to the end of the corridor. 'The car is in the back – through that door. The driver will take you to the Grand.'

'Who was DOA?' Weaver did not want to leave without knowing.

'Mrs Macauley,' Blanchett said with a sigh.

'I thought she broke her leg.'

Blanchett stopped again, as behind them the lift door closed with a loud *clank*. 'She did.' He paused. 'And then she had a heart attack.' He shrugged, as if it were all in a day's work. 'It's got nothing to do with you.'

It didn't? Then why tell Weaver to pretend that Mrs Macauley had worked the meeting? Not that she could confirm or deny it now. Maybe that was the point.

Still, it unsettled him to have his own professional discretion questioned. Weaver had the security clearance required and then some; he could have been drafted into a confab with the Pope and still been good to go. So why was he now so obviously distrusted? The meeting must have taken an entirely unexpected turn, and clearly, he had heard something he wasn't meant to hear. Much less understand.

4

JOHN PAUL HARBINGER HAD MADE $167 MILLION in a hedge fund currency coup. Yet not all the money in the world could alter the fundamental fact that JP was a horse's ass. Though usually a nice one.

JP himself knew this, and had moved to the UK at least in part because, despite his new wealth, his fellow Americans still regarded him as a doofus. He saw England as a land where he could reinvent himself, given the money at his disposal. And he remained Weaver's friend because he trusted Weaver not to tell on him.

With his new fortune, JP had bought a flat in Belgravia for his trips to town, and for his main residence spent £4 million (a bagatelle for him) on a Queen Anne jewel in Wiltshire called the Dower House. It had a façade of faded pink brick, sash windows lovingly restored, eight bedrooms (thanks to the additional Victorian wing, safely hidden from view at the front), and thirty acres of land. The house dated from 1705, JP had proudly told Weaver, and was listed in Pevsner's *Buildings of England*.

Weaver was not in the least jealous of his friend's property, since he could envisage nothing but the duties that must come from owning it: spending a fortune on gardeners to keep the grounds in shape for the annual open day, buying a round in the local pub to show he was congenial and not a snob, paying the 'staff' just enough to win their loyalty without triggering the resentment of the local gentry (who were accustomed to paying far less). Too much to worry about; none of it appealed.

But for its mile of double bank fishing on a world-famous fly-fishing river, he would have gladly made do with a second-hand residence the size of a children's doll house; to Weaver, the fishing rights were where all the value lay. He had visited his friend in England four times before, three of them – not coincidentally – between May and October, the rich sweet interlude that constitutes the British fly-fishing season.

Turning off the main road, Weaver drove through landscaped parkland, studded with mature oak and copper beech trees. JP's house was less than ten miles from the motorway, but sat in utterly unspoiled countryside. Weaver had grown up in Vermont's semi-alpine topography, which was spiky as a troubling electrocardiogram; and New York City possessed the same contrasts – the height of its man-made towers was mountain-like, and the grid-like streets below were the equivalents of mountain passes. But here the terrain, if not exactly flat, rose and fell only gently and with warning. The surroundings were peaceful and undramatic, though now the hawthorn blossom was out, punctuating the hedgerows with explosions of tiny pinkish-white flowers.

He parked on the edge of the circular gravel drive by the front door, which was painted white beneath a handsome pediment. The front entrance was rarely used. He went round to the back, where he found JP's wife, Sue, in the kitchen feeding their Labrador and instructing the cook.

Sue was blue-eyed and blonde and would have been the stereotypical spouse for a man with new money had she not also been considerably educated and, about everything but money, twice as smart as JP. They had met at Harvard Business School, during which time she had had a succession of well-heeled suitors, including a Jordanian prince and the son of a Hollywood mogul. Throughout, JP had been her dobbin-like friend; it was only when he started at Goldman Sachs, while Sue was still looking for work, that they became a couple.

She was from California, where JP refused to live, so she had to be content instead with bringing over a rich supply of items from that cultural epicentre. Given JP's new-found Anglophilia, their marriage was therefore one of move and countermove, a chequers game between JP's romanticism and Sue's own belief that life between Malibu and Marin represented the apogee of human achievement. When JP insisted on installing an Aga, she put in a restaurant-sized range; when he bought at auction a large canteen of Georgian cutlery, she spent three thousand dollars on enamel knives ordered from a shop in San Francisco's Japantown.

Towards Weaver, Sue was thoroughgoingly semi-friendly. 'Hello stranger,' she said now, sounding a little subdued, though supplementing the greeting with a kiss on both cheeks. Weaver always felt she regarded him suspiciously, even though his friendship with her husband pre-dated the latter's wealth; he could hardly be accused of liking JP for his dough. Perhaps she resented the fact that Weaver came from a bygone era, when JP was neither rich nor married to her, though it was never clear which of these two aspects of her husband's past irked her the most.

Weaver put down his bag and unzipped it, then took out two packages. 'This is for you,' he said, setting a gift-wrapped box of cognac with a fancy bow on the kitchen table. 'And this is for JP,' he said, handing over a new English-language anthology of Russian poets of the Silver Age.

'Thank you,' said Sue with a dutiful smile. It was an old joke, first perpetrated accidentally by another guest: Sue didn't drink, and JP had not read a poem since grade school.

'Mrs Wilson, you remember Mr Weaver,' she said to the cook, as if it were a further instruction.

Mrs Wilson stared blankly at Weaver and said, 'Yes, of course.'

'You're in the wing,' said Sue to Weaver. 'Hope that's okay — same room as last time.'

'That's great,' he said brightly, admiring her memory since he knew they had a lot of guests, and it had been almost two years since he had last signed the visitors' book. He wasn't fussy anyway, and was relieved not to be in the main house near the master bedroom; on one occasion Sue and JP had argued so fiercely that the noise had come through the walls. It was hard to have breakfast with a couple whose relationship had been reduced just hours before to a series of 'fuck you's'.

Sue said, 'You probably want to get down to the river; I know JP's waiting for you. Leave your bag and jacket here, you can take them up later. Just don't stay too long, please; we've got guests for dinner. You can fish tomorrow – if you want to. I suppose you will.'

He did as instructed and walked out the back, through the formal parterre, bounded by old-fashioned iron railing, the cost of which had made even JP flinch – per foot, he said, it was more expensive than the house itself. Weaver proceeded through a little kissing gate, fashioned by a local carpenter and stained to suggest a history it didn't possess, and onto a tractor-wide path that cut through the grass of the wildflower meadow, where a medley of cowslips, red campion and ox-eye daisies was emerging. The breeze was picking up a bit, but he could hear the river's flow.

He found JP standing awkwardly on the freshly mown grass strip that ran along the river bank. He was tall, well over six foot, but gawky and unprepossessing, with curly hair and skinny bones; if it came to a fight, no one in their right mind would put money on JP. Weaver watched for a minute as his friend cast to a pool formed on the far side where the little river widened, slowing its flow; on the near side, right in front of them, the current was much swifter.

JP had taken up fly fishing in college, at Weaver's behest after they had first become friends. He'd fallen for it in a big way, perhaps because ostensibly fly fishing did not require any special athletic ability – JP was no athlete. But it did require coordination, a certain physical grace, which made it the more galling for JP that he would never be anything but mediocre when he cast a fly. Even with tuition from the school at Orvis in Vermont, and Hardy-endorsed instructors in the UK, casting proved a skill impossible for him to master, though God knows JP had spent enough money trying.

Weaver was uneasy with his friend's discomfort when they fished together, but his irritation had gradually been replaced by respect for JP's deep if unreciprocated passion for the sport. Weaver's own father had once fished with Weaver and his friend, on a rare weekend trip to Vermont intended to forge some connection with his son. Weaver had found JP deeply embarrassing that day, from his inability to tie a blood knot to the countless times he tangled his line in the bank's tag alders. He had said to his father, 'Sorry to have brought him. He's hopeless.'

His father had shaken his head. 'But he loves it. That's all that matters.'

JP cast again now, aware from the corner of his eye that Weaver was watching. He was always proud of the length of line he could hurl across a river (*hurl* being the appropriate word). His pride collapsed, however, as he overdid it, and reached the willow branch on the far bank, where his fly stuck. He pulled at the leader impatiently, almost to breaking point, until Weaver walked towards him and gently intervened.

'Let me help,' he said and took the rod from JP, then laying it down held the line and walked along the bank ten feet or so. There he stood and tugged the line gently, then not so gently up and down. The branch suddenly released, and the fly flew through the air, then settled with a small bump on the water and headed downstream.

'How did you manage that?' asked JP, as Weaver handed back the line and rod. He sounded more resentful than pleased.

Weaver laughed. 'Because I've snagged a lot more flies than you, I guess.' He watched as JP false cast twice and then let the fly go, where it fell short of the pool by three or four feet.

JP shook his head as he hauled in line. 'Your turn,' he said, handing over the rod. It was split cane with a cork handle, eight foot six inches long and incredibly light. From Hardy and Co, or possibly handmade by some artisan JP had unearthed through friends in a famous fishing syndicate that was located nearby but would never, ever have JP as a member. Weaver drew the line back and made one false cast, then flicked it forward casually, feeling the line surge. The leader gradually unfurled, and the fly, a Grey Wulff from the looks of it, landed with the faintest kiss just above the pool.

'Jesus,' said JP. 'If you knew the hours I spend practising.'

'I've been doing it since I was four years old, JP.'

JP shook his head again. Weaver pulled line in as the fly joined the downstream drift, false cast to dry it, then set it down once again just upstream from the middle of the little pool. The river there was deep and deceptively placid. A leaf fell from an overhanging branch; at first it twirled slowly in the indented disc of water made by its weight, then picked up speed and sailed downstream quick as a man could run.

JP said, 'The rise won't be for another hour or two. You won't get a strike now.'

Weaver's line immediately tautened, and JP cursed again. A few minutes later, he grudgingly netted the fish for Weaver. It was a nice Brown, maybe a pound and a half, which Weaver was happy to let go.

Then JP said, 'Did the Reverend ever fish?'

'No.'

'Of course. Your Real Dad taught you, like he tried to teach me.' JP looked wistful. 'My old man's idea of fishing was to drag a net through Timkins Lake, then boil the catch in an empty oil barrel.' He sounded like he was sucking a lemon. He added more equably, 'So how's life?'

'Can't complain.'

'You hate New York, don't you?'

Weaver shrugged. 'It lets me fish.'

'Amazing,' said JP, sounding oddly pleased. 'You have to live in the big city so you can spend time in the countryside.'

It was an irony not lost on Weaver. He said, a little tetchily, 'What can I tell you? They pay me well; and I'm lucky to have the job.'

JP nodded absent-mindedly. His focus on his own money could be intense and unremitting, but he was rarely interested in the finances of other people, perhaps because even Weaver's salary of $187,000 was pocket money to him.

'How was Stockholm?' JP asked, his attention back.

'Interesting,' Weaver said neutrally. He was a little surprised JP had registered where he'd been. Not always the case.

'You should have learned Chinese instead of Russian.'

'I had a head start with Russian.'

'I have a friend at *The Times* who says the Chinese want us to lift some of the sanctions on Russia. Apparently, they tried to raise it at the summit when they saw the White House guy, Hofstadter.'

When Weaver said nothing, JP pressed him. 'What do you know about that?'

'Less than your friend.'

JP quickly looked at Weaver but seemed to find nothing there. 'I thought maybe you'd know. You were there, after all. Though I suppose if it were a secret meeting it wouldn't have got down to…' JP stopped, but Weaver could imagine what his friend was thinking. …*wouldn't have got down to your level. To a bit player like you. Who I entertain because he is polite and decent company, and for old times' sake. But who is – let's face it – in a distinctly minor league compared to my own life in the Majors.*

These thoughts were not reflected in anything JP had actually said, but as with most friendships, especially of such long duration, the unspoken weighed as heavily as the declared. After an awkward silence, JP changed the subject. 'Your pal Tomic called me this morning.'

'Elek did?' He wondered why.

'Yes. He was probably looking for you. I didn't actually speak to him. He left a message on the London landline. He didn't leave a number; do you have it?'

'It's on my cell phone back at the house.'

JP had taken the rod back and cast an absent-minded fly halfway across the water, then almost by accident managed to mend his line without the usual small explosion on the water's surface. Watching his line, he said, 'I wonder if the Chinese have been talking to the Russians about sanctions.'

'JP, I wouldn't know.' Why was his old friend curious about this? Maybe a Western show of leniency — weakness really, in Weaver's view, sparked by greed — would affect the bond markets or something. JP would have been terribly excited to learn about the meeting between Hofstadter and Kuzmin; it was clearly not the first rendezvous they had had, which made it even more imperative not to tell his friend anything. God knows, Weaver had been warned enough to keep quiet.

The evening before, still in Stockholm, he had been asked by the hotel to move rooms. He had done so grudgingly, only to find himself transferred to an opulent suite with a view of the harbour reserved for some dignitary who hadn't shown. An ice bucket with a bottle of Bollinger had arrived from room service as recompense for the disruption; he poured a large glass full of fizz, and took a long drink, feeling after his day that he deserved it.

He was rattled by the meeting in what he now thought of as the Banker's House. What actually had he heard that would be so damaging if it were widely known? Something that lay somewhere in the thicket of Kuzmin's demands and Hofstadter's ineffectual defensive parries. He tried to remember the final exchanges; normally, he could have repeated almost the entire conversation between the two men verbatim. But not now — for some reason, the words in his head were just an aural stew of stray phrases. Weaver could feel again the tension that had filled the room while Kuzmin waited for Hofstadter's compliance. The tension, but not the words.

Maybe it would help if he wrote down what he could remember. He got up and found a fresh notebook, then poked in his bag for a pen, fruitlessly. He felt in his pocket and found the red pen Mac had given him. He clicked it to extend the point and sat down again. He was about to start writing when from nowhere the voice of Tomic came out loud and clear. 'I was not impressed by the dinner last night,' his friend was saying. 'Were you?'

And Weaver heard himself replying, 'It was okay. The wine was good.'

'Just not enough of it,' Tomic said.

It seemed the pen had been recording his conversation earlier that afternoon.

Intrigued, he sat and waited for more, but at first there was only silence. Had it stopped altogether? Then he heard steps and the sound of a swing door. Of course, he had got up from his seat in the amphitheatre, summoned by Blanchett. Sure enough, he now heard the man's voice demand, 'You know who I am?'

Weaver was completely fascinated. He didn't touch the pen again for fear of erasing something, and sat spellbound while he heard the conversation as he and Blanchett travelled in the BMW to the Banker's House, and then as he worked the confidential meeting between the representatives of the world's two most powerful presidents. He was so engrossed that he ignored his room phone when it rang. He didn't want to think who was at the other end. Probably Blanchett relaying more threats from Hofstadter.

Weaver had got the name 'Galkin' right, he discovered on hearing it again, but almost immediately after that, the well ran dry: the recording stopped, tantalisingly, just after the mention of someone named 'Dan Berry', whoever he might be. Kuzmin had pronounced it clearly enough – 'Dan Berry,' Kuzmin had said. 'That's the one. Here are his details.' And then... nothing; the tape had run dry.

There had been other names after that and Weaver struggled to remember them. One had been a Russian name, he was certain, since Kuzmin had said something about 'a native name', only to be cut short by a panicky Hofstadter. Did this mean there were two names for the same person? And there had been reference to a Polish joke as well – was it somehow tied to the 'nickname' for Hofstadter? He thought so, but wished the joke had been explained.

Though he was now more concerned with the dialogue that was missing, Weaver tried to understand the meaning of what was on the tape. There had been a reference by Kuzmin to an arrangement. But for what – and why? Because Hofstadter owed the Russians money? No; Kuzmin had said explicitly that the debt had been repaid. From what he remembered of Hofstadter's protestations, it seemed that a lot was being asked for by the Russians. If only he could hear the final part of the conversation again, when Hofstadter had reluctantly acceded to Kuzmin's demands. But there was only a prolonged silence from the recorder, terminating in the same-sounding imperilling beep that had startled the Russian security man and Blanchett, too.

At ten he had just ordered room service (a Caesar salad) when the room's phone rang again. This time he answered. It was Tomic, suggesting a drink and complaining that it had been hard to track Weaver down. From the background noise, he sensed Tomic was calling from one of the hotel bars downstairs. He had spent enough time with the Hungarian to tell when he had been drinking; his voice grew high and thin, though contrarily, his face turned heavy, beef-like and sweaty. In person, he would work his tie knot up and down like a bellringer's rope.

'Not tonight, Elek,' said Weaver.

'Really? I covered for you at the session,' Tomic said. 'You owe me one.'

'Okay, drinks on me, but it'll have to be another time,' said Weaver.

'Spoil sport,' said Tomic. 'I'll have to ask Mrs Macauley instead.'

The senior woman had been respected, but also been a slight figure of fun. Her clothes had looked pre-war – the Crimean War, according to Mac. Now Weaver said nothing, remembering Hofstadter's threats.

'Have you seen her today?' asked Tomic.

'No. Why? Should I have?'

'Not at all. Someone said she was looking for me, but I couldn't find her. What did Blanchett want, anyway?'

He hesitated, realising that Tomic would have seen Blanchett summoning him from the doors in the auditorium. Weaver was a lousy liar according to his ex-wife, and had never developed the useful facility of actually believing the lie he was telling. He spoke slowly to Tomic, trying to sound offhand. 'I had to translate a letter they had from some Russian science *apparatchik*. A potential defector, apparently.'

'Couldn't Mrs M have done it instead? She wasn't working our session; *my* session, thanks to you.'

'I don't know. You'd have to ask Blanchett.'

'He's a mine of misinformation, as you know,' said Tomic.

Weaver laughed, then replied, 'I've been spared up until now. I don't think he even knew my name before today.'

'Probably not. But anything interesting in the meeting?' He seemed as interested as Blanchett had been; hopefully, Tomic could be similarly put off.

'Not to me. I couldn't understand most of it. I wasn't sure what to call a quark in Russian. Do you know?'

'*Tvorog*,' said Tomic.

'That's the dairy product,' said Weaver, and they both laughed. Weaver was relieved to sense that his friend seemed to have lost interest in Mrs Macauley, and then Tomic asked, sounding more cheerful, 'You are off next week? Fishing?'

'That's right. Let's have dinner once I'm back at work,' Weaver proposed.

'Great. Send my regards to JP if you see him. And see you back at the ranch,' said Tomic; he was fond of American lingo. 'Ciao for now,' he added, which he also liked to say, and hung up the phone.

Weaver drank some more champagne absent-mindedly. His thoughts were on the gurney and the still unreal-seeming fact of Mrs Macauley's death. A freak accident, and then an ensuing heart attack. So he had been told. But what if that weren't true? Could someone have pushed the woman down a convenient flight of stairs? Why? To put him in the interpreter's chair instead? But Hofstadter didn't trust him. This was followed by an even more chilling thought – what if they would now want him out of the way as well? Did that explain the presence of the Russian security man in the arrivals hall at Heathrow?

He let this paranoid thread run only so far. Stop it, he told himself. A day from now he would be at JP's in England, with nothing more to worry about than what fly to put on the end of his line.

Yet as Weaver now stood on the river bank, he was still struggling to make sense of what he'd heard, never mind why he'd been there to hear it. The Russians had a hold on the American government, and they were exercising it. That was clear, but not much else was, including what the Russians wanted in return.

JP, with his large financial brain, might understand it, not that Weaver could trust JP's discretion. But Weaver might as well learn what he could.

'JP, tell me. Do you know anything about laundering?'

JP looked startled. 'Money laundering?'

'I wasn't thinking of pillowcases.'

'Only from a distance, pal. A nice safe distance. Why do you ask?'

'It just came up in one of the trade sessions I worked. I didn't really understand it.'

'I don't think you want to.' But he proceeded to give a quick exposition which even Weaver could follow. Money came in dirty and got returned clean from new and healthier association: a sleazy casino owner with three hundred grand in cash 'loaned' it to a hotel owner keen to build another hotel; then it got paid back through a reputable bank that the casino owner had an account with... That one was relatively easy to follow, JP explained, but others were complicated, with shell companies and multiple territories involved, all of which – and this was the point – served to make the money trail virtually impossible to untangle.

When he'd finished, Weaver asked, 'How often do banks play a *knowing* role in this?'

'Respectable banks, you talking about, or just the fly-by-night ones in the Seychelles?' He let his fly lag downstream and looked piercingly at Weaver. 'But really, why are you asking?'

'No reason. I read something else about it in a magazine. It was on the plane.'

JP was still staring at him. 'You were always a terrible liar, Weaver.'

'I'm not lying about anything,' he said firmly.

'Just by omission, pal. Just by omission,' and JP looked ready to say more when there was an enormous splash not ten feet from the bank.

For once JP managed to stop himself from jerking the fly out of the trout's mouth. He even let the fish run downstream for a while, and was adroit enough reeling it in that the trout eventually, fatally, tired. Five minutes later, Weaver knelt on both knees, and gently sliding JP's net into the water, lifted it with its captive and laid them both on the bank.

JP was jubilant, and Weaver happy to see him take so much pleasure.

'Come on,' JP said at last, after he'd put the fish in his creel. 'We better get back. There's still time for you to have a rest before our guests arrive. You must be beat.'

'I am a bit,' he admitted. 'Who else is coming to dinner?'

JP rattled off a list, with such casualness that Weaver sensed it had been constructed with the care a social climber gives to a staircase. The reporter from *The Times* who he'd mentioned, which made Weaver nervous; less ominously, the local MP, who had shaky hands ('don't let him pass the decanter,' JP said); a woman named Lily who had helped Sue decorate the house; a man who sold… By now Weaver had stopped trying to keep them straight; there seemed to be about a dozen people coming, though it was the reporter he wanted to avoid. 'Oh, and Louise, a new friend of Sue. A bit of a goer, in case you're feeling lonely.'

Was he? No more than the next man suffering from a disastrous divorce; no more than your average thirty-plus-something interpreter who'd come to see an old friend and do some fishing. Or come for the fishing at the invitation of his old friend. He was not so much lonely, he felt, as deadened much of the time. Weaver had loved his now ex-wife; had moved to a city he loathed so she could move on with her career; had struggled to understand her unhappiness, not recognising how much of it had to do with his own. Consequently, he was thunderstruck when she left him. After that, he had picked himself up as best he could, and tried to resume a life he felt had been fractured for good. The dullness of his work had weighed on him, $187,000 or no; so had his loneliness and the propensity to feel half-dead in half a dozen languages; so too the growing uninterest in anything except the weekend days spent floating a fly, cast upstream only in traditional fashion.

JP said, 'I want to show you something before we go back. Follow me.'

They walked along the grass path by the river bank, which curved fifty yards or so ahead of them. When they reached this bend, Weaver stopped. 'What's that?' he asked, pointing ahead. A small building had been erected since his last visit, built so it overhung the river by a couple of feet on new wooden pilings.

'It's the boathouse,' JP said proudly as they walked towards it. 'If you can call a canoe a boat.'

It was no bigger than a large garden shed, but beautifully constructed, with a tiled roof and steep gable. The sides were built of hardwood: new oak, Weaver guessed, subtly pale in the lowering sunlight of late afternoon. JP opened the door on the near side, and gestured Weaver to come in. A chunk of the bank had been dug out, large enough to moor a wooden canoe, which was chained to a copper ring looped over a post that had been pounded into the dock that jutted into the river.

'I take her out most days,' said JP. 'It was handmade in Vermont.'

Weaver nodded, dutifully stunned. It would have cost a fortune to ship over from the States. He noticed a camp bed in a corner of the walkway. 'Someone sleeping here?'

JP looked embarrassed. 'I have a couple of times. Marriage has its ups and downs,' he confessed, sounding sheepish before getting hold of himself. 'You should know.'

5

HIS BEDROOM WAS AT THE END OF the house's large tucked-away wing. Weaver read for half an hour on the four-poster bed, then took a quick shower, dressed, and went downstairs, where he found several guests already in the drawing room.

It was furnished liberally with English antiques: furniture no longer in vogue, but old enough and fine enough never to be out of favour with those who knew. There were a few stray touches of Sue's trendier taste: a white ottoman partially covered by a fake zebra hide, and an Eames chair JP tried to hide in a corner. The room was brightened by colourful rugs and rich cream curtains that were pulled back – it was still light and the room looked out towards the river over the parterre – and there was none of the faint decay Weaver associated with a house like this; that sense that the past was better than now, the dust purposely left untouched like the faintest sprinkling of picturesque frost. Not here: Sue was almost German in her West Coast obsessive hygiene, and found intimations of decrepitude offensive. She was working to oligarch standards rather than the tatterdemalion habits of the English upper class.

JP gave Weaver a stiff whisky and soda – there was no ice – while Weaver looked at the assembled company. The locals were informally dressed, the London guests smarter, and conversation between them did not look to be easy. JP introduced him to the woman named Louise and to his journalist friend from *The Times*, who rejoiced in the name of Tom Penningale Jones. He was on the short side, with a freckled face and boyishly floppy, sandy-coloured hair.

Louise turned to Weaver. 'How do you know JP, then?' She was plump and lively and had very curly blonde hair.

He explained and Penningale Jones looked at him with new appreciation. 'You're the guy who's come from the summit in Stockholm.'

'That's right.'

'I was there, too, hoping to see your President.'

'He didn't show.'

'I know. He sent Hofstadter instead. Did you see him at all? I was at his press conference. What a monster he is,' he said half-admiringly.

How best to respond? Fortunately, the door from the hall swung open. A woman came in who caught Weaver's attention at once, and not simply as a diversion from Penningale Jones, though Weaver could not have said why. She was small and pretty, but the other women in the room were also attractive, and tall and athletic looking, except for Louise. Yet this new arrival had a confident air about her that struck Weaver even from twenty feet away.

She wore a simple white cotton pleated dress, belted at the waist, with a single-strand gold necklace but no other jewellery. Her legs were bare and lightly tanned, the colour of her heeled sandals, though a thin scar ran down the side of one of her calves. She had swept her hair up into a loose top knot, and it made her face all the more striking: a small, rounded jaw, large appraising eyes, and lips set in a wry smile, as if she had seen it all and found it mostly funny.

He forced himself to turn back to Louise.

'I love languages,' she declared. 'But I wonder, do you think you'll have a job in five years?'

'Is there something I should know?'

'People say automatic translation is getting better and better. Computers will soon be doing the job instead of people.'

Penningale Jones shook his head. 'I think he'll have his job for a while. If you've ever used Google Translate, you'd know what I mean.' Weaver had used it plenty in fact, and it was getting scarily better all the time. The day wasn't that far off when non-human translators predominated, though he hoped by then he would be out of the business.

Sue came over, bringing the new arrival with her. 'This is Lily,' she announced, then went towards the door to the hall, where new guests were coming through.

'What a nice dress,' Louise said, looking at Lily. 'And your hair looks great,' she exclaimed.

'Thanks. To be honest, I just piled it up and prayed it would stay. Fingers crossed, but so far so good.' Her voice was unexpectedly deep. Weaver noticed her eyes were hazel, mainly brown but with discernible flecks of green, and very wide apart. She did not look English, but he couldn't place her.

It seemed the new arrival already knew Louise and Penningale Jones, so Weaver introduced himself. When she shook his hand, hers was soft and cool. She seemed entirely at ease; Weaver realised he was not.

Louise turned to Weaver. 'JP said you speak five languages.'

Weaver shrugged, hoping not to be challenged on his German, which was the one outright exaggeration on his CV.

'All of them slowly, I bet,' said the younger woman in white.

Louise gave a little gasp at the rudeness of this, and even the jaded figure of Penningale Jones looked startled. But Weaver laughed, genuinely.

For something had happened. It had begun when this woman had entered the room, and now it emerged full blown, triggered by one acerbic remark.

He could not have described what it was. Since his divorce, he'd had 'dates', been set up by friends, met women online, and even spent time in someone else's bed – there had been a whole night with a sister of the bride at a wedding in Cape Cod, though that had not survived his return to New York. Yet nothing had replaced the emotional deadness which occupied the place he'd once reserved for the love he felt for his wife. This made the sudden rush of feeling now seem welcome, and frightening. But he had also instinctively made the automatic calibration performed by single people everywhere, and his heart sank at the concluding measurement: Lily was out of his league. She was too pretty, too confident.

It was true he could speak multiple languages at will, but the words were never his own, and he had nothing else of manifest appeal to offer. Okay, with a short fly rod he could supply a roll cast and lay a Royal Coachman like a soft feather before the nose of a suspicious rainbow trout, but was this really a useful attribute for courtship? Of course not. The *coup de foudre* he had felt diminished to the usual mental drizzle. His spirits sank.

Fortunately, they soon filed into the dining room, the walls of which were covered with crimson damask. There were place cards before each setting on the long oak table, which was deeply polished. To his dismay, Lily veered off to her seat at one end, while he was placed down at the other.

Behind the head of the table hung an immense oil portrait of a red-cheeked squire, holding a shotgun. Louise joined him and JP, looking gravely at the painting. 'What a lovely portrait. Family?'

JP's father had owned a general store in one of Vermont's smallest towns; his mother had descended from French-Canadian trappers who'd crossed the border in search of game that was easier to poach. Weaver waited with interest for his reply.

'Very distantly,' JP said, avoiding Weaver's gaze. With many things, there was a faint but discernible gap between JP's vision and the reality. It was not full-blown cognitive dissonance but near enough. Weaver sometimes worried that by the time JP reached old age, he would claim to be the distant heir to some sleeping peerage.

'It looks like a Romney,' said Louise eagerly.

Even for JP, this was a step too far. 'No,' he said, with a regretful shake of his head. 'Possibly "school of".'

'I wonder,' said Louise, with flattering dissent. 'I know Philip Mould. I could ask him to have a look.'

'That would be great. Excuse me a minute,' said JP. Weaver saw that Sue was signalling him.

Weaver went and sat down at the table with Louise, thinking furiously of what to talk about. She got there first. 'JP tells me you're from one of Vermont's grandest families.'

'That's a contradiction in terms,' he said.

Louise didn't laugh, a bad sign. 'No, seriously,' she said, which also seemed a contradiction. 'He said they virtually founded the place.'

'Did he just?' asked Weaver. 'I'm not sure stepfathers count for much.' Trust JP to make him a Mayflower mogul; his old friend was no longer content with having an ordinary acquaintance at his table.

For dinner they served themselves from large chafing dishes set out on the vast sideboard: venison stew with mushrooms and a red wine reduction; rice; green beans covered in buttered almond slivers. Mrs Wilson was probably happier baking scones, but she was no mean cook. She came in to check if any more was needed. Like the benevolent squire in *Tom Jones*, JP called out, 'Thank you, Mrs Wilson. It's delicious.' One of the local wives raised a snooty eyebrow at her husband across the table.

The food was good; conversation with Louise less so. She had the habit of saying, 'You know how it is,' which proved trying. Deflecting questions about herself, she peppered Weaver with them instead, sometimes disconcertingly. She asked out of nowhere, 'What do you especially like?' What did she mean? Professionally? Sexually? Seeing his mystification, she explained, 'I mean which language.'

'I work mostly in French and Italian these days, but I suppose Russian was always my strong suit.'

'Not any more, then?'

'No, since sanctions started there aren't any meetings to give me interpreting work to do. There's some translation work,' he said, thinking of the failed Ukraine harvests, 'but it's not the same thing.'

'I used to see a lot of Russians in London,' she said, sounding wistful. 'My brother-in-law owned a club in Knightsbridge. It seemed like it was all Beluga and bubbly,' she said, her eyes dreamy at the memory. 'That's how I met JP,' she said. 'He used to go there.'

'Really?' It was hard to imagine JP clubbing.

'Not to the disco,' said Louise with a knowing smile. 'There was a card game in one of the back rooms. Poker. A lot of Russians played.' She lowered her voice as she added, 'I think they took more than a few roubles off our friend.'

This Weaver could imagine. JP was always happy to pay if it let him feel he belonged. Weaver asked, 'Is the club still there?'

'Yes, just off Sloane Street. I'd take you there but it's changed – he sold it and the clientele's mainly Chinese now. Oh,' she said with a hand raised to her mouth as she looked down the table. 'I don't want to offend anybody.' Weaver looked at the company; it wasn't clear if she had someone here in mind.

'Are there *any* Russians left in London?'

'A few. Though the rich ones keep dropping dead,' she said, then giggled. She looked down the table again. 'Oh dear, I keep putting my foot in it. You know how it is,' she added for the umpteenth time.

Weaver's patience finally sagged. 'I don't actually,' he said a little sharply. When she looked puzzled, he felt bad for his snappishness.

They worked their way through the courses: there was cheese, there was pudding, then finally more good claret and crystal decanters of port. Some slight social progress had been made, perhaps, as the women did not retire. Weaver was waiting for the end of the meal, knowing it would be followed by coffee in the drawing room, where he could try to talk some more to Lily.

But he found himself cornered after dinner by Louise, until at last Sue intervened and walked him over to the open French doors. 'You've done your duty,' she said with a little smile. 'Go join the boys now,' she said, pointing at JP and several male guests, all smoking cigars on the terrace outside. It seemed gender segregation was not defunct in the UK after all.

JP was talking to Penningale Jones and motioned Weaver over to join them. 'Meet my old pal, Weaver. He's the interpreter I told you about. Tom is on *The Times,*' he added as Weaver tried to mask his slight sense of alarm.

'We met before dinner,' Tom said to JP. 'We were both at the Sweden summit.' He turned to Weaver. 'We've been talking about a rumour making the rounds that China wants the Americans to lay off the Russians for a while. Maybe even have talks with them again.'

'News to me,' said Weaver, trying to sound casual. There had been such rumours before, rapidly spread around the office to lift the spirits of the inactive Russian interpreters. But right now he didn't want to get within a million miles of talk about the Russians.

'I know,' Tom said understandingly, 'it sounds unlikely.' He was mistaking Weaver's expressionless face for scepticism. 'I thought if anyone would know it would be you. JP said you're a Russian specialist.'

'I used to be. Service seems to have been discontinued.'

'Is that really going to last? Non-speaks, I mean. Unless your lot are already talking to them unofficially.'

The silence that followed was awkward. JP was looking away towards the river; Tom watched Weaver intently, as if close attention could effect a useful response.

'Sorry,' said Weaver at last. 'This is all above my pay grade. I was stuck with the autumn trade discussions. Those were in Italian and pretty low level.' He thought of Lily again, and said, 'I'm going inside. See you later on.' As he went through the French doors, he cocked his head and saw JP talking while Tom listened. The image of Hofstadter barking at him returned.

Inside, the party seemed to be winding down. Most people were saying thank you and good night to Sue; several seemed to be staying the night. There was no sign of Lily, and he managed

to duck Louise's invitation to have another drink. He thanked
Sue, and made his way upstairs and along to the wing.

He was undressed and about to listen again to the red pen's
recording of the Stockholm meeting when there was a short
tap on the other side of the bathroom door. 'Come in,' he said,
grabbing his shirt to go with his boxer shorts. He was too slow;
the door opened immediately and he saw Lily standing in the
light of the shared bathroom between their bedrooms. She was
still in white, but this time in a towelling bathrobe, with its belt
drawn tight about her waist. He noticed she had tiny feet.

'Oh, it's you,' she said, sounding amused.

'You were expecting someone else?'

'Louise.' Then, '"You know how it is."' The imitation was
near-perfect.

He laughed. 'What can I do for you?'

'Not what you think, if that's all you wear for visitors. I just
wondered if your room was as hot as mine.'

'Is there a problem?'

'You tell me,' she said, standing aside as he came closer. She
moved through the open door on the other side of the bathroom
and he followed her. He saw she had her hair down now – it was
brown with blonde highlights, and impressively straight and fine,
falling like released silk down the back of her robe.

As he crossed the threshold of her room, he felt like he was
entering a sauna. 'Golly,' he said lightly.

'So it isn't just me.'

'Why the hell is it so hot?' It was like a Greek island in August;
a windless Greek island.

'I can't open the window and the radiator's on full blast. I can't
turn it down.'

He went and tried it; she was right – the valve wouldn't budge.
He tried the window, with the same lack of result. He was
conscious of his pale winter skin and of cutting a semi-ridiculous
figure, especially when Lily giggled.

'Sorry,' she said without a hint of apology in her voice. 'I thought someone else could get it to move; I'm not that strong.'

'I don't think Arnold Schwarzenegger could open it. You better come cool down, while we figure out what to do.' Weaver retreated through the bathroom, and she followed him this time. She closed the bathroom door to keep the heat out and they stood awkwardly in his bedroom.

He said, 'Listen, we'd better swap; I'll go sleep in your room.'

She stared at him. 'Why? So you can boil too? Don't be silly.'

'I'm glad you realise it was a half-hearted offer. Seriously, though, you better sleep in the bed here. I can sleep on that.' He pointed at the small pink sofa by the dressing table.

'Don't be ridiculous. How tall are you?'

'Five eleven and three-quarter inches.'

'That's impressively precise.'

'My old man's six foot, so the quarter inch has always mattered.'

'Well, you're never going to fit on that sofa.' This was true. She went on, 'It's small, but so am I. Five foot three if you're curious. Though I'm still growing.'

She went to the large armoire and opened it. Finding a blanket, she went and spread it out over the sofa, placing two of the cushions at one end and plumping them. Finished, she looked at Weaver. 'If you want to change, I can wait in the bathroom.'

'Change?' he asked.

She laughed, in a pure soprano peal that surprised him since her speaking voice was at least a register lower. 'You don't wear pyjamas?'

He waited a moment. 'Not when travelling.'

She laughed again; he realised how much it pleased him that she did. She said, 'Then you could pretend you're at home.' She curled up on the sofa, still in her robe, and pulled the blanket over herself while he turned off the overhead light and, feeling his way in the dark, got into the bed.

There was a rumbling laugh from the sofa, almost uncontrolled. Then a loud sigh. 'This reminds me of summer holidays when you never knew who you'd end up sharing a room with.' She yawned loudly. 'How do you know JP anyway?'

'We were at college together. University, as you would say. We were members of the same fraternity for a while.'

He remembered the circumstances. He had never been a big club man, and had joined DKE reluctantly and was then about to quit, when he discovered that his frat brothers were hazing this geeky kid (JP) so badly that Weaver felt he had to intervene. Once the hazing had stopped, he'd had enough and did quit. He imagined his 'brothers' had not been sad to see him go.

He told Lily as much, and she said, 'But he stayed a member of the fraternity?'

'He did.'

Lily said, 'Let that be a lesson to you: no good deed goes unpunished.'

'It was a long time ago.'

'But you've remained friends,' she mused. 'I know you two are always on the river, but is JP any good at fishing?'

'He works hard at it.'

'I take that as a no, then,' Lily said. 'But other than fishing, I wouldn't have thought you had much in common. Do you do business with him?'

'Business? What business would I have with JP?'

'I don't know. He travels a lot, or used to; he was always doing deals in different countries.'

'Most of them from an office in New York.' He remembered a visit he'd made there back in his own Vermont days. JP had worked in a Sixties skyscraper on Sixth Avenue, and was puffed with pride at a recent promotion that gave him his own office, instead of a desk in the open-plan where you had to shout to be heard above the raucous traders on speaker phone. The view from JP's tiny soulless cell on the sixty-seventh floor had been straight into another tower block; if you stood right by the window and looked straight down, ignoring the vertiginous rush, you could just see the street below and the people there moving like tiny ants in a primitive video game. To Weaver, that image encapsulated his dislike of New York: heights and *anomie*.

'Do you understand how JP got so rich?' Lily asked.

'Not really.' Did she mean the details of JP's Big Deal, or the companies involved? He could only remember the immediate aftermath – when JP and Sue had come to Vermont, and instead of staying with Weaver and his wife in their modest white pine house, had taken a suite in the Woodstock Inn. It was the first and only time Weaver had tasted Chateau Petrus.

Lily said, 'You must be one of the few blokes who liked him before he made his money. I'm speaking frankly.'

'You seem to make a habit of that,' he said, but not aggressively, since what she said was true. JP had never been popular, especially when he was poor. It wasn't the geekiness that accounted for this; it was the combination of geekiness *and* a certain relentlessness in pursuing whatever JP was aiming for: frat membership; admission to Harvard Business school; a job at Goldman Sachs. And eventually, when his ship came in, there was all that money as well – which, as a result, meant he showed not the slightest concern about anyone else's desires or dreams. He remained thoroughly affable, but the lack of interest was clear. That was what put people off.

Lily said, 'How did you get into this translation game? Did you read Russian at what you call college?'

'Russian and French. I mainly work in French these days. And Italian.'

'Obviously. It must be frustrating, having a skill and not getting to use it. But they'll have to start talking again, don't you think?'

'Don't hold your breath.'

'I know. We'll probably all get blown to kingdom come sooner or later. Though that journo friend of JP's thinks the Russians are just as scared of us as we are of them. But what about Stockholm? Did you need your Russian there?'

This was at such odds with what he'd just been saying that he hesitated, wondering how to reply. He was not only a bad liar, but also a reluctant one.

'I was sent there for French and Italian. Like I said,' he added pointedly; he didn't like being put on the spot.

'Sure, but that's not what I asked.' When he said nothing, she went on, 'Never mind. I used to know some interpreters. I worked in the Foreign Office for a couple of years. You have to be discreet, and letter perfect. Not just okay, but absolutely fluent. How did you get so good?'

'Because I'm a spy. Bolshevik born and bred.'

She gave a small laugh to acknowledge that he was joking, but then waited him out. Finally, he relented: 'My mother's Russian, though she grew up in Paris. I would have been a terrible spy.'

'Was she a White Russian?'

At least she knew what that was. 'Sort of, I suppose. Her grandparents fled Russia in 1920, during the Civil War. My mother was determined I should know Russian like a native, even if her idea of a native was roughly fifty years out of date. She made sure I knew French, too. She never spoke English when she was alone with me.'

'What did your father think about that? I'm assuming he was American.'

'We always spoke English when he was around. Though he could speak Italian – Brooklyn Italian, admittedly. But it meant I had a head start when I studied the language.'

'Your parents sound an odd pairing.'

'They were. That's probably why I have a stepfather now.'

'Where did your real parents meet?'

'In Paris. My father was at the embassy for three months chasing some swindlers. He worked for the FBI. Still does.'

'But I thought you grew up in Vermont. Like JP.'

'I did,' he said, flattered that she knew this. Had she been asking about him? He hoped so. 'My father was the SAC in Burlington.'

'SAC?'

'Special Agent in Charge.'

'How grand.'

'Not really. There wasn't that much to be in charge of: just a lot of drug dealers to chase, smuggling dope across the Canadian border.'

Which was not such small beer, in fact. The dealers he helped send to jail would have paid a lot to have his father killed.

'Did your mother do anything?'

'Yes. She worked for a writer named Anatoly Demidov after he came to America. He settled in Vermont. God knows why.'

'She knew Demidov?'

He hadn't been confident she would recognise the name. 'Sure. So did I. She was his PA for over ten years.' He remembered the countless hours spent as a boy in the compound near Woodstock, waiting for his mother to drive him home. There was always some drama that kept her there: *People* magazine wanting to profile the home life of the creative sage, or the *New York Times* looking for a quote; sometimes just a Russian émigré asking for help. Even the great man would grow tired of the demands on his time; sometimes he would come over to the young Weaver, sitting in an oversized chair, and get down on his knees to play. He was fond of the boy because he spoke Russian.

'Do me a favour.'

He had learned not to say yes right away. 'What's that?'

'Two favours, actually. First, don't tell JP I stayed in here. He'd get the wrong end of the stick and tell half the world that you and I made the earth move.'

'What's the second favour?'

'Try and accept that I'm not entirely stupid. I know who Demidov was.'

'Okay,' he said quietly. This was not someone to condescend to.

'Admittedly, I never went to university,' she said, still sounding cross.

He was surprised. She seemed too – prosperous? Cultivated? – not to have gone to college. 'How did you work for the Foreign Office without a degree?'

'*De façon détournée.*'

By the back door.

'It was at the embassy in Paris,' she said, warming to her theme. 'I got lucky when one of the FCO boffins took an interest in me.'

'FCO?'

'Foreign and Commonwealth Office, to initiates. Foreign Office to the world at large.'

'Got it. I take it his was a strictly professional interest?'

'Oh no, I had to sleep with him twice a week.'

'I hope it was worth it,' he said.

'It got me holiday pay.' Her voice was without any give at first, then she gave her high-pitched laugh and said, 'Moving on deftly, how did you end up in New York?'

'My wife was desperate to live there. My ex-wife.' What initially had seemed the expression of a stray desire had gradually built into a campaign to move to that city.

'And you caved?'

'Pretty much. Which was infuriating when the marriage went south.'

'I wouldn't know; I've never been married. Close, but not quite.'

'What, you changed your mind?' he asked.

'No,' she said emphatically. 'Things came up.' She said nothing more.

What were 'things'? he wondered, as they both stayed silent for a moment. 'Just as well,' Lily finally said. 'It would probably have ended badly and I have never been a fan of divorce.'

'Are you Catholic?'

'Not very.'

'You lapsed early?'

'Don't be rude. You're not Catholic, are you?'

'My stepfather's a Congregationalist minister.'

'And he brought you up?'

'He certainly thought he did.'

'And RD's your real father, right?'

'How did you know I call him that?'

'JP. I was asking him about you. Strictly as a matter of politeness.'

'Yes, JP calls him that, for Real Dad. I don't see him much.'

'You don't get on?'

He ignored this. 'He lives in San Francisco. Other coast, so our paths rarely cross.' He was not about to explain it further, and he felt the old wound from over twenty years before. Once in a blue moon, he and his father might spend an afternoon together, usually fishing since that committed them only to mild proximity on a river bank, and a minimal obligation to talk.

'So Weaver's not your birth name? What was it, then?'

'Fontana.'

'Why isn't that your name now?'

'I was being raised under Weaver's roof after my parents got divorced. He thought the least I could do in return was adopt his surname. My mother thought so as well.'

He remembered that awful summer. He had been thirteen years old, and capable of some resistance. Not enough; the pressure from them both to take the Weaver name had been unendurable.

'What did your real father think of that?'

Weaver said, feeling rueful, 'He didn't speak to me for three years.'

'I am sorry about that,' she said, quite deliberately, then went silent. It was not uncomfortable, this silence, but he was glad when she kept talking. She said, 'So you have two dads.'

'Sort of. You just have one, I take it.'

'No. When I finally tracked the bastard down, he'd gone and topped himself the year before.'

She didn't sound the least upset about it, but he was beginning to see she was all carapace with him. He wasn't optimistic about getting through to a softer interior. If there were a softer interior.

'What is *your* full name?'

'Lily Churchill. And no, I'm not. Americans always ask.'

'What do you do for a living now, Lily Churchill?'

'This and that.'

'Sue said you helped her decorate the house. I assumed you were an interior designer.'

'Did you?' She sounded half-amused. 'Maybe I've missed my calling.'

Neither spoke, until Lily sighed and said, 'I think I'm talked out for now, or maybe listened out. *Spokoynoy nochi.*'

'You speak Russian?'

'I know four words in at least half a dozen languages. *Bonne nuit. Dors bien,*' she said without a trace of English accent. There was a pause. Then, 'Good night.'

In the morning when he woke, he tried to remember what he had told Lily about his time in Stockholm, wondering if he had been indiscreet. He wanted reassurance and got up, but the sofa was unoccupied, its blanket neatly folded and placed at one end.

When he went in to shower, he found the door to her room open, but the room empty, the bed made. Coming back, he found a yellow Post-it note on the shower door. It said:

I can't promise anything too exciting, but if you're at a loose end in London it would be nice to see you. Here's my number...

Weaver planned to leave for London before lunch, as JP and Sue were driving north for JP to fish the Derwent with friends the next day, and Weaver wanted to get out of their hair. Since he'd be back at the end of the week, he left his jacket in his bedroom (he had packed another one, a blazer, which seemed more suitable for London), along with his second pair of shoes and a file of notes from the summit's first-day trade talks in the bedroom. In the chest of drawers, he left his Olympus digital recorder, which he wouldn't need in London. He played it briefly and was at first startled to hear Russian spoken. Had he taped the meeting with *two* devices? But he realised it wasn't the words of General Kuzmin he heard, but those of a low-level Ministry *apparatchik* railing against fishing restrictions in the waters off

Japan. It must be an old recording, he thought, from the days when international trade talks included the Russians.

What should he do with the red recording pen? He was worried about leaving it here, but more worried about taking it with him, though he could not have said exactly why, since so much of its content was still a mystery. He decided to leave it there, but also to hide it. He could collect it when he returned on Friday, stay two nights while fishing with JP, then fly out Sunday morning to New York in time for work on Monday.

There was a tall bookshelf on one wall, and he tucked the pen behind a volume on a middle shelf. Empson's *Seven Types of Ambiguity*, pretty clearly one of Sue's books. She had done a post-grad year at Stanford, studying English, before changing directions and going to Harvard Business School. It seemed a fitting place to hide the pen, and he hoped that by the time he retrieved it he might have resolved the ambiguity about what it had recorded.

He fished until late that morning with JP, catching two brown trout and watching JP lose a third. On the river, JP said, 'I don't know why you're renting an Airbnb when I've got a place sitting empty in Belgravia. Where is the place, anyway?'

'Holland Park,' he said. Even JP couldn't sniff at that. 'Probably easier all round.' He knew that Sue only came up to town on yoga-less days to shop; increasingly, JP didn't come at all. But there were limits to the hospitality he felt it right to accept from his friend. 'I liked that woman Lily,' he said, trying to move round this slight awkwardness.

'More than Louise? She was very taken with you; she would have stayed the night if she hadn't been driven down here by Tom – and he had to get back to London last night. But I'm sure she'd be happy to see you again.' He looked at Weaver. 'What's putting you off? Her overbite? They can fix that.'

Weaver shook his head dismissively. He said, 'I thought I might look Lily up while I'm in town.'

'I never thought you liked Asian women.'

'What's that supposed to mean?' JP, almost uniquely among Weaver's acquaintances, could be both crass and elliptical in a single sentence. There had been something foreign about Lily but Weaver hadn't thought much about it. The homogeneity of Vermont's citizenry was the one thing he disliked about his home state, and variety the only thing he liked about New York.

'She's half Vietnamese.' JP glanced at Weaver. 'I thought I told you that.'

'Refugees?' He was thinking of the boat people.

'Hardly. Her maternal grandparents both came from Vietnam, and went to Paris before the war. Lily's mother grew up there and met an Englishman, who brought her over to the UK. That's the story, anyway.'

What's the real story, then? Weaver wanted to ask. Until this trip he had never even heard Lily mentioned by JP and Sue. JP clearly didn't have a clue that Lily had stayed the night in Weaver's room. That was a relief.

JP went on: 'Look her up all you want, but it won't get you anywhere. She's got a partner.'

'Oh.' Of course she would. He was surprised by how disappointed he felt.

'A very rich partner.'

He must be very rich indeed, Weaver thought, for JP to mention it.

JP continued, 'Who happens to be a woman, I'm told. Though Lily's kept that very hush-hush. There were men in the past, but apparently she's moved on a gender.'

'Why "hush-hush"?' asked Weaver, feeling oddly defensive on Lily's behalf.

JP didn't laugh. 'Her family – her father's family, anyway. Very county, very staid. They would probably disown her if they found out. That, at any rate, is the *on dit*.'

6

The house in Holland Park was as pretty as its picture on the website. Weaver had sailed in, dropped his car off at an outlet of the rental agency in West Kensington, then taken a black cab to Holland Park. There, on a side street off Abbotsbury Road, he had booked an Airbnb in the basement of a large stucco-fronted house.

An ageing white-haired woman in a housecoat and bedroom slippers answered the buzzer. After mutual introductions, the woman, who was called Dorothy, led Weaver down a staircase to a good-sized sitting room with a wall of glass facing a large garden in the back, with flower beds running along each side.

Dorothy explained how the television and Wi-Fi worked, then took him along a short connecting corridor to the bedroom at the front. It was small, slightly claustrophobic, with an old-fashioned dressing table and two big bolster pillows on the double bed. Off the corridor there was a little kitchen, and a bathroom with a power shower Dorothy seemed especially proud of.

Weaver was tired enough to take a nap, a rarity for him. But he woke refreshed, then went for a walk down to Holland Park Avenue. This part of the neighbourhood reminded him of Manhattan's Murray Hill. Once the home of the middle class, it had been transformed by hipness and the attraction of its tree-shaded streets into residences only afforded by the truly rich.

Crossing over to Notting Hill, he walked around for a bit, then ended up at Leo's Brasserie, where he had eaten several times before on earlier stays. He sat at an outside table and watched a couple feed their tethered Jack Russell most of their dinner while he ate an expensive and very good steak, and drank two glasses of red wine.

He thought about the coming days. He had expected to be spending them on the river at JP's, not knowing when he first made his plan back in New York that JP and Sue would be away all week. He would have five days on his own in London.

He had known the city on and off since his father had been stationed at the embassy when Weaver was only a boy. Later, during his post-graduate years, Weaver spent three months ostensibly doing research in the British Library. Thereafter, he visited every couple of years or so, initially as an itinerant translator with meagre resources; recently as a more high-powered traveller en route to an international summit or conference. But he knew few people there, and unless he had business to conduct in the city, usually spent his time in the country fishing at JP and Sue's. He would be having dinner the following evening with Alek Ragoulin, an art dealer of Russian extraction, and there was an old girlfriend from college he could call – but she lived out by the M25, west of the city, and was married with two small and very demanding children. It seemed a long way to go to visit a playground.

He would usually have been happy about the prospect of wandering around the city, trying not to spend all his money on unnecessary fishing gear from Farlow's, and using most of the day unambitiously, reading for pleasure. In New York, he usually got home drained most days, too tired for anything more than a takeaway carton of Szechuan chicken with cashew nuts, consumed in front of the television with a couple of beers, and then to bed. When he did read it was rarely in any language other than English – there was already too much French and Russian to read at work. Occasionally he would read Italian, for its sonorous beauty, and once in a while German and Spanish as well – though he knew neither adequately enough to read them easily. Mostly he read American fiction, a mix of thrillers and more literary fare.

But he was not relaxed now: he could not get the meeting in Stockholm out of his head, the sense of crisis Blanchett had projected, and the revelation that it was Hofstadter he was interpreting for, and Russian he was translating. He had been present at something of critical importance, he knew that much, but not what it was. Was he really expected to forget all about it? He wished he had brought the red pen with him. There had been a loan made to Hofstadter, and though apparently repaid long before, it seemed the mere fact of it would cause a scandal. Why else had both Blanchett and Hofstadter warned him off so emphatically?

He thought of calling Lily. What had she written in her note? He found it now in his wallet. *If you're at a loose end in London it would be nice to see you.* He hesitated, and wondered why he did. Because JP said she was gay? Possibly, since he had found himself so struck by her that he had immediately wanted more than friendship. He couldn't specify whether he wanted sex or love or the rare combination of the two, but from what JP had said, none of the three were going to be on offer from Lily, so he decided not to phone her. Not yet, at any rate.

He decided against a nightcap and returned slowly to cross Holland Park Avenue in the fading light. Back at the house, he stood for a moment in the ground floor hall; no sound came from upstairs. He went downstairs and into the bedroom, where he fell asleep right away.

The next day was equally uneventful – to start with. He slept in until nine, then walked to the Underground at Notting Hill and took the Central Line to Bond Street. He went south and moseyed around the elegant arcades off Piccadilly and stared at the dress shirts in the shop windows of Jermyn Street, thinking of his father, who had taken him to London the summer after his first year in college. His father's clothes were largely dictated by FBI regulations (dark suits, black shoes, always a tie) but he had proved an enthusiast for Turnbull and Asser. This in contrast to the lean pieties and thin sweaters of Weaver's Yankee stepfather, a college chaplain who felt the penury of his post was a signal of its virtue.

He ate a sandwich in the top floor café of Waterstones, then browsed idly for half an hour in Farlow's on Pall Mall, where to justify his lingering he finally bought half a dozen flies, a mix of mid- to large-sized Mayflies. Weaver could tie his own flies, but though he had good hand-to-eye coordination, he was less good at fine work, which meant that it took him forever. One Vermont winter, when the extra income had been sorely needed, he reckoned he had made roughly two dollars an hour for the dry flies he sold online.

Next he went over to St James's Square, where he bought a day ticket at the London Library. He sat in the reading room one flight up, slumped in one of its comfortable leather chairs. He usually got his dose of news online, so was pleased to find the day's newspapers spread out on one of the tables. He was skimming through them a little drowsily in a nearby chair when, coming to *The Times*, a story on the foreign affairs pages had him wide awake. The by-line was from the Washington correspondent. The President was back in the States, after a holiday in Wales and Ireland: a photo showed him and the First Lady coming down the steps of Air Force One, both waving.

Then he read the following:

Controversy has arisen about the possibility, floated in an interview broadcast just hours after the President's return from Europe on Saturday, of his granting a presidential pardon to the former professional basketball player, James 'Skip' Washington. The ex-NBA star was convicted last year of having sex with several underage girls, and sentenced to an eight-year term in a Federal penitentiary. If pardoned now, he will have served just eleven months of his sentence.

Weaver put down the paper. The library had lost its sense of calm; something about the paper's item was unsettling him. Why? Memories of the Stockholm meeting were proving tantalisingly elusive. Images of Hofstadter's reddened face and Kuzmin's hearty guffaws were coming back vividly, but unaccompanied by the words that had been spoken.

He wished there was someone he could talk to, to share his unease and growing sense that he had a secret which was dangerous to have. Normally he would have talked to Mac, with his unblinkered, sardonic take on everything. But Mac could be fatally indiscreet, the last thing Weaver needed now, having been warned off talking so severely.

Then he had another thought. Leaving the library, he went into the little park in St James's Square. He fished the piece of paper out of his jacket pocket, tapped the numbers on his phone. He wasn't confident that what he was doing was sensible, but he needed desperately to talk to *somebody*. He sat down on a bench just as the call went through.

It went straight to voicemail. A voice he recognised said, 'Hi, it's Lily. If it's business please send me an email, not a text.' She gave her email address then paused before saying, 'If it's personal, leave a message and we'll see.' He stood up from the bench, feeling unprepared. Why had he not thought he might be asked to leave a message? Flustered as the voicemail beeped, he tried to think of what to say: *Hi, it's Weaver, the guy from the sofa down at JP's. I hope you'll remember me.*

He couldn't bring himself to say anything like this, nor the frankly ludicrous words that followed in his imagination: *And despite JP's explanation of your preferences, I somehow have a strong urge to see you again. Just as a friend, of course… Blah blah blah* he said to himself, running out of words, even these crazy ones. Thankfully, he discovered that his thumb had terminated the call before he had the chance to utter a word.

What credibly could he have said to her? He couldn't talk to her about the depravity of a professional basketball player – what would that possibly mean to her? Yet he knew he'd like to see her again, despite all of JP's naysaying, and he sensed it might subdue the new-found anxiety mounting him like greedy ivy on a tree. But would *she* want to see *him*? Her departing note at JP's had suggested he call, but maybe she was just being polite. He could imagine her groaning silently if he got through. She wouldn't feel an obligation to assuage his loneliness. Why should she?

7

Dinner with Alek Ragoulin was at one of his many clubs. This one occupied a townhouse on a street north of Piccadilly, behind the Burlington Arcade. Ragoulin was waiting for Weaver in the small bar near the front.

'You are very prompt,' said Ragoulin, shaking hands. 'I thought we'd have a drink before going in for dinner.' He cut an exotic figure: lean with an aquiline nose, he could have stood in for Eustace Tilley of *New Yorker* fame. Though there was nothing fey about his personality, or his business practices, which, as more than one other art dealer had made clear, were hard-nosed.

Tonight he was dressed in a suit of light wool the colour of rust. In a setting that seemed quintessentially English, he looked ineffably foreign, but Weaver was not at all surprised to find Ragoulin a member here: the man moved effortlessly in and out of virtually any zone occupied by the upper class.

It was in Paris that they had first met, almost fifteen years before, and Weaver remembered it vividly. He had been in the city doing some research for his dissertation at the Bibliothèque Nationale, and his mother had insisted he make his presence known to her ancient Russian cousins. An invitation followed, and dutifully, if grudgingly, Weaver had slogged out to the 3rd arrondissement, north of the Place des Vosges. There, in a grisly *appartement* with low ceilings and shabby furniture but magnificent views, he paid his respects to his very distant cousin Oscar, a nonagenarian who had been born in Moscow at the end of the Russian Civil War.

To Weaver's surprise, more than a dozen other people were

present too, many of them – according to Oscar – kinsmen. He noticed Ragoulin, a tall, elegant figure, at once; along with Weaver, he was about the only person present born after Sputnik.

They got on from the start, helped by Ragoulin's entertaining indiscretions: that cousin Oscar had an illegitimate daughter in Marseille; that elderly Vladimir, leaning on his stick as he stood across the room, had done time in La Santé for credit card fraud; and that Sophie, sitting on the sofa, still striking-looking in her ninth decade with a shock of snowy hair, had been one of the 'girls' of the notorious Madame Claude.

These remarks were all made without any moderation of volume, much as if Ragoulin were describing the progress of some seedlings recently planted in his garden. Almost as an afterthought, Ragoulin explained he was an art dealer, specialising in Russian painting; Russian himself, he had spent all his adult life in the West. His customers were, originally, Russian émigrés, largely of the ancient anti-Bolshevik cadre who made up this party, although, he explained with an optimistic glint to his eyes, the new Russia was not only creating wealthy individuals – formerly unheard of – but allowing them to work and live in the West. These oligarchs were keen to civilise themselves, Ragoulin said dryly, and he had decided it was his duty to help them do it. 'They think of art as an accoutrement,' he declared. 'A Kandinsky drawing here, a Constructivist painting there. Culture doesn't come cheap, of course, and I am happy to say that business is very good.'

For all this cynicism about the art he bought and sold – or rather about the people he bought and sold it to – Ragoulin turned out to have a genuine interest in modern Russian writing, and since Weaver had spent perhaps too many years studying many of those authors, they had plenty to talk about. Weaver was a little discomfited to learn that Ragoulin had a particular attachment, bordering on devotion, to the poetry rather than novels of Anatoly Demidov, since this was not an enthusiasm Weaver shared. The fact that Weaver had only been a small boy when his mother worked for the Great Man did not seem to dilute Ragoulin's joy in meeting someone who had seen the Nobel laureate in the flesh.

As the party wound down, Ragoulin insisted that they meet again, and before Weaver left France, they enjoyed a long lunch in a bistro by the Luxembourg Gardens. Weaver was amused by Ragoulin, and by the alternating currents of cynicism and passion in him. But he was also glad that he wasn't rich enough to be a Ragoulin client: there was a roguish yet hard-bitten aspect to the man that displayed *caveat emptor* like a billboard.

After this, they lost touch; Weaver was living in Vermont and not travelling much, and Ragoulin was slowly transferring his business to London, where most of these oligarchs seemed to live. Once Weaver joined the State Department in Manhattan, however, they re-established contact, and whenever Ragoulin was in New York, they had lunch or dinner together; similarly, when Weaver was in London he always stopped by Ragoulin's office on Bond Street.

'How are things?' asked Weaver now. With Ragoulin conversation usually centred, almost exclusively, on what the Russian had been doing, but at the moment – between thinking about Stockholm and the inaccessible Lily – this imbalance offered a welcome diversion for Weaver.

Ragoulin added water to his whisky from a small jug the barman set on the bar, then pushed the jug towards Weaver. He said, 'Business has been a bit stale, to be honest, but it always is when the weather warms. Of course, my countrymen are low in number in the UK now, and Americans seem to think it would be unpatriotic to buy Russian art. Still, one can't complain too much. There has been an enlivening transaction recently, with a man named Zadkin. A Jew, like many of the oligarchs, and therefore always a little fearful about his standing with the Moscow powers-that-be, even though he married a woman whose mother is said to have been in the old KGB. But that could just be talk; it usually is. He's planning to move to Israel but anxious to keep his Russian passport. One of the second wave of tycoons, a recent arrival on these shores who lives in one of the most expensive houses in Weybridge – that's England's Scarsdale, I suppose.' He added a little sourly, 'Zadkin seems so eager to spend his money that one can only assume it's of dubious origins.'

Ragoulin sighed, then said more happily, 'Still, a sale is a sale, whatever the source of the money. It's clean by the time it gets into my hands.' He turned so his back was to the group of dark-suited City-looking types in the corner. He added with the hint of a confidential smile, 'Especially as there's an antique samovar I have Zadkin interested in. Said to date from the time of Peter the Great.'

'Does it?'

'For all I know, it may even have been owned by Peter himself. But I can't in honesty go that far. Not even for the likes of Zadkin.'

They went in for dinner, which was simple but good: a slice of paté, grilled chops, and then a Welsh rarebit Ragoulin insisted on. Between them they drank a bottle of house claret, taking an extra glass apiece with their savoury.

Coincidentally, Ragoulin knew Tomic – Weaver could never remember how or why – and he mentioned him now. 'He was supposed to be in London today.'

'Oh really? He said nothing to me.'

Ragoulin shrugged indifferently. 'His plans changed when he was in Stockholm. Maybe he went to Russia instead.'

'Russia?' Weaver asked, startled. 'Why would he go there?' Tomic had said nothing about going to Russia.

'I know, it's surprising. I can't believe his superiors – your superiors also, yes? – would be happy about it if they knew.'

This was true. It remained legal to travel to Russia, but it was definitely discouraged.

Ragoulin added, 'I believe he has a cousin there. A banker.'

'He mentioned him when I saw him last week. He said the cousin's dacha is near Morozov's.'

'Lucky cousin,' said Ragoulin, implying something quite different.

'It's rather odd, though. Tomic hates the regime there.'

Ragoulin shrugged, then said musingly, his eyes softening, 'I gather the cousin's place is lovely; it's in the Valday Forest. Perhaps that's why Tomic goes.' Ragoulin nodded to himself, no longer musing. 'It must be that, since my friends tell me Tomic's cousin has close ties to the FSB and to Morozov himself. The cousin is a financier *and* a spy.' He shrugged. 'Families!'

Weaver said nothing, since as far as he knew Ragoulin had no family at all. Ragoulin seemed happy to move on in any case. 'So how was Stockholm?'

'Busier than I expected. I covered some of the trade talks. I was doing French and Italian translations. I wouldn't call it interesting, but it was pretty intense. I think people are starting to realise they don't really want a trade war.'

Ragoulin seemed to lose interest, now that the modesty of Weaver's role in the Swedish proceedings had been established. 'Come on,' he said, 'I'll walk you out to find a taxi – let me just sign for dinner.'

Ragoulin was headed for Chelsea, so they walked to Piccadilly and said goodnight there. As Weaver started to thank him, Ragoulin interjected, 'I meant to say, I have something you might like.'

'Really?' said Weaver gently. Was it his turn to receive the dealer's treatment from the man? He rarely bought anything from Ragoulin, and when he did, it was usually a volume of some minor pre-Bolshevik poet. He doubted if all his purchases over the last few years would have paid for this evening's dinner.

'Relax, my friend,' said Ragoulin, laying a long hand on Weaver's shoulder. 'It is not a purchase but a gift.'

'That is too kind, Alek—' he said, starting to protest.

'I hope you will like it. It's not a rare book, but by a young writer I think very good. A Russian writer.'

Weaver could visualise the author: Ragoulin's enthusiasms were inevitably young and female. His comparative flamboyance meant many of his clients thought he was gay, which, as he once explained during a boozy lunch, made seducing their wives much easier.

'Come by the office the day after tomorrow. Wednesday after lunch, let's say, or will you be fishing then at your friend's place?'

'No, I'll still be here.'

Ragoulin nodded. 'Good. Any time after lunch will find me there.'

Weaver thanked him for dinner, and Ragoulin nodded in acknowledgement. 'I think the book may surprise you. Make sure you come by.'

8

WEAVER'S FATHER WAS ALWAYS HAPPY TO TALK to strangers. Weaver was like this too; he found life was both more interesting and usually more pleasant if he exchanged a few words with the checkout lady at the supermarket. His stepfather, the minister, had made it clear he found this mild *bonhomie* irregular; despite his pastoral vocation, across a retail counter he was all Yankee reserve.

On the ride back to Holland Park, however, Weaver let the taxi driver do the talking: business was down; the tourists had less money; the driver's golf game was suffering from the recent heavy rain. Weaver sat back and let the garrulous patter flow over him as he felt an easy contentment after his dinner with Ragoulin. Stockholm now seemed well behind him.

He had the taxi pull over short of the side street where he was staying, thinking even a little walk would do him good after his heavy meal. He got out and handed over his debit card through the front passenger window. Handing it back, the driver said, his voice lowered, 'Not that it's any of my business, but do you see that Merc ahead of us?' Weaver looked up and saw a small dark Mercedes estate slowing down, then pulling over to the kerb. One of its brake lights was flickering, as if on the way out.

'Yeah. What about it?'

'He's been with us the whole way since Piccadilly,' the driver said. 'Mind how you go.'

And the taxi drove off, leaving Weaver standing uncertainly on the pavement. *What am I waiting for?* he wondered after a minute. Did he really think the Mercedes was following him? Who could it be then? He thought of the Russian security man last seen at Heathrow. Could it be the Russians? But why? He tried to dismiss the thought, but started wondering who else it could be. There was no one.

He nonetheless went back towards Holland Park Avenue, away from his Airbnb's side street. Circling, he walked slowly for ten minutes until he approached his house from the opposite direction. The streets were quiet here, virtually devoid of traffic. He heard a car turn into the street behind him, and he moved into the covered porch of the nearest house, ducking down when the car came by. He could only see its shadow, then standing up again saw a blinking brake light on the passing car. It was a Mercedes.

Back at his house, he found the ground floor dark and quiet. Once downstairs, he went into the little kitchen and made a cup of instant coffee. Going out to the sitting room, he turned on a light in the passage before sitting down in a wingback chair next to the vast glass windows facing the back garden. Something was amiss, though when he looked in his bedroom, nothing seemed changed. Was there a faint smell that hadn't been there before – of furniture polish perhaps? Whatever the reason, he had the nagging sense that someone had been in the flat. Probably the landlady, he told himself, trying not to feel spooked.

Returning to the sitting room, he was checking that the sliding door was locked when something buzzed on the little table next to his chair. His phone; he wondered who was trying to reach him. But when he looked at it, he saw a text message instead, which had landed during dinner with Ragoulin:

Call me at home tonight. NOT at the office. Repeat: NOT the office. Mac

Mac was by nature talkative but steady. Something had to be very wrong to account for this unusual terseness, the sense of barely suppressed panic.

He dialled Mac's home number and waited, hoping Peter wouldn't answer the phone; Peter was Mac's husband, and disliked Weaver enough not to disguise it. Weaver's friendship with Mac was accordingly confined to work, where they ate lunch together, usually twice a week.

Though there had been ten nights or so in the immediate wake of his marriage's breakup when, while Weaver hunted for an apartment, Mac and Peter had put him up on their living room sofa. More enduringly, they had adopted Parker, which Weaver had encouraged for the dog's sake despite knowing how much he would miss him. Curiously, Parker seemed to prefer Peter over Mac, even though Mac loved the dog to bits, which Peter most emphatically did not.

'Peter,' Weaver said, hearing Mac's husband answer. The connection was bad, and he found himself having to shout. 'It's Weaver. I've had a text from Mac asking me to call him. Said it was urgent.'

'He's not here. There's a leaving party at work.'

Weaver remembered: Bizhan, a Farsi interpreter so quiet that no one would be sorry to see him go, simply because no one would notice he had gone.

'Is Parker okay?'

'As far as I know.'

As if on cue, Parker barked in the background. 'Please stop shouting, Weaver,' shouted Peter. 'It gets him riled up hearing your voice.'

Good, thought Weaver. 'When will Mac be back?'

'I'm the dog's keeper, not Mac's,' Peter snapped.

'Okay. I'll call back.'

'If you must. Parker's bedtime's soon.'

'Don't worry, I'll disguise my voice.'

He ended the call, then against his better judgement checked his emails on the phone. There were forty-seven of them, none looking urgent – except one from Pauline; its subject line read tellingly, *WHEREABOUTS?* The email said: *Where are you? I was expecting you in the office today. P*

This surprised him. He had filled out the form for taking leave, back when he was planning to go to Vermont for his first fishing of the season. The convention was that approval could be taken as given unless your manager actively objected. But Pauline had said nothing other than a cursory 'See you in ten days.' Had she really forgotten he was on vacation?

He contemplated writing his report on the summit – standard practice for his department, and one way to work his way back into Pauline's favour, since everyone was dilatory about filing from the field. He wondered how to characterise the meeting between Hofstadter and Kuzmin, then stopped this train of thought before it derailed. What was he thinking of? If he wasn't meant to have been there, how could he possibly report on that meeting? But Pauline must know something about his involvement, since Blanchett had phoned her to find a substitute for Mrs Macauley. Weaver would have to play it by ear with Pauline when he returned to work, and find out then how much she knew.

He went to the bedroom, where he looked longingly at the duvet and pillows, tempted to lie down. That would be fatal – he sensed that once in bed he would sleep right through until morning. The travelling, the work, the fishing and late night of the dinner party – all were catching up to him. But tired as he was, he determined to stay up to talk with Mac, and find out what was so urgent.

He returned to the sitting room, switching its lights off as he walked down the passage. He sat down in the chair by the sliding door. He was in the dark.

9

He was wading the Battenkill in Vermont, near Route 22. Moving in the low water by the bank, he found the soles of his waders were slipping on the gravelly bottom, and each step had to be taken with care. He smelt cigar smoke and looked upstream for... another fisherman. Then he was looking for Lily, the woman at JP and Sue's house. But no one was there.

His line tautened and he felt the strong tug — a good fish, two pounds at least. But he was slipping on the gravel, and by the time he found his footing and lifted his rod, the fish was gone, free and invisible in the fast-running river. Disappointment filled him with a dull ache.

Was he still dreaming or was he awake? He sat still, feeling his senses slowly stirring as he came out of sleep. He figured it was now the middle of the night — what had wakened him?

His phone buzzed, startling him until he realised it must be Mac, who was the reason why he was sitting here in the first place. 'Hi,' he started to say, after grabbing the phone.

But Mac went first. 'Where the hell are you?'

'I'm in—'

'Don't tell me! Don't tell me!' He was shouting, unheard of for Mac — Peter was the emotional one.

'What's the matter?'

'Haven't you checked your emails?'

'I'm on vacation.'

'Jesus. You'll find one from me — and one from Pauline.'

'I saw hers.'

'Then you know she wants you back here yesterday.'

'She knew I was off this week. I arranged it ages ago, before she stuck me with Stockholm. So what's the panic?'

'How would I know? The office has been crawling with people looking for you.'

'What people?'

'The Secret Service, a bunch of them, along with Blanchett and some asshole from the White House. Pauline told them you and I were friends, so they decided to give me the third degree.'

'What do they want?' he asked.

'They want you, Weaver. And I don't think it's to give you the Medal of Honour. Blanchett speaks to me once a year at the Christmas party but didn't even remember my name. He sure knows yours, though.'

Mac described the sudden appearance of these people in the office, the harassed look on Pauline's face as she took them first to the floor's conference room, then five minutes later escorted them to Weaver's workstation.

Mac said, 'They questioned everybody: it was just like a movie, one by one in the conference room. I told them I didn't know you that well. They didn't believe me, thanks to Pauline, who told Blanchett we were pals. What they really wanted to know is where you are. Don't worry; I stayed *shtum*.'

'Thanks, Mac.'

'Don't thank me – I don't think they believed a word I said. They acted like you had defected or something. The funny thing is that I really *don't* know where you are.'

'Well, I'm—'

'No!' Mac shouted, then seemed to pull himself together. 'I think this call is safe for now, but they'll trace it eventually.'

'Isn't that a little dramatic?'

'You wouldn't say that if you'd talked to these guys. So please, please promise me you'll get rid of your cell. Don't call me from it; better still, don't call me at all.'

'Jesus,' he said.

Mac must have sensed his slight disapproval, for he said touchily, 'I only mean, have somebody else make the call. Okay? Somebody who they won't trace you through. And have them use a burner and make sure they call me here at home. Not the office, whatever they do.' He added, urgency returning to his voice, 'I tell you what: if I find out what this is about, and you're good to come back, I'll say that Parker's fine. But if there's trouble ahead, I'll say Parker's sick and I'm taking him to the vet.'

'This is starting to sound like a Bourne movie,' Weaver said to lighten things, shaken by this bout of near-hysteria from his normally placid colleague.

But Mac was talking again, even more frantically. 'If you'd seen how many fucking people they sent to the office, you wouldn't be making jokes.'

'Yeah, you made that clear enough. Did Pauline say anything to you?'

'She said you've ignored her email and she can't reach you by phone. Her text bounced.'

'She hasn't got my new phone number. I haven't registered it in the directory yet.'

'Keep it that way for now. But tell me – did something happen in Stockholm? The Secret Service guys kept intimating you'd done something terrible. Did you?'

There was no upside in telling Mac the truth. Hadn't the White House Chief of Staff ordered Weaver to keep his mouth shut? Not to mention the detailed threats of that State Department slimeball, Blanchett. It was too big a risk telling his friend, and it could jeopardise Mac's job as well as his own. The less Mac knew the better – both for Mac and for Weaver. Weaver said, 'Of course not. And actually, the summit was really boring and really hard work. Worst of both worlds.'

'Oh,' said Mac, 'so you're not the American Kim Philby.' He sounded almost disappointed. 'Anyway, did you go to the big dinner?'

'Yeah,' said Weaver. 'I was too jet-lagged to enjoy it, and the food wasn't great. Even you might get tired of gravadlax.'

'No reindeer?'

This was more like the Mac he knew. He said, 'Just the antler.'

But Mac's jokiness didn't last. 'Maybe by the time you're back, Pauline will have calmed down. And maybe by then we'll know what this is all about. In the meantime, I'll sniff around.' He paused, then said, 'I've got to go.'

And before Weaver could say anything more, Mac hung up.

Weaver looked at his watch; it was now four a.m. Even had he felt less agitated, going to bed would seem pointless. As it was, he turned on the sitting room lights, and sat down again in the chair.

The prospect of an untroubled week on his own was receding fast, but could be retrieved. But not here in this flat. The combination of Mac's warnings, the presence of the Russian security man at arrivals, and even a Mercedes with a flaky brake light – they all created a sense of exposure, of vulnerability, that resulted in one clear and repeating message: GO.

The agitation caused by these thoughts resulted in a sudden exhaustion that overcame his fear. Once again, he fell asleep in the chair; this time without interruption, and as far as he knew, dreamless. When he woke it was almost eleven o'clock, and he quickly showered and dressed, then packed up the few items he had taken out of his bag. It was canvas, with a long strap and brass zippers, and seemed infinitely expandable. A graduation gift chosen unexpectedly by his stepfather, though maybe not surprising, with its implicit hint that Weaver should travel more and sleep elsewhere.

Upstairs, he left the keys to the house on the side table in the hall. He called out several times, but nobody seemed to be home. Should he leave a note? No. He had paid in advance in full.

Outside, he started to walk towards Holland Park Avenue while he took stock. Two young men on e-scooters sped past him, unexpectedly close and spookily silent, but there was no sign of the Mercedes as he reached the top of the street, and he headed for Daunt's, the bookshop a couple of blocks away up leafy Holland Park Avenue. He'd need to sit down and browse listings of hotels on his phone – maybe find one in Bloomsbury, something modest but acceptable, the kind of hotel visited by untenured American academics while they researched the sole Malory manuscript in the British Library. It would be a comedown from the Airbnb, perhaps, but should be anonymous, and safe.

10

A HIGH AND HAZY SUN HAD WORKED its way through the morning mist, its light now glowing like resin in the warming air. There was traffic backed up on Holland Park Avenue, and he worked his way through the two lanes of cars, waiting for yet another e-scooter that was manoeuvring almost silently through the waiting vehicles. He stopped outside Daunt's for a moment, looking at the titles on display. He'd better buy some books to read, he thought, since he had brought only an old favourite, Robert Traver's *Trout Madness*, which even when rationed would rapidly would run out of (re)read pages.

He was in the shop pondering which shelves to turn to when someone caught his eye: another customer who'd come in just after him. A young man, roughly Weaver's height, dark-skinned, wearing a leather jacket and jeans, and white Converse All Star High Tops. As the man stopped and took a book from the display on the shop's side wall, packed with face-out copies of the new releases, he was standing sideways to Weaver, close enough to allow an unimpeded view of an impressively long straight nose. And close enough for Weaver to see that the pages of the book the guy was looking at were upside down.

Weaver didn't wait but got moving, leaving the shop and walking fast up the incline of the pavement towards the centre of Notting Hill. Any thought of coincidence was evaporating fast, along with the possibility that this man in the High Tops just liked to read books upside down. The sense of threat, however baffling and unspecific, was starting to overwhelm him.

Turning back, he saw the yellow light of a taxi for hire a few cars back, but saw too that it was stuck in heavy traffic. Getting into a stationary taxi would make him impossibly easy to follow.

Weaver went down the first left turn he came to – a sign said it was Clarendon Road, a smaller street with no traffic. He looked back as he turned, but there was no one following him. He walked fast, hoping to nab a cab on this side street and get out of the neighbourhood. But none of the cars that came by was a taxi.

He carried on walking, and was halfway to the next cross street when he heard a quiet hum, and turned round. It was a motorcycle – no, another scooter with a man riding it. Weaver turned and kept walking, as the faint hiss of the scooter grew louder behind him. As it drew nearer, the scooter seemed to slow down, and Weaver instinctively stepped to the side as it drew alongside. He turned just as the driver's hand reached out.

His bag! The man was trying to grab it, but thanks to Weaver's instinctive swerve away, missed the strap. The scooter had now passed Weaver, and the driver quickly accelerated. For the second time in minutes, Weaver saw a pair of Converse High Tops on a stranger's feet.

The man drove the scooter close to the cars parked on the other side of the street, but then executed a wide sweeping turn that brought him back to Weaver's side of the street, and facing him. The machine mounted the kerb with a small convulsive jerk and came to a halt. It was roughly thirty feet away from Weaver, and the driver stepped off the machine's little ledge. He turned his head and Weaver again recognised the long-nosed profile; it was the same High Tops man he'd seen in Daunt's just minutes before.

The man calmly unbuttoned the top half of his leather jacket and reached inside. When his hand emerged it held a pruning knife, which had a row of ugly serrated teeth.

Waving the knife, the man said, 'Your bag. Put it down and walk away.' The words were spoken with a slight accent. Not Russian, not Polish. But definitely East European.

Bravado seemed pointless when Weaver had nothing to fight with. He turned, ready to run, only to find that two more scooters had arrived behind him. They both stopped on the pavement about fifty feet away.

Weaver weighed up his chances against three assailants, and found there were none. He put down his bag, and started to cross the street quickly. To Weaver's alarm, High Tops also started to cross the street.

He didn't want the bag; he wanted Weaver.

Weaver stopped, then went back and picked up his bag. He forced himself to walk towards the sharp-nosed man in front of him. Weaver held the bag by its leather handle, swinging it loosely. Once, twice – on the third swing he let go, then watched as the bag sailed through the air.

High Tops seemed confused, reflexively trying to catch the bag while also trying to get out of its way; Weaver ran towards him, hoping to get past. But High Tops dropped the bag and, kicking it aside, moved to block the way. He raised the knife in his right hand, but as Weaver came towards him, High Tops stepped back, then suddenly flinched as the back of his leg hit the scooter he'd parked behind him. He stumbled, and lowered his arms to try to keep his balance, and seeing an opening, Weaver instinctively moved closer and threw his clenched right hand in a punch that was awkward but had all his momentum behind it.

It hit High Tops square on the mouth, and he fell backwards, landing hard on the pavement next to the scooter, his mouth spilling blood. For a moment he lay completely still, his eyes shut.

High Tops was out of action, but when Weaver turned he saw that behind him the two men had left their e-scooters and were advancing on foot: one out in the middle of the street, the other on the pavement. They were now so close that they would reach him in a matter of seconds. Weaver quickly grabbed his bag, his sole protection. He looked wildly about for help, but the road remained eerily empty of traffic.

Then out of nowhere, a high-pitched wail broke the air. Glancing quickly up the street, Weaver saw a revolving disc of blue. A police car was approaching at speed, its light continuing to flash, while the siren grew that much louder. Someone somewhere must have called the cops.

The car halted just short of Weaver, angled across the street to block any cars. It was a small, unprepossessing vehicle; as if the cavalry coming to the rescue were riding Shetland ponies. But it was enough to send the two men back onto their scooters and zooming towards Holland Park Avenue.

A uniformed cop got out of the patrol car, his belted waist holding handcuffs, nightstick, and taser. On the pavement, High Tops was still lying on his back, moaning softly through a hand held across his mouth. Blood ran under his fingers onto his leather jacket, where it dripped down, staining the pavement.

The policeman approached Weaver warily, while his colleague stayed sitting in the driver's seat, talking into a radio.

'What happened here?' demanded the lead cop.

Weaver shrugged. 'We had a difference of opinion. I didn't want to give up my bag.'

'So why is the blood all over *him*?' the cop now demanded.

'I didn't start this, officer.'

'I didn't say you did.' His tone was less aggressive. 'We've been watching out for this gang for the last hour or so. We think they moved down from Kilburn, looking for easier meat. We better get an ambulance.' He called this out to his partner in the car, then looking past Weaver, he said loudly, 'Damnit – there're the other two.' He pointed and Weaver looked down the street, where in the distance he saw the two accomplices nearing Holland Park Avenue.

The policeman looked at the mugger on the ground, who was moving, though not a lot. He said, 'You'll need to give a statement. Wait here; the ambulance should be along soon.' He signalled to his partner, who took off in the patrol car, starting up its siren. It was unbelievably loud.

Weaver watched silently in the disconcerting afterglow of what had just happened. He hadn't been in a fight since junior high school. After Weaver had legally changed his surname from Fontana, a well-meaning teacher had announced this in class. During break, Phil Docherty had declared that as far as he was concerned, Weaver was still a wop. Weaver had punched him spontaneously, and before Docherty could hit him back, other kids had broken them up.

The memory of that aborted fight had always seemed unreal, but there was nothing unreal about this one: the injured man dripping blood on the pavement was proof of that. There was, however, something *staged* about the episode; whatever the police said about Kilburn and watching this trio, Weaver had the strong feeling that the attack had been planned – and with Weaver as its target.

A door opened in one of the houses bordering the street, and a young man in green corduroy trousers and a rollneck sweater came out. He lifted a hand to catch the policeman's attention. 'I saw it all,' he said loudly and walked out to the pavement, where the policeman moved to talk with him, while keeping an eye on Weaver's assailant.

Weaver also looked at High Tops, who groaned when he took a step closer. Weaver glanced down Clarendon Road again. The two accomplices must have long since reached Holland Park Avenue, and were probably heading for the Underground, where they'd ditch their machines and proceed anonymously down into the bowels of the station.

In the distance another siren sounded. The ambulance. That was quick, he thought, and soon it was parked, half on the pavement, just short of High Tops, still lying on the pavement. A paramedic in green uniform got out, joined by the driver as they unloaded a stretcher out of the back. They were soon tending to the bleeding man, while the policeman turned to talk with the local witness. Weaver stood by, dumbly watching, glad they weren't asking him how the man had got hurt. Yet.

He resisted the impulse to flee, then wondered why he should resist it. He sensed he would be here for some time, while the cop took down the witness's account and his colleague chased the other two men. Weaver would have to go to the police station, and if he did that he could see nothing but trouble ahead. The only person hurt was this scooter-rider, and unless this witness from a house had seen that Weaver was the potential victim rather than the 'perp', there would be no evidence that Weaver had been acting in self-defence. It was just conceivable, in fact, that the person charged would be Weaver. After all, he had been the perpetrator of the only actual violence.

The paramedics gingerly slid High Tops onto the stretcher and lifted it waist high. They moved a careful step at a time towards the open back doors of the ambulance. Neither they nor the policeman were paying Weaver any attention.

Time to go. The e-scooter had been moved by one of the ambulance crew and stood against a low front garden wall. Picking up his bag, Weaver casually took a couple of steps and stood by the wall. He stepped forward and put a foot on the running board. He tentatively turned the throttle, hoping it worked like a motorcycle. It did, and with a sudden jerk that belied its lack of noise, the scooter started rolling.

'Hey!' the policeman called out in surprise, but by then Weaver was thirty feet away and moving.

11

IT WAS A STRANGE LITTLE MACHINE, THE adult version of a kid's toy. As he headed through the upper streets of Notting Hill, his bag hanging from its strap around his shoulder, Weaver felt like a grown-up with a lollipop. The scooter was surprisingly speedy – he had assumed it would be incapable of more than jogging pace, but he found it was keeping up with cars in the lunchtime traffic.

He was trying to go north, basing his navigation on the position of the sun and vague memories of the neighbourhood. He had just turned left onto Kensington Park Road when he felt a sudden series of shudders around his chest. He swerved and almost came off the scooter in his surprise, then regained his balance and realised it was his phone stirring.

Westbourne Grove lay ahead, he remembered, a road big enough to make an inconspicuous abandonment of the scooter impossible. On the left side of this street he could see a new block of apartments, brown-bricked, with a lobby at the nearest end. Stopping, Weaver dismounted and parked the scooter next to the side wall of the building, near the entrance to the block. He did not look around, trying to emulate the confident air of someone who knows exactly what he is doing. He walked briskly towards Westbourne Grove, alert for a shout that never came.

He wanted to get far away before the police returned and came looking for him, or some new assailants did. He should have hopped on the Underground at Holland Park after leaving Daunt's, but that might well have brought High Tops along right behind him. There would be another station around, though he had no idea where he'd take the Underground to. Right now, he just wanted somewhere private, somewhere safe.

Then he remembered the vibrating phone and fished it out of his pocket. There was a single message: *Couldn't hold out any longer. Sorry. Mac.*

The phone vibrated again, and the number on display was strangely familiar, but it wasn't Mac's. Curiosity overcame his caution, though his 'Hello' was tentative, almost suspicious.

'This is Lily. You called me yesterday.'

'I did,' he managed to say. 'Sorry to trouble you,' he added, struggling to gather his thoughts.

'You're not,' she said cheerfully. 'I was in a really boring meeting. Who is this, anyway?'

'Weaver. The guy from the other night at JP's. Remember?'

There was a pause. 'I do.' Her tone was inscrutable.

From noise in the background, he realised she was not alone. He heard her voice, distant now, addressing someone else. 'Give me a minute.' There was a chair scuffed and then her voice, again far away, saying, 'Tell them I'm on a call, Charles.'

'Hello again,' she said after a moment. 'As I was saying, you rang me.'

'I did – yesterday. I thought it would be nice to see you again.'

'Have things changed today?'

He did his best to laugh. 'No, not at all; I'm glad you've called back.' He realised he was slightly breathless. Why? The scooter hadn't exactly been hard work.

She said, 'Are you okay?'

'Why do you ask?'

'Don't answer a question with a question – it's maddening. You sound a bit… strained.'

His defences were second nature to him, an emotional armour built up over the years, yet he felt something inside himself give way. He remembered how, on first meeting Lily in JP's drawing room, his conventional composure had cracked. That seemed a world away in time, but was just three days ago. And since

Mac was near-hysterical, he was no use to Weaver now. Maybe, somehow, this woman Lily would be.

He took a deep breath, then said, 'I was going to ask you for coffee, or a drink; I could use one, frankly. There are some people after me.'

She was silent for a moment. 'Say that again.'

'I said. People are after me and—'

'I thought that's what you said.'

'One tried to steal my phone – and my bag.'

'That's not good, though this *is* London. Not everybody here acts like Mary Poppins. Did you manage to keep the bag?'

'Yes. The police showed up. They said they'd been watching the guy. There were two others with him, and until the cops arrived, I thought I was a goner. They had weapons.'

'What, knives?'

'Yes.'

'That's bad,' she said flatly. 'Couldn't you just hand your things over? What's a phone compared to your life?'

'More expensive,' he said, and she laughed, with the high pitch he remembered from JP's. He added, 'Though I had the impression they wanted it as well.'

She didn't reply for a moment, then said, her voice measured, 'You've had quite a shock. You should go lie down for a while.'

'I can't.'

'Where are you staying? Can't you go back there?'

'I was in an Airbnb in Holland Park. But I've checked out of it now.'

'Why? I thought you were in London until JP and Sue come back.'

'Yes. But last night I took a cab back from Piccadilly and the driver thought we'd been followed. I know,' he added when she stayed quiet, 'it sounds crazy. But the car he spotted kept driving around looking for somebody.' He continued, a little abashed. 'You're probably wondering how much you should believe.'

'I am a bit,' she admitted. 'I mean, it's not every day I get a call like this.'

'I was... I was just...' He couldn't think of what else to say.

'It sounds like you've been in the wars.' Her tone was that of a doctor, making sympathetic noises while thinking *WTF.*

'This must sound bonkers,' he said, using the English word. Somehow it seemed crucial that this woman believe him, but in the face of her silence, he felt he was floundering, fatally. And his hand was beginning to throb. Should he cut his losses? He said wearily, 'Let's just forget about it.'

There was a moment's silence and he imagined she was about to agree, but instead she said quietly, 'What did the man who attacked you look like? Was he English?'

'I didn't think to ask,' he said, thinking it a pretty peculiar question. 'Does it matter?'

'Possibly. Think: what did he look like?'

He pictured the man getting off the scooter, and then he remembered his voice. Weaver said firmly, 'He was East European; I could tell when he told me to put my bag down. The other two looked foreign as well.'

'Russians maybe?'

'Not Russian.'

'Why not Russian?' she persisted.

'How do I know? I just didn't think they were Russian. I grew up with one, after all. I'd say maybe Albanian, or Romanian. Something like that. What does that matter? What have I done to the Albanians?'

'Half the gangs in the UK supposedly come from there. Now, where are you?'

'Notting Hill.'

'Why don't you stay there? I'll come and get you.'

Had he heard her correctly? He ignored his standard policy of stoic denial and said, with what even to him reeked of insincere equivocation, 'Are you sure?'

'Anything to get out of this meeting. Where exactly are you now?'

He told her.

'Give me an hour; I've got to find some transport and I'm way east of you.'

'Thank you—'

'Save the thanks; you can buy me the candy floss later. But listen: don't just wander around. Get off the street and go into a shop, preferably one where you can sit as long as you like. A coffee place would be ideal; there must be lots of them in that neck of the woods. I'll text you when I'm getting near. I'll be in a Zipcar.'

'What's a Zipcar?'

'Google it. You're not *that* old.'

'Okay. I can't thank you enough—'

'No, you can't. Find a coffee shop and stay there. Pronto.'

He was in a less genteel corner of the Notting Hill neighbourhood, which meant there remained, amongst the brasseries and spritz bars, evidence of its past: a bookie's shop, a Co-op, a garish two-storeyed pub. And straddling the class divide, an independent coffee shop, with a large front room that had smoked windows all along its storefront.

He bought a cappuccino and two croissants, and found a table in the back. He took *Trout Madness* out of his bag, then put it back; he felt too anxious to concentrate.

He was surprised by Lily's reaction. He hadn't actually asked her for help, and her offer to collect him had been unsolicited. He was uncomfortable being looked after, and unused to it. His mother had raised him with intelligence but also considerable detachment, so this sense of dependency was new territory for Weaver, though his unease was tempered by relief.

He looked at his phone. A call had come in while he was talking to Lily. It was Pauline, phoning from her office in New York; against his will, he knew her number by heart.

The voicemail message she'd left was characteristically direct. 'Weaver, this is Pauline. You are now officially absent without leave and this has been approved by Sam Banchett. I did not grant you permission to take this week off. If you wish to retain your employment with the Department of State, I suggest you call me immediately and make plans to come back to work asap.'

Now Weaver understood the recent text from Mac: his friend had given Pauline his new phone's number. Weaver couldn't really resent Mac's surrender; he could imagine the threats that had been made.

Pauline's threats to Weaver, on the other hand, made little sense. What was she playing at? Had she really forgotten he was on leave, and did she honestly think he'd gone AWOL? No, she must be operating under instructions, doubtless from Sam Blanchett in DC, who must have flown back from Stockholm to New York City, rather than to Washington. Weaver was in trouble; that seemed clear. But why were they so keen to have him come back?

A text arrived with another shudder from his phone – *where are you now? L.* He texted back to say where, and almost immediately she replied: *I'm around the corner.*

Outside it took him several minutes to find her. Eventually he spotted her, parked on a double yellow line. She was sitting upright behind the steering wheel of a car so small he wondered if it were legal. Paradoxically, its size would have made it conspicuous even if it hadn't been a glossy white and green, with *Zipcar* in large letters along the door panel.

'Hi,' he said simply, sliding into the front seat.

'Hi back,' she said. She was dressed for corporate work, in black cotton trousers and an oversized pastel-blue blazer that was half-hiding a white silk T-shirt. She wore the same single-strand necklace he had seen at JP's.

'Fancy car,' he said.

'You'd rather I arrived on a scooter?'

'What is it with scooters here? The guy who tried to take my bag was riding one.'

'They're all the rage, especially among the younger breed of hoodlum.'

She swivelled in her seat to look at him closely, and his eyes were now close to her face. She was wearing very little makeup, but that she did have on was carefully applied – the mascara just so and undisguised, some faint hints of blush on her cheeks, and lipstick the palest shade of peach. Her hair was drawn back with a tortoiseshell claw clip, although a few strands were escaping.

'So, are you okay?' she asked.

'I guess so,' he said.

'Why don't you tell me what happened? Take your time.'

A normal enough request, one he should have expected, but he felt ill-prepared. He thought for a moment while she waited, until he sensed she was suppressing growing impatience. He could hardly blame her; to interrupt her working day and drive all across town, only to find him mute.

At last he said, 'I'm not a fan of conspiracy theories, but there's been a succession of strange things happening to me.' He looked at her, and she gave a small encouraging nod, though he couldn't help but wonder if she was going to believe him. 'I did my best to ignore them, but I'm thinking now I should have paid more attention. I could have been...' He stopped short of 'killed', which sounded too melodramatic. 'Hurt.'

He didn't know if she was buying his story; she was looking around and checking the mirrors.

'You probably think I'm paranoid,' he said.

'I probably do. Go on, try me.'

'What do you mean?'

'It means, tell me what's happened. Then I'll assess the evidence and let you know.'

He must have still looked baffled, for she explained, 'Let you know whether you're paranoid, that is, or whether you're right to be scared. One gets you my full assistance; the other gets the Mental Health Act invoked. Either a ride to my place, where we can think things through, or a trip to the nearest psychiatric institution.' She gestured with her hand. 'Get started; I haven't got all day. What were these "strange things"? Tell me and then we'll see.'

So he told her about the Russian security man from Stockholm popping up at Heathrow. He mentioned his dinner with Ragoulin, and then told her about the Mercedes with the tail light on the blink. As she listened, Lily was rolling her upper lip against her lower one, a tic he did not know how to interpret.

He said, 'But I haven't told anyone where I was staying, except JP, and even him only in vague terms.'

'A mystery for now, then. So go on.' When he paused, she asked, 'Did it occur to you that maybe the Mercedes was fixing your location?'

'No, it didn't,' he said, taken aback by the thought. 'But that would be a first – a burglar waiting until the occupant had come home.'

'Who said it was a burglar?' she said cryptically. 'Anyway, it's just a thought. Go on.'

And he described how, not even two hours before, the trio of muggers had appeared, after he'd seen one of them in the bookshop wearing Converse All Star High Tops. She nodded and interrupted, 'Everyone I know used to wear them.'

'I did too, in high school. I couldn't believe what they cost.'

'Not anymore,' she said. 'No longer the hipster's choice. But go on: how did you manage to keep your phone and your bag?'

'The guy tried to snatch them as he drove by. He missed. Then, when he tried again, I stopped him.'

'How'd you do that?'

Weaver said more quietly, 'I hit him.'

Lily's eyes widened.

'Don't look alarmed. I don't go around punching people, but I didn't have much choice.'

She nodded. 'Anything else exciting happen?' she asked, and he could not read her tone.

'That's all, Your Honour,' he said. 'The defence rests.'

'Right,' she said slowly. She looked like she was trying to make a decision. 'Time to go,' she said at last.

Startled, he asked, 'What did you have in mind?'

She smiled quickly, semi-automatically, but her tone was serious. She said, 'If you're right about even half of this, then you've got a problem. There's no point skirting that. We need to figure out what's going on and what you should do. That is, unless you have a pressing appointment elsewhere.'

'I think you know the answer to that. I'm easy,' he added, feeling anything but. 'But I don't see what I can *do*, other than stay out of harm's way.'

'We'll talk about it later,' she said, then reached out and gripped the steering wheel tightly. She had small hands, with slender fingers. She said sharply, 'Don't look at my nails.' Her voice softened. 'I bite them.'

Starting the engine, she pulled out quickly, then turned left smartly onto Westbourne Grove. After no more than fifty yards she suddenly swung the wheel and kept turning it. Shop fronts and a double-decker bus and people on both pavements swam before Weaver's eyes. After what seemed an eternity, the car finished its seemingly impossible U-turn unscathed – though only just, as the bus driver pounded his horn. *The advantages of a dinky car*, Weaver thought ungenerously, feeling slightly sick, though he admired the unhesitating panache with which she had conducted the manoeuvre.

'Sorry,' she said, sounding a little embarrassed.

'Do you always change direction like that?'

'There was a Mercedes that came and parked behind us, a little dark estate. It started up when we did, and turned left when we did. It was just behind us. I thought it best not to take any chances.'

'Are you serious?'

She nodded. 'Mercs are not uncommon in this part of town. But why take a chance?'

He decided not to point out that her hundred-and-eighty-degree turn had involved its own kind of risk.

She said, 'We need to think about who might be after you. And why.' He could not tell from her voice if she was humouring him;

if she were, she was doing it very well. 'But first things first. How did they find you?'

'The Mercedes, maybe?'

She shook her head as they stopped at a pedestrian crossing. They had left Notting Hill, heading east. The buildings now consisted of blocks of flats, mostly council estates. 'I think they already knew where you were staying.'

He saw the sense of this. 'But how?'

'You tell me. Who knew you were in the country?'

He thought for a moment. 'My colleague Mac in New York knows I'm in the UK, but he doesn't know where – he probably thinks I'm fishing with JP. Normally I would be. My colleague Tomic also knows I'm on vacation this week in the UK, but nothing more specific.'

'Where is he now?'

'In Russia at his cousin's *dacha*, near Morozov's palace. The cousin is a banker with ties to the FSB, apparently, though Tomic is himself pretty fiercely anti-Russian.' He paused momentarily. 'Oh, and I called my mother before leaving the States to explain I wouldn't be coming home this week.'

'Did you tell her why?'

'No.'

'Didn't she ask?'

'No,' he said again. He added, deadpan, 'She was too busy hiding her disappointment.'

Lily laughed. 'But what about in this country? Did you tell anyone where you were going when you were at JP's?'

He thought about it, then shook his head. 'Not that I can think of.'

Lily made a small *moue*, and said, 'What about the man you had dinner with?'

'Ragoulin? He's more a close acquaintance than a close friend. He wouldn't be interested in where I was staying.'

Lily looked pensive. 'I've heard the name. I think JP may know him.'

'No—' he started to say, then stopped. 'Actually, he has met him. He came with me once to Ragoulin's gallery. Well, sort of gallery. It's a couple of rooms upstairs on Bond Street. JP and I'd had lunch together, so he came along; he was starting to buy art anyway.' He vaguely remembered now: JP had been impressed by the prices Ragoulin was asking for his latest haul of Russian portraits – there had been a particularly bad one of Tsar Nicholas II for high five figures which Weaver had steered JP away from, leading him to an excellent Russian Expressionist picture that was about the same price.

'I see,' she said, concentrating on her driving.

'JP and Sue know I'm in London, of course. He suggested I stay in their apartment in Belgravia.'

'Why didn't you?'

'It seemed too complicated. JP always says it's just an apartment, but it's enormous, bigger than your average house. And they have tons of security and lots of staff coming in and out, all in a place that feels like a tomb. And besides, he's always so generous I don't want to overdo it.'

'Did you tell him where you were staying instead?'

'Only that it was in Holland Park. That's all.'

'So there's no one you can think of who knew exactly where you'd be staying?'

He thought again for a moment. 'No,' he said finally. 'I only knew myself a couple of days ago.'

'When you drove in on Sunday, could someone have followed you?'

'It's possible. But I think I would have noticed – I'm sensitive to traffic when I drive.'

'Sensitive to traffic?'

He smiled, happy to be laughed at, though he was slightly irked by the relentless questioning; he couldn't see how it was going to help him. 'Also, I didn't drive straight there. I had to drop the rental car off in West Kensington, then I got a taxi. It took me a while to find one, too. It wouldn't have been that easy to tail me to Holland Park unobserved.'

'Hmm.' Lily didn't sound convinced.

They had turned south onto Cleveland Terrace and its row of substantial stucco-fronted townhouses, and were nearing Paddington Station, which on this western side seemed to be under construction, swathed in enormous sheets of opaque plastic.

Lily pulled over but left the motor running. 'That's Paddington,' she said.

'I know,' he said. He waited, the silence awkward, feeling an immense but unexpressed reluctance to go. Sighing, he said, 'I better get out here.'

She turned off the engine. 'Get out? What do you mean? Where are you going?'

'I don't know. I guess I'd better find a hotel.'

'Don't be stupid. I thought you needed help.'

'I did.'

'Do.'

'Do what?'

She shook her head in exasperation. 'You *do* need help. Now be quiet while I think.'

He did as he was told, and they sat in silence for a few minutes, Weaver staring ahead. Eventually, he snuck a sideways look at Lily. She had her eyes closed and her head was nodding gently. Was she asleep?

Then she opened her eyes, and turned her head towards him, resting her cheek on her shoulder. In a murmur she said, almost whispering, 'Give me your phone for a minute.'

He hesitated, then took the iPhone out of his inner pocket and handed it over. To his alarm, she promptly tucked it into the side pocket of her blazer. She hunched both shoulders and sat up straight.

'What are you doing?' he asked, now alarmed.

'It has to go – don't you see that?'

'No, I don't. It's brand new. It cost a fortune, and work won't pay me for another one.'

'You are being ridiculous. Or just naïve.' She sat up, sniffing with disdain – he wanted to wipe it away, as if it were sweat on her Cupid's bow. 'You have to assume the worst. Let's at least agree someone's looking for you. We'll talk later about who it could be. But assuming we're right, then your weakest link is your phone. How else do you think they knew where you were? The phone can tell them who you've called, who's called you, and give them your texts and emails as well. Most important, if they're any good at all at this, and have the resources, it gives them your location. *Capisce?*'

'Got it.'

'Now, who had access to your phone?'

'No one,' he said defensively. 'I bought it last week on 47th Street from an electronics store. It's been with me ever since.'

'Twenty-four seven?' She was watching him. 'This is important.'

After a moment he said, a little self-consciously, 'I live alone.'

She looked unsurprised. 'Join the crowd – well, not a crowd, I suppose. But think hard: was there any time when you didn't have your phone? Not just in London, but since you bought it.'

'I told you, no,' he said impatiently, but for some reason this sounded hollow. And then he remembered. 'Unless…'

'Unless what?' There was nothing jokey in her voice.

He said, subdued now, 'Before a meeting at a summit, sometimes you have to hand over your phone.'

'Why? Are they worried you'll take photos?'

'No. They're worried you'll record the meeting.' And he thought of the pen with its digital recorder, tucked away behind *Seven Types of Ambiguity.*

Lily had both arms stretched out, her palms flat on the steering wheel. She was looking at her nails again, pensive. He said, 'So they took away my phone during… a meeting I worked. I only got it back afterwards.'

'Ah.'

'That's not all. As I said, the Russian man who took my phone in Stockholm showed up at Heathrow.'

'How do you know he was Russian?'

'Because I saw him before, in Stockholm.'

'You saw a lot of people in Stockholm. How did you know he was Russian?'

'Because at one point he spoke to me in Russian,' he said shortly, irked by her persistence.

'At the summit? What was a Russian doing at the summit?'

'He wasn't...' He stopped, looking for a way out. 'It's complicated,' he said at last, weakly.

'It must be,' said Lily. They sat in silence for a moment. Lily sighed, then said, 'You'll have to tell me at some point if I'm going to help you.' She shrugged. 'But let's skip it for now. Tell me more about this man.'

'He was waiting when I came through customs.'

'Waiting for you?'

'I think he must have been. I didn't see him greet anyone else.'

'But he didn't greet you – why was that?'

'I think he must have missed me – I was helping an old lady I sat next to on the flight, and when we came out of arrivals her whole family were waiting. The place is chaotic at the best of times.'

'That settles it,' she said, sitting up straight to look in the mirror. She opened the car door, and started to get out.

'Where are you going?' he asked, sounding plaintive.

She was out of the car by then and leaned to poke her head through the open window. 'I'll be back. Sit tight.'

He nodded reluctantly, feeling like an obedient dog that privately has no conviction his masters know what they're doing. Lily walked towards Paddington, looking both ways along the street. Did she think they were still being followed, even after her stunt with the car? Then her hand shot up, and a moment later a cab stopped next to her on the pavement. Weaver watched with mounting dismay as she spoke to the driver, then climbed into the back of the taxi.

What was she doing? Was she going to leave him after all, here in this ridiculous excuse for a car, while she went off to

God knows where? He could think of nothing that might have precipitated her sudden exit, unless… well, unless she was crazy as well as mystifying.

The taxi hadn't moved, and he wondered what was going on. He could make out the back of her head in the taxi, then it leaned forward and disappeared. To do what? Had she dropped something? The rear door opened and Lily climbed out. She was walking back to the car when the taxi did its own U-turn, rather more easily, and came back, heading towards the Zipcar. As he passed by Lily, the driver leaned out his window and gave her the finger.

'What was that about?' Weaver asked as Lily got back in the car.

'He's not happy, that's for sure.' She started the car and pulled out onto the street. At the corner she turned left, and soon they were driving away from Paddington.

Weaver waited a while to speak. 'What did you tell him?'

'I asked him to take me to the British Museum, but then I said I'd changed my mind and got out. He wasn't very pleased.'

'What was the point of that? And what have you done with my phone?'

'Got rid of it, of course. I did tell you it had to go.'

'Did you give it to the driver?' His voice was disbelieving.

'Of course not. It's now tucked neatly underneath the cushion of the passenger seat. I turned it on silent, so if somebody rings it won't be heard, even if a passenger is sitting on it. At some point, someone will find it – probably the driver, when he checks the taxi at the end of his shift. By then your phone will have seen half of London.'

'So?'

'So if you are being tracked *via* the phone, you'll be leaving a trail that's completely misleading. They'll see you were in Notting Hill, but after that it's anybody's guess. You understand now?'

'I guess so,' he said, looking out his window as they crossed Edgware Road, heading east. The traffic was light, but they were on back streets near Seymour Place, a once unfashionable district of nineteenth-century red-brick mansion blocks that Weaver had seen before and admired. Quiet, central, comfortable yet handsome, unsung. His idea of a tolerable city neighbourhood, yet even it now seemed spooky, threatening.

'When did you decide to come to England?' Lily asked.

'Only after I was told to attend the summit in Stockholm; that was at the beginning of last week. I confirmed things with JP when I got to Sweden; that was Wednesday. I booked my flight to London then, too.'

'So "they" couldn't have planned in advance to find you here – you didn't know yourself until Wednesday. Something happened to make them come after you, and that must have been in Stockholm.'

He realised he wanted to tell her more, but stopped himself. He barely knew this woman. He said, 'I only worked some low-level trade meetings – so what?'

'I don't think the French targeted you over their exports of *fromage frais*. I don't believe you think so, either. Try another language – *ponyal*?'

'What do you mean?' Her use of Russian was disconcerting.

When she didn't reply, he started to feel he had to give her something, or the conversation would stall completely. But how much more should he tell her? He thought of the threats issued by Blanchett and Hofstadter, though their impact was waning – people were after him without his saying a word to anyone about the meeting. And why worry about losing his job when the immediate concern was staying safe?

He looked over at Lily, who did not return the gaze. Deliberately, he felt. But she had believed him, or at least suspended judgement, before receiving any confirming evidence. He was thinking this to reassure himself when suddenly Lily looked into the rear-view mirror, then shouted, 'Jesus!'

'What's the matter?'

'The Mercedes is back. I thought *I* was being paranoid, but I wasn't.'

'How did they find us?' It was hard to credit the Mercedes happening on them by chance while trawling through west London.

Lily sighed as they stopped at a traffic light at the junction with Marylebone Road. 'The phone, of course. There would be a lag while their control people waited for your phone to reach another transmitter. That's why I dumped the bloody thing, but they had time to catch up while we were parked at Paddington. My bad,' she said, sounding disgusted with herself.

'Can you lose them?'

'Probably not.' But her voice brightened as they moved through the green light and turned east on the crowded lanes of Marylebone Road. 'Okay. Marylebone Station is just ahead. You know it?'

'Quaint and picturesque,' he said.

'Well, picturesque your quaintness later. Here's what I want you to do.' And she told him while he listened intently, suppressing his slight resentment at taking orders, though he felt bad that he had dragged her into this.

It took two minutes to reach the station, a surprisingly modest Victorian building of warm red brick, with a vast wrought-iron and glass canopy under which taxis queued and cars dropped off passengers. It was a small station, almost cosy, which somehow made the threat of the Mercedes seem grotesquely out of place – and the more menacing for it.

When Lily pulled over into the entrance, Weaver had the door half open. He jumped out and kept moving. Once inside the station, he swerved left, away from the platforms in front of him, shrugging off a sudden impulse to walk straight ahead and hop on the first train leaving London. Instead, he half-walked, half-ran along a small precinct of shops. Near the end of them, as he approached the dark atrium of the western entrance, he found the station bar, and went through its swing doors into a small anteroom.

A barman stood behind the counter. Weaver nodded, and kept moving into a larger adjacent room, which held only a few customers. The bar here was unmanned, and Weaver strode across the room to the windows facing the little street in front, where some forty yards along he had just hopped out. There was no sign of the Zipcar or of Lily, but as he peered out the window a Mercedes saloon swung into the lane under the station's portico. Two men got out, dressed in light grey suits; both wore ties, and one had on dark sunglasses. They conferred briefly, then the one in shades headed towards the main entrance. The other man came along the pavement towards the bar, where Weaver was watching him through the window.

Weaver kicked himself – he should have kept going out the side entrance of the station. Too late now. And it would be just his luck if he retreated back to the precinct of shops and ran straight into the other man. A classic pincer move.

He had to do something. He went back to the table closest to the bar and took off his jacket, hooking it on the vertical posts of a high-backed chair. He put his bag on the seat, and pushed the chair into the table until the bag was out of sight. Then he quickly went behind the bar.

Rolling up his shirt sleeves, he began to whistle, a little tunelessly, and grabbed a towel and started polishing the glasses that were drying by a little sink. The guy in the suit was outside, looking around; any minute he would enter the bar. Instead, to Weaver's consternation, the barman next door came into the room.

The bartender looked at Weaver down the length of the wooden bar top. He was medium height, wide in the shoulders, balding with a big unkempt beard. 'You the new guy?' he asked.

Weaver nodded. 'That's me.'

'Mary's shown you the ropes, yes?' Weaver nodded again, and the barman said, 'The till's been acting up. If there's any problem, just give us a shout.'

He headed back to the other room. An old man in a duffel coat, who had been sitting with his wife by the window, made his way to the bar. 'Another pint of Stella, please. And a large Coke for the driver,' he joked.

Suppressing his panic, Weaver forced himself to smile and pulled an empty glass from the row above the till, then stuck it under the lager hose and pushed the button. As the glass filled, he looked over the old man's shoulder at the new arrival in the suit. He stood a few feet away, scanning the room. When he finished, he looked straight at Weaver.

'Will be with you in a jiffy, sir,' said Weaver with a heavy Irish accent. It would not have passed in a drinking hole within shouting distance of the Liffey, but it would have to do for now.

The man in the suit shook his head impatiently, then walked through the room and into the smaller bar. Weaver hoped he would go out into the precinct, and join his colleague in a search of trains out on the platforms. This would give enough time to escape and find Lily, he thought, waiting to press the button for the beer's second half.

'If you're the new guy, who's the bloke next door?'

The barman was back, sounding unsure whether to be puzzled or angry.

Weaver shrugged and tried to sound jaunty, still in Irish mode. 'I'm the new guy, all right, but one who's gone to the wrong place. A thousand apologies; I've just learned this is not the Black Horse.'

He was around the bar by now, leaving the pint of beer as he collected his jacket and bag. He had reached the door before the barman started shouting.

Outside, there was no sign of Lily. Then he spotted the little white car down a side street, parked illegally in front of a Travelodge. It was straddled across the kerb, half on the street, half on the pavement. But there was no one in the driver's seat.

12

WHERE HAD LILY GOT TO? MAYBE SHE had got scared and run away. He could hardly blame her – why should she put herself in jeopardy for a man who was still effectively a stranger?

He looked up and down the streets, but there was no sign of her. He wanted to run away himself, but felt he had to give Lily the chance to reappear. Could she be waiting in the lobby of the Travelodge? Starting to cross the street, he stopped himself as a taxi barrelled towards him. It braked hard, coming to a halt next to him, now back on the pavement.

The window in the rear came down and a low voice said, 'Get in.'

Weaver hesitated, until the voice, familiar now, said urgently, 'Hurry!'

He got in and fell into a seat as the cab pulled out and sped towards the Marylebone Road. They just made the traffic light.

'What—' he started to exclaim.

Lily put a finger to her lips. *'Murmure, s'il te plaît.'*

'Okay,' he said in a half-whisper. Was she worried about the driver hearing? For a fleeting second, he wondered if this taxi was the same one that was now host to his phone – right now nothing seemed impossible. But then he remembered the beefy middle-aged face, flushed and angry, leaning out of the window. This driver was twenty years younger, with spiky hair bleach-dyed the colour of sweetcorn, and a faded green tattoo of a spider on the back of his neck.

'What about the car?' he asked.

Lily shrugged and, reclining in her seat now, switched back to English just as the driver turned up the music on the radio, as if tactfully sensing they didn't want to be overheard. She said, 'With any luck it'll get towed. Expensive, but safe. And I'll pay the fine it's accrued with Zipcar,' she added ruefully.

'What about our friends back there?' he asked, making a mental note to pay her for the car rental.

'They'll be some time, especially if they search each train. And they may have trouble with the Merc: one of its tyres has been vandalised, I fear. Scandalous.'

'How did you manage that? Your fingernails?'

'Steady on, or I'll have you dumped at Euston Station.' She flung open the front flap of her dark green leather backpack. As she rummaged in it, he caught sight of a jumble of pens, a small notebook, lipstick, a credit card – and a Stanley knife, its blade now retracted.

'Do you always carry a blade with you?'

'Always.' There was triumph in her voice.

'What were they going to do to me, anyway? They weren't armed as far as I could tell.'

'I wouldn't be so sure about that,' said Lily. 'They wouldn't have attacked you in public. They'd have hustled you into their car and taken you somewhere they could have an interesting… conversation. Then they'd have disposed of you – note the euphemism – since otherwise you'd be the evidence against them. They'd make sure they got your bag, too. They seem to have a thing about your bag. What's in it?'

He thought of the digital pen hidden at JP's. 'Nothing they want, believe me. Clothes. A book or two. Some trout flies I bought,' he said, wondering why Lily was so sure of what the men would have done to him.

'Well, we should be okay now. The only signal they'll get from your phone is in the other taxi, and hopefully it's with a fare out in Lewisham. Or better still, Heathrow. It would be useful if they thought you'd left town.'

With the patience of a veteran, the driver worked through stop-and-start traffic eastwards. They passed the British Library and King's Cross, where an informal depot of buses stood gathered like an elephant herd, holding them up for a few twitching minutes. Finally they continued east, and Weaver wondered where they were going. 'None of this looks familiar.'

She laughed. 'You're out of date, Weaver. "Go east, young man, go east." This is the Pentonville Road, and we are heading towards the lively centre of post-modern London. How well do you know the city?'

'Clearly not as well as I thought. I lived here for two years, but I was just a kid.'

'When was that? During the Blitz?'

'I'm only a little older than you.'

'No. I'm a spring chicken. But tell me, was your father here on business?'

'He was working for the FBI, like he does now. He wanted out of Vermont and this was his chance. My mother went along with it, but she wasn't happy. So they went back to Vermont, but then *he* wasn't happy. When San Francisco came up, he jumped at it. My mother didn't jump; she stayed in Vermont. It was meant to be temporary, but she met the Reverend and that was that.'

Why was he telling her his family history? Why would she care? And where were they going?

As if reading his thoughts, Lily pointed ahead of them. 'City Road,' she announced as the driver left a large roundabout, 'home of the British Digital Highway. All the hi-tech companies with offices in London are here. Don't worry, we're almost there.'

They turned off the Digital Highway onto a narrow side street, lined on each side by older buildings, mixed constructions of brick and glass that looked as if they had a manufacturing history behind them. Then without a word from Lily, the driver pulled over and stopped.

'After you,' said Lily, opening the kerbside door.

'I'll get this,' Weaver said, hoping the driver would take a card.

'No, it's all done,' Lily said, as if explaining it to a child.

'How's that?'

'I have an account. Come on, follow me.'

13

T**HEY WALKED ALONG** L**EONARD** S**TREET,** A **NARROW**
claustrophobic road that made Weaver feel even tenser.
The buildings looked to have been warehouses and factories,
reconditioned into flats and offices whose brick and masonry
origins were not effectively disguised by the modern-day addition
of pane-glass windows and chrome-lined entrance lobbies. One
of the newer-looking buildings had a second entrance at its far
end, barred by a heavy metal door which had a CCTV camera
mounted above it. There was a small metal box attached to the
door frame. Lily stopped in front of it, and taking a key from her
bag, opened the box, then punched a code on an internal pad.
She looked up directly at the camera. A second later came a heavy
click, and the door opened.

Inside, they went up a stairway, Lily's heels clacking on the
concrete steps like the keys of an antique typewriter. She didn't
stop at the first floor, where a locked fire door led into the
building. They kept going, finding the same fire door on each
floor, until they reached the fourth and top floor, and another
massive steel door barred their way.

'This is worthy of Fort Knox,' Weaver said appreciatively.

He thought of his childhood time in the Demidov compound,
where despite every effort to simulate an average American
household – board games, a playhouse, the Demidov boys in jeans
and T-shirts – there was always a disturbing amount of security:
the compound with its high fence, only putatively intended to keep
out the deer; the buzzer at the locked entrance; the unpublicised
presence of guards; the master's own reluctant willingness to

keep a shotgun in his bedroom closet, ready for the day (though it would have been at night) when KGB or GDR assassins might slip through the defences to try to kill the famous exile.

Lily replied, 'The security's inherited. The former tenants said they were financial specialists, but my own sense is that they were high-class loan sharks. That's a cash business, so they needed to be careful. Whereas if someone robbed *me*, they'd be lucky to find a tenner in the petty cash box.' She was opening another metal box now, and entering another code. 'I didn't see any point dismantling the systems. It never hurts to be careful. I have a panic button in every room. They're also inherited.' She was looking up at yet another camera. Her face registered on some invisible screen somewhere, the PIN code went through, and when Lily gave a push, the door clicked and opened a grudging inch or two.

'Get the door, will you?' she said. 'It makes my shoulder sore.'

He soon understood why, for the door was not only steel but lead-lined. He had to push hard before it moved at all. How on earth did Lily do it? At last, it was fully open, and they stepped inside.

He hadn't known what to expect. The office was one large open-plan room, with walls of exposed burnt-orange brick, and a floor of narrow oak boards. It seemed to be part workspace and part meeting room, and had a partition wall at the back with closed twin doors. To his left there was a meeting table, which consisted of a long lozenge of grey slate balanced on two sawhorses of tubular steel, with half a dozen leather chairs around it. The windows, tall sash ones, had wooden shutters, now folded back, and looked directly across to offices in the adjacent building, scarcely twenty feet away.

Lily went to close the shutters, and while she adjusted their slats, Weaver looked at the room's walls. Mainly silk screen prints, with thin brushed-chrome frames, and all contemporary – boldly coloured yet anodyne, if costly. To one side of him, in a brick alcove, there was a fridge and a dishwasher beneath a long counter, with a bulky coffee machine on top and a water cooler standing at the end.

God knows what sweatshop had once filled this floor, or how many immigrants – Jews long ago, Huguenots perhaps, Bangladeshis more recently – had been squeezed in, but the present effect was of the room's good taste managing to survive the large amount of money thrown at it. Whatever her business, Lily must be doing well; or had so much money that it didn't matter if she was.

Then he had the stray suspicious thought that perhaps the office wasn't hers. Or that it was some sort of Potemkin village, erected to deceive visitors that a thriving business was in operation. He remembered Mac telling him a story of how, in an earlier corporate incarnation, he had been sent to perform due diligence on a company his own firm was buying, and found an impressive-looking setup in an East Side townhouse. A little probing, however, revealed that the office's file servers had been rented for a day; the staff were off-duty waiters, aspiring or 'resting' actors to a man (there were no women on show); and the business about to be acquired for a hefty price proved effectively non-existent. Could that be the case here?

'What's wrong, Weaver? You look as if you've swallowed a fly.'

'Nothing's wrong,' he said, still looking around. Trying to sound bright more than dutiful, he said, 'What a nice office.' He added, more clumsily, 'And thank you for coming to get me. I'm very grateful. I—'

Lily was shaking her head impatiently. 'Let's skip the *politesse*, okay? You know, the "I couldn't possibly" and "I insist"...'

'Okay,' he said simply.

She looked at him, impressed. 'That was a quick surrender.' Her easy tones were back in charge. 'Are you sure you're not English? I mean, are you always this easy?'

'I don't feel easy.' He exhaled nosily. 'My odds don't look great to me at the moment.' The tumult of the morning was getting to him, he realised.

Lily was shaking her head again. 'When I work with somebody, I want them upbeat, confident of a happy future.'

'What's in it for you?'

'For me?' She looked startled.

'I mean, am I a client?' He gestured at the space around them. 'You seem to be doing well. Whatever you do for a living.'

'Oh, you think so? Good.' Her tone changed, now more businesslike. 'What I do is help new businesses. I thought I told you that at JP's.'

'No. JP said you were an interior decorator, and you didn't deny it.' But then, JP had said a lot of things.

She laughed, that fine peal he had found so attractive in the country, and found he did in the city, too. As it subsided, she said, 'I probably should have been; Farrow & Ball's loss, I guess. No, what I do is help people who've managed to raise a lot of money for their start-up and then don't have the faintest idea what to do with it. I do scale-ups rather than start-ups. Some don't really need any help; they only hire me to keep their backers happy. Especially true if they're crooks, of whom I assure you there are lots.'

'Even in hi-tech?' he asked.

'Especially in hi-tech. Your average-looking nerd may seem incapable of delinquency, but believe me, that sometimes comes with the dweeb *persona*. I'm exaggerating, you'll be surprised to learn. For the most part, my clients have legitimately received what seems to them a sudden windfall of venture cash, and my job is to keep them from frittering it away. What you see here,' she swept a hand expansively, 'is what happens when they don't listen to me.'

'Why? You run off with the money?'

'Smart aleck,' she said, but lightly. 'All this trendy décor came at a knockdown price from a start-up that spent its money fast and very unwisely. It was more a fold-up than a start-up, to be honest. They paid me well, listened carefully, then took absolutely none of my advice.' There was an air of performance to her talking, thought Weaver, but it was highly entertaining – life with Lily must never be dull.

'Anyway,' she said, her tone indicating she wanted to change the subject; so Weaver, who didn't, quickly asked, 'How did you get into this line of work? It doesn't sound like an obvious career.'

She shrugged. 'I was back in London and at loose ends. A friend of mine had invested in a start-up with some foreign entrepreneurs who didn't understand that in the UK there are things called laws and regulations. They also didn't know English well enough to function at a micro level; not enough to get started, anyway. I offered to help out: I found them office space, then a receptionist and a lawyer – they were going to need one; I saw that right away. Then I had a look at their books and realised they were burning through the cash they'd raised, most of it my friend's. It was a good thing I looked: I kept them out of bankruptcy court by three hours. I had to explain to them that flying first class to Moscow to see "Luscious Tanya" did not constitute a legit business expense.'

'Moscow?' he asked, before she could move on further. 'Why Moscow?'

'Well, they weren't Chinese. I told you they were foreign.'

This set Weaver wondering. Russians had in the past come to London *after* they'd made their money, fair methods or foul; not in order to make it. She shrugged and went on before he could press her on this. 'Enough about me already. The object of the lesson here is you. You want something to drink?' She pointed towards the kitchen. He would have been most satisfied with three inches of whisky, but thought it prudent to say no.

She went and tinkered with the shutters again; Weaver was relieved that they were no longer visible to people in the building next door.

Lily motioned him to sit down at the table while she kicked off her heels, leaving them lying on the oak floor, and sat down herself at the end of the table. Seated upright in her chair, she looked surprisingly tall.

Weaver took a seat at the side of the table, facing the now-darkened windows. Out of nowhere Lily had produced a pad of lined paper, which she put on the table; in her hand she now held a pencil. It could have been a board meeting.

'How do we start?' he asked.

'I've been thinking about that. I suggest we begin with "who", then we can move on to "why".'

'And after that? What do we do then?' There was very little hope in his voice.

Lily ducked the question, saying only, 'By the time we get through both "W's", we should know what to do next.' She drew a horizontal line across the page and frowned. 'Okay, so who sent you to Stockholm?'

'My boss. Pauline Fullerton.'

'What was the assignment?'

'To attend the summit and interpret French sessions and if needed Italian. That was it, more or less.'

'More, or less? I thought your forte was Russian.'

'It is, or was, I should say. The Russians aren't invited to these meetings nowadays.'

'Do you get on with Pauline?'

'Not really.' And he explained about her two communications, as well as Mac's panicky call. 'He was really upset,' Weaver added. 'The Secret Service interviewed him because they were told we were friends – that would have come from Pauline.'

'What did these agents want?'

'They wanted to know where I was. But Mac didn't know; he still doesn't. Neither does Pauline. I told you, nobody does.'

She nodded. 'Did you book your own plane tickets?'

'Yes.'

'How did you do that?'

'By going online. And I phoned the Airbnb to confirm. Two ways to track me down, I guess.'

'You're learning fast; a pity it's so late.' This was not said scathingly, he realised, but with what sounded like real regret.

How did she know all this stuff about wired phones and hacked emails and surveillance of every type? She added, 'What about this dinner you had with Ragoulin?'

He was surprised she remembered the name. He said, 'He might want to know where *you* were staying, but not me.'

'He's like that?'

'Vigorously.'

'Have you done business with him?'

'Not really. I've bought the occasional book. But books are a tiny side-line for him, done more for love than commerce. And I'm definitely small beer: I doubt I've spent more than two or three hundred dollars there over the years. He usually tries to give me the book; I have to argue to get him to take some money.'

'A philanthropist,' she was half-crowing. 'Rare among Russians.'

'No, just a generous man.'

'Does he fish?'

'Not that I know of.'

'I was just checking. JP said you viewed the world through a piscatorial lens.'

'JP said "piscatorial lens"?' He gave her a 'come on now' expression.

'Perhaps those weren't his exact words,' she conceded. 'But he says you're obsessed. Don't worry, he said it admiringly, though I think there was a certain amount of jealousy in play.'

'JP is only jealous of people who have more money than he does. That counts me out.'

'Let's keep going,' she said, tapping the end of her pencil on her notepad. 'Anything unusual you have to do in Stockholm?'

'It was just trade sessions. Why are you so focused on Stockholm?'

'You have a better alternative?' Her voice was scathing. 'What else, or where else, would you suggest? It's not just the guy at Heathrow or one Mercedes following you, or the muggers on the street. It's all of them happening together. They're obviously linked – duh – and why would anyone go to so much trouble if they could have picked you off earlier in New York?'

She was looking directly at him now, and speaking quickly. 'Nobody knew you'd be here; you've said you didn't know yourself until last week. Something happened then to trigger all this. And where were you? What happened in Stockholm that you haven't told me about?'

Lily wasn't letting up. In any good cop/bad cop scenario, she would be the deceptive, initially sympathetic one who then zeroed in for the kill. She said, 'I can't help you if you don't tell me what happened. What were you privy to? And if you say, "just some humdrum trade meetings," I'll scream.'

His anxiety was returning. If he didn't tell her the truth, he sensed, she would send him on his way. Once outside, what would he do? How long would it be before this puzzling and frightening 'they' found him? The safety offered by this temporary sanctuary suddenly seemed both terribly fragile and worth hanging onto at all costs – for the lack of anywhere half as safe to go.

'It *was* run-of-the-mill stuff,' he said reflexively, but then as Lily started to groan, he relented at last. He said quietly, his voice barely above a whisper, 'There was another meeting I worked.' Then a little more loudly: 'An unofficial one.'

There, he had done it.

'Congratulations,' Lily said.

'For what?'

'Coming clean. Go on.'

'I'm not supposed to talk about it.'

'Why not? Is it hush-hush because the meeting was with a country we – I guess I should say *you* – weren't supposed to be talking with?'

He struggled to control the look of acknowledgement on his face. Too late.

'Ah,' said Lily, 'so I'm right. Don't tell me directly if that will soothe your conscience. Though we really haven't got the time for pious rectitude. These people are after you.'

Of course they were; he was just struggling with the need to accept it. Because once he did that, he knew fear would envelop him. There was a deceptive feeling of safety in sticking one's head in the sand, even if it never lasted. 'I was told to keep my mouth shut, not say a word to anyone, or face some awful consequences. By the man in the meeting and by the State Department guy who took me there. But I don't even know what it is that's so secret. It makes me feel like the unwitting carrier of a disease.'

Lily was nodding happily. She said, 'Tell me about this meeting. For starters, where was it?'

'Not at the summit hotel. It was in a private house outside Stockholm.'

'Whose house?'

'A German banker. That's what Blanchett told me.'

'Who's Blanchett? Let's take a step back. Who asked you to the meeting and how did you get there? Et cetera. Start at square one.'

He described the abrupt entrance of Blanchett into the conference hall after lunch, his signalling Weaver to come over. How they'd been driven to the house, been stopped at the entrance to the room by the Russian he later saw at Heathrow, and how he had turned over his phone. And then sat down between Hofstadter and General Kuzmin, with no one else in the room.

'Hofstadter? The White House guy?' He nodded. 'And Kuzmin's the name of the Russian meeting him?'

'Yes. He was on his own. He's a general; not that senior, but a Morozov intimate.'

'Wait a second. Before you get too far. If you didn't interpret for the trade meeting in the hotel, who did?'

She asks the strangest questions, he thought, not for the first time. 'Tomic. He's Hungarian – well, he came with his parents from Hungary as a boy, so he's American really.'

Lily nodded. 'Okay, that brings us back to the meeting itself,' she said, looking at her notepaper as if they were moving through a printed agenda – though there still weren't many words written down. 'Don't look so alarmed, Weaver.'

'I was warned three times not to talk about it.' He didn't like the sceptical look on her face. 'Look,' he said, 'it's bad enough admitting there was a meeting – it was meant to be a complete secret.'

He paused to let this sink in, then went on: 'As for what was actually said in the meeting, only Kuzmin, Hofstadter and I know for sure. And US government interpreters are forbidden from discussing anything they've heard, or even mentioning any meetings where they were present. Otherwise you couldn't have confidential discussions between different countries, or secret negotiations. Oh sure, we joke among ourselves about the people we interpret for: which one swears a lot; who's shown up drunk; who pretends they understand a foreign language when they don't. But we don't repeat what's been said.'

'Not even to your boss – this woman, Pauline?'

'Not even to her,' he said, then remembered Blanchett's penchant for questioning the interpreters. 'In theory anyway.'

He was watching Lily, trying to gauge what effect this was having. It looked like none. He added, 'I tell you, they'll fire me if they learn I've talked.'

'It sounds like they're going to fire you anyway.' She looked annoyed again. He noticed this was inevitably indicated by her lips pouting cynically. 'Getting fired is the least of your problems right now.'

Weaver remained silent. 'Come on,' Lily said, for once openly showing her impatience. 'I haven't got time to cajole you.'

'The problem is I don't know what I can do to stop them before they get to me. I'd give them what they want, only I don't know what they want...' He paused, worried he was sounding melodramatic.

'What they want is you,' said Lily, nodding encouragingly, like she was leading a frightened kid into the pool for the first time. A pool that only had a deep end.

'But I don't know why. I don't even know who "they" is.'

'Yes, you do; we both do. Something was heard by you which they think you understood, even if you aren't sure yourself what you "know". "They" means the Russians, and from what Mac told you, the Americans too. That's the why *and* the who; see, we've already covered a lot of ground.' Lily stared at the notepad, twiddling the pencil back and forth between her fingers, her lips pursed. Then she lifted her head, her eyes innocuous and innocent. 'Now, tell me about the meeting with the Russian general, yes?'

He started visualising himself in the room with Hofstadter and Kuzmin. Seeing them – but not hearing their words.

What was wrong? He had been blessed, if it was a blessing, with an auditory memory (echoic, some called it) which roughly matched the better known 'photographic memory'. It was an invaluable attribute to possess in his line of work, but now he found himself coming up... soundless. He could visualise the scene in detail, but almost all the words Hofstadter and Kuzmin spoke still escaped him. He stared down at the table, wondering why his memory was failing him just when he needed it most. While the cherry-red pen sat useless, hidden in the guest bedroom at JP's. Why the hell had he hidden it?

'You okay?' asked Lily, leaning forward. There was a gentleness in her voice, and he liked that, then kicked himself for liking it, since it suggested he wanted sympathy. 'Once you get started,' she said, lively again, 'it should come more easily.'

Seeming to sense he was still struggling, Lily got up from her chair. 'I'm going to nip to the loo,' she said. 'So you have a think. Help yourself to a drink; there's wine and water in the fridge.' She gestured towards the kitchen.

Weaver watched as she walked through the open-plan office and disappeared through the twin doors. He got up and wandered to the kitchen, where he found bottled water in the fridge. He was pouring some into a glass when he heard a creak from the stairwell, then watched as the heavy door slowly opened. There was a step, then another, and a voice that called out, 'You've got to do something about this door, Lily. Half killed me this time. Let me send a couple of the housekeeping chaps round to see what they can do. Lily?' The voice was male, elderly.

Weaver stiffened and took a couple of steps towards the conference table, and the man came into view. He wore an old Burberry raincoat, unbuttoned, and beneath it a dark suit and creased white shirt. He had a long thin face with a smallish pear for a chin, and the knot of his tie was slightly askew.

The stranger looked at Weaver. 'You're not Lily,' he said.

'She's in the back. She'll be out in a sec.'

The man nodded. For all his rumpled attire, his eyes were sharp, enquiring; they moved around the room, with occasional glances back to Weaver. Then, like a courtier retrieving his manners after they'd momentarily wandered, he said formally, 'I hope I'm not intruding. I just wanted a word with Miss Churchill.'

Weaver was uncertain how to respond, but then Lily emerged through the double doors, walking quickly in stockinged feet. 'Charles, it's not a good time.'

'Not to worry. I happened to be in the neighbourhood,' he said, his eyes now focused on Weaver. Lily started to speak again but he kept talking: 'Just to say we've had some news of our dealer friend. Worth a phone call, I think.'

Lily said loudly, 'Let me ring you later. I've got a visitor, as you can see.'

Charles nodded equably enough, but he went on regardless: 'You might try him after this gentleman—'

Lily cut him off. 'Not now,' she said pointedly, though Weaver sensed fondness in her reproach. 'We can talk later.'

Charles did as he was told and turned to leave. Weaver went to help him with the door, which looked almost as difficult to close as to open, but Charles had already moved through the entrance. As Weaver pushed the door shut, he could hear the man shuffling slowly down the stairs.

Collecting his water glass, Weaver went back to the table, giving Lily a look full of questions as she sat down. 'A client,' she said, as if that answered any questions, and motioned him to sit down again. The old man's appearance was not going to be more fully explained.

She said, 'I meant to ask, why did they pick you to interpret? Were you the only one there who knew Russian?'

'No, but the senior interpreter, Mrs Macauley, had a heart attack. A fatal one.'

'I'd have thought there'd be two interpreters; one for each side.'

'Usually that's the case, but sometimes not, especially if both sides trust the interpreter. And I think Kuzmin was comfortable with Mrs Macauley. This wasn't his first meeting with Hofstadter. I'm sure of that.'

He found himself remembering Kuzmin's comments about her. Not the words themselves, but the tone: knowing, sardonic. Kuzmin hadn't rated Macauley's skills but seemed to see her as harmless. With this judgement had come contrasting uncertainty about Weaver; Kuzmin had been measuring him up. *That* Weaver could remember.

He said, 'Kuzmin's English isn't great, but I was really there for Hofstadter. He doesn't have any Russian.'

'From what I've seen on the news, he doesn't seem to have much English either.'

He smiled, but was feeling frustrated by the loss of his auditory recall. Again, he could visualise the scene unfolding as he'd sat down between the two men; he could remember the timbre and tones used. But the words still wouldn't come.

'What's the matter?' Lily finally asked. Gently again.

He was trying to buy time, waiting for some mnemonic to trigger the recall. 'There were no long introductions, they just pointed me to a chair, and everybody else left the room. At first the conversation was pretty banal. I found myself wondering what the point of their meeting was; Hofstadter himself asked that. He really didn't want to be there. It must have been the Russians who insisted on it. Though oddly it was Hofstadter who did the talking at first.'

'And Kuzmin just sat there?'

'Kuzmin was biding his time, listening to Hofstadter's *spiel*. Then finally he spoke up.'

'And what did he say?'

Weaver held up a hand. 'Let me think,' he said. For noise was filling his ears: white noise, like a wave machine, or an air conditioner picking up speed. The noise subsided slightly, now supplemented by a human voice. A voice – Kuzmin's. Weaver kept thinking in silence. Words from the meeting were returning, but in a choppy flow, rarely with the coherence of sentences. Then more came back to him; he could hear Kuzmin's initial platitudes while Hofstadter kept asking why he was there, until Kuzmin turned to the matter at hand. 'There seems to be a debt,' Weaver said, thinking of the mystifying financial to-and-fro.

'Go on,' said Lily warily.

He described things hesitantly, since only snippets were returning to him. He remembered that Kuzmin had talked elliptically, with references to 'clean linen' and 'dirty clothes'. He relayed what the General had said as best he could, and soon there was no longer any scepticism on Lily's face – she sat upright in her chair, listening intently. 'He seemed to be working round the subject,' Weaver explained, 'and then he said something about the debt. Hofstadter got very worked up by this and tried to cut Kuzmin off. He said it wasn't relevant because the loan had been paid in full and a long time ago – it was clear to me it was years, not months. But Kuzmin went on, and now I can remember his exact words: he said the debt owed hadn't just been to the "German bank" and someone named Galkin, but also *"to us – or to be candid, to our President"*. And here's the thing,' he went on, spurred by a memory coming back, 'Kuzmin also mentioned "another individual". It wasn't entirely clear, but I sensed that the loan was also to this other person, and not just to Hofstadter.'

'Any chance you can think of a name for this mysterious other person?'

'No, but not because I can't remember it. Kuzmin was about to say it, but Hofstadter cut him off – "Stop!" he said. He was almost shouting.'

He stopped for a moment, tired from this brief but intense period of concentration.

Lily said quietly, 'Bingo.'

'Meaning?'

'It seems we know what the blackmail was about.'

'I guess so…'

'It's simple enough,' Lily said. 'A loan was made, probably through the German bank, but the loan was Russian-guaranteed, probably because the borrower didn't have enough collateral to satisfy the German bank. It had the added plus of making Hofstadter beholden, I suppose. From the sound of it, Morozov personally guaranteed the loan.'

'Yes, he did. I'm not sure, but I think the Kremlin may even have supplied the money. Though from what Hofstadter said, the debt was paid off. And some time ago.'

'That's immaterial. The fact of the debt is bad enough; it's the hold the Kremlin has on the White House. It seems clear enough,' she added, but then she sighed. 'There's just one problem.'

'What's that?' he asked.

'I don't believe it for a minute.'

Startled, Weaver looked at Lily questioningly. 'Why not?'

'Because your President would never have needed to borrow money from the Russians, and would never have been stupid enough to do so.'

Weaver saw at once that this was true. The President was straight as an arrow, and a career politician whose assets were unremarkable and listed in full when he took office. He lived high on the hog, thanks to his wife's money, but there had never been a hint of fiscal impropriety on his part. Or financial sophistication, which the complications of the loan and laundering, as Weaver understood them, would certainly have required.

He said, 'But what if Hofstadter borrowed the money himself? Or for his company in California. It seems more likely. This happened before the election, from the sound of it. Hofstadter would have still been in Silicon Valley.'

'That leaves us with the same problem,' Lily said. 'The President wouldn't jeopardise his position to keep his Chief of Staff out of a financial scandal. They may be cronies, but not co-conspirators. I just can't see it.'

'Great. So what does that do for me? I've overheard a blackmail threat.'

'We'll figure it out, but first we have to keep you safe.' Lily got up and stretched both arms. She said, 'Another break seems in order.'

He joined her at the sink as she filled his glass from the water cooler. He noticed a line of white vases on the waist-high bookshelves that ran along the wall underneath the windows. Each vase held a solitary porcelain rose, its dark green stem just visible beneath pink unfolded petals.

'Those look almost real,' he said, wanting her to talk long enough to disguise his failing memory until it came back. If it came back.

'They're hand painted. I do like them, but not as much as real ones. If I had my way, which means if I could afford it, I'd have fresh flowers delivered every week,' she added simply.

He was watching her; she seemed to mistake his scrutiny for amusement. She said, 'Don't laugh – I know, it's a girly thing. I had a friend who had an affair with a magnate. As the affair progressed, the man told her she could have three wishes, which he'd do his best to grant – note the male *caveat* of "do his best". But actually, her requests were pretty modest, and practical. She asked for an Uber account, an account at Harrods Food Hall, and – this the master stroke – a twice-weekly delivery of fresh cut flowers to her flat. Mobility, sustenance, and beauty – clever, no?'

He nodded, tickled both by the wishes and by Lily's admiration for them. 'So what happened?'

'She got dumped, of course. And he cancelled the standing orders two hours later. When she tried to use the card for the Harrods Food Hall, they confiscated it. Speaking of cards, do you have one?'

'Sure.'

'Have you used it here in London?'

'I paid for dinner with it the other night, and used it to book the Airbnb when I was still in Stockholm. Oh, and for the taxi last night.'

'Please don't use it again. It would take exactly one phone call to trace that back from the card company. Use cash only from now on.'

'I'll have to get some then.'

'How? By using your card?' she asked tartly.

'What am I supposed to do? Stand beside a bus stop with a tin cup?'

Lily pursed her lips. 'I'll get you some cash. You can pay me back when this is over.' The pitch of her voice was moving higher now, a sign, he was beginning to see, that she was on edge as well. He realised that her story about her friend the mistress was meant to distract him and lessen his stress. But it looked like she was anxious too.

As they sat down again at the table, he said, 'Tell me, where does this get us? Or me? I mean, if it is the debt getting known that they're worried about, then I know what they think I know. But what can I do about that? Assuming it is the Russians who are after me.'

'That seems a pretty safe conclusion.' Her dryness was not reassuring. 'We're well past the point of no return. The problem is, we don't know what the leverage consists of. It can't merely be Hofstadter still owing the Russians money or they'd just have the loan called through the German bank. And anyway, you said the debt had been paid.'

Weaver nodded, and Lily said, 'But that can wait – there's a bigger issue, an elephant in the room.'

'What elephant?'

'It's simple: why are the Russians after you? Because you know they have a hold on Hofstadter and, presumably, the President? So what? What would they care if you blabbed, enough to try and hunt you down? The only people who'd look bad if it came out are Hofstadter and the President. And Hofstadter would just say you were lying. His word against an interpreter with a grudge.'

'What grudge?'

'Who knows?' Lily said brightly. 'They'd find something, believe me. Yes?'

'I guess so,' he said warily. Clearly there was more to come.

'But that's to ignore the elephant, and we can't afford to do that – not if we want the Russians to leave you alone.'

'You're losing me,' he said.

'Think, Weaver. What is the blackmail *for*? Generally speaking,' and the sharpness had returned to her voice, 'you employ blackmail to get something, usually money. But in this case I think it's something else, something the Russians want badly enough to spend all this time and energy blackmailing Hofstadter. And coming after you.' She took a breath, then said quietly, 'Surely you can see that.'

Could he? He wondered. So far, he felt he'd been swept up in her energetic orbit, carried along like a hitchhiker who accepts the ride without first asking where the driver's going. Maybe this was a mistake; maybe he should rethink everything, and go back to the starting gates. If only he could go back far enough to shake off his pursuers.

She looked intently at him. 'You seem tense, Weaver.'

He took a deep breath and exhaled. 'I am tense. I'm thinking maybe I ought to get out of here – London, I mean. Get on a plane for New York and go back to the office. That's what Pauline asked me to do. Then I can try to sort this all out.'

She was shaking her head. 'I think that's the last thing you should do. In fact, I think right now that would be insane.'

'Seriously?' This seemed extreme, almost melodramatic. 'Why? The worst that can happen there is I get fired.'

'That's what you think. I'm not sure you'd get back in one piece, not if they're watching the airports. I think you ought to lie low for the time being; at the very least, wait until I talk with your friend Mac.'

'*You'll* talk to him?'

'Yes, I'll ring him. You're too risky right now; they'll have tapped his work line – that's child's play – but hopefully they haven't got to his mobile yet. You'll have to give me the number.'

'But why will you call him, not me?'

'If they are listening in and hear me, I'll just be some mystery lady.'

'Okay.' He sighed at the need for such precaution.

'Come on,' she said. 'There's not much to be done about the Russians for now, except hide from them. Until we can persuade them to leave you alone.'

'Is it easier for them to silence me than trust I'll be too scared to talk?'

Her own silence confirmed that yes, it was. Eventually, Lily said, 'I don't think it will be easy to get to Morozov or even anyone who speaks for him, like Kuzmin. So I think it's the other side we have to go to first.'

Weaver replied, 'I told you, it seems the White House is looking for me, too. You said yourself, if I go to them for protection, they won't help me.'

'Another reason to stay over here. The Intelligence services here would go spare if the Americans did anything to you in the UK.' She shook her head. 'That's not going to happen, so at least you should start a conversation with them.'

'How do I do that? Hofstadter will have concocted some story about me. The Secret Service told Mac I'm a bad guy who's gone AWOL. Pauline seems to have bought their story.'

'Yes, but you have another way in.'

'What's that?' He was growing impatient now; despite her candid assessment of the danger confronting him, Lily was being frustratingly opaque.

'Mr Fontana. SAC Fontana, if I'm not mistaken.'

'Absolutely not.' He spoke before he even had time to think.

'I beg your pardon?' she said with a sarcastic sweetness to her voice. 'Why not?' she added more sharply. 'I don't know the state of play in *la famiglia* Fontana, but I can't imagine your own father wouldn't help when the chips are down. And they're down now, that's for sure.'

'I don't want his help. Anyway, he's not part of this, and the powers-that-be will know he's my father.' Though from what Mac had said, it had been the Secret Service swarming the walls of their office, not the FBI.

'He'll have some friends among his colleagues back east, now won't he? So we do have an in.'

'No,' he said, stung. 'It wouldn't be right. And from what Mac said, the Bureau isn't involved. All the people in the office were from the Secret Service.'

He was starting to feel peculiar: the same unsettled feeling he had experienced in the London Library. Only this time he couldn't phone Lily – she was right there. Something was stirring, memory fragments triggered somehow – perhaps by what Lily had said. 'You said something a minute ago.'

'What was that?' asked Lily.

'I can't remember,' he said.

'You don't seem to remember anything,' Lily said, her patience fraying.

He ignored this, not wanting to obstruct the memories of the Stockholm meeting that were coming in and out of his head, like a light repeatedly turned on and off. And words were coming back to him. 'Do me a favour.' He pointed at Lily's laptop. 'Google "Skip Washington" and *The Times*.'

'Skip?'

'Yes, Skip. It's his nickname. Please just do it.'

He waited while she turned to the screen, typing quickly. After a little while, she said, 'Do you mean some basketball player?'

'Yes.'

She kept reading from the screen. '*The Times* says the President plans to issue a pardon for your friend Skip. He's in prison for having sex with underage girls. Charming.'

'That's our man, I think.'

'Do you?' Lily was looking at him with disbelief.

'Yes. I understand now why Kuzmin said attention would be on Washington. He meant the ball player, not the city, and look — there's Skip in *The Times*; I bet he's in the *New York Times* as well. And Hofstadter used the word "pardon". I didn't understand that either: I thought Hofstadter was confused by what Kuzmin was saying — but that didn't make sense; there was nothing complicated in what Kuzmin said. And actually, Hofstadter was asking if Kuzmin wanted a presidential pardon. That was the "arrangement" Kuzmin referred to.'

'I'm not sure I get it. Why would the Russians want a pervy African American basketball player released from prison?'

'That's what I need to find out.'

They sat in silence for a moment, then Lily put down her pencil and pushed back her chair. 'Let's leave it for now.' She sounded like a detective turning off the tape recorder at a suspect's interview — Weaver half-expected her to state the date and time. She said, 'I'm going to go out for a bit. I have some errands to do and your friend Mac to ring. I won't lock up or you'll be locked in. But do me a favour.'

'What's that?' asked Weaver, happy to be the useful one for a change.

'Don't go out yourself.' She looked at him and he gave a slow nod. Lily said, 'Try and relax; I may be a while. You know where the fridge is, and there are snacks in the cupboards above it. I'll bring back something more substantial for us to eat.'

'What's in there?' He pointed to the double doors towards the back.

'It's where I live,' she said with a reluctant smile. 'I know they say don't take your work home with you, but this place has almost fifteen hundred square feet; it seemed crazy not to use some of it myself. The rooms were already there. I'll show you.'

She got up and walked quickly across the oak boards and opened the double doors. Following her, Weaver found himself in a small set of rooms. There was a sitting room, a small bedroom he only caught a glimpse of, a little kitchen and a bathroom that looked newly extended.

The décor was shabby genteel, incongruous after the modish hi-tech décor of the office space next door. The sitting room had two armchairs, a sofa, and a side table with a small stack of magazines. A large worn kilim covered most of the wood floor, and there were framed watercolours and some pen-and-ink drawings on the walls. Two low bookshelves were partly hidden by the sofa, and he kept himself from crouching to inspect the titles.

Lily said, 'If you want a shower, there are towels in the bathroom cupboard.'

'I'll wait until I find a hotel. I'll look one up while you're gone.'

'With what?' she said.

He remembered he had no phone now. And there wasn't a spare laptop in sight. She went on, 'It's a bad idea anyway. You need to hole up somewhere. It might as well be here, especially if I'm going to try and help you.'

They were standing in the sitting room, and Lily pointed at the sofa. 'You're welcome to sleep here; it's a sofa bed. Or there's a futon.'

'The sofa bed's fine. I'm used to them.'

'Why's that?'

'My ex-wife had me sleep on ours during the last happy months of our marriage.' He looked at Lily intently. 'You sure you want me here?'

'Not desperately. But hotels are easy for them to check one way or another, especially if you book online. Your emails will have been hacked into, so even if you're safe from the phone now, there are other ways to find you if you're not careful.'

She was leaving the room when she stopped. 'I just remembered: Chip may show up.'

'Who's Chip?'

'My assistant. He won't bother you.'

'That makes a change. Is he American?'

'Why?' She looked baffled. 'Oh, you mean his name. No, he's British born and bred. I need him. He helped me with the move here and is strong as an ox.'

'That sounds like a euphemism for "bodyguard".'

'It's not. Now settle down and have a rest. When I'm back we'll talk about what to do next. And remember, don't go out – I want there to be a "next" to come back to.'

14

WEAVER WAITED UNTIL LILY LEFT BEFORE GOING out into the open-plan office, where he retrieved his bag and took it back into the little sitting room. He felt drained of energy, wiped out, though at unanticipated intervals anxiety swept through him on unwanted adrenalin waves. He needed to sleep but his curiosity about Lily made him want to look around first.

Lily had closed the door to her bedroom, but unable to suppress his curiosity, Weaver opened it, telling himself that was okay provided he didn't cross the threshold. The room was small and snug, though a pair of pale green curtains were open to let in natural light and give a partial view of the street below. The walls, unlike the exposed brick in the office at the front, were wallpapered in a repeat pattern of birds perched on cherry trees. The bed was a small mahogany double, with an old quilt laid across it. A pile of books sat on a bedside table. On the table there was also a framed photograph of Lily, looking ten years younger, sitting on a restaurant terrace with a man about the same age, both smiling for the camera. The man looked tall, and had swept-back straight black hair, and striking facial features – high cheekbones, strong chin. Handsome by any standard, Weaver was forced to concede. Snow-capped mountains reared up in the distant background. The Alps, Weaver figured.

He closed the door and retreated to the little sitting room, then inspected the bookcases behind the sofa, looking for something good enough to read, but unexciting enough to put him to sleep. There were two sets in French: a complete Flaubert and a partial one of Balzac. The other books were in English:

a mix of fiction, mainly written by women (and most of them Americans), and some current non-fiction: *From Start Ups to Sell Outs*, *Equilateral Thinking*, Malcolm Gladwell, a Michael Lewis, nothing unexpected given what she'd said about how she made her living. His eye caught a small cache of children's books, faded hardbacks – *The Secret Garden*, a broken-spined Beatrix Potter, others he'd never heard of – and then, surprisingly, a few books in Russian. Mandelstam's poems, *Eugene Onegin*, *A Hero of Our Time*. This seemed odd. Gifts, maybe, from Russian clients?

He was leaning over the edge of the sofa to take the Pushkin from its shelf when a voice behind him said, 'Looking for something?'

Startled, Weaver turned and found a young man with bleached hair, dressed in green combat trousers and a black T-shirt, standing in the little hallway. He held a hammer in one hand and his expression was hostile.

Weaver thought of the men on Clarendon Road that morning. He sat down on the sofa, showing a calm he didn't feel. Leaning back against the cushions, he said, 'You must be Chip.' It had better be.

'Who the hell are you?' The man tightened his grip on the hammer.

'A friend of Lily. She said you'd be coming along.'

This seemed only partly to reassure the man. 'What's your name?'

'Weaver. I'm not here on business. Lily offered to put me up. That's why I'm in here,' he added, gesturing around the room.

'Oh,' said Chip, his aggression subsiding. 'Sorry about this,' he said, swinging the hammer in his hand. Then he used it to gesture vaguely towards the doors to the office. 'We've had some problems here. After Tolya.'

'I can see,' said Weaver. *Who or what was Tolya?*

'Somebody tried to break in one night. I wasn't here,' he added. Lily on her own with an intruder was worrying. 'What happened?' he asked, happy to see the hammer lowered now, and held loosely. 'That steel door could keep out an army.'

'Oh, they didn't try and jimmy it. They were trying to break the code.'

Just your average sophisticated burglar.

'It was part of the general weirdness,' Chip said, then noticed Weaver's puzzlement. 'You know, since…' He hesitated.

'Since?'

'Since Lily moved in,' Chip said, a touch too smoothly. 'Anyway, when she's back, could you tell her I've run the errands? She'll understand.'

'Right. I'll tell her.'

'I'll leave you to it then,' Chip said, sounding relieved. He went back out to the open-plan area.

Fatigue returned, gradually. There was something familiar about Chip. Was it the eyes? Large, lively, and surprisingly blue. He'd seen them before, but somehow not quite the same.

He got up and went into the office, where he found Chip going out the door, his back to him. High on the nape of his neck, beneath the razored hair line, sat a patch of faded green tattoo.

Yes, he'd seen Chip before: the tattoo and those eyes, glimpsed in the rear-view mirror of the taxi that had brought Weaver and Lily here from Marylebone.

15

WHY WAS SHE HELPING HIM? HE WAS thinking this dimly, dreamlessly, as he dozed, slumped at one corner of the sofa. A voice said 'Weaver,' only it sounded like 'waver' to him as he perched between waking and sleep. His ex-wife had called him that, and more, when he hesitated about their plans to move to New York. Now louder, the voice said, 'I'm back.'

Back? Back from where? He roused himself and sat up to find Lily standing in front of him, lips set and eyes alert, like a mother returning home to find her teenaged son half-cut amid emptied parental bottles.

'All right,' he said abruptly, to suggest he was alert. 'What's the story?'

'I brought dinner is the story right now. And also this.' She held up something in one hand, shooting it free of the leather sleeve of her jacket.

'A phone?'

'A burner phone.' She tossed it onto the sofa next to him. 'Here's the number,' she said, handing him a slip of paper. 'Better memorise it, though if all turns out well, you won't be using it for long. It's calls only.'

'A dumb phone,' he said, missing his iPhone despite himself.

'It will do for your needs. I have to be able to reach you. Nobody else does,' she said sternly.

They moved into the office area, where she had laid places at the slate conference table. From a large plastic bag she took out takeaway cartons one by one, then got a bottle of soy sauce from the cupboard. The takeaway seemed a regular event for

Lily. She put a serving spoon into each carton, and they sat down.

'Did you get hold of Mac?' he asked, trying not to show the impatience he felt.

'I did. Who is Peter?'

'Mac's husband.'

'You might have warned me.'

'Why, what did he say?'

'He acted more like a watchdog than a husband. I thought I'd have to give my National Insurance number before he'd let me speak to Mac.'

'That sounds like Peter. But what did Mac say?'

'He said, "Tell him Parker's sick. You got that? Parker's sick. Over and out." Those were his exact words. Who is Parker?'

'The dog. The one that used to be mine. Did Mac say anything else?'

'Yes. He told me he'd taken Parker to the doctor. That's why I was confused: he said "doctor", not vet, so I thought maybe Parker was human. Anyway, he said "they" don't know what's wrong with Parker, or if they do, they aren't telling him.'

He saw it now: Pauline wasn't saying anything to Mac about what they wanted from Weaver.

Lily was watching his reactions. 'Not good, is it?'

'No. It's a kind of half-assed code we agreed. It means I'm still in the shit, but they aren't letting Mac know why. Maybe I should call him tomorrow. Just to see if he learns anything else.'

Lily shook her head. 'He's going to call us if he does. Me, actually. And from a pay phone.' She paused. 'You're looking glum, Weaver. Come on,' she said, trying to sound cheerful herself. 'Let's eat.'

She took his plate and served them both. Two noodle dishes, some spiced vegetables with unfamiliar flavours, spring rolls and a container of egg-fried rice they shared. Despite his nerves, Weaver discovered he was ravenous, though he tried to eat slowly.

Lily got up and brought over a jug of water. As she filled his glass, she said, 'There's a bottle of white wine in the fridge, and red in the bottom cupboard.'

'Great.' He got up. 'Do you want a glass?'

'No thanks.'

'You don't drink?'

'Not a lot.' She added, 'JP's dinner party was an exception. I found I used to like a drink when I felt bad, but it got to where I felt bad because I'd had a drink. Or twelve.'

'Twelve will do it every time…' he said, and sat down again.

'Don't hold off on my account.'

'Better to keep a clear head.'

She nodded. 'So Mac's news is bad news?'

'Yes. It means the Feds are still looking for me and it isn't safe to come back.' He finished a spring roll, trying to take modest bites. 'This is good. Is it Vietnamese?' He regretted this before the words were out of his mouth.

'Vietnamese?' She looked at her chopsticks quizzically. 'What makes you think it's Vietnamese?'

There was no point dissembling. 'I guess because JP said you were part Vietnamese.'

'Did he now?' she said, nodding in a way that seemed ominous. 'It's true, I am.' Still nodding, she said, 'I suppose you find that interesting.'

There was a bitterness in her voice which he had not heard before. He couldn't help thinking that it derived from something other than her heritage. Something rawer than social disdain.

'Do you cook?' he asked, hoping to steer the conversation in a safer direction.

'Only in self-defence.' She smiled, as if at a private joke. 'I had to learn when I was still very young because Mum was at work. Otherwise, I would have starved. Can *you* cook?'

'I guess so, but can't be bothered most of the time.'

'We'll have to stick to takeaways.'

He wondered how long she thought she'd have him as a visitor.

He said, 'I may be a little rusty but I do know how. It's a benefit of having an Italian for a father. He had no hang-ups about making dinner.'

'I guess you do look a bit Italian. Except for your green eyes.'

'Italians have more green eyes than any other country in Europe,' he said crossly.

'Ah, my turn to stereotype, I guess.' She did not seem bothered by this. 'I still think you should call your father, by the way.'

'Why?'

'Because he wants you to.'

'I doubt that,' he said. Then her words sunk in. 'You spoke to my father,' he said, and this time it was not a question.

She nodded, as if this wasn't news. 'He said to call him at Sally's. But you need to use a pay phone. I can tell you where to go, and I'll give you a card number.' She seemed to recognise the need to acknowledge his angry surprise. 'Weaver, I'm doing my best to help you, even when you're not helping yourself. You have to trust me; that goes without saying. If anyone has reason to doubt, it's me.'

'Oh?' he asked quietly. 'Does that explain Chip?'

'Chip? Was he here?'

'Yes, he said to tell you he's run the errands.'

'Oh good,' she said emphatically. 'It's quite interesting, actually. You see—'

He cut her off. 'It turns out we've met before.'

'You and Chip?' She didn't wait for a nod, saying, 'How funny. What are the odds on that?'

'Pretty good, I think,' he said.

She had adopted an unconvincing look of bafflement. He was glad to discover she was a bad liar. He said, 'After all, it wasn't very long ago that he and I first met. Outside Marylebone.'

She had the grace not to look away, and met his stare. 'Well spotted.' She briefly laid her head on one shoulder and exhaled a whistle of breath. 'I bet it was his tattoo.' She sighed. 'You'll just have to take my word for it, but I had reason to be careful. Not

everyone appreciates my efforts, you know. I do have the odd
enemy. I know you think I'm sweet and shy and demure—'

'I think nothing of the kind,' he protested. 'Not a single one
of those three.'

'Really?' She looked startled, but only momentarily, and then
what he now saw as her standard mask – breezy, confident –
slipped back on.

And the mask, thought Weaver, was precisely why he felt an
underlying layer of scepticism about *her*. Her assistance had been
entirely welcome, but also too immediate, too forthcoming, to
make sense.

More was coming back to him, small snatches of the dialogue.
In addition to Galkin, Kuzmin had mentioned someone named
Dan Berry – now Weaver remembered how, when he'd replayed
the conversation that evening in the hotel, the name had come
just before the recording cut off. There had been something as
well about a nickname – unspecified, since again Hofstadter had
cut off Kuzmin before he could say what this nickname was. And
there had been a Russian name, one that he could not remember.

But he decided, in any case, to keep what he did remember in
reserve until he was completely sure about Lily, and positive that
she had no agenda of her own.

She was looking at him, unwilling to go on, a defiant take-
it-or-leave-it pout to her mouth, which worried him. He said as
definitely as he could, 'Not really. Okay?' He nodded to emphasise
this, and she smiled.

'But why did you call my father?' he asked, still curious and
still unhappy.

Lily shrugged good-naturedly. 'Somebody had to. Now finish
your rice, there's a good boy.'

16

HALF AN HOUR LATER, HE TURNED ONTO a side street north of Old Street. It was still light, but the Technicolor pageant of the morning had given way to a monochrome blanket of grey cloud.

He was surprised to be using a pay phone, but Lily had said reports of their death had been somewhat exaggerated. There were still a few of them in London, she explained. Many had been vandalised, but the one he found, following Lily's directions, looked relatively unscathed; it was made of steel and glass and open on three sides. It sat on the corner of a street of small shops and another one of gentrified terraced houses.

He slowed down, looking around casually but thoroughly. He had made a zigzag trip here, and was confident he wasn't being followed, but Lily's conviction that his phone had been tampered with in Stockholm worried him: what if they had somehow tampered with something else?

There was a man using the pay phone, so Weaver walked past and stared at a newsagent's window, full of cards advertising everything from second-hand bikes to French tuition. He wished he did not feel so exposed. He remembered the misleading stillness on Clarendon Road that morning.

Weaver was wearing the last of his clean clothes and was more awake now. He had taken a second shower, long and cool, back in the flat, and emerged wearing only a towel to find Lily in the little sitting room, piling up dirty laundry she was unearthing from his bag. She seemed unfazed by his near-nudity, remarking that she had seen him this way once before – at JP's. 'I'll put these in the machine while you're out,' she had said from behind an armful of clothes, 'but first, why don't you go through them and make sure there's nothing fishy in there.'

'Fishy?'

'Look for anything the size of a silicon chip and give a shout if you find one. I think you're clean. I'm pretty sure they tracked you by your phone. But it's best to be certain. And check out the rest of the stuff in your bag while you're at it – the books and your sponge bag. I didn't want to snoop, though that didn't seem to stop you while I was out.'

There was no change in her tone, so it took him a moment to digest this. 'Is that what Chip told you?'

'No, the camera did. And the camera never lies. Don't worry, you were better than most; you didn't actually go into my bedroom.'

He remembered standing in the doorway, looking at the picture of her and some man, happy in the Alps. He said, 'I was lucky not to have tripped one of your panic buttons. Do you really have one in every room?'

'Of course not.' She gave a smile of quiet enjoyment. 'I had them taken out. Even *my* paranoia doesn't extend that far.'

Now he took out the piece of paper with what seemed the world's longest sequence of numbers short of pi; he could never have memorised it. According to Lily, his father had said he should call him at Sally's, but that was not its official name, which Weaver could not for the life of him remember. Fortunately, by using Lily's laptop, Google had come to the rescue: there were only a few bars anywhere near Putah Creek, and The Steelhead Grill rang a bell when it showed up listed onscreen.

He dialled the number, then when prompted added the sequence of credit card numbers Lily had supplied. When he'd said he was worried that the numbers could be traced back to Lily, she had scoffed. 'Your father said the bar is ninety miles from his San Francisco office and about the last place they'd know to look for him. If somebody somehow managed to trace the calls to the UK, they wouldn't get further than a pay phone in Islington.' As for the card, Lily explained that it would take even an intelligence agency several weeks to track it down, since it was an account in Switzerland, and would need a court order to pry loose. 'Even then,' Lily told him, 'they'd find that though the card hadn't expired, its owner had.' The set to her eyes as she said this discouraged further questions.

Weaver waited as the phone in California rang twice and a croaky high-pitched voice declared, 'Steelhead.' He recognised the unexpectedly falsetto timbre of the bar's owner, a bear of a man named Salvatore Giacomazzo, known to regulars as Sally.

'I'm looking for Bob Fontana. Is he around?'

'A minute,' Sally squeaked. 'Bob,' he called in a comparative baritone. 'Phone.'

The Steelhead Grill was a few miles from Putah Creek, a catch-and-release river that had dried out years before but, through the efforts of mad fishers and conservationists, often one and the same, had recently been revived. It held placid stocked browns and a few wild and hard-to-catch rainbows, and was the closest decent fly fishing to San Francisco. The midges swarmed on its water, and sometimes on your neck, but small Mayflies worked a treat throughout the season, which was rarely true of Californian streams and rivers.

His father fished there on at least one day of most weekends, staying in a local motel; in winter, when the fishing shut down, he would often still drive up for lunch at the Steelhead. Weaver had been there twice with him, including during the last trade session he had worked with Russians several years before – held, appropriately, in Sebastopol, on the banks of the Russian River.

The bar-and-grill was one long dark room, with a row of booths with padded seats of dimpled leather, worn to the colour of morello cherries. The bar itself was a long heavy shelf of maple, where at the far end his father liked to perch on a chrome-legged stool. The contrast between the big man, bigger now with the bulk of age, and the skeletal chair stuck like a snapshot in Weaver's head.

'Fontana,' a voice said in the deep familiar rumble.

'Is that the SAC of the San Francisco office?' asked Weaver.

'It is,' he said. There was a pause, then his voice brightened. 'Is that you, kid?'

'Hi, Pop,' he said.

'Hang on a minute. I'm going to take this in the back room.'

Weaver waited while he heard his father's rumbling tones and Sally's alto. After a minute, his father picked up again and someone put the other phone down.

His father said, 'You got my message then. Are you okay?'

'So far.'

'I got the phone off the hook about you yesterday. Your mother came first, but that's only because she'd already had a call from your Uncle Billy.'

'Billy Malone?' Who was only an honorary uncle, and that only during Weaver's early childhood.

'None other.'

'Is he still on the books? I'm surprised he hasn't retired.'

'Next month. He's the Legat in Paris.' Legal attaché, Weaver remembered; his father had held the post in London years before. 'Talk about a soft berth to end your career. He called your mother first, which is strange since she could never stand him.'

'That is weird.'

'Your mother gave him short shrift, apparently, so he had no choice but to try me. He was hoping I'd know where you were. Your mother had another call about you, from some Secret Service guy in New York. He also wanted to know your whereabouts. That got your stepfather pretty worked up – he even called me to ask about it.'

'A secular concession.'

His father laughed, but it was a thin, token effort, which suggested he was feeling tense too. He said, 'When I talked to Malone, he seemed to think you were in England.'

'He did?' He couldn't see how Malone had learned this. Then Weaver thought about his telephone, and Lily's suspicions that it had given away his whereabouts. But to the Russians, according to Lily.

'Any reason he should know that?' his father asked.

'Not that I can think of. I am in London, but it's probably best if I leave it at that. Can you let Mom know? It might be better coming from you if it's that vague. I really don't want her calling me, and it isn't safe to call her.'

'Sounds like you're in hot water, son.'

'I'd say chest high. It's a long story.'

'That's okay. I'm not pushed for time, so why don't you take yours – time, that is – and tell me all about it? Your mom said you were at the summit in Stockholm; is it to do with that?'

'Yeah. There was a secret meeting between a Russian general and Hofstadter from the White House.' There seemed no point prevaricating.

'What about it?'

'I was the interpreter.'

His father whistled appreciatively. 'That's the big time. But why's that got everyone and the maid looking for you?' And before Weaver could go on, his father asked, almost uncannily, 'Or did you hear something you weren't supposed to hear?'

Weaver said, 'Maybe. At first, I thought it was about Hofstadter and a woman.'

'Something extramarital?'

'That's what I was wondering.'

'That wouldn't really damage the President,' his father said. 'What would one more indiscretion by Hofstadter do that the others didn't? Thanks, I'm good with coffee,' he said, talking away from the phone. Sally must be asking if his father wanted a beer. It was still morning in northern California, but once there would have been a beer and another and another. Lately his father had slowed down, scared by a liver count that his internist claimed he'd never seen on a man who was still alive.

'Is that all?' asked his father, returning to the phone.

'No. There was a loan the Russians guaranteed. A German bank was involved.'

'Loan to who?'

'I thought at first it was the President.'

'Really?' This was polite but sceptical.

'I know, it seems improbable. So I guess it was Hofstadter, but I can't be sure.'

'It makes quite a difference,' said his father reprovingly. He was silent for a moment. Then he said, 'I guess you might as well know: the Bureau has investigated Hofstadter in the past, before I became the SAC. He did business in Silicon Valley, and had money from all sorts; it seemed pretty clear there was a lot of mixing of corporate and personal expenditure. I think some of his girlfriends were pretty expensive. We never found anything we could pin on him, but the file's still open. Malone was the Deputy SAC then, and some people thought he didn't push hard enough to build a case against Hofstadter. They were two peas in a pod.'

'How's that?'

'Malone wasn't called The Goat for nothing. And Hofstadter had a nickname, too. Something Polish. Malone would know what it was.'

'Okay, but why is it the Secret Service who are looking for me in the States? I'd have thought it would be the Bureau.'

'Usually it would be, but this way I figure Hofstadter, with or without the President, is directing the show – the Secret Service will be reporting to him. That wouldn't be the case with the Bureau. We're independent, whatever Hofstadter likes to think.'

'Then why is Malone sticking his nose into things?'

'Because he's based in Europe, and can look for you over there, I guess. The Secret Service don't have many assets on your side of the Pond; the offices are pretty much in name only – they don't have any real investigative capacity. That's one reason. The other – and here I'm only guessing – is that Hofstadter has some sort of hold on Malone and can get him to do his bidding. Malone can't be operating officially; I'd bet my bottom dollar that the Bureau Director doesn't know anything about this.

'I'd have said you were safer here in America, but there's no point coming back if you're going to be arrested on landing at JFK. I think for now, you'd better keep your head down; disappear for a while.'

Weaver said, 'There's no point lying low if I don't know what to do when I re-emerge.'

'I understand. But tell me, do you have any idea what the Russians want from Hofstadter?'

'It's more what they want from the President; at least I think it is. Kuzmin – that's the Russian – said something about an arrangement, and then mentioned Washington. At first, I thought it was the city, but now the papers are saying the President wants Skip Washington released.'

'It's going to happen. Apparently, he was going to pardon Washington, but that was going to be a step too far. It's not as if Skip is innocent. The President is going to commute his sentence to time served instead. God knows why.'

'And God knows why the Russians would want him to do that. It doesn't make sense to me.'

'I can't see a link myself. Maybe "Washington" is just a coincidence and they want something else. Did you take notes?'

'I was ordered not to, and a Russian security guy tore up my notebook anyway. It was all hush-hush; we met well away from the hotel where the summit was going on.'

Weaver was asking himself whether to tell his father he had taped the meeting. Not yet, he decided. It wouldn't serve any purpose until Weaver had the pen in his hands again; even then, the missing part meant he wouldn't be able to listen to the enigmatic remarks Kuzmin had made about the 'arrangement'.

His father said, 'I don't get why that means you're in trouble. You were just doing your job.'

'That's what I thought.' He gave his father a brief account

of the past two days' events: from the Russian security man at Heathrow through to the close calls he'd had on Clarendon Road and then at Marylebone Station.

When he finished, his father asked, 'Who were these guys?' He sounded angry.

'They weren't English; I'm sure of that. Lily's sure of it too – that's the woman who called you. Which wasn't my idea, by the way.'

'I'm glad she did,' his father said quietly. 'Is she your new gal?'

His father's diction remained Runyonesque. 'No, just a friend.' It would be hard to explain her ride to Weaver's rescue and his refuge in her odd mix of office and apartment.

'Seemed pretty sharp to me. But mind how you go. Her phone may soon be tapped.'

'Got you.'

'And mine might be too. It will take them a little while, since the DC people can't exactly ask my staff to wire their own boss. The Secret Service will have to send their own team, if it comes to that.'

Weaver thought for a moment, and looked around. An old lady was walking her dog, a grey-and-white mongrel mix. A middle-aged man was sitting in his car about thirty yards away, but looked like he was doing a crossword; Weaver could see the pencil in his hand. He said to his father, 'Can I leverage what I know with the Bureau then? *If* I can figure out what I know,' he said, realising the absurdity of this.

'If you discover what the Russians want, I'm confident the Bureau will leave you alone; I can't speak for the White House and the Secret Service. They're a law unto themselves. But start by talking with Malone.'

'Are you still friends?'

His father waited for a moment, then said, 'Not really, but he doesn't know that. He doesn't know a lot of things,' he added, and there was a new note of bitterness in his voice.

'Like what, Pop?' Weaver asked.

His father sighed. 'He came on to your mother one time. Can you believe it? Some pal.'

'No wonder Mom can't stand him.'

'I know. I wasn't exactly wild about it myself. But she only told me after we'd split up.'

'Did you ever tell him you knew?'

'What would be the point? It's not like we're working together anymore. He still thinks we're buddies, I guess. Though the fact he called your mother instead of me suggests he didn't want me to know that he's looking for you. I said I'd try to reach you, but I also said I didn't know where you were. He wants you to call him, though if I were you, I'd have your gal friend call him first.'

'Why's that?'

'To check the lie of the land. Billy and I may go way back, but so do he and Hofstadter. Don't forget that.'

'Where do I have her call him? Is he at the embassy in Paris?'

'Yes, but he said he was going to London. He's probably over there now. If your friend rings the embassy, he said he'd make sure the switchboard knows he's there. All his phone conversations are logged, whether he's in Paris or using the London legat office. Another reason to have your lady friend make the call.'

'Will Malone understand who she is and what it's about?'

'Yes. I've already left a message, and his should be the next call coming into me here. Your gal—'

'Her name is Lily.'

'Lily it is. Let Lily call him and he'll know by then what you should do next.'

'How do you know he'll want to help?'

'I don't – for sure. He's about to retire before #MeToo comes and bites him on the ass. If he were accused of personal misdemeanours – that's the fancy term for fucking around – he could lose his pension. So he won't be inclined to stick his neck out, not if the White House is saying you've sold the pass.'

'Is that what Malone said?'

'Well, he didn't call you Benedict Arnold, but he certainly hinted at something like that. I don't think he believes a word of it, but he's not about to say so. That's when I realised you were in trouble. Though Hofstadter has been dumping on the Bureau whenever he can; I guess he's taking revenge for our investigation. But if I read it right, I think Billy will do what he can for you; it just may not be a lot. I'll keep my ear to the ground, though I'm not likely to hear the train coming until it's too late. The Bureau has no role in this, and Hofstadter will know I'm your dad.'

'I don't want you sticking your neck out.'

'What are fathers for? Listen, keep me up to date but only when it's safe to. I can get here in ninety minutes and I'll be around at the weekend anyway. I've got a room reserved at the Nickerson Inn on Friday and Saturday.'

'I'd hate to have you waiting around if I've got no news.'

'Don't worry. The midges aren't bad so I'll be in the river all day. My regards to your lady friend. I mean Lily. I liked her.'

17

WEAVER WALKED BACK TO LILY'S BUILDING SLOWLY, changing direction frequently, doubling the distance he would have normally taken. The sinking glow of the sun lit the street ahead of him like a film set's idea of evening, rosy pink and warm. His father had clearly been impressed by Lily, and if she were going to front for Weaver with Malone, then it only seemed right that she knew more of what he was starting to remember.

He thought about Malone. Weaver had not seen him for over twenty years, but remembered him as an avuncular figure (hence 'Uncle Billy' to the boy) who had taken him fishing for blues off Long Island. Malone had also often visited the Fontana family in earlier, happier times in Vermont, fishing the Battenkill and Middlebury rivers with Weaver's father, whose acquaintance with him dated from days working together as Special Agents in Manhattan, and nights spent carousing at Costello's Bar in Midtown. After his parents divorced, Weaver had not seen Malone again – Weaver's mother could not abide him, and it seemed with good reason. From comments made by his father over the years, Weaver knew that Malone, whose near-legendary personal peccadilloes gave him the nickname of 'The Goat', was that slightly dubious thing, a 'character'. But he was also highly intelligent, and back in an era when any new Bureau recruit needed an accountancy qualification or a law degree, Malone, a smart kid from Brooklyn, had managed to acquire both, while also tending bar at night to make ends meet. Once at the Bureau, he rapidly became known for his ruthless diligence in pursuing financial crime.

On Leonard Street, Lily buzzed him through and he went up

and found her sitting at the slate table, laptop open before her. He went behind her and looked over her shoulder. She was reading an academic article, apparently; Weaver got to '*experiencing excessive stress acutely or severe stress chronically can be highly detrimental to memory function*' before Lily covered it with her hand.

'How did it go?' she asked, sounding nervous herself.

'I don't suppose I could use your laptop.'

'I don't suppose you could. Not a good idea.'

He decided not to argue. He might kick up at the extremeness of her precautions, but he could hardly contest them on the basis of some superior knowledge.

Lily said, 'So tell me about your call.'

'You're supposed to make a call yourself tomorrow,' he said. 'I bet you already know that. But listen, I've got another name for you to check. It was Kuzmin who mentioned it: "Dan Berry." As in strawberry. Or blueberry. That's how he pronounced it.'

'I'll check it out,' said Lily. 'I have some news too: good and bad.'

'Start with the bad.'

'They're on to you,' she said, and pushed a folded tabloid newspaper across the table. 'The police want you to "help with their enquiries".'

He picked up the copy of the *Evening Standard* and scanned the article. It began ominously:

Metropolitan police are searching for a man, thought to be American, involved in an incident on Clarendon Road in Notting Hill earlier today. Another unnamed man is being treated at St Mary's Hospital, Paddington, for serious injuries. The man police would like to speak with is described as six feet tall, dark brown hair, of athletic build, and dressed in a dark blue jacket and khaki trousers. He left the scene of the incident on an e-scooter that was later recovered near Westbourne Grove. A police spokesman said: 'Anyone with any information is asked to call the incident room on...'

'At least they don't have a picture of me,' said Weaver.

'Look again.' He did, and saw a fuzzy black-and-white shot of a man on a scooter. It had been taken probably fifty feet away, and must have come from a resident of one of the houses on Clarendon Road. The face – his face, Weaver thought with a start – was in profile, but partly obscured by a tree branch. You would have seen it was Weaver if you already knew him, but it was not clear enough to help anyone else pick him out of a line-up.

'It didn't take them very long to get this out,' he said.

'Uncharacteristically efficient. Suspiciously so.'

'I wonder why they think I'm American.' He thought back; he hadn't said anything to the man he'd hit, but there had been a few words with the policeman: '*We had a difference of opinion… I didn't start this, officer…*'

'What we can't do is let you get arrested. That means,' she said, tipping her head at the newspaper, 'that you need to keep staying out of sight. When were you planning to go to JP and Sue's?'

'Friday. They're not back until late tomorrow.'

'Did you have anything planned before then?'

'Nothing.' Then he remembered his appointment. 'Hang on. I'm meant to see Ragoulin. He's expecting me tomorrow on Bond Street.'

'Cancel it. It's not safe.'

'Ragoulin's not safe?'

Lily hesitated. 'I meant it's not safe to go out.'

'He said it was important.' Was it? He didn't know, but Ragoulin had acted like it was.

'I don't want you going anywhere.'

'I could take a minicab. Or get Chip to drive me.'

She shook her head. 'No way. Not until I've talked to this man Malone.'

'I'll need to let Ragoulin know. He'll be disappointed.' Would he? He had seemed oddly insistent that Weaver come by.

'Poor guy,' she said, again without the smallest note of sympathy.

'You said you had some good news.'

'I did. There's ice cream in the fridge. Pralines and cream, and raspberry sorbet. If you're nice you can have both.'

They sat sated, having finished both cartons of ice cream, though Lily was still licking her spoon. They might have been on a teenager's date in a small town, eating sundaes at a soda fountain after watching a high school basketball game.

'Come on,' she said. 'Let's make your bed. You need to get some sleep.'

'You're the one with the busy day tomorrow. What time are you phoning Malone?'

'Nine. I'll go out to make the call. You lie in as late as you like. Or are you an early riser?'

'Inveterate,' he said.

'That's a fancy word for it. What's Malone like?'

'I haven't seen him in years. But he was always very affable. Maybe too affable for some.'

'How's that?'

Weaver hesitated. 'He has what might politely be called a wandering eye. People used to call him "The Goat".'

'He sounds like something out of *Guys and Dolls*.'

'He is a bit like that. He and my father worked together. They've always kept in touch. They both like to fish.'

Malone actually *loved* to fish, and though he was happiest wearing waders in a trout stream, with a nickel cigar hanging out of his mouth, he was perfectly content with any kind of angling: a spinning rod off one of the piers at Manhattan's southern tip, pike fishing on a lake in Maine, and on one occasion even spending half his savings to fish for marlin off the Florida coast.

'They were in New York together?'

'Yeah. Poor guys.'

She laughed. 'Where is your office?'

'Just off 42nd Street on the East Side. Way over; by the river.'

'Near Costello's.'

'Costello's?' He was incredulous. 'The bar?'

She nodded, surprised he was so surprised. 'I went but it wasn't there anymore. Somebody told me it closed down years ago.'

'How did you hear about it anyway?'

'It was a Hemingway haunt.'

Was she pulling his leg? 'You like Hemingway?'

'I liked hardboiled fiction full stop. My dad's collection of old paperbacks was about the only thing he left behind. Hammett, Chandler, James M Cain. I used to read them under the covers with a torch.' She smiled fondly at the memory. 'How do you know Costello's?'

'My father was a regular. It was his local when he worked for the Bureau there.'

'But you still don't like New York.' She watched him thinking about how best to answer. He must have been taking too much time, for she said, 'Don't tell me – there's no trout fishing.'

'That is one of many reasons.'

'Like I said before, JP says it's the only one that matters to you.'

When had she been doing all this discussing him with JP? Lily seemed to spend a lot of time talking with the man. Weaver said, 'Well, people never thought JP was the most sensitive guy, or frankly the sharpest knife in the box. When he made his pile, suddenly he became a genius. Now it seems he understands what makes everybody tick.'

He retired to his quarters in the little sitting room and was reading *Trout Madness* on the sofa but without feeling its usual sedating effect when Lily came in, folded sheet and duvet draped over her arm. 'Up you get,' she said.

He helped her pull out the bed and make it, tucking in a bottom sheet and laying the duvet loosely on top. 'I've got a blanket if you think you'll need one,' Lily said. He shook his head; it was warm in the room.

Lily went out and he got into bed with another book from her shelves that he'd missed during his earlier inspection. *The*

Dreadful Lemon Sky, a John D MacDonald that he had only read half a dozen times before. Despite its familiarity, he found it hard to concentrate, and wondered if he should go and say goodnight to Lily. Best not, he decided.

She came back in anyway, carrying some printout pages in her hand.

'More Google alerts?' he asked.

'Nah; no point waiting when it's quicker to do it myself.' She waved the sheaf of pages lightly, then glanced briefly at the top page. 'I've been doing some digging. Into both Hofstadter and the First Lady's past. Her ex-husband wasn't always a monster, apparently; she sat on his board when he was still starting up, along with his then-close buddy Hofstadter, and at first they had a lot of success – or at least raised a tremendous amount of investment capital, which they promptly spent on expansion. But as is often the way, there seems to have come a critical moment when the cash flow was drying up and they were desperate for a new capital infusion. They didn't want more investors because they were already heavily diluted; they just wanted a loan to tide them over. A big loan.

'And that's where it gets interesting. No one wanted to lend them a dime, but just before the creditors took over, the cavalry rode to the rescue with seventy-five million dollars. Technically it came from a German bank, which had once tried to do some business in California: wealth management for Silicon Valley tycoons, to be precise. Guess which German bank.'

'You tell me.'

'Herr Galkin's, of course. It turns out the First Lady's then-husband had sat on the board of his California company a few years before. So the association with Galkin went back some time; it must have paved the way for the later loan. There's the chain then: from the German banker to Hofstadter and his partner; through the latter, and considerably diluted, to the First Lady, and thus, very remotely and not until she married the man, the President. But behind the German bank lies…'

'Moscow.'

'As his name suggests, Galkin's half-Russian – and well connected with the Morozov regime.'

'How bad does that look today?'

'That's the point I am coming to in this lengthy exposition you have so patiently sat through.' He laughed but also sat up a bit. She gave a knowing smile and went on: 'The person we haven't considered in all of this is the First Lady. Her involvement would be highly embarrassing for the President.'

'Of course – I just didn't think of it.' He was glad Lily had made the possible connection, but mortified he had not. 'The President would stand by her – they say he's besotted. But Hofstadter would want to protect his boss and the administration; I can see him caving in to the Russians. It seems obvious,' he said now.

'Unfortunately, it isn't,' Lily said. 'There is absolutely no evidence that the President's wife had anything directly to do with the loan, directly or indirectly. In fact, I've discovered she left the company before Hofstadter had even gone to Moscow, much less secured the loan. If it came out that the money came originally from Moscow, then it might make Hofstadter and his then-business partner look both crooked and foolish – but it would blow over in forty-eight hours. It would only be mildly embarrassing for the First Lady, if at all, because she'd once been part of the company. But it's nothing to do with the President – at the time of the loan, I don't think she'd even met him. So I think the "other individual" you say Kuzmin mentioned must be the former partner of Hofstadter out in Silicon Valley. Not the President's wife.

'Once again, we're back where we started: not sure how the Russians are blackmailing Hofstadter, though pretty clearly they are; and not sure what they want in return. I've looked high and low for this Daniel Berry you mentioned, and I haven't found anyone by that name who seems even faintly connected to the Russians. Unless the Russians have a sleeper agent by that name who moonlights as a marriage counsellor in San Diego and has half a million followers on YouTube.

'Anyway, I'm done in; bedtime for me. And you should get some sleep. Sorry I don't have better news, but tomorrow we'll start afresh.' Yet she gave no indication of leaving. 'Before I go, I meant to ask you something.'

'Okay,' he said, steeling himself.

'Before all this excitement, were you planning to stay in New York?'

'I don't know.' He wanted to say something less feeble. 'I'm not sure I will now that I've finished paying off my ex-wife.' He sighed with mild exasperation, and decided it was his turn to change the subject. 'What about you? How did you get to Paris anyway?'

She seemed a little unsettled by the question. 'It's a long story and it's late.'

'I'm happy to have the abridged version. You strike me as a night owl anyway.'

'Maybe, but I was thinking of having a run in the morning.'

'You run a lot?'

She shrugged. 'I did athletics at school.'

'School in England?'

She looked at him as if to say, where else? 'Both my primary and my secondary schools were two miles and fifty-seven yards from my front door. They're across the street from each other. I ran it every morning and every afternoon.'

'Good training.' He was making conversation to reduce his anxiety, but found he was also genuinely interested.

'That was the rationale, though it was really to keep from getting harassed on the way there. There was a bad estate down the road and the kids on it decided I was stuck-up and foreign to boot. Still, it did make me faster.'

She sighed, and Weaver stayed silent; he didn't want to interrupt her flow. He was glad when she sat down in the armchair. She continued: 'Running was the one thing I could do well, short legs and all. There was no point playing the violin or being brilliant at chess; I still would have been bullied. It's the same for boys. If you're good at sport you don't get bothered; you might even be popular, not that I ever had to worry about that. But I ran the hundred metres for the county, and that was enough to be left alone. That's all I wanted,' she said, a little plaintively. 'Just to be left alone.'

'What happened when you left school?'

'I told you; I didn't go to university. I didn't even finish my A-Levels. I just wanted out. So I went to France.'

'Why France?'

'Because it wasn't England. My mother had relations there, and I went to live with them.'

She sat back in her chair, then began talking again. 'God knows what my mother's clan made of me when I showed up. I must have seemed kind of exotic to them, being half-English. I felt a complete fish out of water; and though my French was fluent, I only spoke a little Vietnamese.'

She explained that the relatives lived in two or three apartments (depending on the money coming in) on the southern edge of the 13th arrondissement, the Quartier Asiatique. The family had originally arrived during World War One, the men employed as labourers, and even after so many years and several generations, its members remained almost without exception semi-educated, distinctly working class, and thoroughly Southeast Asian. When Lily's mother married an Englishman, the family elders were appalled.

The family business was confined to a single pho restaurant that served cheap and plentiful meals to the local Vietnamese and Chinese communities. However alien her cousins found Lily, they had no compunction about putting her to work; she waited table, language deficit or no. The hours were long; the pay, after deducting her contribution to the apartment's rent, was negligible; and having fun never figured on the menu.

Unsurprisingly, Lily found she missed her mother, and missed England, but she was determined to stay in Paris for however long it took to make her move a success. The problem was that the avenues to this seemed blocked by the sheer grind of her working life; there was not only no light at the end of the tunnel she found herself in, but no end either.

Then one day two Western men came in for lunch. They were speaking to each other in English, and when she explained the Vietnamese dishes in English rather than French, their interest was piqued and they asked Lily about herself, something no other customers had ever done. They must have liked the food as well, for they came back the next week, and the week after; soon they were regulars. Both worked at the British Embassy, though it was the elder of the two men who took a particular shine to Lily. Whether this interest was avuncular or lecherous was not something Weaver felt he could ask, since it might interrupt Lily's unprecedented account of her personal history.

One day, the older man, who was called Boyd, asked Lily if she could type. She said she could, omitting to mention she typed with two fingers; soon she was working part-time in the typing pool at the embassy. There, it was rapidly discovered that she was a bad typist but a good linguist, and since her employers were not keen to use French natives for sensitive work, she was given French documents to translate into English for consumption back in Whitehall. She was a fastidious translator but also a quick one, and her hours at the embassy were gradually extended, to the point where she was working only the odd shift at the family restaurant.

Mr Boyd, as Lily always thought of him then, continued to serve as her patron, and he was pleased when Lily's immediate superior praised Lily for her work ethic and for the intelligence she brought to any task. Learning of the obvious gaps in her education and her complete lack of qualifications, which Lily wisely never lied about, Boyd somehow wangled her into the residential courses INSEAD arranged for Foreign Office staff.

'Boyd must have liked you a lot,' said Weaver, trying to keep all suspicion out of his voice.

'He did,' said Lily. 'He was a grammar school boy from Leicester. He didn't really fit into the Foreign Office, though he was as bright as anyone else in the outfit. He told me once that in his family people said "serviette" instead of "napkin", as if I knew what that signified: where I grew up, we didn't say either. He was slightly eccentric but hid it; on the surface he seemed completely conventional. He shared my love for all those tough guy writers; I think part of him wished he'd been American. Which is hilarious, since he was such a classic English type: retiring, modest, un-macho; the kind of quiet boffin everyone at school goes to for help with their homework.'

Lily paused, thinking, then went on: 'I'm not sure why he took me under his wing, except that I didn't fit either. And he thought I was clever. He was quiet, and rather shy; he told me once that the self-confident public school boys he worked with had terrified him when he first started. Not that you'd ever know it. And when he relaxed and did the talking, he was the most articulate man I've ever known.'

Is that where she gets her gift of gab? thought Weaver. 'Were you lovers?' he found the courage to ask.

'None of your business,' she said crisply. 'But I'll tell you anyway,' she added, unable to hide a smile, 'since I'm a believer in the value of gratuitous information. The answer is no. Some toad called Harrington who works here for MI6 told me that he'd once asked Boyd if he'd ever tried it on. He said Boyd was outraged; Harrington thought Boyd might actually hit him, he was that angry. I was so happy to hear that; it meant Boyd actually did value me for more than my figure. And because of that, so did I.'

By now she was also making decent money, enough at any rate to leave the restaurant entirely behind her, and just enough for her to rent a minute studio on the rue Monsieur le Prince. 'It was so small it could only fit someone my size,' she said, her voice fond rather than indignant. 'But I loved it. It was in the 6th arrondissement and it was all mine. And then the embassy bigwigs decided to overlook my lack of academic credentials and make me a member of embassy staff. Between better work and having my own place, Paris seemed unbelievably exciting,' she said wistfully. 'I'd probably still be there if I hadn't come back to London.'

'So why come back?'

She said simply, 'Mum died.'

She went quiet now, as if the memory of her return from France signalled the end of what she was willing to recount. Weaver sensed that if he pressed her to continue this potted personal history, she would simply ignore him. Her more recent history, it seemed, was out of bounds.

He risked another question, nonetheless. 'Do you still see Boyd?'

'We've kept in touch,' she said. 'A bit.'

'Do you still call him Mr Boyd?'

She gave a half-laugh but didn't answer.

'What's his first name?' Weaver asked; he didn't want to leave this alone. 'Actually, never mind; I know it already.'

'What do you mean?' Lily demanded.

'I've met him, haven't I?' He could picture the raincoat, the long face with its small round chin, standing in the doorway. 'It's Charles.'

Lily shook her head, not in disagreement but as if dismayed by his discovery. She stood up, ostentatiously yawning. 'I need to ask you about presidential pardons but it will have to wait. Bedtime for us both. Try to dream about fishing. Tomorrow, don't go out; stay here and try to remember more about the meeting. I know it would just be your word against theirs, but it would be good if you could remember more about what the Russians wanted.' She thought for a moment. 'What if we had you hypnotised?'

'What if we didn't?' he said with an edge.

'You are remarkably unadventurous,' she answered with equal sharpness. 'Sleep well. I'll leave your door open; it gets too stuffy otherwise. But the alarm's set again in the office so please don't go out there.'

'Okay,' he said, briefly reassured by the security. 'Goodnight,' he added, as she went out to her bedroom. He was unaccustomed to being bossed around; at work, he usually held his own, even with superiors like Pauline. So why was he being so compliant with this woman? But then he was not used to anything remotely resembling the events of the last twenty-four hours: the violence, the fear, the confusion. Lily's confidence had served as a lifeline, and this landscape of cat and mouse seemed her natural turf. It wasn't remotely his. So it made sense to put all his trust in her.

Well, not all. For questions remained which made him uncertain of her: how did a member of a typing pool get to do important work for the Foreign Office in France? And what more 'interesting' job had she then got? But he was in no position to investigate her now. There seemed no choice but to let Lily's experience – greater than she let on, he sensed, whatever it really consisted of – direct their actions, even if it meant he bridled at times and had to fight his natural instinct to go his own way.

She had called him 'unadventurous'. That stung. Did she really think he was? Or was she annoyed that he had figured out that 'Mr Boyd' and the old man in the doorway were one and the same? Either way, he wanted to prove her wrong, and demonstrate that he was not some passive victim, helpless without her direction. Time to come clean, he decided, putting aside his caution.

He called out towards the dark well of the passage between their rooms. 'Lily.'

'Yes, Weaver,' she said faintly but dutifully. She must be in bed.

'There's something you need to know.'

'Yes.' The reply was not even a question; he sensed she was almost too tired to care. He waited, thinking how to phrase it, until she said impatiently, 'What is it?'

'I taped the meeting.'

18

Early riser though Weaver actually was, Lily beat him to it. When he emerged into the outer office, she was sitting at the slate table, fingers busy on the keyboard of her laptop. She was looking hot and bothered, and Weaver wondered if she'd been out for a run. He could see white trainers underneath the table and bare legs, one with the trace of a scar he remembered from the Dower House. She wore a T-shirt emblazoned with the words *University of Life*.

'Morning,' Lily said, sounding a little subdued.

'I'm ready whenever you are. Are you booking a Zipcar?'

'We're not going to JP's,' she said flatly. She stared, grim faced, at her laptop.

This was very different from the night before, when she had come half-running into his room, still drawing the tie strings of her silk dressing gown, barely able to contain her excitement. Barefoot, she had perched impatiently on the small armchair next to the sofa bed while he explained how his taping of the meeting had come to pass.

He and Lily had eventually agreed that the next step would be to retrieve the pen from JP's; they would leave after rush hour in the morning, which would mean a late morning arrival, hopefully when JP and Sue should still be on the Derwent. How they would secure entrance to the house, much less the guest bedroom in the wing, was something they decided to think through during the drive down.

Now Lily gestured wearily at the phone. 'I've had a call from him. Two men came by the house yesterday evening. The cook spoke to them. She explained JP was away but she got the impression it was you they were looking for. They were foreign. Since then, there's been a car with two men in it parked on and off down one of the lanes.

'JP was also trying to reach you. He said he couldn't get you on your mobile; somebody else answered it. Probably the driver of the taxi I hid it in,' she said. 'I thought JP's asking was a bit off. As far as he knows, we only saw each other at his house. Anyway, I said I didn't know where you were.'

'Why?'

She shrugged. 'JP is not Mr Discreet.'

She was right: JP thought of confidences as convertible debentures. Weaver thanked God that he hadn't spilled any beans of consequence when he was with JP on the river bank. 'I know, but why is he looking for me?'

'Unclear. He said that if I heard from you, you should call him. But he's away today.'

'We knew that. He and Sue aren't back until tomorrow night.'

'I mean he's incommunicado. He said there's no signal where he's fishing on the river,' she added. She got up and walked to the window, looking lost in thought, then came back to the table and sat down. 'I've got some more bad news. It's in today's *Times*. The London *Times*.' She slid her phone over to him.

He read:

Police want to speak with a 35-year-old man in connection with an unprovoked assault in Notting Hill yesterday morning. TF Weaver, a US State Department employee, is thought to have been staying at an Airbnb in the neighbourhood of Holland Park, but his current whereabouts are unknown.

The small accompanying photograph at the end of the article was the mug shot used for his State Department ID.

He said with annoyance, 'I like "unprovoked assault". Jesus, the

Brits are doing the Russians' work for them. They've sentenced me before I've had a trial.'

'Believe me, the Russians aren't interested in a trial,' Lily said. She took her phone back and tapped at the headline. 'I think it's the Americans behind this; that's how the police know your name now. The Secret Service will have been pushing the authorities here.'

'You think the Secret Service fed *The Times*?'

'Not directly. That was probably MI5. Or maybe Tom, JP's friend: he's at *The Times*. He might have recognised you from the police photo. I don't know for sure.' She paused, then said, 'I need to ask you something.' She sounded reluctant, as if it were the last thing she actually wanted to do.

'What's that?'

Lily said, still speaking slowly, 'I'm not quite sure how to say this, but have you ever had… troubles?'

'Troubles?' He was bemused. Lily looked exhausted, and little wonder: she hadn't got much sleep, between the late hours when they had finally called a halt to their post-midnight confab and her early start. But behind her fog of fatigue, he sensed that she was agitated, even upset. He said, 'If you mean financial problems, then yes, I've had plenty of them. In the past,' he added.

'No, not those.'

'Do you mean legal troubles? The IRS audited me one year when I actually made some money in Vermont, but that was largely out of disbelief, theirs and mine.' He grinned but she didn't seem satisfied. It was Lily who looked like she had troubles now.

'I was thinking of personal problems.' She was searching for words, and he sensed she was avoiding some. 'Emotional ones, maybe.'

'Ah,' he said, catching on. 'Do you mean "mental health issues"?'

'Yes,' she said, giving a cursory smile, grateful he had got there at last.

'Now that you mention it,' he said, inhaling deeply, waiting while he saw worry start to flood her face, 'the answer is no.' He stared at her, not remotely tempted to joke now. Something had happened. 'Spit it out, Lily: what have you heard?'

'Did you ever spend time at the Madeline Adgerton Health Facility?'

'The what?' He was thinking hard. 'God, I'd forgotten its full name. We just called it Mad Maud's.'

'And you were resident there?'

'Yes, until I got fired.'

'Fired?'

'Well, what you'd call "made redundant", actually. The state makes cuts, and heads roll. Mental health was never a strong part of the legislature's agenda in Vermont. Still, I got unemployment until I went back to school.'

'You mean you *worked* there?'

'Sure. Initially, I was just an orderly. Mopping floors and organising the meds. But then I was promoted and became Dr Deakin's assistant. He did the initial assessment of all the incoming patients. I had to sit in and make sure he had copies of the relevant court orders, and also in case there were any ructions. A lot of these patients had pretty severe problems with anger management.'

Lily laughed at this, and he was relieved to see her own relief. She said, 'I thought you were an interpreter. Not an attendant in a loony bin.'

'I was an impoverished grad student, trying to finish my PhD.' He added quietly, 'Why don't you tell me what this is about?'

'This morning I had a Google Alert. Here, have a look.' She typed something, then passed her phone back to him. It was an online gossip column in Vermont called *Rootless in Rutland*, and contained the following:

Alarmed but not surprised to learn of Federal authorities' interest in local boy TF Weaver, whose mom worked for many years at the compound of Anatoly Demidov during the Nobel Prize winner's years in Vermont. The younger Weaver, a translator for the State Department, seems intent on becoming as famous a thorn in federal authorities' sides as Edward Snowden, and is said to be peddling a tell-all book of diplomatic secrets to NYC publishers. Hard to take him too seriously, however, if you know that – according to his ex-wife, contacted yesterday in Manhattan by RR – Weaver spent three months in his twenties at the Madeline Adgerton Health Facility. Aka Vermont's finest nut house…

'Well,' he said, putting down the printout, 'I'm not buying my ex-wife a fucking Christmas present this year.'

Lily's smile was perfunctory. He said, 'This would hurt more if any of it was true.'

'I thought you were the injured party in the marriage. What's all her anger about?'

'I don't know.' He sighed with mild exasperation. 'Between her and Pauline, I have two people happy to badmouth me to the world.'

'Was Pauline already down on you?'

'And then some. She put me on report for a while last year. I had translated a joke made at a trade convention that wasn't part of the written speech, and the joke was pretty lewd. Careless of me but hardly criminal – it wasn't my joke, after all. But Pauline jumped at the excuse to give me a formal warning. She really doesn't like me.'

'But why?'

'I'm not sure,' he said, thinking about it.

'Is she chippy or something?'

'Chippy?'

'Class conscious.'

'Maybe she is. I hadn't thought of it that way. But Mac got half-tanked at the Christmas lunch and told her I was a *Mayflower* descendant. Pauline brings it up all the time, as if I thought I was something special because of it. But it's not even true. It's my stepfather who has the blue blood, nothing to do with me.'

'I know that scenario. My father wanted people to think he was to the manor born, but his birth name was Cahill, not Churchill, and his own father worked on the Docks in the East End. But never mind about me; I have to say, your divorce settlement doesn't sound very fair.'

Weaver shrugged. 'I should have fought harder in court, but by then I was so tired that I just wanted it over. I think my ex was counting on that. She has remarkable stamina when there's money at stake.' He added, 'I did draw the line at paying child support.'

'I didn't know you had kids.' Her voice had gone flat.

Weaver's laugh was not a happy one. 'I don't. The child's father is indisputably the other man, a derivatives trader since you haven't asked, but my wife's lawyer was happy for the judge to think otherwise. My wife was six months pregnant, swore that I was the father, and did her best to attract the court's compassion for a newly impoverished single mother. If I hadn't said I'd insist on a DNA test, she would have been happy for me to pay the bills for the new arrival.'

'God, you have been through it.'

He didn't like the suggestion of victimhood. 'Not really,' he said, regretting his marital confession. 'But obviously someone's briefing against me to *Rootless Rutland*.'

'Hofstadter wants to cut you off at the knees before you have time to stand up.'

'Elegantly put, but what does it mean?' It was his turn to sound impatient.

'It's simple: by painting you as an unstable thug, already in trouble at work, they hope no one will believe anything you say.'

'It's not the Russians then?'

'The Russians aren't interested in assassinating your character; they want to assassinate *you*.'

'You sound pretty confident of that.'

'I am,' she said. And added bitterly, 'They're only happy when an enemy of the state is dead.'

Great, he thought sourly. It didn't bear thinking too much about; he needed a plan. He said, 'If we're not going to JP's, what do we do?'

'Let me see what this Goat man has to say. I'm going out to ring him now. You stay put.'

'For how long?'

She gave a one-shoulder shrug. 'I don't know. I may be some time. But I'll be back for sure by teatime. We still need to go to JP's to get the recording, but only when he's back. Safer that way. Meanwhile, please don't move while I'm out.'

'Should I expect more visitors?' He said it with a smile but the prospect was unnerving.

'No, only Chip and Charles know the code; on his good days, Charles actually remembers it. You're American: have another shower. Or read about trout life in Michigan. Snoop around if you have to, but don't go anywhere.'

'There's one other problem,' he said.

'Yes?' she said warily.

'The very end of the meeting isn't on the tape. And that's when they talked about what the Russians want from the President.'

'Are you serious?'

She sounded incredulous, which was not the response he was hoping for. 'I am,' he said steadily. 'But the good news is that I remember some of it. There was a Russian name I'm hoping will come back to me. And a Polish joke.'

'Polish joke?'

'Kuzmin called it that, I think. Kuzmin laughed at his own joke – very loudly, almost maliciously. Hofstadter didn't like it one bit.'

'And all this has just come back to you?' she asked, making him wonder if she sensed he had been holding back this information. Probably. But he had been waiting until he was sure of her. Was he sure now?

He nodded. 'So go on,' she said. 'What do you remember?'

'The Russians were demanding that the White House make an announcement.'

'About what? Don't tell me you want to revisit Skip Washington.'

'I don't. But they wanted the release of somebody and the announcement was supposed to be about that.'

'So when will they make it?'

'What – the announcement?' Lily nodded impatiently and Weaver went on: 'That's the weird thing; if it is for some unknown reason Skip Washington, then they've done it already—'

'And you said Hofstadter agreed to this?'

'Reluctantly, but yes, he did.'

Lily looked disappointed. 'I guess you just have to keep trying to remember – at least until we get the pen back.' She left unsaid the fact that the pen did not hold all the conversation of the meeting. 'Keep at it,' she said eventually, 'and pray that more comes back to you. Maybe another shower will help.'

19

BEFORE SHE LEFT, LILY LENT HIM HER laptop, and he took it back to the little apartment and sat on the sofa, checking his emails, using VPN. He approached them warily. There were several increasingly shrill ones from Pauline that formed a gathering storm, and a brief one from Tomic; he asked Weaver to call him as soon as possible, though he gave no explanation. There was also one from his mother, expressing concern about the phone call from the Secret Service asking where he was and mentioning the earlier call from 'Uncle Billy' – 'that awful man Malone.'

He held off replying to any of them, and spent the morning alternately dozing and reading. Neither seemed to reduce his stress levels, and he wondered why Lily had to be gone so long.

Lunch was a tin of tuna he found in the kitchen cupboard. Only then did he write to Ragoulin, cancelling their meeting, explaining that he had been 'called away'. Weaver hoped he would think this was just an excuse for going fishing earlier than planned.

Within five minutes, Ragoulin had replied.

My dear Weaver,
   I read your email with great dismay which I would express by phone but yours seems unavailable – is it dead?
   That aside, I implore you to come to my office. As well as the book I mentioned, I was planning to show you several letters from an American lady to Anatoly D after his return to Russia in 1991. They are unsigned, perhaps because the letters are personal, indeed intimate.

    I have been given this correspondence in order to assess
its value and suggest potential purchasers of the letters. My
custody ends tomorrow, when I have to return the letters to the
Demidov archive.
    I would send you scans of the letters were the risk of
interception not so great. So I feel most strongly that you should
visit the office and look yourself at this correspondence.
With warm regards,
Alek

On first reading, Weaver was mystified; he had a residual
but limited interest in Demidov from his mother's connection
and his own memories of the man, nothing like the intensity of
Ragoulin's interest. But rereading the email, he saw why Ragoulin
felt he had to see these putative letters from 'an American lady'.

Could Weaver's mother really have had some secret passion for
the writer? And would his mother have written so indiscreetly?
She must have known that correspondence sent to Russia would
be examined by the FSB, even in the briefly democratic days of
the 1990s.

Weaver knew his mother's handwriting; he would be able to
tell at once if these letters were hers. *If* he were to see them, that
is. He went into the open-plan office and looked out the window,
trying to decide what to do. Lily thought he had agreed to her
diktat to stay put; disobeying would be a kind of betrayal – and
that after all she had done for him. Wouldn't it?

It took him forty-five minutes to reach Bond Street. He started
on foot, and made a circuitous progress under a cloudless sky. On
Theobald's Road he jumped on a bus, the only passenger getting
on at that stop.

He was tense but confident that he would have lost anyone who
might be following him, though on reaching the axis of Oxford
Street and Tottenham Court Road, he got off and detoured into
the clogged streets of Soho until he was himself lost. Operating

by feel, memory of Google Maps, and the position of the sun – as helpful navigating in a city as in countryside – he eventually emerged uncertainly into Golden Square.

From there he approached Piccadilly Circus, full of foreign teenagers, lazing on the steps of the grimy fountain on its north side. He was slightly out of breath. Fishing two weekends a month didn't really constitute a workout. He had thought of joining a gym in Manhattan's midtown, where he could stop each evening on his way home after work. But something in him balked at that; it would symbolise the complete urbanisation of his life, something he resisted. Now he vowed to start leaving for work half an hour early; if he got off the bus at Times Square, he could walk the mile and a half east and arrive at the office at the same time as usual.

He realised with a start that odds were, he wouldn't be going to work anytime soon. He looked at his watch, a battered old Longines, a present from his father on his twenty-first birthday. Ten minutes to go. He walked west along the graceful parts of Piccadilly, then turned right and north, passing Ragoulin's club, where they had dined two nights before. It seemed a year ago.

Ragoulin's office was a hundred yards north of the old Time-Life building on Bond Street, upstairs from a gallery specialising in post-Impressionist painting. Entrance was through a modest, recessed doorway where he buzzed for the first floor; there were no names listed to identify the tenants.

'Hello,' a female voice said questioningly through the intercom.

'I'm here to see Alek. My name's Weaver.'

'Oh,' she said. There was a pause he wondered about, then she said, 'You'd better come up.'

She buzzed him through and he walked up a steep stairway, lined by prints of Russian paintings. At the landing, he knocked on the door and went in. In the anteroom a pretty young woman stood behind her desk. He saw through an open door Ragoulin's office on the right, with its view over Bond Street; it was unoccupied.

'Mr Weaver?' The voice was soft, almost imploring,

'That's right. I have an appointment with Alek at three.'

'He's not here,' she said, obviously puzzled. 'There's nothing in his diary, and when he left for lunch he said he wouldn't be back this afternoon.'

'Really? He said it was important I come by. Did he leave anything for me?' She shook her head. 'Any kind of message?'

'No, nothing.'

'Could you try his phone?' She looked reluctant. Weaver said, almost plaintively, 'I've come a long way to see him. He arranged it this morning. I can show you his email if you like.' She looked like she needed reassurance.

He was reassured himself when she said, 'I'll text him.'

As she tapped the number on her own phone, he waited, feeling mystified by Ragoulin's non-show and by the lack of any message. The tone of Ragoulin's email had been urgent, just short of threatening; it seemed inconceivable he could have forgotten their appointment.

The young woman put her phone down. 'Funny. His phone is switched off. Alek *never* leaves it off.' She was looking more concerned about this than about Weaver's wasted journey.

'Do me a favour. Have a look on his desk and see if he left anything for me.'

She was taken aback, as if he had suggested something improper. Weaver said, 'I'll wait here.'

She went into Ragoulin's office and came out after a minute. 'Nothing, I'm afraid,' she said.

'No letters? He was going to show me some. They might be in Russian. Handwritten.'

'No, I'm sorry.' She closed the door to Ragoulin's office and went back to her desk. 'I'll try him again.'

But the phone was still switched off. Her manner was gradually easing with Weaver, and off her own bat she tried the landline number at Ragoulin's home, a spacious flat near Cheyne Walk in Chelsea. There was no answer there, either. She said carefully, 'Would you like to wait for him here?'

Weaver wondered what to do. Had something happened to Ragoulin? An accident? Catastrophic possibilities filled his mind. Weaver pushed them away. He had better get back.

He said, 'When you hear from him, please give him this number. Tell him I have a new phone.'

Outside he looked around carefully but saw nothing suspicious. He walked quickly now towards Piccadilly, starting across the pedestrianised area between the two branches of Bond Street. Just beyond, two men were chatting, seated on a bench. They were dark, almost copper-coloured, and then he realised the men were lifelike statues: Roosevelt and Churchill.

An old lady in a sage cloth coat, hardly required on a warm May day, stood examining the seated figures. As she turned away her eyes met Weaver's, and he felt a peculiar sense of recognition. The old woman's face broke into an undiluted smile, and she lifted the cane she was carrying and jabbed it in the air. 'My helper!' she cried.

It was Mrs Golubova. Unchanged from the airplane – the same coat, the stick, her glasses hanging from around her neck. Next to her was her daughter.

'*Lyogok na pomine,*' she went on. *Speak of the devil.* 'I was just discussing you.'

There couldn't have been very much to say, thought Weaver. 'How nice to see you, Mrs Golubova.'

'This is my daughter, Nina,' she said.

He looked at her companion, ready to extend his hand. Standing next to her mother, she seemed almost outlandishly tall, but it might have been her heels. Forty-ish, attractive, with expensively cut ash-blonde hair, though her eyebrows were dark, and her eyes brown – and watchful. She was dressed in a short pink Dior jacket over an immaculate black skirt. Nina nodded, and flashed a fleeting automatic smile.

'I thought you were in the countryside,' Mrs Golubova said accusingly.

'I was. But business calls, and I had to come into town.'

'Of course. We have come in today for the shops. Nina looks after her mother as a good daughter should.' Nina gave the faintest of stoical smiles, like that of a teacher introduced to the parents of an idolatrous pupil. Mrs Golubova went on, 'But I am so glad to see you again. I have been wondering how I might thank you for your kindness, but knew no way to reach you.'

'It doesn't matter,' he said, impatient to get going if he were to beat Lily back to the apartment. 'Very nice to see you,' he said, trying to make it a definitive farewell.

But Mrs Golubova was not to be deterred. 'Not yet, not yet. I must give you something to show my gratitude.'

What was she proposing? A silver ashtray from Asprey's? A Hermes tie? None of the immediate options seemed practical, let alone desirable. She was looking wildly around, then spied the dark green wooden hut ahead of her. Under its large canopy, dark blue buckets were crammed with bunches of fresh spring flowers. A cardboard sign was pinned to the side of the stand: *Flowers £12.*

'Ah,' the old woman exclaimed, and jabbing at the pavement with her stick walked with surprising speed, Weaver and her daughter following. Ignoring a customer ahead of her, Mrs Golubova pointed a finger of her free hand at a mixed bunch of curly-petalled tulips. 'That one,' she commanded, and her daughter fished out the bunch and handed them to the aproned vendor. With a theatrical sweep, the man took a sheet of green paper from his side of the cart and quickly wrapped the flowers. He gave the package to Mrs Golubova while her daughter handed over the money.

Mrs Golubova turned to Weaver and extended the bouquet. 'For you,' she declared. 'While they last, you can remember me. You said you no longer had a wife, I believe, but surely a *Krasavchik* like you has friends among the ladies. I hope one of them is here in England,' said Mrs Golubova. 'If not two!' She grinned. Nina was waiting patiently enough, but was staring at the Patek Philippe window display, unwilling to join in.

'England can be very lonely for people,' continued Mrs Golubova. 'The people can be very cold. I hope your friend here is a warm one.'

He had forgotten how nosy and insistent the old woman could be.

'Mama,' said Nina quietly but firmly.

Mrs Golubova took the hint. 'I hope you enjoy the flowers. And your lady friend does too.'

'Thank you,' he replied, and the old woman beamed. 'It's very nice to see you again,' he said. 'Perhaps we will meet on another airplane someday.'

She tittered at the thought of this. Then she waved at him, as if he were already moving away. 'Goodbye my good, good man,' she said, and Weaver found himself dismissed.

20

WHEN HE RETURNED, LILY'S LAPTOP WAS OPEN on the table but there was no sign of her, though the twin doors to the apartment were wide open. She had beat him back. He stood for a minute by the computer and idly touched the keyboard. The screen refreshed and he was staring at a photograph, black-and-white, part of a *People* magazine article he dimly remembered from years before. The picture showed two young men at a picnic table, both fair and looking serious, almost defiant, their gazes fixed on something slightly to the side of the lens. Between them sat a small boy, darker-haired and wearing shorts, his bare legs visible underneath the plank seat of the picnic table. He was looking shyly at the camera. Sitting on the side of the table nearest the viewer, a woman in a light patterned blouse had her back to the camera. Next to her, with his face turned so that the beard around his strong chin was visible, was Anatoly Demidov.

He was about to read the accompanying text when he heard steps on the wood floor and Lily emerged from the apartment. 'I hope you didn't come back on my account,' she said.

'What do you mean?'

'I thought you'd done a runner.'

'Of course not,' said Weaver. He was pleasantly surprised by her calmness; he had been dreading an explosion. 'I'm sorry, I know I said I'd stay here. Ragoulin was insistent.'

She shook her head and he realised she was struggling to keep her equanimity. 'I thought I could trust you.'

'You can. You should know that by now.'

'Oh? Everybody else seems to think you're a fantasist.'

Who was this 'everybody else'?

He said, 'You saw those thugs at Marylebone.'

'What about them?'

'They were real enough. You know that.'

'Maybe they were right to come after you. Maybe *they're* the good guys in all of this.'

He ignored this. 'And the guy on Clarendon Road? What about him?'

'Who knows what really happened there? For all I know, it *was* an unprovoked attack.'

'And the meeting in Stockholm?' He felt like he was slapping at midges. As soon as he squashed one, another appeared.

'I only have your word for it. Again. Funny how that keeps being the case.'

'I have the meeting recorded on the pen at JP's,' he said, trying to sound definitive.

'We can't listen to it now, can we? How convenient.'

He was running out of ammunition, and starting to despair of convincing her of anything. Lily went on: 'You don't answer to me. If you think you'd be better off without my help, then go ahead. Believe me, I have nothing vested in this.'

Nothing vested. The words sunk into him, her indifference more wounding than her anger. What had he expected from her? Affection? He barely knew her, so why did he feel so let down? There was no point continuing on a self-deluding basis, so he said, 'You've helped me a lot, but I'd better take over now and handle it on my own.'

Did he mean this? No. Would he do it? Without question. If she couldn't even believe in the existence of the recorder, then there seemed no point staying.

Lily was biting her lower lip when he looked at her, her eyes fixed on the laptop screen. 'I'll just get my stuff,' he announced.

He had almost reached the door to the living quarters and was wondering where on earth he was going to go, when she said, just loud enough for him to hear, 'Don't you want to know about Malone?'

He stopped. Her voice was cool, neutral, and it took him a moment to understand she was asking him to stay. In his guilt over his own aborted meeting, he had completely forgotten about her call with Malone. He walked back to the table, and sat down. 'Yes, I do.'

'Good.' She sat forward and put her forearms down on the table. 'He wants to see you. Tomorrow. In the flesh.'

'Where?'

'We'll need to work that out, but somewhere in south London. He may be able to help.'

'How?'

'You have to remember, I was just the messenger. At first he wasn't going to tell me anything. He said he can't do much for us with the Brits. MI5 is working with the police and Malone's worried that they'll find you, and so am I. But he's also worried about being spotted with you.'

'So will he help me or not?'

'I think so, but he didn't exactly commit. If you can tell him what the Russians have on the White House, Malone says the Secret Service will back off. And trust me, the Brits will then follow.'

'How do you know?'

'I have it on good authority. Let's leave it at that.'

'Charles,' he said bluntly.

Lily shrugged. 'Until then, as far as the British know, they're chasing a traitor who the White House desperately wants found. The Special Relationship at work… Anyway, I don't think it matters why Malone wants to help, as long as he actually does.'

'I can't fulfil my side of any bargain until I have the recording of the meeting. You said yourself that otherwise it's my word against theirs – unless I can show the tape.'

'That has to wait until JP's back. It's just too risky otherwise.'

'We'll need to explain that to Malone. I guess the tape could be the quid pro quo.'

She began to describe her call. Initially Malone had been very suspicious: he began their conversation by asking for the password that Fontana had given her on the phone.

'What was it?' asked Weaver now.

'Quechee Gorge. Your father had to spell it out for me.'

'It's a landmark in Vermont. Scarily deep. My mother almost dies every time she has to drive across it. To tell you the truth, so do I. But go on.'

Malone had asked her many questions, lots of them personal; she felt he was still checking her out. But the question Malone put most emphasis on was why she was helping Weaver. Since Weaver himself wanted to know why, he paid special attention to this part of Lily's account. But she skirted the issue, something Weaver was learning she was good at, and whatever she'd said must have satisfied Malone, as she concluded by saying, 'So he wants to meet with you.'

'But?' He sensed hesitation on her part.

'I don't know; I just found him slightly cagey. He kept saying how close he'd been with your father, but here he is hunting down his great friend's son. You said he's based in Paris, but he's in London now, using an office at the American Embassy.'

'Yes, my father thought he was coming to the UK.'

'Because Malone knew you were here? So he came over from Paris?'

'It sounds that way. But I'd like to know how he found out. It was probably the White House – even Hofstadter himself. But how does Hofstadter know what country I'm in?'

'The Russians would have told him – if Hofstadter was desperate enough to ask.'

'Why desperate?'

'Desperate to find you, Weaver. Sorry, but there's no point ducking it: I think we can forget any idea that Hofstadter is going to be sympathetic. But with Malone, it seemed almost as if he hadn't made up his mind. So I didn't say anything about the recording.'

'Good,' Weaver said. Lily no longer seemed so angry with him, and he was immensely relieved that he hadn't left. He said, 'I'm sorry I went out, but Ragoulin insisted I go see him. He said he has some letters written to Demidov. I thought they might be from my mother.'

'*Billets-doux*?'

'Something like that.'

'And were they?'

'I don't know. When I got to Bond Street, Ragoulin wasn't there. I don't know what happened. He didn't even leave a note.' He added with emphasis, 'I was very careful. I'm sure I wasn't followed.'

But Lily wasn't listening. She said, 'Maybe he didn't want to see you after all. Maybe—' Lily stopped for a moment, then said, 'Maybe he just wanted to get you there.'

'But why? Nothing happened.' He realised he was still holding the bunch of flowers, and put them down on the table. Lily stared at them and he wondered what she was thinking. Did she really still distrust him – could she possibly think she had been helping a compulsive liar?

'I'm just checking, Weaver. It's what I need to do.'

Or was paid to do. 'You don't believe me then?' he asked.

'I've learned not to believe anyone until I've got the facts.'

'Great. After all, you thought I was a fantasist. Maybe you still do.'

Lily shook her head. 'The thought did cross my mind, but no, I didn't really think that. And I don't now. Sometimes it pays not to be suspicious, and I guess this is one of those times.'

Now he pointed to the laptop and its photo of the celebrity family in Vermont. 'Why were you looking at that?' he asked.

'Looking at what, you great big snoop?'

'The article on Demidov. It must be thirty years old.'

'I wanted to see if it was true.'

'What was true?' He expected her anger, but not this sudden distrust.

'Your story about your mother and Demidov.'

'And did you find what you were looking for?'

'Not yet. But the photograph,' she pointed to the laptop, 'doesn't make sense. Wikipedia says he had three sons, but they weren't that far apart in age. Look at the photo. The little guy is much younger than the other two.'

'He is,' he said without looking.

'So is it a mistake?'

'You could call it that, I guess. The little guy isn't Demidov's son.'

'How do you know that?'

'Because the little guy is me.' He ignored her expectant gaze. 'You could have asked, you know.'

'What would be the point if you were going to lie to me?'

'Thanks for the show of faith.'

'You're welcome.' She sounded happier now. She looked him up and down. 'You need a haircut.'

'Is that all you've got to say?'

She parted her lips a little as she considered this, a contemplative look on her face. 'Malone sounded like he's pretty old school. You don't want him thinking you're some kind of Julian Assange.'

'He knew me when I was knee high to a grasshopper.'

'All the more reason to show him you're still your father's son. And like your dad, an upright citizen. So I'd better do it. Don't worry, I've cut worse. I think. Let me get some scissors.' But she made no move to get up, and he noticed she was staring at the flowers. 'Are those for me?' she demanded. 'To make amends for going out?' She reached for the flowers.

'I thought you'd like them,' he said, torn between honesty and a generosity that was accidental.

'I don't mean to sound ungrateful but these aren't very fresh,' she said. 'You wuz robbed. Where did you buy them?'

'Actually, I didn't buy them. They were given to me.'

'By Ragoulin? I thought he wasn't there.'

'He wasn't, but something remarkable happened. I ran into Mrs Golubova. You know—'

'I remember. The old Russian lady on the plane. Where was this?'

'On Bond Street. I had just left Ragoulin's and there she was. I don't know who was more surprised.'

'I do,' Lily said sharply.

'What do you mean?'

She said neutrally, 'Go on.'

'There's not much to say. She started thanking me all over again. Her daughter was with her. I can't say I liked her very much. Bling, blonde, buxom; you know the type, I guess.'

'I do. So how do the flowers come in?'

'Mrs Golubova said she wanted to give me a present. To say thanks. There was a flower stand on Bond Street.'

'Don't you think it seems a bit pat – she just happens to be outside Ragoulin's when you come out? What are the chances of that?'

'But how would she have known I'd be there?' A disturbing thought emerged, one he tried but failed to dismiss: Lily was the only person who knew about his appointment, though she had also ordered him to cancel it.

He continued, 'She said she was grateful to me for looking after her at the airport.'

Lily was still looking sceptical, so he said, 'Look, we barely spent a minute together today. If it was some kind of set-up, then it couldn't have produced much. She bought the flowers on the spur of the moment. And no, she didn't ask me where I was staying.'

'Maybe she didn't have to.'

Weaver watched as she stripped off the enveloping wrap of green paper. Then she rolled off the elastic band around the stems, and spread the flowers, fan-like, on the grey slate tabletop.

'Oh, come on,' he protested. 'She could hardly poison the flowers ahead of time.'

'I'm not looking for ricin,' said Lily, head down to examine the flowers, her fingers going nimbly through each set of the frilly petals. 'I'm looking for this,' she said, and held out a hand, palm flat in offering. On her palm he saw a tiny translucent disc, no bigger than a fingernail.

'Get your toothbrush,' said Lily. 'We haven't got much time.'

21

THEY WERE OUT OF THE BUILDING IN three minutes. He left his toothbrush, in fact, though at Lily's prompting he made sure his passport was in his jacket pocket as he came out from the apartment into the open-plan office. Lily was standing by the slate table studying her phone, her fingers moving quickly as she texted, her handbag hanging from its strap around her shoulder.

Outside the sun was in their eyes as they went west. Lily walked astonishingly fast, her short legs piston-like as they moved down Leonard Street. 'I'd run but it would draw attention,' she said between breaths. Over the rooftops a kite appeared, a hundred feet up, floating in the breeze, a faint silver streak against the sky's sheet of blue.

The street was one-way in the direction they were heading, and after a black cab passed by, Weaver glanced behind him and saw there was no other traffic coming. For a moment it seemed they were out of harm's way, especially since Lily had slowed down.

It was then that the car came out of nowhere from the end of the street. A dark Mercedes estate, driving the wrong way.

The cab that had passed them braked sharply, and the driver hammered on his horn. The Mercedes reacted unexpectedly, swinging to one side of the street and climbing the pavement, where it narrowly missed a man in a pale suit, who threw himself against the side of a building just in time. The Mercedes edged forward, aiming to squeeze through the gap between the taxi and the building, but inexplicably the taxi driver moved even further over, blocking its way.

Now it was the turn of the Mercedes driver to hoot his horn, the two horns competing like a brass duet. Lily turned around. 'Run!' she shouted and was two steps past Weaver before he even moved. He sprinted after her, but even at full tilt struggled to keep up. After forty yards he saw a large building ahead on the right, a brick-and-stone Victorian church, set well back from the street. A fence ran next to the pavement with a pair of ornamental gates in its centre. Lily slowed, opened the right gate, and went through. She started running again, along the paved path bisecting a churchyard of ancient headstones and grass. Weaver followed as she ran towards the church at the end of the path. In the distance, the battle of the horns continued, augmented by the sound of angry shouting.

Next to the chancel at one end of the church, a small one-storey annexe had been built. Inside they found a young woman wearing a wool cap, sitting behind a desk. Before she could speak, a flustered-sounding Lily said, 'Is there a loo we could use please? We're due in church but got stuck in traffic.' When the woman pursed her lips, a pleading note entered Lily's voice. *'Please.'* She waved a hand in Weaver's direction. 'My husband's about to burst.' She gave a little laugh. 'I don't want him to desecrate the place.'

The woman relented. 'Okay. It's just down the hall.'

What now? wondered Weaver, following Lily along a corridor, past a door marked *TOILETS*. At the end of the corridor, she opened another door and stepped right onto the street outside.

Following her out of the building, Weaver found Lily already moving, peering anxiously ahead. In the foreground, high in the sky, another kite seemed to be floating up and down, like an indecisive gull. 'What is it with these kites?' he said as he caught up with her.

'Where?' Lily demanded, and he pointed up. She said, picking up the pace, 'Keep walking. That's not a kite; it's a drone.' She pointed ahead to a line of parked cars. 'Found it,' she said, and went and stopped at the third car. An old Golf, little larger than the Zipcar, and from the multiple dents on its side, with an eventful history.

While Weaver stood on the pavement, wondering what she was doing, Lily went round the front of the car. She stopped by the kerbside front wheel, then crouched down; he could see she was feeling around the tyre.

'Shit,' she said crossly, and stood up. He realised she was looking for the key.

'Wait a minute,' Lily said, but she was talking to herself. She waited momentarily for a car to pass, then crouched again, this time by the other front wheel. She stood up with a key in her hand. 'Quick,' she said, clicking open the car doors. 'Get in the back.'

'What? Are you my Uber driver?'

'Just do it please. You'll find a blanket folded there. Lie down and put it over you.'

He did as he was told, though it didn't make a lot of sense. Was she taking him some place where he might be spotted? An image came into his head of an underground parking lot, badly lit with bleak concrete pillars, and two cars arriving quietly to make a transfer of goods. Goods? The thought alarmed him. He was the goods.

Lily started up the engine as he lay along the seat, scrunching up his legs to fit, making sure he was thoroughly covered. 'Who left the key there?' he asked, as he felt the car begin to move. His voice was muffled underneath the blanket.

'Chip,' she said. 'I know he's dyspraxic but God it gets ridiculous sometimes.' She gave a harsh half-laugh. 'He said he'd put the key on the right front tyre, so naturally he put it on the left one. Now, no more talking.'

'Tell me where we're going first.'

'You'll see. It'll take a while – an hour or maybe two. The rush hour traffic's already started.'

The car was light, tin-like, and he felt every bump, every touch of the brakes as Lily drove. Soon he was feeling slightly sick. He took slow deep breaths, trying not to make too much noise, not wanting to distract Lily. After about ten minutes they stopped – he assumed at a light – and she said, 'I think it's okay.'

'Can I sit up now?'

'No.' Her voice was firm. 'I just meant there's no sign of their car.'

'Great. But why am I still hiding under a blanket?'

'So you won't show on CCTV. From what Malone said, MI5 and Special Branch are pulling out the stops. As far as they're concerned, you're Code Plato. That's the name they use when terrorists are on the loose.'

'They think I'm a terrorist?'

'They don't know what to think; they only know what the American authorities tell them. Malone said requests are coming here from the White House, which means it's all systems go to find you, Weaver. You must know there are more surveillance cameras in London than grains of rice in China. Or something like that. Malone doesn't think they're looking for me – yet. And anyway,' she added, almost offhand, 'somebody's got to drive.'

'What about Chip?'

'He's been busy with other things. Thank God is all I can say.' The light must have changed; they were moving forwards again. She said, 'I've got to concentrate now. Motorways unnerve me.'

'Where are we going?' he asked again. They couldn't be going to the Dower House, so where was she taking him?

'Somewhere safe. Well, as safe as anywhere else. Why don't you get try to get some sleep? I'll wake you when we get there.'

The next thing he knew, a voice said gently, *'Miliy, prosnis.'*

What was his mother doing here? And where was he? He stretched a leg and his foot pressed against the inside of the car door; then something whirred inside him, a component clicked, and a word popped out of his mouth like an offering. 'Sukolov,' he announced, then yawned. 'Can I get up now?'

'Yes, you can sit. But what did you say?'

'Sukolov. That was one of the names I forgot.'

'You going to give me some context for it? Who is Sukolov meant to be?'

'I think he's someone the Russians value, so someone they want... released, I guess. He had another name in America which Kuzmin was about to say when, once again, Hofstadter shut him down. And there was also something mentioned about a nickname, which Kuzmin seemed to find hilarious. I *think* he said it was a nickname but he didn't say what the nickname was.'

'Okay; it can wait. I'll need to go back to work on my laptop. But we're almost there.'

Weaver sat up now, and blinking sleepily saw a Londis shop, a newsagent, a Chinese takeaway that also offered fish and chips. Then a few fields, one with a scraggy horse standing desolately by a wire fence. Next a row of semi-detached houses, where Lily turned in behind a low retaining wall, its stone crumbling in places like leftover cake. Behind the wall was a sand and gravel track that ran parallel to the road, with inlets cut at right angles for the cars of each house. They drove slowly along this, bouncing and bumping with each pothole. The houses were dingy: some had curtains, some did not; all had walls coated with grey pebble dash.

Lily pulled into the parking space of the last but one. A strip of lawn was bordered by a thin line of rose bushes between the grass and the parking space. At the neighbouring house, an old tricycle sat in the doorway; the lawn there was littered with toys; a kid's plastic wheelbarrow lay tipped on its side.

As she neared the house, Lily reached in her bag for a key, but when she touched the door it swung open. 'Christ,' she exclaimed. 'How many times—'

'Must be a safe neighbourhood,' Weaver said, and she gave him a sour look. He followed her into a narrow hall that led to the sitting room. This was neat if sparsely furnished, with a long green sofa, large easy chair and a plasma screen TV against one wall. A solitary bookshelf held a line of paperbacks.

'Come on through,' said Lily, and he followed her into the

kitchen at the back. There were dirty dishes in the sink, an open box of cereal on the table. Through a large window behind the sink, he saw another strip of grass and an empty clothesline. Behind it, stretching into the distance, sat another dank and treeless field. There was a small fridge against a side wall and Lily opened it, then almost as quickly closed it, shaking her head.

There was the sound of a motorcycle, coming closer. Weaver looked at Lily, but she didn't seem alarmed, and a few moments later the front door opened and Chip came in, carrying his helmet.

'Hullo,' he said, addressing a point in the room somewhere between them. 'You've been all alone after the motorway.'

'Good,' Lily said. 'You know Weaver.'

Weaver said, 'Hey,' and Chip nodded back.

Lily said, 'Where's the taxi?'

'Parked near the office,' said Chip. He paused, then said, 'What were you thinking of for dinner?'

'Weaver, what do you want?' asked Lily. The clock on the kitchen wall said it had just turned six o'clock.

Food was the last thing on his mind. 'Anything,' Weaver said.

'There's nothing to eat here,' she said. 'Looks like takeaway to me. If you get it, Chip, I'll buy. But no pies.'

'I love pies,' Chip protested.

'And pies love you,' said Lily, nodding like a personal trainer appraising an obese client. 'But not tonight.'

'Should I go to Madame Lee's?' Chip asked.

'No,' Lily replied firmly. 'Honestly, if just once you'd let me take you to Chinatown, you wouldn't set foot in Madame Lee's again. Her sweet and sour pork is sick-making.' She paused, thinking. 'Pizza,' she announced loudly. She said to Chip, 'An extra-large one – no mushrooms. Some beers for you, and a bottle of white wine – Sauvignon.' She cast an appraising look at Weaver. 'Better make it two bottles. I'll get my wallet.'

When Chip had gone, the noise of the motorcycle tailing off outside, Weaver looked at Lily. 'What are we doing here?'

'Hiding. Best I could think of at short notice.'

'Whose house is it?'

'Chip lives here, but I own it.'

Weaver gave her a puzzled look. She said, 'He's my brother. My half-brother. We share a father, or at least the dickhead legally known as my father. Chip's mum was one of the few women my father didn't manage to marry. I told you that after my mother died, I tried to find the bastard, but I found Chip instead.'

'And what happened then?'

'He wasn't doing much of anything when I came along. He works for me now. I don't pay him a lot, but at least he's got a roof over his head.'

'Who else knows you own this place?' he asked.

'No one,' she said.

'What about JP and Sue?'

'No.'

'So did you buy this place as an investment?' he asked, sounding more dubious than he meant to.

Lily laughed. 'It's not that bad. It belonged to my mother and she left it to me. I grew up here, since I was eight years old and my father fucked off.' She was looking at him as if this should have been obvious. 'Come on, I'll show you where you'll be sleeping.'

Upstairs, the front bedroom was a tip: the bed unmade, a man's clothes (presumably Chip's) all over the floor, a pervasive odour of sweat. Lily reached around Weaver and shut the door. 'Chip will be going out later,' she said. 'Wednesday's quiz night at the pub. Sometimes he gets lucky.'

'Lucky?'

'He pulls a girl in the pub. I can't deprive him of that; the one excitement in his life. That means you're in the other room,' she said, going past the bathroom to the back. She opened a door onto a slightly smaller room – tidy, odourless, a large double bed made with a bedspread neatly laid on top, a chest of drawers, round mirror on a stand on top, a bedside table and lamp. 'You'll have to share with me.'

He looked at her, but the eyes gave nothing away. She said, 'The bed's plenty big enough, so don't get excited.'

'I won't,' he said with a studied calmness he didn't feel. 'JP's explained.'

'Explained what?'

In for a penny. 'You know, about you.'

She was looking mystified, biting her lower lip again. Weaver could not have explained why he found this so attractive, since it usually presaged an eruption of anger, but he did. He added hurriedly, 'When will Malone tell us where I'm meant to meet him?'

'Eleven o'clock tonight. He's using a clever wheeze for communicating. No phone or emails. So he's putting comments up on a site along with a location postcode. I'll find them there when the page is refreshed.'

'What site is it?'

'Quechee Gorge, of course.'

22

DINNER WAS PIZZA WITH A SALAD LILY concocted out of some lettuce she unearthed from the fridge. She had gone up and changed clothes, and now wore a pair of paint-stained cotton shorts and a grey sweatshirt that had *YALE* in bright blue letters on its front.

They sat in the sitting room with plates on their laps and watched the Channel Four news. There was no mention of the row over the impending Rome summit meeting of the USA and China, and nothing about Skip Washington.

Chip didn't say much, and ate quickly. When Lily turned off the TV, he went upstairs, then came down a few minutes later wearing a leather jacket and with his hair gelled. 'Go get 'em, tiger,' said Lily as he left.

After Chip had gone, Lily opened her laptop and sat at a rickety pine table in one corner of the room. She kept typing away while Weaver suppressed his growing irritation at his confusion; he could tell he was tired. 'Tell me,' Lily said, without turning her head to look at him, 'is this pardon a one-off thing for the President?'

'He can grant them anytime he's in office. I remember RD complaining once that someone he put away was freed by a presidential pardon. And there's always a bunch of them at the end of the President's term.'

'I've got our friend Skip here. Not clear if he's out yet.'

'Where was he serving his sentence?'

'Let me see.' While Lily checked, Weaver sat quietly, too tired even to read. What would happen next? A blur of images, like moving postcards, came to him rapid-fire: the Mercedes screeching to a halt; the drone he'd mistaken for a kite; then, out of nowhere, the image of Lily's double bed upstairs, which he struggled to keep out of his head.

'He's in some place called Atwater in California. High security,' she said, as if Skip Washington had graduated *summa cum laude*.

She was typing quickly still. 'Found it,' she suddenly said.

'What?'

'A list of "pardons and commutations" granted this weekend.'

'So there were *others*? Jesus, I hadn't even thought of that. Goddamnit. Skip Washington is the only one in the press.'

'Well, there are plenty more. Must be twenty of them. It looks like almost all the rest were convicted of white-collar offences. Sheesh,' she said, shaking her head, 'as if that doesn't count.'

'You've got the list?'

'I just found it. Hold on a second. Here we go: Aaron, Comiskey, Davis…' she read aloud while he half-listened.

When she paused, he said, 'I don't suppose there's anyone named Dan Berry?'

'Nope.'

'How about Sukolov?'

This took a little while, then she said, 'No. The only one with an "S" was serving five years in a Connect-icut prison.'

'Connecticut – you don't pronounce the second "c". You probably say Mitch-igan as well.'

'I probably do,' she said patiently. 'So Con-net-icut it is. The Danbury Federal Correction Institution. Sentence commuted by Executive Order.'

'What did you say?' He sat up, suddenly focused.

'I said a "Federal Correctional Institution".'

'No. You said "Dan Berry".'

'Are you being sniffy about my pronunciation?' Lily said defensively.

'No, no,' said Weaver impatiently, afraid of being distracted. 'Don't you see? That was what Kuzmin meant. He just didn't know how to pronounce it. Dan Berry isn't a person; it's a prison. Who is in Danbury, Connecticut?'

'The man being pardoned there is called Dennis Symons, aged forty-seven, convicted of fraud, and sentenced to five years.'

'Is there anybody else on the list doing time in Danbury?'

After a minute Lily said simply, 'No.' She paused, then said, 'So what should we do?'

Weaver realised it was the first time she rather than he had asked this. 'We could talk to my father,' he said.

'They'll be watching him now. Phone, email, text. All no go. I wish he'd go fishing again. You could call him at that bar.'

Weaver said, 'He's not going to Putah until the weekend. Should we tell Malone about it instead?'

'I don't trust Malone. But I know someone I do trust.' She stood up, her mobile in one hand. 'I just need to make a call. Maybe two. Back in a mo.'

When she came back, she was carrying a glass of wine in each hand. 'This seems to me well deserved for us both,' she said. Handing Weaver one of the glasses, she sat down along the sofa from him.

'Any luck?' he asked hopefully.

'They're working on it. They'll ring me once they've found out anything.'

They? He was about to ask when she said, 'Do you want the television on?'

'Not unless you do.'

'No. Let's just talk. You don't have to pretend to listen, provided you let me do the same.'

He tried to laugh but was overtaken by a yawn. Lily said, 'You must be tired.'

'All that running.'

'You did well.'

'I didn't do anything. Thank God that cab came along.'

'I'm not sure God had much to do with it.' There was a hint of a smirk on her face.

'How's that?' He stared at her.

'Think about it.' Her smirk grew more pronounced.

How slow he was being. 'Don't tell me; it was Chip. He blocked the Mercedes.'

'Yes, it was Chip; he's canny on the streets. But you could sound happier about it,' she said, and she was smiling openly now.

'I was too busy running to notice the driver.'

Lily was sitting up. 'We should cut your hair now. Come on.'

Reluctantly, Weaver followed her back to the kitchen, where she brought out a high stool, with a soft vinyl seat and chrome legs, not unlike the one Weaver's father liked sitting on in the Steelhead Grill. Taking a tablecloth from a drawer by the sink, Lily shook it out and tucked it around the now-seated Weaver, then turned down the collar of his shirt. A large pair of thin-pointed steel scissors had materialised; she held the blades open and poised above one of his ears, ready to start.

'Aren't you going to ask me how I want it cut?' he asked.

'No,' she said simply.

She started in then, focusing quietly on the task at hand, from time to time standing back to examine her work. Without a mirror, Weaver didn't have a clue how much hair she was taking off, or how adroitly; taking his cue from Lily, he didn't ask.

The silence didn't last, though by tacit agreement their conversation was unrelated to what had brought them here: being on the run. Instead, Lily made small talk, like a local barber, the kind who knew the previous night's baseball scores and the name of the town's oldest citizen. Gradually the tenor of her chatter changed from patter to probing.

How did he get into the interpreter game? He explained he'd lucked out in New York when he'd been accepted for the training programme at the State Department. Two years of low-paid slog followed, supplemented by tutoring rich high school kids, teaching them French and sometimes Russian to beef up their

CVs for college applications. The kids were usually diligent, well-mannered and often very nice; the parents were demanding and occasionally unpleasant, especially as the admissions deadline neared.

Did he go to Russia often? No. He had visited as a graduate student, but except for three days a couple of years back (another dire trade conference, held in St Petersburg) he had not been back. And of course, now he couldn't go. Not that he missed it.

Was it that grim? Yes, and then some.

What about fishing? What about it? He did it as often as he could – more now, since he had no wife to complain he wasn't around on weekends.

Did he keep the fish he caught? Not so much anymore, and he only kept fish he would eat himself.

Then, oddly, *What do you think about when you're fishing?* Nothing about himself. Absolutely nothing. That was the beauty of it. What did that poem say – 'In a field / I am the absence / of field.' Perfect. In rivers, Weaver sometimes felt in some sublime way that he had left his personality behind on the bank.

His answers grew shorter as the questions continued. He realised he had already relayed most of the information they contained. It struck him, as the questions continued, that Lily was not really looking to learn more about him, but rather testing him for consistency. Which meant she still doubted him.

He had a question of his own. 'Tell me something,' he said as Lily stepped back again, this time to admire her handiwork. 'If Mrs Golubova wanted to find out where I was staying, how did she know where I'd be?'

'Who knew you were going to Mayfair?' she asked.

'Ragoulin, of course. But why would he cooperate with the SVR or whoever it is? He's made his career doing business with exiles, people who hate the regime.'

'Which regime? I've never heard he's had any problems, whoever was in power.'

'I didn't realise you know him.' How had she neglected to mention this?

'I don't. I know *of* him.'

'How?'

He watched her closely, but she was concentrating on his hair. 'I better take some more off. How did *you* meet him in the first place?'

Weaver sat back against the tubular back of the chair and started telling Lily about it, a little hesitantly, since she was still trimming the hair on both sides of his head with a certainty and speed that were slightly alarming.

When he'd finished the history of his friendship with Ragoulin, Lily asked quietly, 'How does Ragoulin know Tomic?'

'I've wondered that myself. Not through me.'

She nodded, apparently satisfied. 'Done,' she announced, and untied the tablecloth from around his neck. 'Next time I'll do your eyebrows.'

He liked the 'next time'. 'Where did you learn to cut hair?'

'Right here.'

'But who taught you?'

'Mum.' She ruffled his hair above one ear. 'You asked how my mother made her living. This is how.'

'Cutting hair.'

'You betcha,' she said like a native of Kansas City. 'I always liked the way Americans say that. Anyway, Mum had a little salon in the precinct of shops down the road. Right next to Madame Lee. I don't know what was stronger, the smell of shampoo or next door's beef with black bean sauce. Once Madame Lee added fish and chips to her takeaway menu, she won the battle of aromas.' She was smiling at the memory, but there was nothing saccharine in her voice.

'Your mother taught you then?'

'From the age of eight. My mother also made curtains – posh ones for rich people when business was good; cheap ones for the neighbours when it wasn't. I knew how to make interlined drapes when I was ten. The plan was that once I left school, I would join her in the salon and help with the curtains. Paris put the kibosh on both.'

'Your mother must have been upset.'

'She never said. She lent me money for the fare; it took me six months to pay her back.' She paused, holding the scissors up in the air. 'If I'd stayed here, I'd be running the salon on my own now. What would my life be like? I wonder.'

'Can't see it myself. You seem a natural city girl.'

'Maybe, but we all have fantasies of alternative lives, don't we? I don't mean wishful ones – you know, what I'd do if I won the lottery – I mean the lives we've left behind: what would have happened if we'd stayed. That's what it sounds like when you talk about Vermont. What would have happened if you'd stayed?'

He shrugged. 'These days Orvis have their own guides. With luck they'd have taken me on. You don't get rich but you do get an awful lot of fishing in.'

Lily poured them each another glass of wine, finishing the bottle, and they retreated to the living room, where *Newsnight* was just beginning. This time there was a story on the coming summit between the US and China. Lily kept looking at her watch, and when Weaver checked his phone, he saw it was almost eleven o'clock.

Before he could say anything, Lily stood up and left the room. A minute later, he heard her moving around upstairs. When she came back, she picked up her laptop and sat in the corner, where a table was jammed against the wall, covered by a jumble of motorcycle magazines. While she went online, he walked into the kitchen and washed the few dishes they'd used, leaving them in a rack next to the sink to dry. He had just finished when Lily called, 'We're all set.'

In the living room she was looking at her screen. 'I found the reference, buried among a bunch of comments that anyone will find entirely innocent.' She said, in a fairly decent imitation of a Midwestern accent, '*Can anybody help? I'm going to Europe this summer and am spending a couple of days in London and Paris. Everybody says they both have beautiful parks. Can anybody recommend some? I don't know where to begin!'*

She said in her natural voice, 'Twelve people answered. One answer was meant for us.'

'How do you know that?'

'Malone said it would have a postcode in the middle of the description, and sure enough, there is. SE21 7BQ. We're meeting in a park.'

She came over to the sofa and collected their glasses, lifting hers first and finishing her wine.

'Time for bed,' she announced. 'We're meeting him at noon, but we're going to have to make an early start.'

'You running first?' he asked, only slightly facetiously.

She shook her head. 'We need to stop and get you some clothes. You don't want to wear the same gear tomorrow.' She made a face.

'No, I don't,' he said.

'I can sort that out,' Lily said firmly. 'Let's go up and I'll find you something to wear for bed. Leave the light on here so Chip doesn't fall over the furniture and break his neck. Or the neck of some girl he brings home.'

23

HE WAS ALONE, STRETCHED OUT ON THE window side of the bed in his boxer shorts and a motorcycle T-shirt of Chip's which Lily had unearthed. Having changed in the bathroom, he came out to find Lily changed as well. She wore a pale lilac wool robe; it was a size too big and stretched down well below her knees. Lily pulled the curtains and turned on her bedside lamp, but then went downstairs.

She returned after a few minutes and got into her side of the bed, drawing the covers up. 'I've had a call while I was downstairs. Dennis Symons was a prisoner in the Danbury Correctional Institute, serving three to five years for mail order fraud – though I bet it was some cyber scam, since all of it seems to be online these days.'

'He *was* a prisoner?'

'Released yesterday. He went straight to Manhattan, where he's currently staying in a hotel, after serving only three months.'

'What's his link to Hofstadter or the President?'

'Not clear, and the link may be to something else altogether. The suspicion is that Dennis Symons might not have been his birth name.'

Weaver said, 'Are you thinking what I think you're thinking?'

'I hope so. You tell first.'

'Kuzmin was about to give the "American name" of the guy they were talking about. Hofstadter cut him off and basically told him to shut up. That's because I was there. But I think it must be the same guy Kuzmin had already mentioned – only by his Russian name. And that was "Sukolov".'

'AKA Dan Berry, or should I say Dennis Symons?' she asked with a smile.

'Exactly. But does the FBI know any of this? Hofstadter may be keeping them out of the loop, but presumably the British don't know that.'

'They've talked to the Bureau, which is how we know that Symons is out and now in New York. But they haven't said they believe Symons could be a Russian plant. Or have the birth name of "Sukolov". And I think it would be better not to mention it to Malone when you see him.'

'Why's that?' he asked, trying to focus on her point. He was starting to feel oddly light-headed.

'Because we don't know for sure that Malone will want to help. After all, the FBI are deliberately being kept out of things in the States; I'm sure he's worried what would happen to him if he were on our side.'

'Does that mean there's a chance I'll find a dozen Secret Service waiting for me tomorrow, ready to hand me over to the police here?'

Lily was shaking her head. 'I don't think so. They wouldn't have any jurisdiction over here, so they wouldn't dare abduct you – this isn't Afghanistan. And the Brits have nothing to charge you with, whatever the *Evening Standard* would like to suggest. Anyway, for now Malone's our only way in with the American authorities. But I'd definitely leave Dennis Symons, or whatever his name used to be, out of whatever you tell Malone. I'll be back,' she said and went downstairs again.

When she returned, he sensed from her sombre look that she wasn't going to tell him who she had been talking with. She got back into the bed, still wearing her robe. 'I was going to make Ovaltine. But there isn't any milk, thanks to Chip. When I'm here I do a big shop; when it runs out, he just waits until I'm here again.'

'It's okay.' He was getting used to her making small talk in tense situations. It was a stress reduction technique he was increasingly seeing the point of.

'I thought hot milk would help you sleep,' she said. 'Though that shouldn't be a problem after the day you've had.'

'Yours was not exactly inactive. What else did you think of Malone? Did he flirt with you?'

'Believe it or not, he did. Even over the phone. He wants to have dinner with me. Jesus.'

'You should have explained you don't like men.'

'I… don't… like men,' she said slowly, quizzically. 'Who told you that?'

'It doesn't matter. It's not as if it's any of my business.'

'No, it isn't. But it's true enough.'

Weaver was feeling a little apprehensive. 'Okay,' he said.

Lily said, 'When I was twelve, I let Rebecca Akers kiss me on the lips.'

'Oh,' said Weaver, trying to sound indifferent. Was he going to have to hear the whole Sapphic history?

'That was my first taste.' She waited, relishing the pause. 'And my last.'

Weaver said, 'Oh,' again, this time with some relief. 'That's all?'

'Afraid so. Sorry to disappoint you. And anyway, what if I had been gay?'

'That would have been fine.' This sounded bogus even to Weaver.

She looked at him and laughed, that fine high chord, so at odds with the smoky tones of her speaking voice. It sounded joyous now. 'I like that,' she said, shuffling her legs under the bedclothes. 'Even if deep at heart you're an unreconstructed pig like the rest of them.'

He ignored the insult, largely because he thought it might be true. Lily reached out her hand to the bedside table and let it hover near the lamp switch. 'You ready?'

'Ready for what?' he asked, just as she turned off the light.

In the darkness, his question hung over them unanswered, and Weaver tensed, lying on his back. Lily said, her voice awkward and rising, 'I meant ready to turn off the light.'

'Don't sound so concerned. I know you're not interested.'

'If you say so.'

This sounded hopeful, or was he desperately looking for anything to keep hope alive? Then she added, 'Sweet dreams.'

Conscious it would sound like a schoolboy's ploy, Weaver nonetheless found himself saying, 'Goodnight kiss?'

'Not a chance. But cheer up; you can kiss me in your dreams.'

'All right,' he said, slightly stung. 'Sleep well. And thanks again for your help. Don't object; I haven't said it for at least eight hours.'

Lily laughed and he sensed her turning onto her side, towards him. 'Okay,' she said in a whisper. 'One kiss.'

He forced himself to turn slowly, then used his bent arm as a prop to raise himself. He leaned over, telling himself to kiss her only once, and that on the cheek if it was clear that's where she wanted to be kissed, then to return promptly to his side of the bed. But as he leant down, he found her arm reaching around his shoulder, bringing him down where she met his kiss with full lips that opened.

He whispered, 'Lily.'

'You don't have to say anything,' she said.

So he kissed her again. Before he could do anything further, Lily started to shudder. Her arms and shoulders shook spasmodically. When he reached his hand out to caress her cheek, it was wet. Wet with tears.

'What's wrong?' he asked as gently as he could.

She shook again, and turned over, her back to him as she began to cry harder. Quietly but uncontrollably. He put his arm around her and with his other hand stroked her hair, saying nothing.

Lily cried for what seemed a long time, then suddenly stopped. She rose and swung her legs out of the bed and sat with both feet on the floor. Turning on the bedside lamp, she wiped her eyes with one hand. Taking a tissue from a box on the night table, she blew her nose.

'Sorry about that,' she said, sniffing and turning to look at Weaver. 'I never cry. I did when I discovered my father was dead, but that was out of frustration – it meant I couldn't kill him myself.' She smiled weakly and Weaver smiled back. She said, 'I am sorry, Weaver; I wasn't trying to lead you on.'

'You're allowed to change your mind.'

She shook her head as if to clear her thoughts, then said, 'I'm not sure why I thought I wanted to do this.'

'Maybe you did want to,' he suggested.

'Possibly,' she admitted. 'You seem such a nice guy. You have the kinds of problems women think they can solve. In your case, I probably could.' Lily smiled knowingly. 'You're very attractive and I get such a charge just *talking* to you that… Usually saying no is a lot easier to do.'

Weaver wondered if this was supposed to make him feel better. Lily went on: 'Anyway, it's probably just as well. You might be back in New York next week.'

'Or six feet under.'

'Don't say that.' Her voice was sharp. 'Anyway, it would just be a one-night stand. That's not ideal at our age.'

'Let's hope it would be at least a *two*-night stand.'

She laughed, if a little dutifully, and wiped her eyes again. 'Now that we're getting all confessional,' she said, 'you should know that I come with a lot of baggage, Weaver.'

'That's all right; I'm not exactly duty free.' He watched her carefully, having learned her face sometimes told him more than her words. 'But do you always say no?'

'Since…' Then she decided to say only, 'Yes.'

'Since Tolya?'

'How do you know his name?'

'Chip mentioned him. Is he the guy in the photograph? On the bedside table in your London place?'

She nodded.

'Do you want to tell me about him?'

Lily didn't say anything. She was staring at the end of the bed. Weaver asked quietly, 'Did he let you down?'

'You could say that.'

'I'm sorry. Where is he now?'

Lily looked up at Weaver. 'He's dead.'

Sorry would sound helpless. 'When was that?'

'Almost five years ago.'

'Was he sick?'

'No.'

She didn't explain and he wanted to keep her talking. 'Did he die here in the UK?' he asked.

'No. In Russia. Tolya was Russian, as you must have guessed, but came here as a teenager with his parents. After Berezovsky died, he was lured back by the Russian government – and promptly arrested. The charges against him were trumped up – corruption, the usual thing – but he was found guilty and given two years. Enough of a sentence that observers would think he really had done something wrong, but short enough not to attract attention from the likes of Amnesty, who had bigger fish to fight for.

'Ten days before he was due to be released, he was stabbed to death. The authorities claimed he'd had an argument with another inmate. They couldn't even tell the family who the other inmate was.'

'Were his parents still alive?'

'Yes, but that didn't help to find out what really happened. Tolya's father was himself already on shaky ground with the Russian authorities; even before Tolya went back to Russia, he was worried about his dad. The old man couldn't investigate after Tolya died, and neither could I. They wouldn't even let me into the country. As for his mother—'

'Heartbroken?'

'Maybe she was. She divorced the father a year after Tolya was murdered. I gather she lives in Gstaad now.' She thought for a moment. 'We never got on. Then it turned out Tolya had made a will, leaving me Leonard Street free and clear. And also the little cash he had in Russia, which I can't collect, of course.' She laughed sourly. 'His mother said Tolya might as well have left it to Ho Chi Minh. She hates me.'

She pursed her lips and looked down at her knees, started slowly to stand up but then sat down again. 'There's something else you should know.'

He said simply, 'Oh,' trying to sound neutral rather than wary.

Lily sensed his tension. 'Relax,' she said. 'I haven't got another brother who's confined to Broadmoor, and no, I've never slept with JP.' She made such a convincing retching noise that he laughed out loud. Then she said, 'Try and keep laughing, will you?' she said. 'You see, when I was in Paris...'

She hesitated; he wondered what would come next. That she'd been the mistress of her mentor Mr Boyd after all? *Quelle surprise*; he could certainly cope with that.

'I worked for MI6.'

'Oh,' he said, not because he was surprised to learn this but because she was saying so.

'At first I was a translator like I told you, but then they had me helping run agents in the field. But they wouldn't make me an officer.' She seemed to wait then for his reaction, which he wasn't sure of himself. Had he not thought this at various points along the frenetic progress of the last six days? Yes, but he felt shaken nonetheless. Why hadn't she told him?

'You ran agents?' he asked, surprised.

'Yes. Why not?' She sounded prickly.

'I just meant you were awfully young to be doing that,' he said.

'Boyd said that too. I wasn't working for him though, not directly.'

'Mr Boyd, you mean,' he said, and was glad when she smiled. 'For how long did you do this?'

'Five years. And two months. Then I had had enough, and my mother died. Other way round, actually. Mum died and I realised I'd had enough. When I came back to England, I said I wanted a proper job in the Foreign Office; enough of the spying business. But it soon became clear that this wasn't a serious possibility. I had more chance of becoming a bloody astronaut than a career FO employee.'

'What was the problem?'

'This was before diversity arrived, and I doubt they were thrilled by the prospect of a part-Vietnamese woman entering the corridors of Whitehall. But to be fair, I think the real issue was my education; it was too "unorthodox" – that means "woeful" in diplomat speak – for me to be considered even an entry-level candidate. Auditing some courses at a foreign business school didn't stack up very well against candidates with Firsts from Oxbridge. I met a few of them; they were clever clogs all right, with all the confidence in the world. All I had was experience.'

'So what happened?'

'I got myself a normal job, with an interior decorator on the King's Road. Back to curtains, I guess you'd say. That's how I met Tolya. His mother came in with him one day to return some fabric she'd decided was not to her oh-so-refined taste, and she was so fucking rude to me that Tolya came back at closing to apologise for her behaviour. And to ask me out,' she added with the hint of a smile. 'I stayed well clear of Whitehall – and Vauxhall. I didn't even see Boyd when he was posted back here. I don't think I was missed.'

'I sense a "but" coming along.'

She nodded. 'Once I started going out with Tolya, they decided they missed me after all. He was the object of occasional surveillance by MI5 and Special Branch; no difference when it comes to it. A watcher must have seen me with Tolya then, and discovered who I was. Anyway, MI5 needed someone to infiltrate the Russian community in London, and MI6 reckoned I was in the perfect position to help their brothers across the river.'

She said this angrily, almost proudly. Did she really think consorting with a junior oligarch was the equivalent of possessing more traditional credentials? But then, Weaver supposed, in the eyes of MI5 it probably was. Instead of a green kid who had to be taught the ropes, here was a street-smart clever young woman who had shown her mettle in action already, and through her boyfriend was now at the heart of a community – the oligarchs – normally closed to the prying eyes of Western intelligence. The masters at Vauxhall must have thought their ship had come home.

Except she wouldn't play ball. Lily was adamant. She told Weaver she wouldn't even have 'the conversation'. She left their phone calls unanswered and messages unread; the one foolhardy soul who had the temerity to approach her in person had received a sharp slap for his pains.

'I wouldn't help them. I wanted my own life, or at least the life I chose, not somebody else's choice for me. And I never told Tolya they'd approached me.'

She shrugged, then stood up. 'Time for bed. I know I said that once before.'

She came and got under the covers. Weaver remained lying on his back. There was nothing he felt he could say.

Then Lily said, her voice a half-whisper again, 'Would you hold me? You know, without…'

'Sure,' he said. 'One order of "holding without", coming right up.' And he turned as Lily shuffled across the middle of the bed and snuggled up to him. He put his arm around her, and semi-entwined, they lay together in silence. After a few minutes, he realised Lily was asleep.

When Lily's mobile phone emitted a faint burr, Weaver himself was asleep, if only just. The clock radio next to Lily's side of the bed said 4:16. She must have been a light sleeper, for she sat up right away in the dark to reach for her phone.

A voice barked at the other end, loud enough for Weaver to hear: 'Is he there?'

'Who is this?' Lily asked. She sounded remarkably unflustered.

'It's Mac. You talked to me the other day. Please get me Weaver.'

'Hold on,' she said, and turned on the bedside lamp, then handed Weaver the phone.

'Mac?' asked Weaver tentatively.

'He's dead,' the voice shouted, then seemed to falter. Weaver realised his friend was sobbing.

'Who's dead?' *It must be Peter,* he thought, but what had happened?

Mac said now, 'I know they killed him. I know it.'

'Slow down, Mac. Tell me what's happened.'

'We went for a walk. Down to Gramercy Park; he loved it there.'

This was news to Weaver. Mac continued, 'Then over to East River Greenway. He liked running there sometimes; you know, along the river.' He started crying again and Weaver waited, mystified. Mac managed to stifle his sobs enough to speak. 'He went off on his own, but I thought I could find him.'

'Okay,' said Weaver, baffled. 'Did you?'

'No,' Mac said; he sounded wobbly. 'A fisherman did.'

None of this was making a lot of sense. Best to ask, Weaver decided. 'Where, Mac?'

'In the water, by the river bank.' Mac was only sniffling now. 'He couldn't have been there long.'

Jesus. 'How did Peter end up there?' he asked, as gently as he could.

There was a long silence, and Weaver sensed he had said the wrong thing. Mac said, 'Peter? What the fuck has it got to do with Peter?' His voice was rising now, and scathing. 'Peter didn't even *like* Parker.'

'Okay—' Weaver started to say, and then he stopped as he understood. Peter wasn't dead; Parker was.

He felt a stab of terrible sadness. Parker had been the one sweet note in the terrible dissonance of Weaver's New York life. A puppy when brought to the city from Vermont, Parker had been as happy in Central Park as in the Green Mountains. He had made the adjustment to urban life much better than Weaver had.

Lily was sitting up now, watching him. He smiled thinly, trying to reassure her. She'd slipped her robe back on but it was open below the neck. He noticed, with the pointless observational power that follows a shock, that she had a tiny mole at the base of her throat, where it sat like a dark miniature pearl.

Mac said, 'I tell you, they killed him.'

Weaver said, 'I'm sorry about Parker, sorrier than I can say. But why do you think somebody killed him? Who would do that?'

'The White House, Weaver. Whatever you've done, it's the White House people behind this, and the Secret Service is doing their bidding. They're all acting crazier than an outhouse fly. You should see Pauline – she used to look down her nose whenever the Service guys came round. Now she's scared to death of them.'

'But why would they hurt Parker?'

'To get at me.'

'Really?' Weaver said. He had never seen Mac paranoid before.

Mac said impatiently, 'Listen, I've been questioned *six* times in the last two days. Once by that slimebag Blanchett, and five times by the Secret Service bullies. They've emailed me and texted me and messaged me – there was even a note slipped under the door to the apartment. All they keep asking is, *where is Weaver?* They know you're in England but they don't know where.' Mac exhaled, then continued, his voice hoarse but still charged: 'I have to be honest with you: these guys can wear you down. I wish I had told them where you were. I wish I'd *known* where you are.' He paused, but only briefly. 'So where are you, Weaver?'

'Come on,' he said, and was grateful for the silence that followed, suggesting Mac wouldn't press the point. And after a moment, Mac said quietly, 'It's too late anyway.'

'I find it hard to believe they'd kill Parker to get at you, Mac.'

'You think so?' Mac demanded loudly. 'He drowned.'

Enough, thought Weaver. 'Mac, Parker could swim; all dogs can. He must have had a heart attack. The East River is freezing, even at this time of year.'

'I'm telling you, they drowned him.'

'How can you be so sure?'

He could hear his friend exhale; it sounded peculiarly hopeless. Then Mac said, 'His legs were chained together when they threw him in.'

24

L ILY HAD GIVEN HIM A FIVER, WHICH meant the old man sitting in the ornate ticket hut handed over a pound in change. Seated in the middle of the rowboat, Weaver lifted the oars over the gunwales and let them down into the water. He hoped he would be getting his money's worth.

It had taken some time to get there. Half an hour after leaving the house, they stopped in Slough, where Lily said she'd wait in the Golf while Weaver went into Marks & Spencer to buy clothes for the day. Just as he'd picked out a shirt, button-down with thin blue stripes, Lily appeared at his side, surveyed his selection, and nodded her approval. She baulked at his choice of sweater, however, and persuaded him to put back the fine maroon one he liked in favour of a staider navy blue. About trousers he stood firm, and bought a standard pair of chinos, and while Lily went back to the car, he paid for the entire haul with cash she had loaned him. Ignoring the female attendant's curious look, he went post-purchase into a changing stall to put on the new clothes.

From Slough, their route seemed completely counterintuitive; each suggestion of the GPS designed to speed their journey drew a different response from Lily. They went south on minor roads, all the way down to Weybridge, land of nouveaux mansions set behind camera-guarded gates and adjoined by many wooded golf courses.

He noticed Lily was no longer looking at the GPS screen. 'You know these parts?'

She nodded, grimly. After a minute she said, 'Tolya's parents' old house is just the other side of that golf course.' She gestured towards a fairway on their right.

'I never used to think of England as wealthy,' he said, thinking it best to keep clear of the subject of Tolya. 'But Westchester County has nothing on this.'

'Most of the money here is foreign.'

'Russians still?' Not every oligarch was being sanctioned.

She nodded, braking as they came to a rare stop light. 'Just a few. But lots of Chinese.'

After this, their voyage became a blur of anonymous conurbations on the far reaches of London, with the sudden intrusion of familiar names: Legoland; Hampton Court; then through Richmond Park, where they had to wait several minutes for a herd of fallow deer to move off the road. They skirted Wimbledon and moved east on an array of little streets into south London, passing through an old-fashioned toll gate of all things, past yet another golf course (this one relatively tree-less), down a hill and through massive iron gates into a park.

Lily drove into it along a broad avenue lined by pedestrian walkways and large oaks, then turned around, reversing direction, watching her rear mirror the whole time. Near the entrance there were lots of free parking spaces, and Lily circled so they faced the interior of the park, then pulled into one and switched off the engine. She said, 'This is where we part company. Malone said you're to go up to the lake,' she pointed to where the park's main road split in two, 'and hire one of the boats. He'll take it from there.'

'That's all he said?' He was feeling uneasy.

'If there's a problem or no one shows, text me.'

'You'll wait here?' It seemed important to know.

'A single woman sitting alone in a car is not a good look. We really don't want to attract any attention – to me or the car. I'll be in the gallery across the main road, refining my aesthetic sense. Or more likely, sitting in the café.'

'Okay,' he said at last, trying to focus.

'Weaver, I'm glad it's okay. But you have to go. I managed to get you here bang on time; don't spoil it now by being late.'

He nodded, and this time got out of the car and started walking. He wondered what was troubling him exactly. Did he want Lily to come with him? Was he worried she wouldn't be there once he was through? He didn't know, and it would take more than a CBT exercise to relieve his festering anxiety. He looked back at the car once and saw Lily in the driver's seat, watching him as she talked on her phone.

Now as he reached for the chain that tethered the little boat to the dock, an American voice said, 'Got room for a passenger, buddy? I paid for a seat.'

Weaver looked up and saw the shoes first: black brogues, highly polished. He took in the rest of the man, a tall figure standing on the wooden dock. It was Malone.

'Bill,' Weaver said. 'Come aboard.'

Malone was a good six foot three, as tall and gaunt as Weaver remembered from years ago. He was skinny, almost skeletal, and bore a resemblance, often commented upon, to the actor Peter O'Toole. Though Malone's face, once handsomely chiselled and the setting for startling aquamarine eyes, was now asymmetrical and a bit beat up – the result of advancing age, perhaps, and the legacy of a youthful taste for brawling. He wore a dark blue suit with loose-fitting shoulders, the once-standard white shirt, and a nondescript dark tie with the knot pulled down below his prominent Adam's apple.

Malone now clambered awkwardly into the stern of the boat, sitting on its plank seat to face Weaver. 'Well, this is a treat, getting rowed around by Bob Fontana's boy. Your old man always made me do the rowing.'

'Same here.'

'You seen him lately?'

'A year ago. We fished Putah Creek.'

'Any luck?'

'Yes. All mine,' Weaver said, grinning. He was not a very competitive fisherman, but he knew Malone was, especially with his father.

Malone pushed them off from the dock. Though the little lake was completely still, they were very low in the water, and Weaver pulled lightly on the oars. 'Where am I heading?'

'There's an island right behind you. We should go to the far side and talk there.'

As they neared the island, Weaver rowed around one side of it, then followed Malone's instruction and pulled into a little backwater pool, tucked between two promontories that were thick with bushes. There they sat in the motionless boat, blocked from view by the little island on one side and the bushes of the promontories on the other.

Weaver looked at Malone, thinking the venue for this meeting seemed faintly ludicrous. Malone seemed to sense this. 'I'm sorry for all the palaver, but I can't have it known I'm seeing you. How did you travel here?'

'I had a chauffeur. You talked to her yesterday.'

'Where is she now?'

'In the gallery across the road. I'll text her when we're done. She won't bother us. Tell me, how did *you* get here?'

Malone looked slightly piqued to have the same question asked of him. He said, 'I drove. Alone.'

'Well, thanks for seeing me. My old man didn't seem sure what part the Bureau was playing in this problem of mine.'

'The Secret Service are running the case – without the Bureau.' Malone paused briefly, then explained: 'The Service haven't got the right people stationed here; that's why I've been asked to help. Otherwise the Bureau have been told to stay out of it. Orders from Hank Hofstadter, the White House Chief of Staff.'

As well as orders to find me, thought Weaver. He said, 'What does your director make of that?'

Malone gave an awkward shrug. Weaver realised his father was right: the FBI Director didn't think anything – because he didn't know about it. Weaver asked, 'Had you come across Hofstadter before this came up?'

He had, according to his father, but Weaver wanted to test him for the truth. Malone hesitated, almost painfully, then said, 'Yes.' And clearly wanted to leave it at that.

But sensing an opening, Weaver asked, 'My father mentioned him. Hofstadter was in California before the White House, wasn't he?'

'Yes,' said Malone slowly. He said carefully, 'That was well before your father became SAC, and before Hofstadter came to anybody's attention. I don't believe your father would have known him.'

'Really? My old man said Hofstadter had a funny nickname. Is that right?'

'Why do you ask?' Malone was staring at Weaver.

He ignored the question. 'Dad said it was something Polish. But he couldn't remember what it was.'

'Something Polish?' Malone said and gave a loud derisory laugh. It reminded Weaver of Kuzmin's glee, while Hofstadter sat silent, the expression on his face alternating between embarrassment and impotent resentment. Malone went on: 'I'll say it is. Polanski's what they called him back then.' He seemed to expect Weaver to join him in laughing, and when Weaver did not react, Malone's tone changed. He said brusquely, 'Nothing to do with me. Don't go tarring me with that brush, you understand?' It was not really a question; more a command.

'Okay, okay,' said Weaver, taken aback by Malone's vehemence.

Malone seemed to calm down. He said, 'Your friend who called me yesterday, what exactly does she do?'

'For a living, you mean?' Malone gave a small nod, and Weaver explained, 'She helps new companies keep their heads when their venture money comes through. I'm not sure if there's a job title for it.'

'No, there wouldn't be,' Malone said. 'She sure seemed worried about you.' Weaver shrugged and Malone went on, 'I called your dad but he said he didn't know where you were.'

'True.' Weaver told himself that it was true at the time Malone called his father.

'Do you know why the Service people are looking for you?'

'No.' Of course, he had a pretty good idea, but since Malone hadn't shown his cards, Weaver thought it best to hide his own.

Malone trailed a cupped hand in the water. 'The White House is convinced you're trying to become some kind of Snowden.' He paused and looked directly at Weaver. 'Are you?'

'Of course not.' He could hardly be accused of leaking a secret without some indication given by the White House of what the secret was. And that was the one thing Hofstadter wouldn't want to do.

'Well then, I guess you can explain this for me.' Malone reached into his jacket with his dry hand and came out with a small envelope which he handed to Weaver.

Inside it, Weaver found three photographs, CCTV extracts from the look of them; slightly grainy. They had time and date stamps in their upper corner.

The first showed Weaver ascending the front steps of a large pale yellow ochre house. The Banker's Swedish pile. He remembered noticing a CCTV camera fixed to the exterior wall above the front door.

He was alone in the photograph, and he also remembered how Blanchett had speeded ahead of him when they got out of the chauffeured car. The time said 15:12.

The second photo, which recorded the time as 15:17, showed Kuzmin and his Russian henchman along with a third and unknown man – Galkin perhaps? – entering the house.

He looked finally at the third photo. It said 15:44, which seemed about right, since it showed Weaver on his own again, but this time getting into the Mercedes saloon in the turnaround at the rear of the Banker's house, where there must have been another camera installed.

'Doesn't look great,' said Malone flatly.

'Why's that? What are they supposed to show?'

'That you had a secret rendezvous with a Russian general, to whom you gave classified information.'

'You're kidding. What secrets does a mid-level interpreter have? For Christ's sake.'

'Why else were you meeting with the General? Don't tell me you were giving him English lessons.'

Weaver weighed up how much he should tell Malone. Lily had counselled caution, but as Weaver had found when dealing with Lily herself, sometimes you could be too cautious – and get exactly nowhere. And he didn't see how he could leave the charge of treason unanswered if he wanted help from Malone. Weaver said, 'I met with General Kuzmin all right. But what the pictures don't show is who else was there.'

'Go on.'

'I was the interpreter at a meeting between Hank Hofstadter and General Kuzmin last week. I heard everything they discussed. And I was the only other person in the room.'

'Hofstadter? Meeting with a Russian general?' Malone looked sceptical. Whatever his orders, he clearly hadn't been fully briefed.

'Yes.'

'Okay,' Malone said mildly, digesting this. 'What did they say that's got everybody so excited?'

'Kuzmin talked about a loan; he used it as a threat. I didn't understand it then.'

'Do you now?'

'I think so.' And Weaver explained what Lily had discovered – the loan to Hoftstadter and its origins in Morozov and Moscow. Weaver tried to keep this brief, and concluded his account simply: 'So far, so Russian. They'd helped a maverick politico – Hofstadter – and figured one day he might be in a position to help them in turn. They didn't know he'd become the White House Chief of Staff. That was a lucky bonus.' He looked at Malone hopefully. 'Does that all make sense?'

Malone nodded. 'Go on.'

'The middleman who handled the loan is named Galkin. I gather he's well known in financial circles.'

Malone laughed. 'You can say that again. In theory, he and his bank are independent, but believe me, he doesn't take a breath without Moscow's okay. He's been known to act as Morozov's personal banker, though God knows Morozov doesn't need to borrow any money.'

Weaver nodded. 'That explains why in the meeting Kuzmin actually said the ultimate approver of the loan wasn't Galkin, but Morozov.'

Malone sat still in the boat, as Weaver watched a dragonfly settle on some nearby reeds. 'It's a good story,' Malone finally said.

'It's a true one,' Weaver said forcefully. He exhaled, realising as he did that his vulnerability was even greater than he'd thought. 'I didn't even realise what I knew until they came after me.'

Malone stretched a long leg out and scratched his knee thoughtfully. 'But without any evidence from you, why should Hofstadter be worried? He must think you have proof somehow.' He let the implication hang like smoke in the air.

'Seems so,' said Weaver, deliberately casual.

'I mean, other than your say-so. Real evidence.' Malone was staring directly at Weaver, his eyes unnaturally blue in the bright light. 'So do you?'

Weaver hesitated. He was suddenly certain that Malone wasn't there to help him; Malone was there to find out what Weaver knew – and, more importantly, what Weaver could *prove* he knew.

'No. No evidence,' Weaver said firmly. 'Except what's in my head.' His phone juddered in his jacket pocket but he ignored it; it had to be Lily. 'You see, I have a word-for-word power of recall.' His voice had lightened, for he was trying to sound boastful, geekily proud of this extraordinary gift. He added, 'It's like a photographic memory, only for the spoken word.'

'That's remarkable,' Malone said, though he didn't actually sound impressed. 'But if this memory of yours is all you got,'

Malone went on, relaxed now that he'd apparently decided Weaver had nothing tangible in the way of evidence, 'then I would strongly advise you to go back to New York and keep your mouth completely shut.'

So Malone really was there on Hofstadter's behalf. He was happy to show disdain for the Chief of Staff if it won him Weaver's confidence – and it almost had. Weaver wondered how Hofstadter or one of his minions would have worked on Malone to get him to moonlight in this role. They must have threatened his pension. Or else Weaver's father had been right and Hofstadter had a pre-existing hold over Malone.

The older man looked sideways at the water, his blue eyes narrowing as he squinted against the sun. He said, without a trace of menace, almost musingly, 'That should take care of things as far as you're concerned. Of course, Russians being Russians, they may kill you anyway.'

The ensuing chilly silence seemed endless to Weaver, but was suddenly broken by Lily's appearance on the nearest promontory. Waving frantically, she was shouting: 'I have to go. I have to go.'

'Coming,' Weaver shouted back. He looked at Malone. 'Something's happened,' he said, and before Malone could object, started rowing quickly to the miniature peninsula where Lily stood. When the rowboat ran aground in the soft mud, Weaver put the oars in and stepped into the shallows. The water soaked his trousers to the knee.

Lily was waiting on the bank above him. She looked flustered. 'It's Chip,' she said, now breathless. 'He's been in a fight. I've got to go.'

'Hold on a minute, kid,' Malone said. 'We're not through.'

'We are for now,' said Weaver decisively. 'I'll call you tomorrow.'

He clambered up the bank, then turned back towards Malone, who was still sitting in the stern, looking grim. 'Your turn to row,' Weaver said, and hurried to catch up with Lily, who was already heading to the car.

25

L ILY HAD BEEN CALLED BY A&E IN the Royal London, the hospital nearest to Leonard Street that had an emergency room. By the time they arrived, Chip had been admitted and transferred to a ward upstairs. Making their way there, they discovered from the nurse behind the desk that Chip was being interviewed by a policeman. 'Make yourself scarce,' Lily whispered, and he remembered it wasn't only the Russians who were looking for him. He went and hid in a lavatory stall, where he waited anxiously until Lily texted him to say the coast was clear.

When he came back to the desk, he found her arguing with the nurse, who didn't seem to believe Lily was a relative of Chip's. Lily looked about to lose her temper, Weaver realised, so he asked her to sit for a moment in the adjacent visitors' lounge, then turned to the nurse and explained that Lily was Chip's half-sister, and there wasn't any other family.

The nurse pursed her lips for several nerve-wracking moments. 'Ten minutes,' she finally said.

Weaver beckoned to Lily, who came over, finishing a call on her phone. The nurse announced sternly that no phones were allowed in the ward, so Lily handed hers to Weaver and quickly followed the nurse to go see Chip.

Weaver was getting a much-needed coffee from a machine in the waiting room when his jacket pocket juddered. He froze reflexively; for a brief moment he was back on Clarendon Road, fleeing on his assailant's scooter.

Who could be calling him? No one but Lily had the number of his new cheap phone. Then he realised it was Lily's phone that was ringing.

The screen showed *JPH*. He took his coffee in his free hand and walked to the end of the hall.

'Hello,' he said quietly.

There was silence at the other end. Then a voice said, 'Who is that?' After a further, briefer silence, the voice said, 'Weaver?'

'Yes, JP. You back?'

'Just arrived home. But what are you doing with Lily Churchill's phone?'

'Answering it,' he said.

JP snorted. 'You still coming down?'

'Of course. Assuming that's still okay.'

'Sure it is. Only you haven't called, so I wanted to be sure. Glad I've reached you, even if I didn't expect you to answer this phone.'

'Sorry, but I lost mine. I haven't replaced it yet. And I got a bit tied up this week.'

'So I gather.' JP let this sink in before adding, 'Come down late morning. We can cast a fly before lunch.'

'Great.'

'Meanwhile, watch your step with Ms Churchill. I wouldn't want to see my old pal get carried away.'

'How's that?'

JP was silent for a moment. 'I need to be fair about her: she's from nothing, you know; I was kidding about the old family stuff. She really should come clean about things. That and all the rest.'

'The rest?' Weaver said mildly, keen to keep JP talking. He might as well hear the whole story, or JP's version anyway.

'I'm sure you've heard it all by now. The tragic downfall of poor Tolya: sob, sob sob. Followed by Lily's gritty comeback as a financial genius. If you believe it.'

'I take it you don't.'

'Well, ask yourself this: how does a gal who left school aged thirteen or whatever end up acting as the fiscal auditor for several hi-tech start-ups? Lily's not dumb, I grant you that, but come on.'

'Have you seen her set-up? The office?'

'No, but how do you think she paid for it? Not through financial wizardry, if that's what you're thinking. And not from the boyfriend either. More like the company he owned – if you can call it a company.'

'I'm confused. She had backing from some Russians; what's the big deal?'

'*Some* Russians? That's a funny new name for the KGB, or FSB or however they style themselves these days. Knowing Lily, she's implied that she's got spook connections all right, but healthy Western ones. Yes? MI5? Or was it MI6? Maybe she's even thrown in the CIA. The girl's got Intelligence associations, that's for sure, but maybe not the ones she'd like you to think. Some Russians came to the house, as you probably know. They asked for you, but Mrs Wilson said they mentioned Lily as well. I wonder how they knew she'd been here.' He paused for a moment. 'Take it for what you will, Weaver; I'm not begging to be believed.'

But when Weaver stayed silent, JP continued: 'The boyfriend worked with Berezovsky, you know. Oligarch *numero uno* for a while. When he fell out with Moscow, you'd think young Tolya would have fallen out of favour too. Far from it – I'm told that's when he started making real money, picking up the Russian bits of Berezovsky's empire which the great man was no longer allowed to own.'

'I didn't know that,' said Weaver stolidly, though his stomach was churning.

JP continued: 'No one seriously thinks Berezovsky killed himself. Whoever got to him had access. The guy had more guards than the President. Yet none of the staff saw anything or anyone, of course.'

'Of course,' said Weaver.

JP took no notice. 'I'm not saying young Tolya did the deed himself; it would have been enough to let a couple of thugs in the front door. But the *on dit* is that he was involved.'

Weaver would have paid good money to get JP to stop talking about the '*on dit*'. He said, 'But Tolya's dead.'

'Oh,' said JP, without missing a beat, 'is that what she told you? Last I heard he was running a gas subsidiary that Morozov takes a particular interest in.'

'Who told you that?'

'The art dealer you introduced me to.'

'Ragoulin.'

'That's the one.'

'When did he tell you this?'

'I bought another painting from him last year. It's in the Belgravia house. He delivered it personally and we had a drink or two together, or maybe four; he's a typical Russian for all the French polished bullshit. I have to say, he knew a lot more about banking than any other art dealer I know.' JP chuckled at this. 'Lily must have come up during our conversation; she was always looking for art for her Russian friends. It turned out he knew the boyfriend.'

'But I thought you told me Lily was gay. What happened to all that?'

'I didn't say she was always gay, now did I? Maybe it was just a phase, after the Russian dumped her. I don't know. It's none of my business,' he added outrageously.

JP waited, assuming Weaver would respond. When he didn't, JP went on, slightly faster now, and less certain. 'I heard about your hookup with her last weekend.'

'There wasn't a hookup, JP.' He wondered who'd said what to JP, or was his friend just guessing – not without a trace of malice? Weaver was trying not to get angry; he wanted to hear what more JP had to say about Lily. He said measuredly, 'Her radiator was stuck – her bedroom must have been ninety degrees. I put her on the sofa in my room. Nothing intimate.'

'Sure,' said JP flatly, which made it impossible to challenge. Then his tone changed, to a livelier mode. 'That explains it. Sue said there was something odd in one of the bedrooms; somebody superglued one of the radiators open. Godzilla himself couldn't have turned it. Sue had to get a workman to chisel it off. We couldn't understand why anyone would want to do that. Now I do. It gave Lily the perfect excuse to go visiting next door.' His tone was just short of hostile now.

'That sounds a little far-fetched to me. Especially since nothing happened.'

'Maybe. But tell me, how was the Airbnb?'

'Not so good. I only stayed a night.'

'And the rest at the Lily Churchill Hotel?'

'Something along those lines. Is that a problem?'

'Not if you kept your eyes open going in. I'd hate to see you of all people taken for a sucker.'

'What would I have to offer? You seem to think she only likes guys with dough, and I haven't got any. I'm just a mid-level schmo in an obscure corner of the State Department.'

'For a mid-level schmo, you seem pretty popular at the moment. I've got Russians on my doorstep and God knows who else on the phone, all desperate to find you,' he said caustically. 'Anyway, I've got to run. Just wanted to check you were still alive, and that you hadn't broken your casting arm wrestling with Ms Churchill. See you tomorrow.'

Weaver pressed *end*. It was worse than he'd thought; Weaver felt sick about JP's seeming confirmation of the doubts he'd felt himself about Lily. Simmering on and off since she had first called him on Tuesday morning, they had been brought to the boil by JP's call. He waited by the nurse's station, until Lily joined him. She said nothing as they walked to the lift.

'How is Chip?' he asked, since that seemed the natural thing to do, though JP's venom had left him anxious and confused.

'Okay. He's badly concussed, so they want him to stay in for now. They may scan him in the morning.'

'What happened?'

'He's not sure. He went to the office on his bike – the motorcycle. He left it outside while he went in to find something to prop the door open. He's usually extra careful, but not this time, I guess: when he came back, two guys were right behind him, the same two who were in the Mercedes yesterday. The drones you saw must have captured us somewhere near Leonard Street, so they were patrolling the area. He reckons they saw him on his bike and followed him. He tried to stop them from going up the stairs and there was a fight. Guess who didn't win.'

'Did the police come?'

'Yes, thank God. Somebody saw what was going on and called 999. Chip said they would have kicked him to death if the police hadn't arrived.'

But would they come again? Weaver thought.

Lily seemed to sense his unease. 'I'm just glad you weren't there,' she said. 'I don't know if they've made the connection, but if they have, they'll be back. We have to stay clear of Leonard Street for the time being.'

'So are we going to your house?' He dreaded the long journey there; he was exhausted by the day.

'Too risky. I don't like the fact they found Chip. We better stay in town.'

'JP's flat?'

'You must be joking. We need a hotel. Not a fancy one; somewhere anonymous.' She looked at him searchingly. 'Are you okay?'

'Sure,' he said. 'I'm fine. Honest.'

'The thing is, Weaver, Chip said that while they were kicking him, one of the thugs kept calling him a prick. An American prick.'

'Chip?' he said in disbelief.

'Yes, Chip. He reckons they thought he was you.'

26

THE PREMIER INN WAS CLEAN, SPACIOUS ENOUGH, inexpensive and, to Lily's apparent satisfaction, entirely soulless. It had the added benefit of sitting on the western side of London near the Cromwell Road, which further west turned into the M4 that would take them towards the Dower House the next day. When they checked in, the receptionist raised a frigid eyebrow at their lack of luggage, but looked more content when Lily asked for twin beds.

Weaver sat on one of them in their room on the fourth floor, while Lily stood and fiddled with the television remote. Right now, he wanted nothing other than to be by a river – preferably *in* a river – concentrating in his own intent way on the mend of his line, the perky float of a fly's upright wings, watching for any hint of a fish, entering the mental state of sheer concentrated nothingness he had described to Lily.

Too much had happened in too short a time. Could it really have been only five days since he'd flown in from Stockholm? He could just about cope with Malone's outline of the dilemma he faced, and he no longer hoped for help from that quarter. But with JP's character assassination of Lily, whom he was watching now while she channel-hopped, he felt only dread. He knew he could not go on secretly doubting someone he thought he could also love.

At last he said, 'JP called your phone while you were with Chip.'

For a moment he thought she hadn't heard him properly. Then she said, 'What did he want?'

'I'm not sure. He was surprised when I answered.'

'He was probably calling me to find you. Did you tell him about Chip?'

Weaver shook his head. Lily said, 'He's never very sensitive when it comes to other people. Empathy isn't something you can buy, so JP reckons it can't be very important.'

'He spoke very highly of you,' he said sarcastically.

She looked at him in surprise. 'What's that supposed to mean?' She turned off the TV with the remote and sat down on the other bed. 'What did JP say?'

'I had an earful from him.'

Lily stared at Weaver. He felt as if he had decided to wade across a river, only to discover he had picked a crossing point where the water was over his head. 'Why don't you just tell me what he said?' Lily spoke slowly, her voice ice cold. 'From your expression, it can't have been very nice.'

'It's the things you haven't told me that are worrying.'

'I'm a private person; you know that. I'll keep my dress size to myself, thank you very much.' There was no lightness to her tone.

'Your business isn't any of my business, but I'm puzzled that there don't seem to be any clients around. I think we've established Charles isn't one.'

'Business goes up and down,' she said, deceptively reasonable. 'You know how it is – forgive me, you obviously don't. In my line of work, sometimes things are slow. It doesn't help that the oligarchs are gone. I used to be able to count on them; their business alone took care of the overheads. And you may have noticed, I've had some other things to do. Not things that pay,' she said, looking closely at Weaver.

Unconvinced, he ploughed on. 'You know Ragoulin, don't you?'

'Never met the man. I've kept my distance, ever since Tolya told me he's the kind of guy who plays both sides of any fence. All the oligarchs, pro-Morozov or anti-Morozov, were happy to do business with him. That tells you all you need to know.' She seemed to think of something else. 'Since I'm the one who pointed out that he must have tipped off Mrs Golubova that you'd be on Bond Street, what makes you think I'm in league with him?'

'I didn't say that.'

'You might as well have – why else ask whether I knew him? All right. What else?'

'JP says the radiator was working fine the day I arrived. He said someone glued it to stay open so the room would be boiling.'

'Guilty as charged,' she said without hesitation.

'But why?' he asked, startled by her quick admission.

'It seemed an ingenious way to get to know you. Is there something wrong with that?'

'Why? We'd exchanged about fifteen words.'

'Can't women like someone for their looks alone? Men do it all the time. And I didn't know then how stupid you are.'

'I've been called a lot of things, especially by my ex-wife, but not that.'

'That's what all dumb people say. Anyway, it's better than boring, though you're sometimes also that.' She took a breath, like taking on fuel. He was startled by her fury, but was not about to back down. She went on, 'Do you mean to say that, for all your "yes ma'am", "no ma'am", "thank you ma'am" bullshit, you've been doubting me?'

'Yes.'

'So what's next on your list?' she asked curtly.

'JP says the Russians showed up at the Dower House looking for me. One of them mentioned you.'

'So?'

He hadn't expected this reply. Why would the Russians connect Lily with JP? She went on, 'My boyfriend was a Russian, as you know. I knew a lot of Russians once.'

'Okay, but why couldn't we go down to JP's yesterday? Why wait?'

'Because I was worried the Russians would be watching the house. I still am; last weekend, when you still had your phone, they could have known you were there, so they might well have thought you'd be back again – and they'd be right. It will be much safer now JP and Sue are there; the last thing the Russians want is someone calling the police. And this way, we know we'll get in. I'm not sure Mrs Wilson would have let us inside, much less go hunting for a pen upstairs in the wing. Not without JP's say so, and we agreed we shouldn't mention any of this to him.'

'All right,' he said, but he was not ready to give up. 'JP said Tolya worked with Berezovsky. Is that true?'

She laughed, but there was no joy in it. 'Tolya would have loved to hear that he worked *with* Boris. Actually, he worked *for* Berezovsky.'

'So that is true.'

'Sure.'

'And he fell out with him over Morozov?'

'No. Absolutely not. Tolya stood by Boris until the end.'

'Was Berezovsky murdered? JP seems to think he was.'

'Almost certainly. He was depressed, but Tolya swore he wasn't the kind of man who'd top himself. I trust his judgement. They claimed he hanged himself, but when people hang themselves, they usually stand on a chair – they need the height to let gravity do the job. I mean, you can't strangle yourself with your own hands, now can you?'

'I haven't tried recently.'

'When you jump off a chair, the ligature marks are at an angle, like a "V". But the marks around Boris's neck were straight across, horizontal. That's what happens when someone else strangles you.'

'You seem to know a lot about it.'

'I should do. Tolya was determined to prove Boris had been murdered; after Berezovsky died, he worked at little else. But fat chance proving anything. First the Russians pressured Tolya to drop it; then they tried to kill him; last and most lethal, they started being nice to him. But why should you listen to me? You have an expert in forensic pathology apparently: JP Harbinger.'

He ignored this, and said, 'Are you sure Tolya didn't fall out with Berezovsky?'

'Oh, is that where we're going?' Her words were coming out *rat-a-tat* again. 'I suppose JP says Tolya helped the killers. Or is it that Tolya did it himself? Is that it? Then why is Tolya dead as well?'

'JP seemed to think he might still be alive. That he's running an oil business somewhere in Russia.'

'That is so fucking offensive.' Lily was glaring at him now. 'If Tolya were alive, then why did I have his dragon of a mother in a Russian morgue screaming down the phone at me, saying I was responsible for getting her son killed? If Tolya was on the Morozov side, then tell me why they tried to break into my London office, thinking Tolya was there? You wondered why I have so much security? Well, that's why: I had Muscovite hoods following me, trying to find my boyfriend. If that sounds familiar, think what it's like for me to go through it twice, this time with a man I barely know. If one of those pigs tells JP he knows me, he probably does – from the days they watched my every move.'

'Then why did Tolya go back to Russia?'

'Because they asked him to, and the poor guy thought that meant he would be safe. They said they'd been labouring under a misapprehension – don't ask me how to say that in Russian – and they wanted to clear things up. I begged him not to go; I pleaded with him. But he said he was sick of living under the shadow of Boris's murder, sick of safe houses that might not be safe, sick of having me involved. He believed them because he wanted to, and that's the last I saw of Tolya. So don't tell me he killed Boris, or that he worked for the SVR, or that he didn't die in the hellhole of the White Swan Penal Colony.'

'Do you know these SVR people?'

'What you mean is, do I help the SVR? No. Could I help the SVR? You bet. Easy as pie. I could have turned you over and been well paid for it. Five hundred thousand, minimum; six hundred at a stretch.'

'How do you know what I'm worth to them?'

'Because that's what they offered me to betray Tolya. You're not as valuable to me as he was, but I guess you are to the Russians.' She said this with a *more fool them* tone that stung.

Lily waved her hand dismissively. 'Listen, my brother's hurt and I haven't got time for this rubbish. I could answer all your questions one by one, but I don't want to. The point is this: if I were working for the Russians, as JP would have it, then why are you still breathing? Why would the Russians be trying to hunt you down when their agent — me, according to JP's scenario — has been with you virtually all the time for the last few days? If you can answer that, I promise not to ask *you* any other questions.'

He shifted heavily on the bed, thinking hard. He had a dozen further questions, exposing inconsistencies in her previous accounts, gaps in her explanations, maybe even a few downright fibs — but all of them added up to nothing when he asked himself how, if Lily was working on the Russians' side, he had survived the week. 'I'm sorry,' he said at last. 'I've been very confused. Even Malone wasn't what I thought he would be. I figured you must be helping someone other than me.'

'I am.'

He looked at her, startled. She said, 'But not the people after you: Russians or Hofstadter's people. Charles came to see me a month ago. He asked if I would reconsider helping with the Russian community, and for MI6 not MI5. I said, what Russian community? All the pro-Morozov lot seem to have left.

'Then he explained. The SVR can't buy anything with roubles now, including paying their agents in the West. They have dollars but they need the money laundered, and to do that they need to buy things.'

'What sort of things?'

'In this country, it's paintings. The oligarchs still here who cooperate are "loaned" dollars by the Russians, through dollar deposits made with the middleman Galkin's crooked bank. The oligarchs use the dollars to buy expensive paintings from a West End dealer; someone you are familiar with.'

Ragoulin, he realised. He could not stop staring at her.

'They are truly bad pictures, I gather; God knows where the Russian government gets them – the bowels of the Hermitage or from confiscated private property. I mean, a lot of them aren't worth a hundred roubles, but the oligarchs sometimes pay a hundred thousand dollars for them. But it's not their money they're using to buy them. It's the SVR's.

'From these sales, Ragoulin takes his commission, then sends the money back to the bank, which in turn repays the Russian government its original oligarch "loans" in what are now-clean dollars.'

This seemed clear enough to Weaver. 'Okay, but what were you supposed to do about it?'

'Find out who Ragoulin's customers are, so MI6 can get MI5 to warn them off. Or throw them out of the country. MI6 is not in the business of helping the SVR's finances.'

'But you said yourself the oligarchs have gone.'

'Most of them, it's true, but there have been plenty of buyers from other places who, for a price, are willing to go along with the scam. Americans even…'

'JP.'

She didn't nod, but she didn't shake her head.

'You're telling me you've watched him for Boyd?'

'Yes, though it got complicated. I hadn't appreciated how jealous JP is.'

'Jealous? Of you?'

'Weaver, use your head. No, he's not jealous of me. He's jealous of his old pal, the easy-going guy who seems to get the girl in all the home movies JP would like to make.' She sighed, as if talking about this were distasteful, so he didn't feel he could ask her to be clearer.

'What made you change your mind? Why did you agree to help MI6 now?'

'Because of Charles. You saw him at my place. It would have been comical had he not been so hangdog and sad. He's not well,' she said. 'He still has all his marbles and is desperate to keep working, but he's struggling a bit. His wife died and they didn't have any children. He has nothing else but the job. When he's working, he's his sharp old self; when he's not – well, as you saw, he's not. I reckon I owed him a lot, so I helped him.'

Weaver said, 'As simple as that?'

'No. It was the Russians so I had no trouble motivating myself. Boyd was counting on that.'

'So you were working for him all this time,' he said, half in wonder.

They sat in silence for a minute.

'Do you still want to go down to the Dower House tomorrow?' Weaver asked at last.

'There's no point dropping out now,' she said. She looked around and stood up, breaking the intense cocoon of their conversation. 'I want to hear exactly what Malone said to you, but first I have to go out for a bit. I need you to stay here. I've said that before and we know what happened. So please, for once, do what I ask. Have your necessary shower, then go to bed and stay there. I may be a while. I need to make some calls and no, I won't be telling you who I've talked to. And I'll get us something light to eat. I was thinking of baguettes – there's a Pret around the corner.'

'Get me two baguettes please.'

'Two?' She was smiling openly now, despite herself.

'Yes, two. Like you, I'm still growing.'

When she came back with a Pret bag, he was dozing lightly with CNN news on the television, though he had been awake enough to watch an item about 'Skip' Washington, the basketball star, who had been released in California the day before. Women's groups had gathered to protest this, and one had picketed Washington's mansion in San Francisco's Sea Cliff neighbourhood – fruitlessly, since Washington had gone straight to his ranch in Montana, flying by private jet. Buried in the middle of the piece to camera was a mention that Washington had been one of twenty-one pardons and commutations made by the President.

Weaver got up from the bed and they both sat down by the window overlooking Knaresborough Place. They ate for a while in silence, watching the end of the news, until Lily finished and said, 'Now, tell me what Malone said.'

He tried to keep his account brief. Lily seemed unsurprised by his description of the photos Malone had shown him, and agreed that they meant he had no choice but to tell Malone about the secret meeting. When he recounted how Malone had pressed him on whether he had any evidence to prove the meeting had taken place, she grew irate. 'He isn't really helping you after all.'

'No, he's not. I think Hofstadter got to him. My old man is going to be awfully upset.'

'Fuck that,' said Lily crossly. 'I'm upset, and you should be too. You said Kuzmin made a joke about Hofstadter. What was it?'

The memory came to him unbidden, first an image of Kuzmin laughing, then the words that had triggered his laughter. There was none of the recent fuzziness. 'Kuzmin said they had video of Hofstadter. I guess they have a repository of stuff about all sorts of people in the West; part of their *kompromat*. Hofstadter's files were called by a nickname he used to have.'

'What was that that?'

'Polanski. I don't know why, but Kuzmin thought this was hilarious.'

'His nickname was Polanski?' Lily sounded disbelieving.

'Yes, but I gather not for public consumption. The word Kuzmin used for "nickname" means it was meant pejoratively.'

'You bet it was. Come on, Weaver, you know what Polanski means. Don't you see it?' she said with impatient affection. 'You must remember Roman Polanski and the thirteen-year-old girl he had sex with. Obviously it means Hofstadter likes young girls.'

'God, it never even crossed my mind.'

'If they have video of Hofstadter with an underage girl, taken during his Moscow trip, no wonder he backed down. That would be more than enough to get him to persuade the President to spring our friend Dan Berry. *That's* what the blackmail was.'

Weaver said, 'It also explains why Malone blew up when I mentioned the nickname to him. He said, "Don't tar me with that brush." I'm guessing he confined his own antics to adults.'

'Yes, though Hofstadter probably has something on Malone. He isn't really helping you after all.'

'No, but he did warn me that I might be prosecuted by the Feds if I go back; equally, I figure I might be a folk hero if I disseminate the recording as widely as possible.'

'You might be both. And what about the Russians then?'

'They're still the biggest problem I have. Malone didn't offer to help me there. Come to think of it, he didn't offer to help me with anything much. He seemed to think just meeting me was help enough.'

She smiled, but only fleetingly. 'All right,' she said, wiping her fingers on a paper napkin. 'First things first. If we don't get the pen back from JP's, you won't have any choice to make. Let's attend to that and then we can discuss how to take it from there.'

He could see Lily was exhausted, and this time she didn't even go into the bathroom to get undressed. He turned away, and tried to keep his eyes focused on the TV until she was under the sheets of her twin bed.

After a long silence, Lily's voice floated towards him. 'Awake?'

'Of course.'

'Thanks for being there.'

'Where?'

'The hospital.'

'Don't be ridiculous. Think of all you've done for me.'

'It's not a competition.'

'I know, though I still don't know why.'

'Why it's not a competition?'

He laughed. 'No, but seriously, why did you decide to help me?'

'We've been through that already, Weaver.'

'Not really. I've asked before. You never answered. Tell me why. Please?'

She sighed, but then began to speak. 'At first, when I heard about you, I thought maybe you were in league with JP and somehow connected to Ragoulin. You have the perfect cover for that, travelling all over the world. So I made it my business to get to know you; I switched rooms and yes, I glued the radiator open. But I admit after we talked that night I found it hard to believe you were an accomplice of JP's, much less in league with Alek Ragoulin.'

'I see,' he said neutrally.

'Then you rang me in London and told me what had happened, and I realised I'd been completely wrong ever to suspect you.'

'And that's why you helped me?'

'No.' She waited for a moment, and he could hear her legs moving underneath her sheets. She said finally, 'It was because I liked you at JP's. I liked you a lot. And it was because you asked.'

'Asked for help?'

'Yes. In my experience, men don't ask – they *assume*.'

'Still, I'm surprised you believed my story so easily. The guy at the airport, the guys in the Mercedes, the guys on the street. It must have sounded pretty far-fetched.'

'It did, but I did believe you. Don't ask me why. Probably because of our late-night encounter at JP's. You weren't a creep and you didn't seem to have JP's propensity for self-deception. It seemed worth a punt helping you out when we spoke on the phone. Anyway, Charles was having one of his bad days, and the conference call I was on was terribly boring...'

'Please be serious.'

'I am being serious, and that was the reason. At first. Then when it was clear who was after you, well, try keeping me away. I hate those bastards. I couldn't sit back and let them do it all over again.' He heard her turn in her bed, and flop her pillow over. She said quietly, 'I'm going to sleep now, okay? Night night.'

'Night,' he said. After a while, when he sensed she was just about asleep, he said in a whisper that was half-offering and half-belief, *'Schlaf gut, meine Schöne,'* thinking it safest to utter this endearment in a language Lily didn't understand.

In the morning, Lily called the hospital and learned that Chip had spent a peaceful night and was clamouring to leave.

She made her bed and sat on it, looking at her laptop while Weaver watched more CNN news.

'Do you want to be there for Chip?' he asked. 'I could take a train down and you can join me later once you have him settled.'

'No,' she said firmly. 'They said regardless of the scan he'll be in for at least a couple more days. He took a pretty good knock from those thugs, but the painkillers are deceiving him into thinking he's all better.'

He nodded and then saw Lily looking aghast at her laptop. She pointed at it. 'Something's happened,' she said.

He went and stood next to her, and read the top lines on the screen. *'Mystery surrounds a West End art dealer found dead in his car outside the house of a Russian oligarch living in Weybridge.'*

Weaver read on in disbelief. Ragoulin had been leaving the oligarch when he fell ill. A passer-by had seen him in distress and called an ambulance. He was pronounced dead at the scene by paramedics, and initial reports indicated he had suffered a massive heart attack.

Exactly at the time when Ragoulin's body was found, Weaver had been waiting for him in Bond Street. The piece itself ended with a poker-faced note that *'Mr Ragoulin's death follows a succession of similar unexpected fatalities in the Russian oligarch community.'*

Weaver scrolled down. There was a photograph of a mock-Georgian mansion, video-camera-guarded gates and all, and another photo below it, of a striking blonde woman wearing a double row of pigeon's egg pearls. She was identified as Mrs Aleksei Zadkin, and Weaver recognised her right away.

'God,' said Weaver.

'I'm sorry. I know you were fond of him.'

'It's not just that. The woman,' and he pointed at the blonde on the screen. 'They say she's Mrs Zadkin.'

Lily glanced at the photo. 'Yes, the oligarch's wife. She certainly looks the part. What about her?'

'Her name is Nina and I've seen her twice: once at Heathrow and once on Bond Street. Each time she was introduced to me by Mrs Golubova as her daughter. And it seems her oligarch husband was a Ragoulin client. Ragoulin even told me about him the other night.'

'Really?' Lily's big eyes grew bigger still. 'Useful cover for the old lady, no? You have to question whether Ragoulin really had a heart attack.'

'You think the Russians killed him?' he asked. It was bewildering to find so many unthinkable things were possible.

'He's about the tenth victim of a heart attack among the exiles living here. After a while, you start to wonder.'

'But why would they do that? You thought Ragoulin was working for the SVR.'

'He was. Or do you think MI6 and I had something to do with that too?'

Her tone had momentarily reassumed its bitterness, but he had no interest in resurrecting his earlier doubts. 'No, I don't,' he said forcefully. 'But maybe he did have a heart attack. People do, you know.' Like Mrs Macauley.

'He wasn't old, was he? And he sounded fit enough from your account of him.'

'Yes, he seemed in good shape,' he said, thinking of the tall, elegant figure. 'I don't understand. If he was trying to help the Russians, and had Mrs Golubova arrive on Bond Street in order to track me, then why would they kill him?'

'Because he knew too much. He tried to give you up to the

Russians, but they still worried he knew what you'd heard in Stockholm.'

'I didn't tell him anything about it. But the Russians don't like loose ends.'

'Exactly. And Ragoulin talked too much.' Lily stood up. 'Come on, we'd better go.'

27

THEY WERE ON THE WESTERN OUTSKIRTS OF London, short of Heathrow, when Lily said, 'I need to stop for petrol. Won't take long.'

'Really?' he said. He could see the gauge from where he sat. 'You're over half full.'

'Actually, I need the loo.' She turned her head and smiled sheepishly.

They left the motorway for the Heston services, a grimly urban outpost in the flat valley land of the M4. Lily stopped at the pumps. 'Might as well fill up while we're here,' she said.

'I'll do it while you go to the bathroom,' he said.

Lily shook her head. 'Sit still; the cap's a little tricky.'

While she filled the car, he sat and looked at the overcast sky. It would be nicely warm on the river, and cloudy enough to make the fishing good. Not that he would be casting a fly. Lily got back in and drove round the corner, where she pulled into a parking slot to one side of the petrol station's shop. 'Won't be a minute,' she said, and hopped out. Her window was lowered, and she bent down until her face appeared in the opening. She stared intently at Weaver. 'I meant to say, whatever you decide, don't be bullied. You should only do what you think is right.'

What was she talking about? Bullied by whom? Before he could ask, she had walked away towards the entrance to the shop. He was tired after a fitful night, and briefly closed his eyes, but it was not time for a nap. God knows where he would be sleeping that night, but a rest would have to wait. Maybe once they'd retrieved his recorder, they could make their apologies to JP and Sue and leave; then just drive, west probably, into the countryside, and find a place to stay. Picked at random, it would be safe. Perhaps a country inn; how nice that sounded. If they ever got there – what was keeping Lily?

Opening his eyes, he became aware of a man standing outside, next to his door. Uneasy, Weaver was about to get out to investigate when the driver's door opened and another, older man in a raincoat got in and sat behind the wheel. Weaver recognised at once the hangdog eyes and pear-shaped chin of Charles Boyd.

'Mr Weaver,' Boyd said, his voice cordial.

'Mr Boyd,' he said back carefully. There seemed no point sounding alarmed. Weaver pointed at the figure standing next to his door. 'Who's the gentleman outside?' he said.

Boyd was busy trying to smooth out his raincoat, and said without looking at Weaver, 'Just someone to ensure our privacy.'

'Where's Lily gone?'

'Queuing to pay, I expect. Don't be alarmed; she knows I'm here.'

'So what can I do for you?' Weaver said this affably enough, but he felt wary. Had Lily set this up? Or set him up? And if so, for what?

'Charles. Please call me Charles. And I will call you Weaver, on Lily's strict instructions. First of all, I want to thank you for calling Mr Symons to our attention. He would have gone unnoticed otherwise, I'm sure.'

'Yes, thanks to Skip Washington.'

'I never understood the appeal of that sport. Too much like netball. I gather he's a household name.'

'Yes, and now a notorious one. The White House knew that even just talking about releasing him would receive the world's attention. Skip Washington gets all the press, and none for the other twenty people pardoned.'

'Clever of the White House, I must say. So thank you all the more for helping unearth the obscure Mr Symons.' He hesitated, though Weaver sensed he knew exactly what he wanted to say next. 'I wonder if you might consider helping out again.'

'What is it you want me to do?'

'It involves Mr Symons and someone you were acquainted with: Alek Ragoulin.'

'Now with God.'

'Do you think so?' Boyd asked wryly. There was a faint sweet odour that had come into the car; not unpleasant. Tobacco, thought Weaver, who had never been a smoker.

Boyd continued, 'We are quite certain that Mr Symons is Russian by birth and by allegiance, and that if we are correct, his real name is Sukolov. We also think, now that he's free, that Mr Symons will, unsurprisingly, want to go home – to Russia. Since he can't fly directly from America, London would be a useful resting place while he decides how best to make his way back. From his point of view, it's better than staying in the US. There he'd be worried that the FBI might get wise to his real identity.'

'Have they? Got wise, that is.'

'They know his birth name was Sukolov, if we've got the right man. But that's about it.'

'How do they know that?'

'We told them,' Boyd said quietly. 'Only yesterday, in fact; that's when we found out.'

Because Weaver had remembered the name. Was Boyd aware of that? Boyd was speaking again: 'At least we were showing good faith by telling the Americans about him. Though without actual proof, it's hardly enough to put the man back in prison, and he has not been willing to talk with the FBI even informally.'

'Yet you think he could be flying here?' It seemed incredible.

'I don't think it; he's in the air as we speak. Touchdown in a little more than an hour.'

They were cutting things awfully fine then. 'Will you arrest him when he lands?'

'Sadly not. We haven't any evidence to let us charge him, any more than the FBI does; neither do we have any reason to refuse him entry. As far as anyone can prove, he's an American named

Dennis Symons with nothing outstanding against him. He knows all this, I'm sure. I don't imagine he plans to stay here very long in any case. He'll move on to Istanbul or Ankara or Helsinki. Some place where he can fly straight to Moscow.'

The car was facing south, and in the distance a small front of dark cloud hung like a large ink smear low in the sky. Weaver didn't believe Boyd was telling him all this just to add him to the loop. There was nothing vague about the man today, and Weaver now understood why Lily had been in such a rush. She knew they would be stopping on their way to JP's.

He looked at his watch; it was nine-thirty. The red pen recorder he'd hidden was over an hour away. 'All right,' he said. 'What would you like me to do?'

'Nothing like getting to the point,' Boyd said, but he was smiling, and didn't seem fazed by Weaver's bluntness; this must be one of his good days. He continued, 'It's your eyes I need, actually. We have nothing on Symons, as I said, nothing to keep him from going where he likes once he lands here. And there is just a chance – so small as to be infinitesimal, if you ask me – that we have the wrong man.'

'What?' asked Weaver sharply. 'You're saying Skip Washington could be the one the Russians want?'

Boyd gave a hint of a smile. 'That would be a step too far; I think we can agree on that. No, it's just that the real spy could conceivably be someone else altogether. Or *not* someone at all, and the blackmail was about something else.'

'So what I told Lily about the Stockholm meeting wasn't accurate? I got it all ass backwards?'

'That would not be my choice of words. And as I say, the possibility is remote. We have every reason to trust your account, which I gather is what led us to Danbury's penitentiary.'

Dan Berry did, thought Weaver.

Boyd added, 'And Symons was the only one from that prison to be pardoned.'

'All right, so how do we find out for sure? And what do my

eyes have to do with it?' The continuing presence of the man just outside his car door was unsettling.

'Symons was meant to be met at Heathrow by Ragoulin, which is another reason to think we have the right man. But obviously that rendezvous is no longer going to happen.'

'And so you need me because…?'

'Because notwithstanding Ragoulin's sudden demise, we think Symons may still be met. It is just conceivable, given your recent experiences, that you might recognise the person who meets him – if anyone does.'

'When did you discover he was flying here?'

'Not until a few hours ago.' Boy looked slightly uncomfortable. 'We had… access to Ragoulin's email account. Not his usual one; it's under a different name. We took it over after Ragoulin was found dead. Immediately.'

'Why was Symons being met by Ragoulin?'

'Presumably to get instructions, and plane tickets perhaps, on how best to travel onwards.'

Suddenly these details all seemed entirely ridiculous. Weaver said, 'Are you telling me the Russians went to these lengths – the secret meeting in Stockholm to blackmail the White House; doing their best to silence me – in order to free one lousy spy?' He was unable to keep incredulity out of his voice.

'This is not your ordinary spy.'

'Really? What makes him so valuable?' When Boyd hesitated, Weaver went on, his voice softening, 'Come on. You know who Symons really is because of what I heard in Stockholm. At the very least I'd like to know why this has half the SVR trying to kill me.'

Boyd had both hands sitting on his thighs, and now brought them together, clasped in his lap. After a long pause, he eventually gave a small judicious nod. 'Fair enough,' he said. 'Dennis Symons, born Dmitri Sukolov we believe, helped run Russian Illegals in the United States. Thanks to your former President, "Illegals" means illegal residents, but I'll stick to the meaning that matters to us – they are agents who insinuate themselves in a foreign country, usually claiming to be another nationality, which in this age of Google explains why they don't have much of a traceable past.'

'I know what Illegals are.' They were commonplace in the spy novels his father sometimes sent him.

'Well then, you may remember that a large number were rounded up some years ago by the FBI. Symons was already planted in the States but somehow escaped the net. The thinking is another group of them went undetected; or else that another group was sent when the earlier ones were exposed. Either way, we calculate that some are still there, and these people have a more specific and more dangerous brief. What that brief is, we don't know; we think Symonds does. Since the FBI exposed the first bunch, these other Illegals must be worried stiff about being discovered; I believe Symons's job was partly to support and reassure them. Not that significant a duty, you might say, but the point is, Symons knows who all the remaining Illegals are.'

'You said "partly" – what else do you think he was up to?'

'That's where it gets more speculative, though we do have a pretty good idea. Symons's cover in the States was to act as an investor in new companies, so he travelled all the time. And by checking the data for his trips – both the airlines and the credit card companies have been cooperative – it turns out that in the course of his putative business travels, Symons managed to visit the city or town of every Illegal who has been caught by the FBI. It would strain credulity to think this a coincidence; some of the Illegals' locations were very remote. I believe the expression is "Podunk towns".

'The key thing is, we have every reason to suspect that Symons continued in this role for all those Illegals who weren't caught and for all the new ones sent to replace those who were.'

Boyd paused while Weaver took this in. Weaver asked, 'But why does that make Symons so important to the Russians? I thought most spying these days took place in cyberspace. You know, with

Russians sitting at their laptops, sabotaging airline schedules and utility companies – any core industry will do – without having to move from their desks in Moscow. Am I wrong? Is that really why the Russians are so desperate to get him out of American hands?'

Boyd considered this for a moment. He said, 'Well, it would still be very useful for us if he would blow the cover of all the Illegals he's dealt with – it would set back Russian subversion that's still on the ground in America for years. But,' and Boyd raised a didactic hand, 'I understand your doubts, and I shared them myself to a large extent. The bunch of Illegals caught by the FBI were resoundingly unexceptional – none had risen to any sort of prominence; none had access to classified information the Russians would be keen to have. There's no reason to expect this new group to have proved more accomplished at subversion.'

'Okay, but I sense a caveat.'

Boyd gave a hint of a smile. 'I should tell you we've now discovered that in addition to his travels across the country, Symons was in Washington DC virtually every month.'

'Doing what?'

'*Seeing whom* is what we'd really like to know. But so far we haven't had any luck there.'

'Do you think Symons will tell you any of this – especially who his contact is in Washington?'

'I have no real reason to think so,' said Boyd. He sounded frustrated but resigned. 'Still, one must never underestimate the Russian capacity for shooting themselves in the foot. They are famously mean, for one thing: I doubt Symons's superiors in Moscow were generous when it came to funding the ventures he was meant to invest in. Or when it came to paying Symons himself. As a result, he apparently couldn't resist trying to make some money of his own. The problem was, he picked a very rum bunch of people and a very rum business to get involved in; eventually he got done for fraud. Part of him must blame his miserly Moscow superiors. That's our hope anyway.'

'Did the FBI tell you all this?'

'Not officially, since the Bureau has been kept out of this affair. Though much of it came from our own efforts, including some exceptional assistance from you,' he added quietly. 'The Bureau was especially helpful with the data collection.' He cast a quick searching look at Weaver. '*Not* the Paris office,' he said meaningfully. It was good to know that Boyd didn't trust Malone either.

28

THERE MUST HAVE BEEN THREE CAMERAS OPERATING in the arrivals area, for there were three monitors for Weaver to watch, each showing a different feed. He soon found himself focusing on the middle one, for it had the best view for his needs, looking down towards the terminal doors from a position high above the exit where passengers left the confines of His Majesty's Revenue and Customs and joined the free market world.

He had not seen Lily again, not since he got out of her Golf and followed Boyd into a large grey saloon. Driven by the man who had stood guard outside Lily's car, they reached the airport in a quarter of an hour, and were deposited outside Terminal Five. Weaver had followed Boyd as he led the way into departures, both of them bypassing the queue at security with the aid of Boyd's wave of his ID and a security guard who seemed already to know him.

Soon they were exploring a part of the terminal inaccessible to the public, going up and down several half-flights of stairs, then along a corridor until they eventually arrived at a small windowless room full of monitors, occupied by a quiet middle-aged man introduced by Boyd as Mitchell. Mitchell quickly explained the internal camera surveillance system, then showed Weaver the monitors displaying the feeds from the arrivals hall, and how to freeze the cameras at any point during their one-eighty-degree sweep back and forth across the waiting area.

'What am I looking for, Charles?' asked Weaver when Mitchell had left.

'Any person you know; actually, any person you've seen before. It can be a man you once worked with, or a teacher from your primary school; any familiar face, let me know at once. I will be with Mitchell down the hall, the room on the left. Take your time; we won't let Sukolov through immigration until I've checked with you. If I'm not there, it means I am talking with Sukolov in the interrogation room, so please don't disturb me then unless it is an emergency. In fact, even if it is an emergency,' he added, and for the first time Weaver sensed something steelier behind the man's old-fashioned courtesy.

They did not have long to wait. After only a couple of minutes, Boyd's phone buzzed. He looked at its screen and nodded. 'Right. He's here and in the queue for passport control. I better go along.'

On the monitors, Weaver could see that the reception area was crowded with waiting people: mainly families, often with small excited children in tow, ready to greet grandma back from her holiday or their father home from a business trip. Weaver worked his way carefully through the thirty or forty people standing closest to the camera; there was no one he recognised. He found himself wishing he hadn't volunteered to help, since it seemed a pointless task, and he wondered how soon he would be able to collect Lily, or rather be collected by her, and get on with retrieving the recorder from JP's house.

Having checked the barrier attendees, he proceeded backwards from the customs exit and towards the front of the terminal. This was also pointless, he felt, since anyone waiting for Sukolov would want to be close to the exit from customs, to make sure the agent didn't somehow slip by in the crowd.

Then a text came in: *You okay? x L.*

He responded right away: *All okay and on board with Boyd. No bullying involved. More later – The Illegal has landed.*

She replied immediately: *!!! xo*

What a funny mix she was. Tart at times, and though never gushy, warm at others. Capable of enthusiasm but often reserved, and also, as the night in her little house had shown, vulnerable.

He tried fruitlessly to banish Lily from his head, remembering the perils of Tomic's 'Third Man', the dangers of distracting thoughts.

And then he saw the man.

Tall, with a long broken-looking nose. It was the same man without question: the Russian security officer who had confiscated his phone in Stockholm, then reappeared in the Heathrow terminal just down the road, where, thanks to the mini-pandemonium of Mrs Golubova's family, Weaver had gone undetected. And now here he was at Heathrow again.

This time the Russian was keeping his distance from the barriers, where the chauffeurs stood waiting with their placards – none of which, Weaver had already noted, were for Mr Dennis Symons. Or Sukolov, for that matter.

Then a solitary man, athletic-looking in a tight-fitting leather jacket, came through the terminal's doors. He stopped almost immediately, and stood next to the Russian, though he seemed to make a point of not looking at him. The new arrival was also familiar to Weaver, who noticed that he had changed his shoes, dumping the Converse All Stars for a pair of simple brown loafers. He seemed fully recovered from Weaver's punch on Clarendon Road.

The man continued to look away from the Russian, but when the Russian's lips moved very briefly, as if talking to himself, Weaver knew they were there as a team. They stayed in position, well back of the barriers that steered the new arrivals into the hall; they were almost at the external automatic doors. Why?

Weaver looked at the people waiting closer to customs as the camera swept across the expanse of the arrivals area; they were unchanged from the characters he'd examined sixty seconds before. Then just as the camera neared the end of its swing, he spotted someone new: a person standing alone at the end of the barrier, almost exactly where the exit from customs merged with the hall. The figure was lost from view as the camera moved on; Weaver waited as the camera reversed itself, and this time the new arrival was the first to come into view. A woman, an old woman. She was wearing a sage-coloured woollen cloak, and carried a stick gripped tightly in her hand. No one coming out of customs could fail to see her there; equally, she could see everyone emerging.

He had to find Boyd right away, he thought, just as the door opened and the man himself came in. He had taken off his raincoat to reveal a light grey suit that had seen better days, and yet another striped tie. He sat down, puffing slightly.

'Is he still here?' Weaver asked tensely.

'He's in the interrogation room around the corner, but I can't keep him there much longer.'

'No luck then?' Weaver asked, more gently this time.

'He readily acknowledges that he is indeed Dennis Symons, but says he has never heard of anyone called Sukolov. He made no bones of the fact he's just been released from a Federal prison, but when I started to try and persuade him he would be better off staying in the UK rather than heading to Moscow, he cut me off. He claims that's precisely what he is planning to do. Said he is here for a holiday, and has no plans to go anywhere other than London, and certainly not Moscow. He said if he isn't allowed to continue on his way, then he wants a lawyer.' Boyd rubbed a cheek absent-mindedly. 'If I hadn't known better, he would have been utterly convincing. Except for one thing.'

'What's that?'

'He didn't seem at all surprised by my accusations; his denial lacked any sense of outrage, or even puzzlement. An innocent man would have been angry or scared or plain bamboozled. Not our Mr Symons. He's Sukolov, I'm sure of it.'

Boyd sat silent for a moment, then said more brightly, 'What about you? Anyone you know?' He pointed to the monitor.

'I was about to come find you.' And Weaver quickly described the waiting pair. He saw from the monitor they were still by the terminal doors, and pointed them out to Boyd.

'You're sure they're the same men?' Boyd asked.

'Absolutely. But there's something else.' He waited for a minute, until the camera reached the spot, then froze it and pointed to the screen. His voice was energised now: 'Do you see the old woman there with the stick?'

'What about her?'

'Her name, or at least the one she gave me, is Golubova, Mrs Golubova. I think she had a lot to do with Ragoulin's death, and she certainly had a lot to do with trying to organise mine.' He explained her presence in the adjacent seat on his flight from Stockholm; her bizarre reappearance on Bond Street; the 'coincidence' of Ragoulin's death occurring outside the gates of her son-in-law's Surrey mansion.

'I'm just wondering why they need three people to stand in for Ragoulin,' Boyd said.

Weaver was glad to have got there first for a change. 'Don't you see?' he said to Boyd. 'They're not here to help Symons or Sukolov or whatever the poor sucker's called. They're here to kill him.'

Boyd had initially resisted Weaver's suggestion that he interview the man. Then after Weaver pointed out that he had actually known Ragoulin, and it was conceivable that Sukolov might still be expecting to be met by the art dealer, Boyd relented. It was unorthodox, no doubt, but he seemed to realise there was nothing to lose by letting Weaver have a go. 'I'll give you fifteen minutes. After that, we'll have to release him. Otherwise, his welcoming party in arrivals will become suspicious and leave.'

'Okay,' said Weaver, wondering how he could possibly work that fast. He had one request: that Sukolov be brought to him here, in the room with the camera feed.

While Boyd went to get the man, Weaver got a coffee from a vending machine down the hall. When he came back, to his surprise he found Sukolov waiting for him, drumming his fingers impatiently on the table.

For some reason Weaver had expected Sukolov to stand out

from the crowd. Someone dashing, flashy even and sharply dressed. In fact, the guy looked every bit the regular American businessman he claimed to be. Medium height with recently cut hair. Dress expensive casual: blue linen jacket, Brooks Brothers shirt open at the neck, pressed khaki trousers, expensive loafers. He had flown club class to London, and seemed to have slotted effortlessly into the role of a well-heeled American businessman.

Weaver introduced himself and sat down across the table from him. Sukolov said, 'I hope you're not going to give me the same song and dance as the old boy did.'

'I'll do my best. And I won't keep you long; you'll be free to go in a few minutes.'

'Really? That's not the impression the old guy gave me.' He spoke with so little inflection that Weaver could tell he had originally been taught English in a foreign country. By a linguistic drillmaster determined to root out any trace of Russia in his voice.

Weaver shook his head. 'It's true all the same.'

'Who are you anyway? Another spook, or just a regular cop? Or immigration, maybe?'

'None of the above. I'm just an interpreter, but with a connection I'll explain. Don't worry: when I leave in a little while, you can leave as well. The only question is whether you'll want to.'

'I don't think there's any doubt on that score,' said Sukolov, and he laughed, the first dissonant note in the stereotype he was so successfully inhabiting; the laugh was too hearty, almost uncontrolled.

'I'm not here to make a pitch, Mr Sukolov.' At the sound of his Russian name, the other man stiffened slightly. Weaver went on, 'All you have to do is hear me out. Then you can be on your way. As I said, that's if you still want to.'

Sukolov was now watching Weaver intently. Weaver said, 'First of all, can you tell me who's meeting you here?'

Sukolov shrugged, unbothered. 'Not sure that anyone is. A friend was supposed to, but he's indisposed.'

Meaning dead, Weaver thought. 'I think you'll find people are waiting for you. At least, there were the last time I looked.'

'Really? I'm flattered.' Sukolov seemed to be enjoying himself.

Weaver said, 'Before you go through immigration, I want to tell you a story. Don't worry: it's a short story. It's also true, which I know because I'm the connection between all the main characters. There are three of them, and all three have been doing their best to find me.' *Less wordy*, he told himself, not daring to look at his watch. He added, barely above a whisper. 'And then kill me.'

Sukolov's expression didn't change, but one hand was now stroking the arm of his chair. Weaver continued: 'Of course, these people are also linked by the person giving them instructions. That's where I get lost, I'm afraid; you'd know more about that than I do.'

Was there a trace of uncertainty now in Sukolov's eyes? Hard to tell. So Weaver told his story. He felt the clock ticking, and therefore made sure the Stockholm meeting itself was quickly despatched, though Sukolov looked impressed when Weaver explained that a Russian general had been a participant. Weaver focused instead on Mrs Golubova and her recurring appearances, but Sukolov seemed uninterested in the old woman. Weaver accordingly changed tack: 'You know Alek is dead, yes?'

'Ragoulin? Yes; I gather he had a heart attack. A shame.'

'There have been a lot of heart attacks lately in the Russian expatriate community.'

'If you say so.'

'Where do you think Alek died?' Sukolov did not answer, so Weaver said, 'Outside the gates of Mrs Golubova's daughter's house. If you doubt me, you can look up the newspaper reports – the house belongs to a Mr Zadkin; he's Mrs Golubova's son-in-law.'

Sukolov remained silent as Weaver moved on and described the sinister SVR man with the long nose; how he encountered him at the secret meeting in Stockholm, and then his presence there at Heathrow on the following day. It could not have been a coincidence, he added. Finally, there was the mugger on Clarendon Road.

When he had finished, Sukolov shrugged. 'I don't see why any of these people would want to harm you. Are you sure you're not letting your imagination run away with you?'

At least he was talking.

'Look,' said Sukolov, 'I'm sorry for your troubles, but to be honest, I don't understand what they've got to do with me.'

'That depends on how important you think you are,' Weaver responded. 'When Hofstadter met with General Kuzmin in Stockholm, guess what they talked about.'

'I haven't a clue,' said Sukolov, making a show of boredom.

'You,' said Weaver, and was pleased to see this made an impact.

'And you said you were at this meeting?'

'Yes. I was the interpreter.'

Sukolov nodded. He said, 'That makes me understand why the Russians want to make *you* disappear, but why do you think this other character, this Sukolov guy, is in danger?'

'Because he knows too much about the identity of the Russian Illegals in the States. The Kremlin's worried the West might find out Sukolov's real identity and offer him asylum, and a lot else, in return for telling all.'

Sukolov was quiet for a minute while he digested this. 'What makes you think a man in the position you describe would be tempted by such an offer?'

'I can't give an ironclad guarantee, and the details would have to be worked out with the gentleman down the hall, but I'm certain Sukolov would be treated well. He'd have to spill the beans, of course, but I'm confident he would get to do so in comfort, and with the promise of a normal life once he'd finished talking.'

'Talking to the Americans?' he asked.

There was a new urgency in his voice, and this seemed important to him. So Weaver took a chance and said firmly,

'No. Just the Brits.' He paused, then added, 'The alternative, if Mr Sukolov refuses to talk, is not something he'd want to think about. If one were Mr Sukolov, that is.'

'And how does our Mr Sukolov know this isn't one big bluff?'

'Ah, let's move on to part two of the story. Come sit over here, please.'

Sukolov came and sat in an empty chair. Weaver held the mouse with one hand while pointing with the other at the monitor in front of them. 'That's the feed from a camera in the arrivals hall.'

None of the trio had moved. As the camera swung, Weaver froze the picture, then stood up and hovered by the monitor, pointing at it with his index finger. 'There is the fetching figure of Irina Nikolayeva Golubova. She will be smothering you in kisses when you go through.'

Then as the camera kept moving after he clicked, it took in the entire crowd of waiting visitors, all the way back to the front of the terminal. Weaver froze it again, and when he pointed, they could both see the two male figures, still standing by the exit doors. The High Tops athlete was looking anxiously around the hall; the Russian bruiser had his eyes fixed on the customs exit.

'That,' he said, leaving the mouse on the table and returning to his seat, 'is your reception committee. Why there needs to be three of them is beyond me. And why *those* three is even harder to understand. Unless…'

'Is that it then?' Sukolov sounded like a moviegoer impatient for a film to end.

'Yes. That's it.'

They sat in silence for a good ten seconds. Finally, Sukolov said matter-of-factly, 'Am I free to go now?'

Weaver tried hard to mask his disappointment. 'Sure,' he said curtly. He stood up. 'Wait here a minute. I'll just go and get the gentleman who spoke with you earlier. He'll take you through.' As he was closing the door behind him, he called out, '*Do svidaniya.*'

*

Boyd was very decent about it, though he must have shared Weaver's frustration that Sukolov would not play ball. Weaver saw no point in telling Boyd about the unusual approach he had taken, and thankfully Boyd did not press him. After Weaver gave his brief account, Boyd got up. 'Stay here for a moment, will you? I just need to hand Sukolov over to Mitchell; I'll let him take him through. I do hope the bugger realises that if we're right, he'll be dead by nightfall.' And Weaver sat, contemplating this prospect, and his failure to convince Sukolov of it, all the while wondering where Lily was now.

A few minutes later, the door opened and Boyd stood in the doorway. He no longer looked dismayed; unless Weaver was mistaken, he was positively excited.

'Weaver,' he half-shouted. 'He's *staying*. He says he wants *asylum*. God knows what you said to him, but it's worked.'

Boyd gradually recovered his equilibrium as he came into the room, though his hands were trembling. 'When I first went back to the room, I thought my heart would give out: Sukolov wasn't there. But he'd only gone to get some water.' He was laughing at the thought of it. 'When he returned he said, calm as you please, that he has decided that he has no wish to go through immigration on his own. And he hoped his application for asylum would be favourably received.' Boyd had caught his breath now, and said more measuredly, 'Weaver, you have my enduring thanks. Job well done – more than well done. I'll take it from here, though I hope to have occasion to thank you again.'

'I hope so too,' said Weaver. Boyd's politeness was catching.

They sat in happy silence for a moment, and then Boyd said gently, 'I hope you wouldn't mind terribly if I were to ask one more favour from you.' He looked embarrassed.

'All right,' said Weaver equably, curious what it could be. He couldn't think what else he could do to help.

'It's nothing very important; it's just that...' Boyd hesitated, then went on in a rush. 'Could you please *not* tell Lily I've let you talk to this man. At least not until some time has passed?'

'Okay. But can I ask why?' asked Weaver, wondering what 'later' meant.

'She was completely opposed to your being involved today. I don't want her to feel she was being ignored.' He paused. 'I don't want her upset.'

Upset? Weaver wanted to laugh. He was certain Lily would be delighted by what had transpired. But there was a concern to Boyd's voice that was touching. 'Okay,' he said. 'Though if you think she was being overly protective of me, I'd say the same is true of you about her.'

Boyd shrugged, but not defensively. 'Lily's a natural at this sort of thing. But she needs… looking after, shall we say. However much she won't admit it. Perhaps you know that already,' he said mildly, his eyes on Weaver.

'I do. Normally I'd say I am a fairly quick study, Charles. But she's a difficult subject.'

Boyd allowed himself a smile. 'Then I hope you'll keep studying.'

Weaver stood up to go, but then Charles said, 'Wait, I almost forgot.' He went to a filing cabinet in a corner, and returned with a padded A4-sized envelope, sealed with thick brown masking tape. He handed it to Weaver; it was surprisingly heavy. 'That's for Lily. It's her birthday tomorrow, so please don't forget to give it to her.'

'I won't,' said Weaver, wondering how he could buy her a present in time.

'She's out front, waiting in her car. Off you go.'

29

They were twenty minutes from the Dower House and the drive from Heathrow had been uneventful. Somewhere Lily had changed clothes – she wore white cotton trousers that looked brand new and a striped blue-and-white T-shirt. 'All you need is a straw hat,' Weaver remarked, 'and you could be a Venetian gondolier.'

She grinned, happy after Weaver had told her what had happened with Sukolov – in a censored version that had him playing no role in persuading the Russian man to stay.

Weaver felt hopeful for the first time since the intruder episode on Monday night. He would feel even better when the red recording pen was in his hands, but he hoped the Russian and American hunt for him was over.

He said, 'By the way, I see what you mean about Charles. There was nothing remotely dozy about him today.'

She nodded. 'I know. He just needs to keep working.'

'What will they do with Sukolov?' he asked.

'Take him to a safe house, give him a large drink and a medical. Then in a day or two, when he's settled, put the tape recorder on.'

'Will they tell the Americans?'

'Not yet,' she said. 'Eventually they'll contact the FBI – but not until Sukolov has told us everything he knows.'

'I got the strong feeling Charles doesn't trust Malone.'

'You're right about that.'

'Yet Charles has managed to get in the FBI's good books by telling them Dennis Symons's real name. How did he know about that?'

Lily looked straight ahead. 'Because I told him right after you told me.'

At least she wasn't trying to deny it. 'Okay, but Malone would have been his FBI contact for this case. Or did Charles go around him?'

Lily waited a moment before saying, 'Yes.'

'How was that?'

Lily shrugged. 'Some other way in, I guess.'

This was unusually vague for Lily, and when he glanced over, her discomfort was obvious. There was only one answer that could explain her agitation. 'My father,' he said flatly. His father had been brought into the loop, and Lily would have been the facilitator. Weaver could hardly complain, he realised, since now the Bureau would know he had helped unearth this Illegal, which was scarcely the act of someone betraying their country.

He reached over and put his hand lightly on Lily's shoulder. 'I don't mind,' he said gently.

Her eyes stayed fixed on the road, but he could feel her muscles relax. After a moment she said, 'When I told your father how Malone sat on the fence, he blew a gasket; he said he was going to go straight to the Director about it. He should be pleased that Sukolov's in the bag now, even if it is a British bag.'

'Charles told me about Sukolov's regular trips to Washington.'

Lily nodded. 'I know. He trusts you. Do you think there's any chance Sukolov was seeing Hofstadter on these little jaunts?'

'You mean, Hofstadter is a Russian asset?' When she nodded, he continued: 'No, I don't think so. It's hard to convey, but if he were used to helping the Russians, he would have behaved differently in the meeting with General Kuzmin. He seemed genuinely nonplussed when Kuzmin insisted they pardon Sukolov. He didn't know Sukolov's alias – Symons, that is – and he was obviously baffled about why Kuzmin placed such importance on "Dan Berry".'

'I thought Kuzmin mentioned Sukolov's name.'

'He did, but it meant nothing to Hofstadter. I am sure of that. And initially he said no to the request. It was only when Kuzmin tightened the screws that Hofstadter relented.'

Lily said, 'If you're right – and I grudgingly concede you must be – then that means Sukolov may have been seeing virtually anyone of importance in the capital.'

'I'm afraid so. We just have to hope Sukolov will tell all. But what about the reception committee in the arrivals hall? Did Charles and co just let them go on their merry way?'

'Unsure. Ask me after I talk to Charles again.' They had left the M4 and were making their way through the lush English countryside. Lily said, 'We're getting close. I'm going to show you the back way and drop you off there. When you get to JP's, I want you to stay down by the river – JP's already there. Leave the house to me.'

'What? Why can't I come to the house?'

'In case it's still being watched. News of Mr Sukolov's change of heart may not have yet reached his fellow Russians in the UK.'

'No,' he said. 'I can't let you face them alone.'

'Calm down. I won't be alone. Boyd has arranged things so I'll have armed support at the house. Your presence would just be a distraction and might provoke the Russians, if they did show up, to do something stupid. Like try and shoot you. They don't have any reason to shoot me.' She paused. 'But I need to know where you hid the pen.'

There seemed no good reason not to tell her, though he slightly resented the way she was taking charge. He described where he'd stowed the pen, and she laughed at his hiding place, behind a book about ambiguity. He said, 'Won't Sue be surprised when you show up instead of me?'

'Don't worry. I talked to Sue this morning; she's happy to have me, and frankly, I don't give a toss what JP thinks. Sue's going to send him down to the river as well, so wait for me there until I text you or come down with the pen.'

'Okay,' he said reluctantly, vowing that if there were ever a next time to this situation, he would be the one in charge. Well, an equal at any rate.

The village was about a mile from the Dower House, with farm fields and woods separating it from JP's holdings. There was also a church on his side of the village, with a Norman tower. Next to it was the rectory, a Georgian house smaller than JP's and recently bought by a London couple who, JP said rather witheringly, kept themselves to themselves.

Lily pulled into the entrance of the church and parked by the iron gate. 'If you go through the graveyard, you'll come to a footpath by the river. Follow that and you'll end up on the river bank below the Dower House.'

'Okay,' he said. He still felt uneasy about her going to the house on her own, but she was insistent, and repeated that Boyd was ensuring there would be armed backup in the house. 'Good luck,' he said when he got out, but Lily was already turning the car around.

He found the footpath and the river, which was narrower here but with deep pools that held some big trout. He realised he had seen this stretch before, on a walk with JP, but coming from the other direction. It was glebe land, owned by the church, but the fishing rights were leased and JP had acquired them. JP had let both sides of the path go uncut, which made walking slow and difficult, but didn't seem to impede the efforts of the local poachers.

It took Weaver a quarter of an hour's fast walking to traverse the path, and he paused only to check his phone from time to time. But there was nothing from Lily. Eventually, the grassy path became fine gravel, its verges neatly mown, signifying he was on JP's land. Here the river curved, and as he came round the bend he found JP himself standing on the bank, facing the water. He was only about thirty feet away but about to cast, so Weaver stood quietly in order not to disturb him. He felt his old affection return as he saw the determined look on JP's face, but then he remembered what JP had said about Lily.

JP managed to get his elbow out of the way for a change, and the line sailed cleanly through the air, the leader unfurled, and the fly settled with the barest pucker on the surface of the water.

'Nice cast,' said Weaver from behind.

Startled, JP jerked his rod skyward, and the fly popped out of the water, undoing the compliment.

JP said, 'I thought you'd stop by the house first. I asked Sue to text me when you arrived. I left a rod for you outside the kitchen.' He pulled in some line and cast again, not quite so well.

'Take your time,' said Weaver. 'Don't let me put you off.'

'I'm better at this than you think, Weaver. Maybe not an expert,' he said, spitting out the word, 'but some of us have a living to make, mouths to feed. My ten thousand hours weren't spent on a river bank, but in a shitty room with a shitty view in a shitty office block. You know the drill.'

After his time in New York, Weaver figured he did, but it was not what he was here to talk about. He said directly, 'I didn't realise you disliked Lily so much.'

JP let his fly lag downstream while he considered this. 'It's not dislike, Weaver; it's distrust. I thought it best to give warning to my old friend.'

'That was big of you.'

'I thought so. What are old friends for, after all? I mean, other than fishing my beats, drinking my vino, consoling my wife when she's fed up with me, and hitting on the women guests.'

It was said so mildly that it actually made the words more toxic. Weaver wondered where he could begin in response. He had never shown the least carnal interest in Sue, and not just from self-restraint and loyalty, though he'd like to think those would keep him in check, but for the more fundamental reason that he was not attracted to her in the least. Saying that now would only make things worse, but what startled him was not the inaccuracy of what JP said, but the hostility behind it. It could not be new, this antipathy, but until the phone call in the hospital and now here on the river, it had been well hidden.

'Probably best I don't stick around then, JP.'

'Am I the only reason?' From his taunting tone, this was not the prelude to an apology; JP wasn't backing off.

'No. I've got people looking for me who I really don't want to see.' He glanced at his phone and to his relief saw that Lily had texted him. *All okay here. L.*

JP said, 'As I told Lily, they were here, asking Mrs Wilson lots of questions while we were on the Derwent. Highly recommended, by the way – the Derwent, I mean. Not that my recommendation will mean much to you.'

JP started to reel his line in. He said, 'I found your little gizmo, you know. The one you taped some meeting with.'

'*What?*'

'Don't look so astonished,' JP said. 'I know people are looking for you, but I still don't know why. I listened to what was on it, but obviously I couldn't make hide nor tail out of the Russian. Don't waste time searching for it in your room. It's not there.'

Weaver was stunned. JP must have searched hard to find the recorder behind the books. 'Where is it? I need it back.'

'Sorry, too late. The Ivans, as Sue called them, showed up after breakfast, just after your friend Lily phoned. They were looking for you, and for it. They were happy to take the thing off my hands.'

'Jesus Christ.' Weaver was stunned. 'Do you know what you've done?'

'What do you mean?' JP lifted his rod and swung the fly at the end of his leader to one side. 'You don't have to worry about the Russians: they seemed more than satisfied. I've got them off your back; not that I expect any thanks for it.' He seemed indifferent now to Weaver's anxiety. 'That's a neat little machine. I knew Olympus were good at cameras, but not with audio stuff.'

'Olympus?' His phone stirred but he ignored it.

'Their logo on the thing is almost as big as the gadget itself.'

And Weaver now understood. JP had found the wrong pot of gold. Weaver had put the Olympus recorder in the chest of drawers, easily found by anyone. JP would have played back the little machine and heard Russian being spoken by... a Russian trade spokesman several years before, when West and East still met. *Got it!* JP would have thought jubilantly, and who could blame him? JP wouldn't know what the voice was saying; he would know only that the words were Russian, spoken on a machine that belonged to Weaver.

Weaver's agitation was now replaced by anger at this inept betrayal. His phone shook again; he barely felt it. 'Why did you do it, JP?' he demanded.

JP turned in surprise. He didn't seem surprised by the question itself so much as the fact that Weaver felt the need to ask it. Weaver said, 'How did the Russians know the recorder was here? You must have told them.'

'I did, old buddy. But don't worry: they don't want you, they just wanted the gizmo.'

Wrong, thought Weaver; the Russians wanted both. He realised that JP didn't think he had betrayed Weaver. Or understand that Weaver was in any kind of danger. For all his malice now, his friend had been stunningly naïve.

JP had reeled all his line in. Hooking his fly carefully to his reel, he picked up his fishing bag and started walking slowly towards the path that would lead to the house. Weaver walked with him. From a distance the two would look like old friends heading back for a drink before lunch. Weaver's phone was now shuddering repeatedly, and he took a moment to look. The screen showed a text from Lily: *I'M SAFE. U R NOT. GO NOW!* Then another one: *MOVE!!!*

But Weaver couldn't bear the thought of letting JP think he had done nothing wrong. 'You could have got me killed, JP.'

'Don't be melodramatic, Weaver. This is England.'

'And they're Russians.'

'Speak of the devil,' said JP, pointing towards the house. Two men were walking down the wildflower meadow path towards them, approaching briskly, their strides deliberate rather than urgent. Professionals, Weaver thought, as instinctively he stopped and took a step back. They wore suits and city shoes, but their shirts were open at the neck. One wore sunglasses, and Weaver remembered Marylebone and the man who'd come in through the street entrance, while Weaver gave his impersonation of an Irish barman.

JP walked forwards to greet them. He called out, 'Back again?' They were still a little distance away and didn't reply. Annoyed, JP spoke more loudly. 'What are you doing here?' His tone had reassumed the Anglophile archness of his British incarnation. 'I said I'd see you in the house if you needed anything else. You have the recorder.'

'We have the recorder, yes,' shouted back the partner of the man from the pub. He must have been the other one in the Mercedes, who had been combing the platforms. Weaver took another couple of steps backwards.

'Then there's nothing left to discuss,' JP declared. 'I'm spending some time with an old friend, so I'd like you to go. Now.'

'Where is the correct recorder? The one you gave us is so much... *der'mo.*'

'*Der'mo*?' asked JP. *Horseshit*, thought Weaver, but he wasn't about to shout out the translation. He was backing towards river and the boathouse, a careful step at a time.

'I don't know what you're talking about,' JP said crossly. 'Now leave the property or I'll call the police.'

Weaver had reached the little boathouse when he heard the noise – *crack*. He looked and saw that the Russian from the bar had drawn and fired a handgun – bang, like that.

JP had stopped at the sight of the gun, but now clutched his chest and, with a loud mourning-like groan, crumpled to the ground, trailing a hand already dripping blood. The Russian was about to holster his weapon when he saw Weaver and raised it again. It was a 9mm Glock, Weaver thought dully; his father owned three of them, and liked to go to a range in Marin for target practice.

Then fear overrode these memories. He sprinted into the boathouse, ducking when he heard another *crack*; there was a small thud when the bullet hit one of the rafters. Weaver jumped into knee-deep water and grabbed the stern of the canoe. There was another *crack*, and the gunwale of the canoe splintered next to his hand. He crouched to reduce his target size while he felt for the chain attached to the little dock, unhooked it and then shoved the canoe with both hands out into the river. Then he took two small steps and dived into the water.

He swam underwater as far as he could, until, almost bursting and desperate to breathe, he surfaced again, and was relieved to see that the canoe was between him and the bank. But before he could get to it, the canoe was caught by the current and started to move downstream at speed. The two Russians were on the bank, scanning the river. Seeing Weaver reappear in the water, the Russian with the gun started to raise his weapon again, but then hesitated. By then Weaver was now downstream enough to make it a long shot for any handgun. But the Russian fired anyway, just as Weaver ducked his head, and something sounding like an air kiss whistled past.

Weaver took another deep breath and dived under again. This time when he surfaced he was just at the bend in the river. He looked back, and there was no sign of the Russians. Weaver started swimming, now with a head-up breaststroke, and soon spotted the canoe ahead of him, snagged on the far bank by a low sweep of half-broken alder branches. Relief at finding the canoe was replaced by fear when he wondered if the Russians were following him on foot. He wanted to get further downstream more quickly, and standing up nervously in the shallow water near the bank, unhooked the canoe from the branches. Using both hands, he pushed the boat out towards the middle of the river; before the water became too deep, he managed to heave himself into the canoe. As it moved out into the river, he wriggled until he was lying flat on the plank bottom, next to the paddles.

As the canoe reached the faster current, he risked it and sat up on the single seat wedged inside the stern. There was a paddle stored lengthwise under the two thwarts, and as he slid it out he heard another gunshot from behind him. Nothing hit the canoe or – Weaver flinched at the thought – him.

The river had curved sharply here, and he was now out of sight of the boathouse. But the current also slowed as the river widened; if the Russians had a car, they could come within firing range again. Picking up one of the paddles, he dug ferociously through the water until he was back in the river's quicker current. He turned his head to look upstream at the bank, half-expecting a bullet in return, but there was no sign of the Russians. He heard shouting, a distant medley of voices, and then another shot.

He paddled all out for twenty minutes according to his watch, which was more waterproof than he expected. The same was not true of his phone, which had been completely immersed when he jumped in and now refused to turn on. He had no way of calling Lily to see that she was safe, or of reaching the police. He told himself Lily had sent at least one of her texts after the Russians' arrival in the meadow, so they must have left her unharmed. But it was a feeble reassurance, and he felt helpless. The river here was going through farmland, and if he left the canoe and set out on foot, he might find himself several miles away from any kind of assistance.

Several times Weaver's paddle struck the bottom as the river became shallower. He tried to tell himself again that Lily was all right, and he realised he didn't give a damn whether she had retrieved the digital recording pen. He wondered if he was suffering from shock, because he was no longer frightened about what might happen to him, nor interested in the many eddying mysteries of the last few days. He had answers enough to most of them – but none that told him Lily was safe.

The river widened, and progress was easy enough through a succession of sweeping bends. He came around the last one, his arms aching, and was relieved to see a stone humpback bridge ahead. It had two arches that divided the river into two fast streams. He was trying to decide which one to aim for when he noticed a figure standing in the middle of the bridge, facing away from him and talking on their phone. On the little road leading to the bridge from the Dower House side of the river there were two cars, one a police car with a blinking light on its roof. The other was a Golf that had seen better days.

30

Nearing the bridge, Weaver had to paddle hard to avoid being sucked into the narrowed slipstreams of water underneath the arches. He made it to a cleared patch of river bank, where the canoe first slowed, then stopped with a shudder on the mud. He got out, then splashed through the water until he stood on dry ground, stretching his legs before cramp set in. He saw that there were two men in the front seats of the police car.

The figure on the bridge had turned round. It was Lily. Seeing Weaver, she started to run, then caught herself, and walked like a school kid admonished for running in the hall. Unable to help herself, she started running again, until she pulled to a stop just a few feet short of the waiting Weaver.

Weaver said, 'You're allowed to hug me; I won't break.'

'I was so worried they'd got you.' She came and hugged him hard, then broke off and looked at him appraisingly. 'You're soaking, Weaver. If you're cold, I can get the blanket out of the car.'

'I'm drying off, so I'm okay,' he said. 'But JP's not.'

'I know, but he's going to make it. Though he won't be fishing for a while. He's lost a lot of blood.'

'What about the Russians?'

'Arrested. They've taken him away.'

'Him? There were two of them.'

Lily looked away. 'The other one's dead.'

'The one who shot JP?'

'Yes.'

'Was he shot by one of your armed people?'

'Something like that.' Lily shrugged; she wouldn't look him in the eye.

'Who shot him?' It seemed important to know.

Lily looked down at her feet, then whispered, 'I did.'

Weaver went and put his arm around her. 'I didn't know you owned a gun.'

'I don't. I only got one today.'

He took his arm away gently. *When would that have been?* he wondered. Was it while he was at Heathrow? Then he understood. 'Your birthday present from Boyd.' No wonder the padded envelope had seemed so heavy.

'Yes.'

'Come on,' he said, aware of the stares of the two cops in their car. 'Let's go to the bridge.'

They walked silently onto the middle of the bridge, where they stood, leaning on the parapet and facing downstream. A fish rose about a long cast away, but Weaver felt none of the usual excitement. 'What happened?' he asked. 'I thought you had armed protection.'

'So did I,' she said unhappily. 'I'd seen Sue and explained I'd left something behind. So I went upstairs and found the pen, just where you said it was. I was coming back down the stairs when I looked out and saw two men in suits cutting across the meadow. The man from MI5 who'd been sent by Boyd had gone outside; Sue says he thought he'd heard a car on the drive in front. So he didn't see the Russians.' She shook her head to show what she felt about that.

She took a deep breath, then went on. 'When I realised they were heading for the river, I ran downstairs and went to my car; I'd left Boyd's package locked in the boot. I never thought I'd need it – that was the whole point of the guy from MI5.

'I ran as fast as I could and the first thing I saw was JP lying on the ground. Then I saw the two Russians by the boathouse; the one with the gun fired at the canoe. I shouted at him to put his gun down and he turned around to look at me. Then the stupid fuck turned back and fired again. He didn't give a damn that some woman had a gun pointed right at him; he was going to try and kill you anyway. So I shot him.'

'You didn't have a choice.'

'I know,' she said. 'But I've never shot anyone. I've hardly even fired a gun.' She rubbed one eye with a balled fist, then said wryly, 'I failed the small arms course.'

'Well, then you must have got all A-stars in large arms.' He was relieved when she managed a smile. He was astonished by what she'd done; no wonder she seemed shaken. 'Where's Boyd?' he asked, hoping to distract her.

'Still with Sukolov – they've gone to the safe house in Wandsworth. Sukolov didn't want to wait to talk: he's spilling the beans already.' She paused for a minute and he waited patiently, glad that she did not want to keep talking about the shooting. She said, 'I want you to know something. It's important. I spoke with your friend Tomic.'

'Tomic? Why are you talking to him?' He told himself not to get angry. 'Did he call you?'

'I called him originally while you went off to Bond Street, looking for Ragoulin. I got Tomic's number from JP. We spoke again while I was waiting for you at Heathrow. You see, it was obvious to me that the greatest threat to your life and limb was coming from one place only: Moscow. My contacts there are either dead or in prison, so I didn't know where to turn. But you had mentioned Tomic, and his cousin, who you said worked in the FSB.'

'That's right. But Tomic's just an interpreter like me.'

'Maybe so, but he's got a great future as a middleman. You'd told me the cousin's place is near Morozov's summer dacha; I was hoping maybe the cousin had an in to the great leader. He doesn't – I suppose it was too much to hope for; it would have been like a local policeman knowing the Prime Minister. But he does know someone almost just as good.'

'Who's that?' asked Weaver.

'The cousin's brother-in-law is a German banker who knows

Morozov. And Hofstadter, for that matter. Does the name Galkin ring a bell?'

'You must be kidding.'

'Fortunately, I'm not. Tomic prompted his FSB cousin to brief Galkin on your situation, starting with the fact you accidentally taped the meeting.'

'They must have suspected I had or they wouldn't have felt the need to come after me. But I don't understand *why* they suspected it,' said Weaver.

'They not only suspected it; they *knew*. When you were in Stockholm, it seems you changed your room in the hotel.'

He remembered the move from his lowly room to a plush suite. 'I got an upgrade. God knows why, but I wasn't complaining.'

'Neither were the Russians. The room you moved to was part of a block booking that wasn't being used. Somebody did somebody a favour and let the Russians have it. I bet some kopeks changed hands to have you moved. It wasn't hard to have the room bugged.'

'Did Tomic tell you this?'

'Yes. His cousin found out from his FSB colleagues.'

Weaver was starting to understand. 'I played back the tape that night. If they wired my room, they would have heard it.'

'So they knew you had a recording of the meeting. They'd also already hacked into your phone. You said yourself, they confiscated it during the meeting.'

'But why? They had no reason to think I'd recorded anything, and at that stage I hadn't.'

'It was a precaution. You got called in when Mrs Macauley had her fall. They were suspicious of that. The Russians do like a bit of research; they must have then discovered your connection to Anatoly Demidov and your father's position in the FBI. They're paranoid enough to think those were infallible indicators that you were some kind of spook.'

'Could they have learned about the Demidov connection from Ragoulin?'

'Probably.'

'I wonder if Ragoulin really did have letters from my mother to Demidov.'

Lily shook her head. 'I doubt it, though I suppose you can always ask your mother.' She laughed as she saw the reaction on his face. 'I think it was just a ploy to get you to Ragoulin's office.'

He looked at her, but her gaze was determinedly fixed on the river flowing away from them. 'It all seems awfully complicated,' he said.

'Not really,' Lily said, and she turned to face him. He noticed that she had her hair up again. She said, 'The Russians were on to you from the time you landed, thanks to your phone. They sent some Albanians to whack you on the street and take your bag. That failed, and the problem for them then was that once I put your phone in a taxi at Paddington, they didn't know where you were.'

'They seemed to find out soon enough.'

'Thanks to Ragoulin, and then thanks to JP.'

'JP was working for them?' he asked.

'No, no – nothing like that. He was just dumb, and naive. And the Russians knew you'd stayed there last weekend because you still had your phone then.'

She stopped and glanced at her watch. He turned to look upstream but saw only a heron, working the shallows for easy fish. Turning back again, he saw the two men in the police car were watching him. He said, 'Have you found out what happened to the reception committee at Heathrow? Did the three of them get away?'

'They detained the two men. Charles said the Russian claimed he was there to collect a visitor – and that he has diplomatic immunity. Sadly, it looks like he does; he's registered with the embassy. So they had to let him go. The Albanian's a different story. He's being held.'

'Albanian? You were right.'

'I have more experience with them. This guy's a real beauty, with a rap sheet as long as your arm.'

'That leaves Mrs Golubova. She's probably the most lethal of the trio.'

'And the cleverest. She disappeared when they stopped the other two. Charles said the CCTV camera caught her one minute, then on its next sweep she was gone. The thinking is, she caught a flight to some European city using a different passport – not Russian, that's for sure. She's probably already landed somewhere. Maybe your old stamping ground, Stockholm, but who knows? It will be Moscow next.'

They stood silently for a minute, side by side, watching the river. 'So what do we do now?' he asked.

'Why is it Americans always want to *do* things? You'll die if you do anything now.'

'How do you know?'

'Because, through Tomic's cousin, I've communicated with the SVR.'

'You have?'

'Yes. Tomic was horrified you'd got caught in the middle of things. So he told his cousin about it, and he then talked to his superiors. They made it absolutely clear to Tomic that if you go public with the tape, they will kill you.'

'Why? Just for revenge? Or to discourage any others?' The threat seemed melodramatic, almost far-fetched, but then he thought of the Russian with the gun, who less than an hour before had shot JP – and tried to shoot Weaver.

'Both. And while they were at it, they'd make certain to discredit you. You'd be found dead in a hotel room somewhere; they'd dress it up to look like a suicide. They might forge a note, or leave drug paraphernalia scattered around, or simpler still, just throw you out a sixth-storey window.'

'Oh, come on.'

'I'm serious. They'd try to trash your reputation to distract from the tape. It's worked before. Even in America,' she added with an edge.

She went on: 'Charles has managed to persuade MI5 that

you're not Snowden Mark Two. And after your father intervened, the FBI Director spoke with the President himself. He knew nothing about Hofstadter's activities, including the meeting you interpreted for in Stockholm – and the hunt-the-rabbit campaign the Secret Service conducted trying to find you. All Hofstadter's doing. Apparently, your father is confident that if you don't rock the boat and stay... what was the word?'

'*Shtum.*'

'That's it. If you do that, no one will bother you. You can even keep your job. Lucky you... No more looking over your shoulder, Weaver, no more hiding.'

He was only half-listening now, waiting to speak. 'I still don't think Hofstadter was a Russian asset. I don't see how he can be the reason the Russians wanted Sukolov released.'

Lily cut in: 'Who is Blanchett again?'

A non-sequitur, he thought, but let it pass. She must still be very shaken still; he could see that, but talking seemed to be calming her. He said, 'He's Pauline's boss. What about him?'

She didn't answer him directly. 'You ask why the Russians were so desperate to get their hands on Sukolov. He was running the sleeping agents – okay, sounds great. But is it that important? I mean, when the FBI nabbed a good dozen of them about ten years back, what struck everybody was how little any of them had advanced in American society. They were all nobodies. And there was no reason to think the ones they *didn't* catch were more important. So again, why the panic about springing Sukolov?'

'Something says you're about to tell me.' He made sure to smile as he said this.

'Because his asset in Washington, the man he went to see each month, was Sam Blanchett.'

'*What?*' Weaver was simply astonished; it seemed almost preposterous. But then he saw it. He said, 'Blanchett was in charge of all the interpreters, which meant he was the ultimate boss of people who were present at every secret meeting the

United States conducted with a foreign power. Nobody even knows the names of the interpreters used for these confabs, but they hear every single word that's said. Blanchett always played dumb – everyone thought he *was* dumb – and this let him ask all sorts of questions interpreters aren't supposed to answer, but that's not easy to do when you're being asked by your boss's boss. If you have access to these interpreters, and power *over* them, then that's worth a lot. Especially to the Russians.'

'I can see that,' she said. 'He won't be long in his post; the only question is if they have enough to prosecute him. I think if you were to poke around, you'd find that Blanchett was the "other individual" Kuzmin talked about in Stockholm. Who helped Hofstadter get the loan from Galkin.'

'That makes sense, and we know it wasn't the First Lady.' But Weaver was thinking now of something else. 'You said you found the red pen. Can I have it?'

'Sure, but why?'

'I've got to decide what to do with it.'

'What are you talking about? Have you not been listening to me? You can't do anything with it, not if you want to keep breathing.' Lily was shaking her head, and looked perturbed.

He said, 'I need to think this through. What happened in that meeting was wrong. You know that. I'm not sure how I could live with myself if I do nothing with the recorder.'

'Even though I've just told you what the consequences would be? If you don't believe me, just ask Tomic. Are you really sure you want the pen?'

'Absolutely.' He wondered why she was being resistant.

'I was worried you'd say that.' She paused, then said out loud, as if to some third party, 'But hope you will forgive me.' As Weaver watched, mystified, Lily reached into her bag, a smart tan leather number he hadn't seen before. She came out with something in her hand: a pen, red as the cherries that end their days in a cocktail glass.

When he reached for it, Lily clenched her fist around the pen and moved a step away from him. Then she turned to face the river and hurled the pen into the water downstream.

He watched, amazed, as the pen sailed through the air and landed in a whirl of fast-moving river. It flipped over, and he saw it caught in the rushing water that came funnelling out from under the bridge. Then it was gone.

Weaver found it hard to believe what had just happened. Any moment he expected Lily to say she was joking and had the real pen in her bag. He looked at her and realised it was gone for good. 'Jesus Christ! What the hell have you done?' he managed to say.

'Well, I think I've saved your life. And possibly mine as well.' She was talking quickly now. 'No one's ever going to know you don't have the tape anymore. When I sent Tomic the segment, I told him to tell the Russians that if a hair on your head is touched, I will send copies of the recording to news outlets everywhere. As well as hundreds of social media outlets. I told Tomic that I know the Russians hate loose ends, but that you and I are two of them they're just going to have to live with. Otherwise, I said the entire world will get to hear about the whole bloody thing.

'Weaver, listen to me,' Lily said urgently. 'I know you well enough to be certain that if you kept the pen, one day you would use it. It's too great a temptation: Hofstadter would do something awful or the Russians would get their way about something else, and you'd release the tape. And then you would die, I guarantee it.'

Weaver looked at her, unconvinced, and for a moment they stared fiercely at each other. Lily was the first to soften, looking away as her phone pinged. She looked at the screen. 'It's a text from your father,' she said. 'He's up early, and he's sent me a link. Hang on a minute.' Then as she read the message she laughed, the singular high chord he usually liked so much – but not now.

'What's so hilarious?' he demanded, still angry.

Lily looked up from her phone, smiling. 'You won't believe it, but Hofstadter has resigned – first thing this morning, Washington time. Effective immediately.'

He kept himself from saying she must be joking. 'Why? Was he fired?'

'Nope, though I'd bet you he was about to be. But this will make you sit up: it's from the wire services. They say Hofstadter resigned, quote, "due to differences with the President". Hofstadter's letter of resignation said, "I cannot countenance the presidential pardons recently given to individuals who should have stayed under lock and key."'

Weaver shook his head in disbelief. 'That is a masterstroke,' he said. Seeing Lily's puzzlement, he explained: 'Think about it. If he'd simply resigned without saying why, there would still be a risk of the Russian blackmail being exposed, since as far as he knows, I still have the tape. But by resigning over a pardon, then even if the tape came out, it wouldn't do as much damage – I mean, it's pretty hard to accuse Hofstadter of procuring a pardon for the Russians when he's just resigned in protest about it.'

'Do you think the President knew this was coming?'

Weaver nodded. 'I'm sure he did. Once the FBI Director called him, the President must have seen the writing on the wall. It was probably his idea that Hofstadter should resign. And the President's in the clear now as well. The link to the loan has been cut with Hofstadter's departure, since the money originally went to him.'

'I wonder if news will leak that Dennis Symons – I mean Sukolov – has defected.'

'That's another reason Hofstadter's going to be okay: he can always say he'd been told by the FBI that Sukolov would defect, so he was therefore happy to have him pardoned by the President.'

Lily said, 'I think this means you're safe, Weaver.'

'Even from the Russians?' he asked with vestigial suspicion.

'Especially from the Russians. The last thing they want is for people to know about a blackmail attempt that's *failed*. What Hofstadter's done is ingenious, and he's covered all the bases. You have to give him that.'

He was confident Lily was right, but wished his relief were greater. Even though it seemed he could stay in his job, he realised he would only return to New York in order to clear his desk. What would Lily think when he said he was going? After all the hurly-burly of the last few days, she might be glad to be shot of him. It felt strange that he would miss this woman so much after knowing her all of seven days.

She looked at him questioningly; now she seemed the vulnerable one. 'You can't stay mad at me forever, Weaver.'

He didn't say anything but silently watched the river instead, and gradually felt himself calming down. Lily looked again at her watch. 'We'd better get going. I need to go see Chip, and there'll have to be an internal inquiry about the shooting which I better start preparing for.' Seeing Weaver's concern about it, she said, 'Don't worry. I told Boyd exactly what happened, and he said any hearing at Vauxhall will be strictly a formality.' She added casually, 'Do you want me to drop you?'

'Drop me where?' he asked, trying to control the rising timbre of his voice. It was like Paddington, where he'd thought Lily was dropping him in more ways than one; only this time was far worse.

'Heathrow, I guess.'

'I thought you said Boyd was in Wandsworth now,' he said, deliberately misunderstanding her.

She ignored this. 'I reckoned you'd want to fly back to New York. I'm not saying they'll have a welcoming parade on Fifth Avenue, but you'll still have your job.'

He was at a loss for words. 'Come on,' Lily said, her voice brittle now. They started down the bridge towards the bank and the Golf. Halfway along, Weaver saw one of the policemen getting out of his car.

The cop's voice rang out: 'Everything okay, miss?'

'All fine thanks, officer,' Lily said, trying to sound cheerful.

'Okay, we'll be heading off then.'

Reaching the Golf, Weaver said, 'You better let me drive.'

'Oh? It's the wrong side of the road for you,' Lily said, but her heart didn't sound in it. The policeman had got into his car, which now moved at speed back up the little road.

'We'll be fine. I've driven lots here. Remember: I'm sensitive to traffic.'

'Okay, but I thought you'd want to fly back.' He was glad to see she was fishing for the keys in her bag.

'I will, but not yet. I'm only going there to say I won't be going there anymore – if you get my drift. There's no rush to do that, whatever Pauline may think, and Orvis will still be there when I go back to Vermont. First, I want to see things through here: you know, make sure Chip will be all right, pretend I care whether JP is all right, and then make sure you get through your internal stuff. That is, unless you have objections.'

She said nothing, which he took as a form of assent. They got into the car; to his relief it was an automatic, which meant there was one less thing to worry about while he dealt with the *bizarreries* of British roundabouts. He was wondering about the Russian for *bizarreries* and was thinking *strannosti* when Lily said, out of the blue, 'Is the autumn in Vermont all that it's cracked up to be?'

He paused before turning on the engine. 'Hard to say,' he said, acknowledging the ambiguity with a shrug. 'But I do know one way for you to find out.'

Acknowledgements

Many thanks to: Andy Russem, Clare Howell, Olga Losynska, Candia McWilliam, Sara Nelson, Andrew Schuman, Sam Radin, James Wolff, Carol Drinkwater, Angela Munro, Jonathan Lloyd, Lucy Morris, Andrew Holgate, Stephen Glover, Susan Sandon, and David Profumo.

Thanks in the United States to Michael Daly, Will Hunter, David L Deen, Dan Rosenheim and James Rosenheim.

At Bedford Square thanks to: Jamie Hodder-Williams for plucking me out of the blue, Victoria Chapman, Polly Halsey, Claudia Bullmore, Bill Massey, and Dan Coxon.

Last but by no means least: Sabrina Rosenheim, the late Sue Freestone, Claire Preston, Anthony and Jenny Forbes Watson, Frank Viviano, Rebecca Gowers, Joaquim Fernandes, Jon and Ann Conibear.

About the Author

Andrew Rosenheim was born in Chicago and came to England as a Rhodes Scholar. He has lived outside Oxford ever since, and is the author of a memoir and nine novels, including the Nessheim trilogy (*Fear Itself*, *The Informant*, and *The Accidental Agent*) and *Hands On*, the first novel to explore AI-generated poetry.

NO EXIT PRESS

More than just the usual suspects

'A very smart, independent publisher delivering the finest literary crime fiction' *Big Issue*

MEET NO EXIT PRESS, an award-winning crime imprint bringing you the best in crime and suspense fiction. From classic detective novels, to page-turning spy thrillers and literary writing that grabs the attention. Our books are carefully crafted by some of the world's finest writers and delivered to you by a small, but passionate, team.

In over 30 years of business, we have published award-winning fiction and non-fiction including the work of a Pulitzer Prize winner, the British Crime Book of the Year, numerous CWA Dagger Awards, a British million-copy bestselling author, the winner of the Canadian Governor General's Award for Fiction and the Scotiabank Giller Prize, to name but a few. We are the home of many crime and noir legends from the USA whose work includes iconic film adaptations and TV sensations. We pride ourselves in uncovering the most exciting new or undiscovered talents. New and not so new – you know who you are!

We are a proactive team committed to delivering the very best, both for our authors and our readers.

Want to join the conversation and find out more about what we do?

Catch us on social media or sign up to our newsletter for all the latest news from No Exit Press.

f fb.me/noexitpress   **X** @noexitpress

noexit.co.uk